ROSALINDA:
PRIDE OF MEXICO

PROUD TO BE ME

DEDICATION TO THE FEMALE BOXERS

*TO THE FEMALE FIGHTERS IN THE SPORT OF BOXING
WHO HAVE WORKED HARD, WHO STRIVE TO BE THE BEST
THEY CAN BE AND REACH THE GOAL OF THEIR LIFE. IF
YOU HAVE THE PASSION, THE STAMINA, AND THE DETER-
MINATION, YOU WILL SUCCEED AND BE PROUD TO SHOW
WHO YOU ARE.*

*IT DOESN'T HAPPEN OVERNIGHT, BUT IT WILL TAKE DED-
ICATION, SWEAT, AND PAIN TO GET YOU THERE. IF YOUR
HEART DESIRES WITH THIS PASSION, FOLLOW IT WITH
YOUR GUT, JUST DO IT BECAUSE YOU WILL NEVER FIND
OUT IF YOU CAN OR NOT.*

*FEMALE FIGHTERS ARE HERE TO STAY AND SHOW THE
WORLD THAT YOU CAN BECOME A CHAMPION. FOLLOW
THAT PATH TO STARDOM AND LET YOUR DREAM BECOME
A REALITY THAT WILL MAKE YOU PROUD OF WHO YOU
ARE.*

JESSE MORENO

CHAPTER ONE

The sun was like a huge flaming torch burning close as the temperature was reaching as high as 112 degrees in a small suburb town in Mexico. Despite the sun rays radiating from above and heating the ground to make it unbearable to walk barefooted, it did not stop the kids who lived next to each other from playing outside in the hot sun. The only place the kids played was under two huge oak trees which had grown several feet tall and had branches spreading enough shade for them to play underneath. Occasionally, a mild wind would blow the heat away from the shade, making it pleasant for the kids to play. The trees were separated a few yards apart, but close enough to give the kids plenty of room to run around and play.

There were three homes side-by-side and had a total of twelve kids among them between the ages of five and twelve. The best thing about having all these kids living next to each other is that they all got along very well and always had a great time playing without having any trouble. They enjoyed running around the yard dressed in clothes that looked like they were homeless; pants with torn knees, clothes that didn't match, but they didn't care how they looked. They just wanted to play and have fun.

Rosalinda, the eldest of three kids, lived in one of the homes. She worked at a grocery store nearby and occasionally babysat for one of the neighbors to raise money for a dream that she had of going to Los Angeles. She also helped her mom around the house whenever she needed some chores to be done. Her brother, Rudy, worked at a farm nearby, plus he was also training to become a professional boxer in his spare time.

The life they had was not an easy way of life and living in an environment to survive by growing their own gardens and chickens for the eggs and chicken for dinner at times. They struggled on occasion, but they also managed to find a way to get by with what they had to eat and maintain the house.

Rosalinda's brother Rudy had a 2011 F150 Ford pickup truck that he drove back and forth to work and the gym where he trained. He helped around the house doing manual things that needed to be repaired because their dad had passed away last year. Because of this, Rudy stepped up to be the man of the house and learned manual labor. His late father taught him to use various power and hand tools when he was younger, which eventually made his manual tasks easier to do.

Rosalinda had talked to Rudy about her traveling to Los Angeles a month ago. Her plan was to find a good job to help support the family with the income she would make and send back with the intentions of making it easier for her mom to live on.

When Rosalinda had enough courage, she told her mom, Francis, what her intentions were of leaving Mexico and traveling to LA. She led her to the living room to have a mother-to-daughter conversation. Rosalinda was hoping that Francis would understand the reason for following her plans and look at the bright side of the picture.

After the conversation, Francis didn't want to accept the idea of Rosalinda going by herself for a few weeks. Francis was afraid that something might happen to her if she was alone or would never hear from her again. But it was a typical concern that every mother has when one of her kids decide to leave the household by themselves.

Rosalinda specifically told her mom that it was going to be a temporary leave for a few weeks, unless she found a good job that would bring her enough money to make their lives a lot easier and better to survive, but she would have to stay longer than she wanted.

It took her mom several minutes to think about what Rosalinda wanted to do, and still did not like her idea of leaving. Francis thought about the things that could go wrong, but the longer she thought about how Rosalinda was raised, she convinced herself and felt that Rosalinda had grown up to be a responsible and smart girl who would take good care of herself, no matter what circumstances she was in, she would find a way to figure things out.

The next day, her mom was trying to give her some of her money for her travel that she was saving up for a rainy day, but Rosalinda refused to take it, even though she did not have a lot of money saved up. She knew she could manage to get there with what she had saved up, and Rudy had given her some of the money that he had saved up for an emergency if he ever needed it. He just wanted Rosalinda to make sure she makes it to LA alright.

Two weeks later, on a Monday morning, and after Rosalinda had the reluctance of having and dreading the conversation with her mom, it was time for Rosalinda to leave. Rosalinda disliked telling her mom about it. The separation of the family, especially between Rosalinda and her mom, was not a pleasant farewell. Francis had tears flowing steadily down her cheeks, trying to hold her composure and it made Rosalinda emotionally heartbroken to see her feel this way. But Rosalinda was expecting that it would turn out like this, knowingly that she had to do what she was planning to do and look on the bright side for the sake of the family. After saying their good-byes and telling her mom that it was just a temporary leave,

Rosalinda hopped into Rudy's truck as Rudy put her carry-all bag and suitcase in the truck bed and jumped into the drivers' side to get it started to leave.

As Rudy started the truck, Rosalinda and Rudy looked through the windshield and saw the family with a sad look on their faces as he backed-up the truck and drove away, glancing on the rear viewer mirror and saw his mom and sisters waving at them until the truck vanished down the road to the bus station.

The day was going to be another very hot day and Rosalinda thought to herself that it was going to be wonderful to get away from all this heat and look forward to this trip. The downside of her trip was about leaving and saying good-bye to her mom and siblings, but she had to do what she had planned and in the hopes of sending back a lot of money to help the family. The other reason she wanted to leave and go to LA was to give her the chance to see the other part of the country and explore the opportunities to become someone important in her life.

Rudy dropped her off at the bus station and said their good-byes before she hopped onto the bus. Shortly afterwards, her journey began. Rosalinda was on her way to Los Angeles as she sat by a window in the bus facing Rudy as he looked on to wave to Rosalinda to leave. It made Rudy sad to see her go, but he knew what her intentions were, knowing that it would be very beneficial for the family to help support the family and live a better life.

Rosalinda was nervous at first because this was her first long trip by herself and traveling out of the country. She took a deep breath hoping that she had made the right decision to do what she felt was right for her. Her mind finally calmed down from thinking about how sad it was to leave her mom, and then she switched her thoughts on the trip which got her excited the more she thought about it.

Rosalinda is a beautiful twenty-five-year-old Mexican girl who dreamed of traveling to Los Angeles on a bus one day with a visitor's visa. And now, after saving her money for a couple of years, she's on her way to make it a reality. The trip will take one day and a half to get to LA, but all she could think of was getting there and exploring the opportunities to earn enough money to send back home and help her family live in a more comfortable way to live.

While on her way to LA, she met a girl, Amber, at a bus stop when she boarded at one of the bus stops in Tucson, Arizona, and sat on a vacant seat next to Rosalinda. During their time traveling together to Los Angeles, they got acquainted, and after having a long conversation with each other, their plans were almost identical about what their intentions were. When they arrived in LA, they stuck together and wandered the area. They were both amazed at how Los Angeles was flooded with so many people rushing down the sidewalks, some dressed classy while others wore casual clothes, and most of the younger generation were dressed in wild outfits to go with their looks and not caring what other people thought of them.

Their belongings were shoved underneath the bus storage, so the bus driver had to take out a couple of baggage that were blocking Rosalinda's luggage, which was a medium-sized suitcase with wheels and a handle to make it easy to pull and drag it by the handle, besides carrying a medium-sized shoulder bag. Amber had a smaller one with wheels, and a smaller size shoulder bag.

After getting their bags, Rosalinda strapped her shoulder bag on top of her luggage with the handle to make it easier to haul around. Amber put her shoulder bag over her left shoulder and grabbed the luggage handle on wheels with her right hand and pulled the luggage behind her as they made their way down the sidewalk. Her shoulder bag was not as heavy as Rosalinda's' so it was easier to carry on her shoulder.

They began walking down the sidewalk against the flow of people passing by as they stared at them because they dragged their luggage behind them, obviously, looking like tourists. Amber noticed two guys coming in the opposite direction as they were passing by them with one guy eyeing Rosalinda and trying to get her attention, but Rosalinda ignored him, although the guy kept trying to get her attention with his smile. It didn't make a difference to Rosalinda as she kept her pace on the sidewalk. Amber looked at the other guy and got his attention with her flirty smile. The guy responded with his own smile and winked at her. As they passed each other, the one that was staring at Rosalinda said hello to Rosalinda. This time, Rosalinda was nice enough to respond to him and said hello in a very low tone of voice and kept walking alongside Amber down the sidewalk, wanting nothing to do with him. Although, it did make Rosalinda and Amber giggle for a few seconds after they passed them.

After walking three blocks down the sidewalk as they looked around the area, Amber spoke out to Rosalinda, telling her that she was hungry and needed to stop somewhere to eat; she could hear her stomach growling.

"I have to agree with you, Amber. My stomach is also telling me that we should stop soon at the next food place we find. Plus, I need to go to the restroom really badly. I don't know how long I can hold it." Amber could see Rosalinda's face looking at how it was an urgency to find a restroom as soon as possible.

They walked another two blocks weaving through the crowd of people as Amber followed behind Rosalinda, pulling her luggage as close to her as she could to dodge the oncoming crowd of people; probably rushing to get back to work since it was lunchtime, or running late to wherever they had to be.

They finally found a small café and entered, seeing people feeding their faces like they haven't eaten in days, and others seemed to be done eating their lunches because of the dirty plates in front of them and having conversations about who knows what with their friends or whoever the person was sitting across from them.

Rosalinda glanced around the café looking for somewhere to sit and noticed a couple getting up from a table with two chairs. That's all they needed. It was next to a window facing the sidewalk and a chance to watch the people passing by to see what sort of people live here and get a slight view of where they might be. She tapped Ambers' shoulder and told her to look at that table and said, "No one seems to be heading towards that table." So, they rushed to get the table before anyone else got it. They sat down and waited for the waiter or waitress to come and clean the table for them or whoever was going to help them, so they could place their orders.

"I have to go to the restroom; I'll be right back," said Rosalinda. She didn't have that much time to explain anything else to Amber other than to take off to the restroom before it was too late.

Meanwhile, a waitress came by to clean the table and told her a waiter will be here to take the order. Shortly after, a waiter came by to take their orders, so Amber placed her order with him and told him to come right back because Rosalinda would be returning soon, and she will also be placing an order.

Rosalinda made her way back to the table, feeling much better and relieved, and carrying a newspaper in her hand. She looked more relieved and relaxed now that she had made it in time and told Amber that her stomach was still growling and ready to eat.

Amber held on to her cell phone, checking her messages, when Rosalinda returned from the restroom and had a weird look on her face as though she read a terrible message and wasn't too happy about it. It got Rosalinda's attention.

"Is everything alright with you, Amber?" asked Rosalinda.

Amber put her phone down on the table and looked at Rosalinda with an upset expression, and then told her, "My boyfriend just became my ex-boyfriend." Then Amber with a frown on her face didn't know whether to yell, cry or be happy about it since they were already having problems with their relationship.

"So sorry to hear that," Rosalinda tells her. "Was that an un-expected thing to happen to you?"

"Well…yes and no. But I wasn't expecting it to happen right now. I knew things weren't going right for us every time we got together at my place. We would disagree on a lot of things that we wanted to do and argue about little things that didn't mean anything. Those kinds of things."

It got quiet for a few seconds until Amber told Rosalinda that the waiter came by to take their orders. "I went ahead and ordered my food. I couldn't wait for you." Then Amber giggled. "But I told him to come back because you were going to place an order too."

"What did you order, Amber?"

"Cheeseburger, fries, and a Coke. That was the cheapest combo on the menu. I have to be conservative because I don't have much money. How about you, Rosalinda? Do you have enough money to live on right now?"

"Not really. We need to look for a place to stay and find a job as soon as possible to help us survive. I got a newspaper on my way back from the restroom to search for a job, and hopefully, we can find a place to stay." Rosalinda caught sight of the waiter and waved at him to get his attention so she could place an order.

"Hey! Waiter! I'm ready to order. Can you help me?" Rosalinda was starving and anxious to eat. The waiter shows up with a flirty smile because he saw what Rosalinda looked like after he got there and stared at her, thinking if he weren't working at this moment, he would ask her out. Rosalinda broke up his thoughts and told him she was ready to place her order, which he did and left.

"Rosalinda! Did you see how he was looking at you?" Amber tells her. "I think he likes you. You are a beautiful girl though. I can't blame him for staring at you. And he's good-looking himself."

"Amber! It's not the right time to think about this. We just got here, and I'm sure there will be other guys who will come across our path. The first thing we need to do is find somewhere to stay, besides finding a job. Don't you think so?"

"I guess you're right. I need to focus on us, and what we need to do to survive. Did you see anything in the newspaper where we can stay for now?" Amber asked, feeling bad because after telling Rosalinda about the waiter, it wasn't the right time to get involved.

"There're not too many jobs available for us that we can start right away. It seems that most of the companies that are hiring want applicants with experience, and the only ones that I found that don't require having experience are places like washing cars, ironing at a laundry cleaner, dishwasher, or housecleaning. We might not have a choice though," said Rosalinda.

"We need to start somewhere and whatever job we could find available. And we need to start as soon as possible because the amount of money we have in our possession isn't going to last us very long." Rosalinda added to her concern. They both went silent for a few seconds, thinking of what the next step they'll have to take.

After five minutes of searching through the newspaper and waiting for their order, the waiter returned with both meals and set them on the table. As soon as the waiter placed the food on the table, Amber quickly grabbed two fries, and then three, stuffing them in her mouth as fast as she could grab them, and then started munching them. When she swallowed the fries, she picked up her Coke and guzzled down the Coke with the straw, sucking for three and four swallows before she stopped. And then she took a deep breath, a sigh of content, and then grabbed the cheeseburger and took a big bite before Rosalinda picked up a strip of her fries. Rosalinda looked at Amber, trying not to laugh because Amber looked like she hadn't eaten in days by the way she was shoving the food in her mouth. Amber stopped chewing and looked at Rosalinda staring at her.

"What!" Amber tells Rosalinda. Then they both chuckled. Amber knew why she was staring at her.

After searching for a day and sleeping at a nearby bus station, the first night, they decided to stay in a reasonably priced motel the second night. On the following day, after searching for a job all day, they finally found a place to work, washing cars, and a small studio for rent that was not too far from the job they were going to start working. The studio wasn't the most elaborate place to stay, but it was just a temporary place to live, serving its purpose for now.

The studio wasn't big, but there was room enough for them to share, even with a queen size bed, until they could find a better-paying job to get a bigger place.

While both struggled to survive by getting minimum wages, like washing dishes and working in a car wash, Rosalinda decided to look for something different because she didn't like washing cars. She moved on and found another job at a laundry cleaner not too far from the car wash. Amber wanted to stay at the car wash because she didn't want to leave a guy named Danny, whom she met and got infatuated with him while working there.

After working for a couple of months, they were making enough money to go out and start doing fun things like eating out, going to the movies, and occasionally, Rosalinda would tag along with Amber and her boyfriend to go out dancing at a nearby lounge called Harry's Lounge. This is the place where Rosalinda met Rob Anderson by accident, a local resident who has been working at a supermarket for the past year.

Rob Lee Anderson was Caucasian, born in Las Vegas, Nevada, and is two years older than Rose. That didn't make any difference to Rosalinda. It just happened one night at Harry's Bar when Rosalinda met Rob.

That night, as Rosalinda was having a drink at the table with Amber and her boyfriend, this guy kept smiling at Rosalinda and winking at her until Rosalinda finally had to walk up to him and ask him if he was flirting with her. And he, being so honest, said, "Yes, I am. Would you care to join me?"

Rosalinda hesitated for a few seconds then accepted. "I think I will. Since my friends are just a couple of tables away from us, I feel okay with it," she told him casually.

"I won't bite you," he tells Rosalinda with a flirty smile. Of course, it made Rosalinda smile and get a good feeling about him, a trusting feeling she felt about him as she joined him for the rest of the night and had fun, joking, laughing, and dancing. Their conversations led them to become boyfriend and girlfriend after having a few dates and liking what each other had to say about one another and how they felt with the relationship. Ever since that day, they had been together, enjoying every minute they had to spare for two months until they decided to live together.

After three months had passed, Amber's boyfriend asked her if she wanted to get out of town and look for a new adventure. It didn't take her but a minute to say yes. She was ready to go with him the next day. She didn't have a lot of belongings to pack, so when her boyfriend came by to pick her up, they were gone in a flash on their new journey to somewhere, not knowing where their destination was going to be. Ever since the day Amber and her boyfriend left, Rosalinda has never seen or heard from Amber again. Occasionally, Amber would cross Rosalinda's mind, thinking about all the things they used to do together. The same things crossed Rosalinda's mind. Rosalinda missed doing things together because Amber always made her laugh or had fun going out to the bars after work and enjoying being with some friends they met at work.

Rosalinda got tired of working at the laundry cleaner after working there for a couple of months and decided to look for a different job. It wasn't that she couldn't do the work, but she was cooped-up in a tiny room, steaming clothes and ironing, which got old from doing the same thing repeatedly.

One day, after working a full day at the laundry, she thought of moving on to a better job, somewhere where she could connect and collaborate with people, to get stimulated and move around in a more free environment. So, after work, she walked straight to her new apartment that she had moved into, and slipped into something a little dressier because she didn't want to be wearing the laundry cleaners' shirt with the emblem when she went looking for a new job. After searching and applying at various businesses for three days, Rosalinda found a busy little restaurant, Maria's Café, that was hiring. When she entered the Café, there were people waiting to be served, meaning that it was a popular restaurant with this kind of crowd and all the tables were taken. The hospitality and the surrounding environment seemed to be well organized and professionally served by the staff who served them. Rosalinda was acknowledged by one of the staff members and after Rosalinda asked for a job application, she was given an application form to fill out. After filling out the job application, she was taken to the manager's office for an interview which lasted about 30 minutes and was asked to come back the next day to start her first day.

The owner hired her, not knowing too much about Rosalinda, other than she had traveled from Texas looking for a new beginning and he needed more help as soon as possible. That was good enough for the owner. The other reason she got hired was that she was an attractive girl with a genuine personality. That was a big plus for her to start right away.

The next day Rosalinda began her first assignment as a waitress's responsibilities. She shadowed another waitress to make sure she learned the routine with taking orders from the guests and what to do afterwards. The staff connected with Rosalinda in no time by way of her personality. Every day and every time Rosalinda worked in the café, she was well liked by many of the local and new guests. She had served their meals and had a friendly welcome from the staff that was already working. Since the first day she started working at the restaurant, her thoughts were to make enough money at the restaurant to send back to her family back home in Mexico. The only thing Rose didn't know at this time, as she worked at this restaurant, was that this was going to be a new turn in her life to begin a journey that she wasn't expecting to happen.

It wasn't in her blood to give up or accept something she didn't want to do it, but she always tried her best to succeed. This was the one thing she remembered that her mom always told her to do: "If you ever want to become somebody, so the whole world will remember you, just do the best you can." And now, she was doing just that.

CHAPTER TWO

Rosalinda was comfortable and felt safe living in her new apartment a few blocks from the restaurant, making it easy for her to walk to work. Buying a car now would add another expense to her cost of living, so it worked out fine being close to work.

During the time she worked there, the people became more and more fond of Rosalinda because of her personality, hospitality, and excellent service. She would always give them 110 percent of her effort. She stood five feet five inches tall and weighed a solid 125 pounds. She had always been a lean and muscular girl who watched her weight by eating healthy. During her off time from work, she always found time to do some workouts at home before taking an hour's jog around the area through a nearby park. Her English was a little rough but clear enough for her words to be understood when she spoke. Most customers ignored her accent because of the excellent service she provided, except for one Friday evening when she was involved in an incident that changed her whole life in minutes.

As Rosalinda was doing her typical serving and doing what her responsibilities entailed that day, three girls were sitting at a table, one was black and the other two were white. As Rosalinda passed by this table carrying a tray of dirty dinner plates and drinking glasses on her arm above her shoulder, the black girl purposely put her foot out in the aisle, just far enough to trip Rosalinda. Rosalinda's foot got entangled under the girl's leg, causing her body to go forward. She tried holding on to the tray to prevent it from landing on top of someone sitting nearby. With her quick actions and reflexes, she missed the surrounding tables and fell straight toward the aisle, falling face down in front of customers sitting close by. The tray filled with dirty dishes went flying right in front of her, missing everyone nearby. Plates shattered as soon as they hit the solid floor, drinking glasses breaking into hundreds of small pieces, scattering in front of her and causing some pieces to roll underneath a couple of customers' tables nearby.

Within a few seconds, Rosalinda managed to roll over and pushed herself up from the floor, carefully not to cut herself and wiping off the leftovers from her uniform as she stood up, leaving stains on her clothes from the food. As she finished wiping most of the leftovers off from her clothes, she was not looking very happy about the situation and her anger was escalating very fast, but she knew that she had to control herself and not cause any trouble with the guest. She stared directly at the guest who had tripped her, still trying to control her anger, and walked toward the table where the three girls were sitting. She saw the girl who had tripped her, and confronted her face-to-face. Rosalinda stood in front of her, leaning slightly towards her because she was sitting down, as Rosalinda tried to control herself because she knew how cruel she could be if she lost her temper. Rosalinda was only inches in front of the black girls' face and the noses almost touching when she told her, "I think you owe me an apology for doing what you just did to me." Rosalinda stood her ground and did not back away from the guests' face, wanting to punch her smirky looking face.

The girl stayed seated at her table as Rosalinda talked to her, then the black girl stood up from her chair and stared into Rosalinda's eyes with the smirky look she still had on her face. As they stood face-to-face, and neither one backing away, their height and weight seemed to be alike, the girl started to curl her fingers onto her palm and making a tight clinch fist as she stared at Rosalinda with a devilish look and said to Rose, "There is no way in hell that I'm going to apologize to you, bitch," the guest tells Rosalinda.

After her remark, Rosalinda, still trying to control herself after the black girl refused to apologize, told her that her attitude and actions would not be tolerated in the restaurant. Since she refused to apologize for the incident, Rosalinda had no choice but to ask her to leave.

The girl kept staring at Rosalinda with a smirk on her face, knowing that she wasn't taking that from her. The girl's thoughts immediately interpreted it wrong, thinking Rosalinda meant it as a racist remark, giving her an excuse to argue. When she refused to leave, Rosalinda got hold of her left arm by the wrist, enough to guide her out the door.

The black girl pulled her arm away, refusing to walk out of the restaurant. She then pushed Rosalinda to one side with her other arm, causing Rosalinda to lose her balance. Rosalinda's quick reflexes prevented her from falling; she grabbed a table nearby to regain her balance. As Rose turned around to face the black girl, Rosalinda saw an arm coming toward her, but this time, Rosalinda was ready for her. She stepped aside and hit the black girl's chest, making her lose her balance as she'd done to her and fell to the floor. It didn't take long before the black girl came back toward Rosalinda. The girl cocked her arm back and aimed it directly at Rosalinda's face. Rosalinda moved to one side, avoiding the swing, and cocked her fist. As the black girl's swing passed swiftly by her, Rosalinda loaded her fist with her power behind it and gave her a left hook, sending her to the floor again. The black girl got up slowly, but she was furious and embarrassed because she knew everyone had watched her fall as she landed on her side with a bounce and hit her face on the floor. She finally stood up and walked straight back to where Rosalinda was standing. She positioned herself into a boxing position and told Rosalinda, "Let's go, bitch!" Rosalinda then took her stance, placing herself into a boxing stance.

Both girls started throwing jabs at each other, mostly trying to protect themselves from getting hit on the face but still connecting light punches on the bodies. As the two girls swung at each other, it did not look like a hair-pulling cat fight, but more of a boxing match. The restaurant manager came rushing from behind the kitchen door because of all the banging and yelling he was hearing. Two of his staff personnel followed him as they approached the two girls. The black girl rose from the floor and was getting ready to attack Rosalinda when the manager saw and heard the girls arguing and began exchanging punches again. The black girl started swinging at Rosalinda again, but Rosalinda tightened her fist and returned a solid blow, hitting the black girl in her face. That's when the guys got between them to break them up. The manager and his employees finally managed to keep them apart and control the situation as the manager demanded an explanation. Both girls got silent, staring at each other, fire coming out of their eyes, wanting to tear each other apart. Rosalinda started explaining, but the black girl intervened, saying that Rosalinda was lying about how it happened.

"Quiet!" yelled the manager to the black girl. "You'll get your turn as soon as Rosalinda explains what happened." The manager listened to both sides of the story and decided the three girls at the table should leave the restaurant immediately.

The black girl turned to stare at Rosalinda and said, "I'm not finished with you yet, you brown bitch. I'll see you somewhere soon. Be prepared for the next time because I will not be too easy on you, so beware. I plan to kick your ass back where you came from." She turned around to face the door of the restaurant along with her friends and started walking toward the exit door. As the manager escorted the three girls out of the restaurant, the customers started clapping for Rosalinda. They were glad that the manager asked the girls to leave the restaurant.

When the manager came back after escorting the girls out the door, he approached Rosalinda and told her that he needed to talk to her in his office as soon as she helped clean up the mess from the incident.

When the black girl stepped outside the restaurant with her friends, she couldn't believe a waitress had knocked her ass down to the floor. She kept wondering who Rosalinda was and how she managed to do that to her. She was going to find out who she was, one way or another, to pay her back for what she had done to her.

Rosalinda went straight to the manager's office after cleaning up the mess created by the incident. When she walked into his office, the manager had a Notice of Employee Termination form on his desk for Rosalinda to sign. Rosalinda wasn't expecting this to happen to her since it wasn't her fault. She didn't know what to say to him other than it wasn't her fault, and she didn't start the fight. She tried to convince him of the truth, but it didn't matter. The manager had made up his mind. She couldn't believe that he had to terminate her that quickly.

"Why are you doing this to me?" Rosalinda asked.

The manager knew she was a well-liked waitress and always did what she was supposed to do in her job, but he felt she was too high risk to keep her employed. Then the manager commented, "Rosalinda, I fear that another incident might occur again if she returns to the restaurant. I have no choice but to relieve you from your duties and let you go." Rosalinda was speechless as she looked at the manager with her teary eyes. She knew this wasn't right, and so did he, but he had to make a decision of what's best for the company as a manager of the business.

After the manager talked to Rosalinda, he knew she wasn't that kind of a person to start any trouble with anyone, but he had to do it for the business. As Rosalinda quietly walked toward the office door with her head facing down at the floor not knowing what she was going to do now. After signing the termination form, the manager spoke out loudly to Rosalinda as she was walking out and one foot out the door when she heard the manager make a remark. "Rosalinda, you did very well, protecting yourself against the girl."

Rosalinda stopped and turned around to look at the manager. The manager continued his remark and then told her, "You should explore the opportunity of training with someone who could make you a professional boxer, or at least give it a try to see if you might like it. By the way you were protecting yourself against the black girl, you seem to have some gift and talent with boxing skills that might help you become somebody in the ring." The manager was trying to motivate and convince Rosalinda to give herself a chance about why she should try it. "Think about it Rosalinda. If you decide that you would like to try it, let me know. I know of a good boxing trainer that might be able to help you get started. He's a good friend of mine and has a lot of good connections with other managers and promoters in the boxing world," as he continued to encourage Rosalinda to give herself a chance to at least give it a try.

Rosalinda listened seriously to the open possibilities of becoming a boxer about what the manager was suggesting to her that she should do with her talent. She thought to herself, 'Maybe this isn't a bad idea.' Rosalinda's thoughts quickly realized that he could be right if it could happen. So, after thinking about it as she listened to the manager, she asked him for the trainer's phone number and how she might be able to get in touch with him. The manager wrote the information on a piece of paper and gave it to Rosalinda without hesitation.

After Rosalinda got the information from the manager, she turned around and started walking out the office door when she heard the manager shout Rosalinda's name again. Then she stopped and turned around to face him again. "One last thing Rosalinda!" said the manager. "Rosalinda..." he paused. "Do you know who that black girl was or what she does for a living?"

Of course, Rosalinda didn't know a thing about her, and then she responded, "No! I don't know who she is."

So, the manager looked straight into her eyes from his distance and said, "She's not only a boxer…she's the featherweight champion of the world. Just think about what you just did to her." He smiled, hoping to make her think twice about what he just told her. Rosalinda remained silent for a few seconds as she looked at the manager, and it did make her think twice, just like the manager wanted her to do. Then she turned around to face the door and continued walking out of his office, not saying another word to him. Rosalinda strolled out of the restaurant, thinking about everything the manager had said to her and making her feel confident about herself.

Walking down the sidewalk to her apartment gave her enough time to decide what she wanted to do. She visualized the scenario and how it could change her lifestyle, giving her the chance to own her own home and help her mom back in Mexico. But she also thought about the bad side. She knew of fighters that were hurt badly enough to keep them from fighting for the rest of their lives. She didn't want this to happen to her. She needed another opinion from someone she could trust, and the only person she could think of was her boyfriend, Rob. She knew Rob would give her some good advice about her situation, and she trusted his decision. Rosalinda was so excited thinking about what she wanted to do, so she started walking at a faster pace, just to get home sooner. When she got home, she tried calling Rob, but he didn't answer. Rosalinda didn't even think what time of day it was and had forgotten about him being at work.

'Darn it!' she whispered aloud to herself. 'I must wait until Rob gets off work, which will be around five-thirty this afternoon.'

During their time together, Rob always picked on Rosalinda, making her fight back like a fighter. He taught her how to defend herself as a boxer and stand in a boxing position. This wasn't too new for Rosalinda because one of her brothers back home in Mexico was a professional boxer, and she learned a lot by watching him spar and fight in the ring. She didn't tell Rob about where she was really from and that her brother was a boxer. This was one of the reasons why she was able to defend herself when she got into a brawl with the black girl at the restaurant. She felt comfortable and confident when the situation erupted, quickly remembering and using the skills from flashbacks on how her brother countered back at his opponent when he was in the ring sparring back home in Mexico. That's why she positioned herself into a fighter's stance like her brother had told her to protect herself.

The more she thought about the incident at the restaurant, the more adrenalines began to flow in her body, making her feel like becoming a real professional boxer and train as hard as she could to be ready for the black girl in the restaurant and get the chance for a retribution. This was becoming a dream for Rosalinda and liked the idea of becoming a world champion boxer. She was being optimistic about what might lie ahead for a career that she wasn't expecting to happen. She finally convinced herself to seek the experienced trainer that her ex-boss told her about and pursue her dream. She dug into her purse and pulled out the piece of paper the manager had given her. She couldn't wait until Rob got off work because she was too excited to find out how and what she has to do to become a boxer, so she decided to get hold of the trainer. She tried calling the trainer several times, but there was no answer. She tried again later, but still no response.

It was 5:45 p.m. when she heard the door open and saw Rob walking into the apartment. She was happy to see him and anxious to ask him about her decision to become a professional boxer. Rosalinda rushed toward Rob and gave him a hug and kiss as soon as he walked in, making Rob wonder what she was up to now because when she does this, he knows that she must want something bad. Rosalinda hugged Rob snugly and kissed him on his lips longer than usual. Rob leaned his head back once Rosalinda stopped kissing him. He stared at Rosalinda directly into her eyes, squinching his eyes, and said, "Okay Rose...I love it when you do this to me, but... what's going on? What do you want this time?" he asked.

All Rosalinda had on her mind was about becoming a professional boxer and how she could help her family with the money that she would make if everything turned out to be something she liked doing.

"Okay my love. I do have something I wanted to ask you." Rosalinda kept staring at Rob with hopes that he would understand. "I'm so excited right now. I don't know where to start!" she tells

Rob. "Well...anyway, to get to the point, I want to become a professional boxer." Rob's eyes widened with an unexpected and surprised look on his face, not knowing how to answer her, especially about becoming a boxer suddenly.

"Let's sit down on the couch to have this conversation," she tells Rob. They talked for a while about what she should do with her life, whether she should try it for a limited time to see if she had the passion and heart of a boxer or just wanted revenge on the black girl she had encountered at the restaurant. Rob sat quietly on the couch listening to Rosalinda as she gave reasons why she wanted to be a boxer.

After Rob listened and gave it a thought, he convinced himself and with his involvement with boxing, he knew what a fighter must do to become a professional boxer. He looked at Rosalinda, seeing how excited she was and wanting his approval. "Rose, is this what you really want to do? Have you given it any thought about what it takes to become a boxer? It's not easy and what you want to accomplish is not an overnighter career. It takes passion, hard core training among other vigorous workouts to get you to that point."

Rob could see Rose thinking about what he just told her, but the look Rose had on her face was a look of determination and it didn't bother her at all.

"I do want to do it, Rob. That's what I want to do. I know I could do it. And yes...I thought about it."

"Well Rose, to me, it's not a bad idea, and you should give yourself that chance. But if you don't like it, or it didn't work out for you, you could always quit."

"That's one way to think about it. But I'm not a quitter," she voices her opinion.

After having the conversation with Rob, Rosalinda tried getting hold of the trainer again, hoping he would answer this time. She heard his voice this time and a hello from him. Rosalinda was surprised that he answered, not expecting a response. They spent 30 minutes on the phone with the conversation of becoming a boxer, but Rosalinda did most of the talking, explaining to the trainer what her intentions were and if he was willing to give her a chance to show him any abilities or potentials that she might have to become a professional boxer.

The trainer listened to Rosalinda's explanations and the request she was wanting from him, giving her the opportunity to show him what she was capable of doing in the ring. When she finished talking, the trainer responded with his answer. "All I can tell you, Rosalinda, is to be here tomorrow afternoon, and then let me decide if you have the potential of a boxer. Is that a deal?"

"It's a deal, Sir. That is awesome, and I appreciate you giving me that chance. What time would you like for me to be at the gym tomorrow?" asked Rosalinda.

"Four o'clock sharp," said the trainer.

"I'll be there, and I'll see you tomorrow," answered Rosalinda and hung up. With the thoughts of training with a professional trainer and being excited, she just hung up the phone without saying goodbye. She thought for a minute and then remembered that she had forgotten to ask him for directions to the gym. Rosalinda was embarrassed to call him back because she didn't know where the gym was located or address. So, she had no choice other than to call him back and did. When he answered, all he did was laugh, knowing she was too excited about the chance he had just given her to start training. Then he gave her the directions to the gym after having a brief conversation about what to expect tomorrow. "I'll see you tomorrow, and don't be late," said the trainer. He said goodbye to Rose and hung up.

It was good news for Rosalinda because the gym wasn't far from where she lived. It was four blocks north of her apartment and kind of hidden off the street. The location wasn't in the best neighborhood, but at least there were lights around the place for security reasons.

"I did it Honey!" she tells Rob. "I know I can do it!"

"I'm pretty sure you can, my Love. There are lots of things you have to remember when you're training. I won't go over them right now until you start your first training day at the gym to see if you're going to be alright with the type of training he has for you."

"Okay," Rosalinda responds to Rob. "The trainer seems to be understanding about what I want to do. So, hopefully, that's a good sign."

"Well for now, just wait until tomorrow and then you can decide if you still want to pursue a boxing career, okay? Let's eat. I'm starving!"

The next day, she arrived at the gym on time, four o'clock sharp, just like the trainer had asked her. He was already waiting for her by the ring when she arrived. The gym wasn't in the best condition for training, but good enough to train and work out. The gym had old and new equipment at their locations to train for certain exercises and workouts. It also had lockers, male and female, for everyone to change into their workout clothes. Some of Simon's male and female fighters were still training with the equipment and two others sparring in the ring.

"I believe I forgot to tell you last night that my name is Simon Foster," as he introduced himself to Rosalinda.

"It's a pleasure meeting you, Simon," Rosalinda responded.

"The first thing before we start, I would like to know a little bit about you, Rosalinda. May I call you Rose instead of Rosalinda? Or would you prefer Linda?" asked Simon.

"I like to be called Rose, if it's alright with you?"

"Sounds okay to me," answered Simon. "Rose, it is."

"Let's go into my office and talk," said Simon. Rose follows Simon in the direction of his office as Roses' eyes scanned the gym while walking behind Simon to his office.

When Rose walked inside his office, the first thing she saw was pictures of him and some of the fighters he had trained, and some had championship belts wrapped around their waist.

"Have a seat, Rose." Rose sits on the chair in front of his desk while he goes around and sits behind his desk. "Okay Rose. What makes you think that you can become a boxer? Doesn't it bother you to think about the damage that could happen to your beautiful face, or you could get hurt by some dirty fighter that doesn't care what you look like or who you are?" commented Simon.

"Maybe it's in my blood, like my brother, or because of the incident that triggered me at the restaurant. It didn't take me very long to respond to her actions. My train of thought was to protect myself, and I reacted without thinking about it. It happened so quickly, and I didn't even have to think about it. I didn't know that I had the ability to do that. I think the manager said her name was Brook Spencer, but she went by the name *Echo* and holds the title as the world featherweight champion."

"I know who she is," responded Simon as he bobbed his head up and down with a slight smile on his face.

"Anyway, it made me think about how much I wanted to get a chance to get in the ring with her and take the title away from her. I don't think she's entitled to be a world champion with an attitude like she did me at the restaurant. She doesn't deserve to be a champion. She's rude and unrespectful if you ask me." Rosalinda's adrenaline was kicking in as she talked about Echo as Simon saw her eyes squinch and noticed her fist starting to clench.

"When the manager told me who she was, it made me think twice about what I did to protect myself with confidence. It made me feel like I could learn to be a professional boxer. So here I am, ready to begin a new chapter with my life."

"You know Rose, Echo is not going to be an easy piece of cake to follow. She's been fighting for a long time and has a lot of experience in her resume. She's fought some tough opponents to get where she's at now. She comes from the city of Chicago where she was almost homeless until a trainer saw her by accident fighting with another female on the street and saw something in her that got his attention and impressed by the way she handled the situation with her defense and counters. Thereafter, he took her under his roof in his gym and trained her. Now she's a world champion."

Rose listened to Simon, but it didn't give her any sign of fear if she were to face Echo someday in the ring. It was now a retribution to Rose, and she was determined topursue that goal to settle what Echo did to her.

The conversation lasted for about twenty minutes before Simon wanted to get started with the fundamentals of boxing for Rose. "Okay Rose, I think I get the picture. If you have it in your heart, you will do good and possibly even become a world champ, depending how bad you want it," remarked Simon. "By the way, it sounds like you have made the right decision if you ask me. I'll try to teach you as much as possible in a short time, and the rest is up to you. What you put into it will be the results. Is that a deal, Rose?"

"What are you waiting for, Simon? Let's get started. I'm ready," said Rose with enthusiasm and eagerness about getting started.

"One more thing, Rose. When you told me you stood up to a champion and protected yourself from someone with that kind of experience, and I'm talking four years, and you didn't let the fear get to you, I think you're going to be alright. You impressed me, and I like that. I think we're going to get along just fine."

"Okay. First, let me show you where all the equipment is located and get you a locker where you can change. It's not a lot, but enough to get you in shape to become a champ." Then Simon smiled.

Simon started Rose in the body bag for about thirty minutes. Then he took her to the speed bag for another half hour. So far, Simon was impressed with how Rose worked out with the equipment. She showed some fatigue, but not enough to say she was tired. She sweated a little, but not enough that it was drenching her forehead. Her clothes were a little soaked from sweat, but that didn't stop her momentum. She jabbed and hit the bags like she imagined the black girl was the bag. Simon asked Rose if she had ever done this before after seeing her train with the bags and weights. He was still impressed by the way she handled the bags.

"No!" she replied. "I only use my boyfriend for a punching bag." She giggled when she answered him. "The other times, I watched my brother train back home in Mexico at the gym. Sometimes he would have me jump into the ring with him and show me how to protect myself against someone who might want to hurt me. That was it."

He smiled and looked at her for a few seconds. He didn't think it was that funny. "Follow me, Rose." He walked toward the sit-up bench, and Rose followed, not saying a word. "Give me fifty sit-ups and call me when you're done," he told her and walked away. Rose positioned herself on the slanted bench and began counting "one, two, three…etc." As Rose got closer to forty, she was hurting and wanted to stop, but she knew it wouldn't be a good idea, so she continued counting—forty-four, forty-five. At this point, Rose was struggling to rise to the next count. She was not going to give up now—forty-eight, forty-nine. As she was ready to do her last sit-up, Simon walked up to her. Her face was red and sweat dripped from her forehead for the first time during her training.

Simon looked at her as she did her last sit-up and reached out to give her a hand to help her up from the bench. "Congratulations, Rose! Most of the guys or gals training here couldn't even reach forty, so good job, and I'm proud of you."

After Rose completed the required sit-ups, Simon asked her about her boyfriend. She didn't want to talk about it, but she felt comfortable talking to Simon since he was her trainer and seemed very understanding and trustworthy. Rose sat on a chair close to the ring, and Simon sat next to her on another empty chair. She started talking about the things Rob and she used to do for fun. Simon just listened to Rose telling him most of her past. All Simon wanted to do was get to know Rose and find out how far she wanted to pursue her boxing career and if she liked it enough to become a professional boxer. Now Simon understood why Rose was as good as she was with her boxing techniques. "I would like to meet Rob one of these days," said Simon. "He sounds like he has been an inspiration in your life to keep you focused."

"He has, Simon. I would have been alone all this time if it weren't for him. He has shown me how to survive by myself, mentally and physically. I love him very much." After that remark, they were both silent for a few seconds. "I am a very lucky girl to be with him," said Rosalinda.

"I have seen many fighters come through my gym, and I have never met anyone who explained it like you. It's all real when you say it from the heart, and you have what it takes to become a world champion. I plan to take you there if you stay with me," commented Simon. "Now, let's get back to your workouts and make a champion out of you, okay?" said Simon.

Rose leaped from her chair and gave Simon a whack on his shoulder.

"Boy! That was a hard hit. Like how a true champion should hit," remarked Simon and laughed as Rose prepared to continue her training.

After observing Rosalinda working out with the equipment, Simon already had an idea of what her training schedule would be like for the rest of the week. They had been training for the last two hours, so Simon decided to call it a night. He told her to rest for a few minutes while he went to his office to get something. Shortly after, he returned with a rough copy of her schedule for the rest of the week.

"Here's a rough training schedule for you, Rose. This would determine if you had the stamina and endurance to become a true champion, or if you're just another wannabe fighter like some of the ones that are or have been training in my gym, and they tell me about their boxing abilities to become professional boxers, but for most of them, it never happens because they don't have the passion to do it."

"I promise you one thing, Simon. I won't let you down and I must follow my dream of becoming a professional boxer, not only because I want to, but because I need to settle a score with the champion, Echo. I know I can do it, and I'll do my best to get there, no matter what I must do to make it happen." Simon saw this determination in her eyes, serious and meaningful as she was expressing her words to Simon.

Rose would be his sixth girl in his entire training career. Two of his girls never made it through his required training schedule for a week. They gave up because of the vigorous training Simon expected them to follow. This time, he had a good feeling about training Rose. Simon knew she was determined to become a good boxer and a champion. He just wanted to prove to himself that he was right by giving her a chance to finish the week of training that he had made for her and had a good feeling about training Rose. *If she can only prove to me that she has the potential, I will promise her that I will take her to the top of the world,* he thought to himself as his mind flashed with a dream of his own. It kept haunting him to find a girl he could train to become a true world champion. Rose followed Simon's training schedule as he instructed her for the rest of the week. He observed her moves and punches and noticed that she wasn't hesitating to throw the punches with all her power, and kept her mind focused on her training. He was sure she was the one he would make into a world champion.

After vigorous workouts at the gym, Rose proved to Simon that she could become a true boxer by the end of the week. She had lost three pounds but only got stronger. She felt like her body was in better shape than five days ago. Rose was eager now to continue to pursue her career as a boxer; she liked it after all.

Simon had her sparring with the other girls the following week. The girls she fought were knocked out or knocked down on the mat. They decided they didn't want to spar with her anymore; she was too good.
Other boxers at different gyms were starting to hear about Rose. Word was getting around in the streets within a few weeks about a new female boxer who was tough and knocking out most of the sparring partners who went into the ring with her.

Another thing that was occurring around her training ringside, since she was a Mexican, was how the gym attracted many Mexican people who just wanted to see her work out. Simon didn't mind having these spectators around if they just watched and observed. Some of the spectators were local fighters who were curious about who she was and how she boxed. The funny thing about Rose spar was mostly male boxers instead of females.

CHAPTER THREE

Rob was always there for Rose. He always tried to motivate her when she was a little tired after training. Rob inspired her by caring and doing many little things to cheer her up. He had dinner waiting for her most of the evenings when she got home, playing soft classical relaxing music to add to the romantic atmosphere and occasionally, he would lite some candles on the table to give the kitchen a scent of pleasure. Afterward, they would just sit on the couch and enjoy the rest of the evening, cuddling, and occasionally, Rob would sneak a kiss or kisses on her cheek as they watched television. Rob would try to do anything to draw her attention away from her long and tiresome training day.

Rob's life had been a struggle since he was incarcerated for two years for doing drugs. His parents were alcoholics and never helped him with anything when he needed help. He lived in the ghettos for a few years before he served his time in prison. Rob survived by stealing and hanging around low-life survivors to buy drugs, which was the reason for being incarcerated. Most of his fighting skills developed from protecting himself and trying to help his friends from other gang members that were in trouble and needed someone to help them out, plus it helped him survive in prison with his fighting skills he picked up in the streets. Once Rob was released from prison, he got his act straight, got a job, and later met Rose. Ever since, he has changed his way of life, thanks to Rose, who saw him as a responsible and caring man. She got to know him very well and decided that he was the one she wanted to be with for the rest of her life.

Rob had gotten off early one Friday afternoon and wanted to surprise Rose at the gym and meet Simon. When Rob entered the gym, Rose turned her head and saw Rob walking toward the ring. She reacted with a great big smile, but when she did, a hard hit from her sparring partner came out of nowhere that knocked her butt down on the canvas. She was embarrassed, but it was for a good reason. She knew she could live with that.

"Hi, Rob! This is a surprise." She looked from the canvas and smiled at him.

Rob was trying not to laugh but couldn't help it, so he just kept it mild and smiled at Rose instead as she slowly worked her way up on her feet. She then crawled between the ropes as Rob kept them apart, managing to get out of the ring. Rob grabbed her and gave her a big hug, followed by a sweet and loving kiss on the lips. "I'm happy to see you here, Rob, and this is a complete surprise," Rose told him.

"I figured since I was thinking about this beautiful young lady and had some free time on my hands, I would pick her up, take her home so she could glamour herself, and then take her out to dinner." He paused for a second. "How would you like to go out with me, my beautiful lady?" Rob finished enchanting her with his charming plans.

"I have to think about it." Rose looked at him. "But since you look so charming and handsome, I guess I'll accept that offer, as long as it's a wonderful place to eat," answered Rose.

"I already have a place in mind where I'm taking you for dinner, so shall we go?" responded Rob.

"Not yet. I have to ask Simon first if I can leave this early. So, hang in there for just a minute and I'll talk to him," Rose tells him excitedly.

"That's cool," answered Rob.

Within a few minutes, Simon and Rose walked out of the office toward Rob. "Rob, I want you to meet Simon," said Rose.

"It's a pleasure to meet you, Simon," said Rob.

"It's also nice to finally meet you. Rose has told me a lot about you, and she really loves you. I've heard so many great things that you have done for Rose, and I would like to talk to you when you have some free time," asked Simon.

"Sure," answered Rob.

"What about next Tuesday, around six in the evening? Does that sound okay with you, Rob?" asked Simon.

"That's a good time for me. I'll meet you here at the gym. Plus, it would give me the chance to pick up Rose," answered Rob.

"It was nice to finally meet you. Looking forward to talking to you," said Rob.

"Oh! Rose... go ahead and take off since you've had a tough training day. Enjoy your time with Rob this evening, and I'll see you on Monday, okay?" said Simon.

"Thank you so much, Simon. And you bet I'll be here on Monday. I'll be ready to start a new week." Rose smiled and giggled as she held on to Rob.

"Well, are you ready to leave, my love? You are a very hand-some and good-looking man. You know that? I'm ready to go." Rose spoke to Rob with a happy and flirty smile. "First, let me go to my locker and get my things. It'll take me just a minute. I'll be right back, okay?" Rose rushed to her locker to get her things, which didn't take very long. Rob waited patiently for her as he browsed around the gym. Rose got her things from the locker room as quickly as she could and fast paced herself out the locker door to be with Rob.

"I hope I didn't keep you waiting too long, Honey. I'm ready. Let's go." Rosalinda grabbed Robs' hand and said bye to Simon, thanking him for letting her go home early. She was thrilled and excited just to be with Rob and especially going out to dinner somewhere that she didn't know where Rob was taking her to. Rob wanted to surprise her because he knows how Rose likes him to do those unexpected and spur-of-the-moment kind of things to excite her and make her happy at the end. Today was the day when he felt like doing something special for Rose.

After they got ready and on their way to her dinner surprise, the minute she saw the street of the restaurant where she used to work, she had a feeling about his surprise. As soon as he parked the car, she had already guessed where it would be. Although, it made her happy that he had selected Maria's Café. Now she would be just a guest and enjoy the excellent service, tasty, and delicious food listed on the menu instead of serving it. She had always wanted to try an entrée on the list and she had always been curious about how good the taste would be, and that night was the night when curiosity would be revealed. Many people ordered it and liked it and would always compliment the entrée afterward, but today, it was her time to discover the taste that she had been dying to try for herself.

They were confronted and greeted by one of her best friends, Rita, at the counter to check them in. Of course, they had to give themselves a hug to welcome each other and then Rob was introduced to her. The hostess waited to take them to their special table at a cozy and intimate corner, which Rob requested having two candles set up to light up when they got there. It brought back memories to Rose as they waited for their meals. She talked to Rob about her experience when she used to work there. As they were talking, Rose had a flash-back of her incident that happened to her at this same place. She held herself back from bringing up the unwanted memory of the incident to keep from spoiling the evening, so she kept it to herself and did not say a word about it to Rob. Some employees who worked with her stopped by her table just to say hello and welcome her. The staff who were working at the restaurant that night, mostly the same co-workers during the time Rose used to work there, congratulated Rose on her new career that she was pursuing as a fighter and they were hearing good things around the city talking about how Rose had been winning all her exhibition fights. Meanwhile, Rob and Rose enjoyed every minute they said to each other that evening and what they wanted to do with their lives.

After finishing their delicious dinner and having great conversations about their background experiences, they went to her apartment and spent the rest of the weekend together, having a romantic moment and doing what they wanted to do to end the day until Monday morning.

Before they walked into the apartment that evening, Rose stopped Rob at the front door before unlocking the door, and grabbed hold of Rob around his waist, snuggled him against her and hugged him. Then she whispers in Rob's ear. "I love you so much Rob and thank you for this lovely evening because it was one of the best surprises I have ever had. So, thank you for being who you are in my life." Rob embraced her tightly and kissed her intimately on her lips for a minute and walked her inside to finish the night in bed.

CHAPTER FOUR

After Rose had a great weekend with Rob, going out to dinner and seeing some of her old friends at the restaurant, she was ready to continue her body conditioning with the training Simon had scheduled for the day.

That morning, after working out for an hour with the punching bag and other exercise equipment, Rose was dripping with sweat from her forehead and her clothes dampened from working out when she saw Simon approaching her with a smile on his face. Rose stopped punching the speed bag, looked at him, and asked, "What's wrong?"

Simon remarked, "I have something to tell you."

"Well?" responded Rose.

"I scheduled your first amateur fight one month from now."

Rose's face lit up with an enthusiastic feeling when he told her. She reached out toward Simon, hugged him, and said, "You just opened the door to my dream. The moment I have been waiting for is finally here," she speaks out loudly. "Thank you so much, Simon. It means a lot to me. Believe me." Rose took a deep breath and exhaled slowly, knowing that she was now on her journey to her career for a real match in the ring with an opponent that she had never met.

This was something that she'd been wanting to find out if she could do it and prove to herself that she will become a professional boxer the more she trains. Rose's mind was in a lively mood just thinking about her amateur fight for the next month and was determined to get her body in the best condition she could ever imagine. It motivated her to start working even harder than before and taking her training exercises beyond her limit. She had a month to get in shape and wanted to be 110 percent ready.

Rose had a part-time job at a small grocery market not far from where she lived. She had to have some income to help her pay for the training. Rob helped pay for the rent and most of the groceries. Before Rose started training, they had a long discussion about how they would find a way to free her time for training until she became a big contender. They both knew she had the stamina to become a world champion. They were going to do whatever it took to achieve her goal. Rose worked at the store for just a few hours a week, and the owners understood her situation with her career, so they accommodated her schedule without any problem.

The following day, Rose had a vigorous workout. She was a little worn out by the end of the day, but it was her choice to get her body in the best condition to withstand all the punishment that she would encounter from the fights. When she got home, Rob had already cooked some dinner for them. He had the table nicely set up with the place settings and a candle in the center of the table. When she walked in and saw this romantic atmosphere, her eyes widened. Rob stood next to the table, waiting for her. It was a big surprise, something she wasn't expecting this evening. She loved it and didn't know what to say. Then she rushed toward Rob, wrapped her arms around him, and gave him a French kiss that lasted longer than usual. Rob didn't mind at all. He enjoyed it and didn't want to let her go. They finally broke apart and told her to go shower and hurry back.

They were truly in love, and Rob would do anything for Rose, whatever it took to make her happy, he would try his best to make it happen. The important thing Rob wanted Rose to do was see her succeed in her career. As the evening passed, they had a pleasant conversation at the table while eating, but in the end, Rose couldn't believe how romantic Rob was to her, surprising her with everything he had done. Rob blew out the candles and guided Rose to the bedroom to end the night, embracing each other romantically and falling asleep.

Rose was ready for her scheduled training at the gym for a few hours the following day. She had about four hours of vigorous training with Simon before going to work at her part-time job at the retail store. Sometimes Rose didn't want to go, but she knew this was the only way to help Rob pay bills and the rent. They were managing to survive comfortably, and still had some funds left over to have a little fun together with what they were both making at their jobs.

Rob was supposed to meet Simon at 6:00 p.m. at the gym. When Rob walked into the gym 10 minutes earlier than expected, Simon was already waiting for Rob in his office. As soon as Simon saw Rob standing at his office door, he immediately called out to him to come on in.

"Hey! Rob, I'm glad you were able to come," Simon greeted him. "Have a chair and sit down but give me a few minutes to finish my paperwork. Then we can talk, okay?" said Simon. It didn't take long before Simon finished his paperwork as Rob looked around his office, admiring his photos hanging on the walls. The photos were taken from Simons' past with his ex-fighters, some who became champions and a photo of Simon when he used to fight five years ago until he hurt his hand that prevented him from ever boxing again. "Okay I'm done. Now we can talk," said Simon.

"I had forgotten that Rose had to work at the store today. She called me from work to let me know that she wouldn't be here, but she wants me to pick her up at the store after she gets off," said Rob.

"She told me that before she left about not being here when you arrived, so I was aware of that, but I didn't know you had forgotten about her working today. It's alright since it's just about getting to know each other and how you can help me with Rose's training. That's the reason I wanted to talk to you if you wouldn't mind using your skills to help train Rose. But first, tell me a little about yourself."

"So, Rob…Rose told me that you had been in prison for two years, but she's very happy that she met you."

"Yes. I was in prison for two years. Before that, I would get in trouble and spent some jail time a couple of other times until I met Rose. And I'm glad that I did," said Rob.

"She also told me you were involved with some inmates that established a workout regimen, had privileges to use some exercise equipment, and sparred in a small boxing ring designated in a se-cured area, just for that occasion," Simon tells him.

"Yes, but it was a tiny place with some old, worn-out equip-ment, but good enough to train and work out," Rob responded. "It kept me in shape, and I learned a lot of fighting; street fighting.. that is, but it was mostly to protect myself from the other inmates. It was a good learning experience though."

"What I was thinking about doing is maybe you can spar with Rose one evening or more if you're willing to get into the ring with her and show her some of your techniques. That way, if she could pick up even another move, different from mine, it would en-hance her technique even more, and would be another advantage to use against her opponent for a win," Simon explained to Rob.

It was now making sense to Rob as he listened to Simon's suggestion and liked the idea.

"I think having you in the ring with her will make her realize what a difference it is when sparring with a male fighter instead of a female fighter. I would like for you to start at a slow pace until she gets used to you being in the same ring with her. Then she'll be able to see what the power difference between a male and a female has behind the punch. Don't you agree, Rob?" asked Simon.

"I do. The only thing that bothers me is, what if she hesitates to punch me with all her power because it's me? What if she won't get in the ring with me? What then?" asked Rob.

"We'll have to change it. The way I look at it, she'll do it because I think she's focused on becoming a champion, and this is one of the alternatives of getting there after I convince her of what we're trying to accomplish," said Simon. "And she'll do what I ask her to do without any questions asked." Simon smiled at Rob with assurance that Rose would do it.

"I think you're right, Simon. You're beginning to know her better as a fighter in the ring than I can at home." Rob laughed and thanked Simon.

After getting acquainted, they finally ended their conversation for the evening because Rob had to leave to pick up Rose at the store. Before Rob left the gym, he mentioned to Simon that he'd accept his offer as a sparring partner for Rose but decided to let Simon talk to her first and convince her of the idea.

Rob went to pick up Rose at the store as soon as he left the gym. On the way to the apartment, Rob had a conversation with Rose to let her know what Simon had to say to him, except the part about Simon asking him to be her sparring partner. He preferred that Simon talked to her first about what he wanted to do.

The following day, Rose had a routine of jogging every morning for three miles to help her build her cardio. Most of the time after she ran her miles and returned home, Rob would still be in bed, but by that time, it was time for Rob to get up and get ready for work. Rose usually got up at five in the morning to start jogging, which gave her about an hour to get ready to go to the gym. She was determined to get herself in condition to be a champion.

CHAPTER FIVE

Simon talked to Rose the day after the conversation with Rob, telling her that Rob would be sparring with her this week starting in two days because he first had to make arrangements with his store manager to get his approval to get the hours to coordinate with Rose's training. When Simon told Rose about his arrangement, she hesitated for a minute. But the more she thought of the idea, the more she liked it.

"I can become a better fighter," she thought to herself. She had convinced herself that it wasn't a bad thing after all. Now she couldn't wait to get Rob in the ring and spar with him. Meanwhile, Rob had made arrangements with his work schedule to coincide with her training to allow him enough time to spar with Rose, at least a couple of hours in the evening.

By the end of the week, it worked out just fine and it didn't affect their relationship of training together. Rose was okay and didn't hold back any of her punching power like Rob thought she might do. Rob taught her some of the techniques he learned at the prison like he used against the inmates. It always worked for him, so it was the first move he taught Rose to learn. She was thrilled to have another way to counter her opponents and a couple more that Rob thought she might be able to use. Rob included some exercises that were different than the ones she had already been doing; more intense and vigorous.

After her first amateur fight, she knocked out her opponent in the third round, which was scheduled for four. For the next few fights, with the help of Rob and Simon, Rose won every one of her amateur fights. Simon thought of having her first pro-fight soon. Instead, Simon had decided to have Rose fight a few more amateur and some other exhibition fights before turning her into a pro-fighter, even though Rose had no trouble in the ring, by doing what Simon and Rob trained her to do and winning all her bouts so far. Simon wanted to make sure she was ready because there was no turning back. Rosalinda was on her way of challenging female boxers with a little more experience that will bring out her real talent and show the skills that she had developed through her past few fights.

Another two months passed, and Simon saw nothing that would keep Rose from fighting as a pro, so he set her first pro-bout with a boxer from Chicago named Keyanna Brighton. She had a 4–1 record. The matchup was perfect for Rose since the fighter didn't have that many fights in the ring. Rose didn't care who it was. She just wanted to get in the ring and fight. She felt confident that she was in good condition and physically ready for her first fight or challenges that she would encounter in the future. Simon had Rose get her professional fighting license to fight and be ready for her first pro fight in Las Vegas. The fight was going to be in Las Vegas and scheduled for six two-minute rounds, starting at 4:00 p.m. on Saturday.

Three days before the fight, they planned to fly to Vegas and arrive at 7:00 p.m. on Wednesday, giving them enough time to rest and settle down before the fight. The weigh-ins for all fighters who were fighting in the event on Saturday night was on Friday. It was to make sure that all fighters were at their official weight for the event. Rose was a little nervous when she arrived in Vegas, but she managed to calm down after a couple of hours in the room with Rob. After settling down, Rob had Rose sit on the couch, wanting to say something to her that had been on his mind since they arrived in Las Vegas. "Rose, I just want to say, I'm so lucky I met you. You changed my life and opened my eyes to see better things in perspective, and I really appreciate it. If I hadn't met you, there's no telling where I would've been. Probably back in prison or out in the streets, trying to survive like it was before." Rose listened as Rob talked to her, thinking that she was also lucky to have met him and have him by her side. "But here I am, with you in my arms, holding on to the best thing that could ever happen to me." Rob kissed her on the cheek then on the lips. Rose embraced Rob even harder as he kissed her.

"I think we better go to sleep, Rob, because I have a big day tomorrow, and I want to be alert and mentally focused in the best way I can. You can understand that, can't you?" remarked Rose.

"Can we continue where we left off tonight, for tomorrow night?" answered Rob.

Rose chuckled at that remark, gave him a sexy smile, and said, "By all means, plus you might be surprised with the things I'm going to do to you afterward." Rose chuckled and gave him a good night kiss and hug. Then they cuddled and fell asleep.

The day before the event, on Friday afternoon, all the fighters had to get weighed in for the official weight class they were fighting. During the weigh-ins, all the fighters in the event had the chance to meet face-to-face with the opponent they were fighting. Some of the fighters tried to intimidate their opponents with bad language or smirky expressions to show them who they were fighting against.

On Saturday morning, Rose was feeling great and had overcome her nervousness. She felt strong and ready for her first battle. The morning slowly turned the clock from hours to minutes, and it was almost time for Rose to start getting ready for the bout. Rob had Rose do some shadow boxing and stretches to loosen and warm up her body. And then he had her hit the mitts for ten minutes to build her adrenaline to help loosen her arms and body some more. She was ready and waiting for this moment to happen.

The moment has come, and it was time for Rose to start her first ring walk as a professional after the ring announcer had announced her name. Simon and Rob walked behind her as she strolled down the aisle to the ring. The fans clapped and whistled as she walked down the aisle. It made her feel good when she heard the fans cheering. The fans' excitement made her adrenaline build up and calmed the nerves in her body. Rose acknowledged her fans for their presence and the support they were giving her as she walked to the ring, and she responded by waving her arms high in the air in return. When she reached the ringside, she entered the ring between the ropes and onto the canvas while Simon spread apart an opening with the ropes for Rose. She recognized a few fans in the crowd who were regulars at her gym and waved at them as she walked around the ring. Rose was ready to fight and wanted to make Simon proud with a win because of all the hard work and sweat she had to endure to get here, but thanks to Simon, he was the reason for being here. Soon the other fighter climbed into the ring, showing respect to Rose as she approached her by touching gloves to say hello as a respectful gesture.

After the ring announcer made the fighter's introductions, the referee called them to the center of the ring and went over the rules of what was legal and what was not before he told them to go to their corners and wait for his command to begin fighting. As soon as the bell sounded and the referee shouted, "BOX!" Rose charged Keyanna with confidence and without fear with her right arm, armed with the power to throw her first punch. Rose had no show of fear and brought out her aggressiveness as she let out the first punch, followed by some jabs. Keyanna had her arms in front of her face, trying to protect herself from the flurry of punches Rose was throwing. Keyanna managed to throw a punch that made contact on Rose's face, but it didn't faze Rose. Rose quickly stepped back and sprung forward with an outside swing that landed right on her opponent's right-side temple, causing her to fall against the ropes. Rose saw the opportunity of a knockout and took advantage of the situation by landing combinations and finishing with an uppercut. Her opponent's legs started to buckle, but Keyanna leaned her body against the ropes which helped her from going down. All Keyanna was doing now was guarding her face as Rose kept punching her body then threw a shot at her face. Keyanna clinched Roses' arms and held on to them, trying to keep Rose from landing any more punches on her face. The referee broke them up and had them return to the center of the ring. It didn't take long before Rose shot another hard punch to her body and followed with some combinations, pushing Keyanna against the ropes, punishing her. By that time, the bell rang, and her opponent was safe for the moment.

After the minute break ended, the referee had the fighters wait at their corners for the bell to ring. The sound of the bell rang for the second round. Keyanna was still recuperating from the last round. Rose started her attack with combinations and punching her body like a punching bag. Keyanna kept her hands over her face, trying to avoid any more punches on her face again. Then she embraced Rose's arms and held on to them until the referee broke them up. Keyanna threw Rose a couple of jabs at Roses' face and followed with combinations. Rose counteracted with an overside swing that caught her Keyanna at the right side of her temple. This time, it sent her to the floor. The referee sent Rose to her corner to begin his mandatory count. At the count of eight, Keyanna still wasn't responding very well or getting up from the floor. She never made it on her feet. Rose could hardly wait to hear the tenth count from the referee so she could be declared the winner at the end of the bout.

All she heard were screams and yelling from the fans for her victory. Simon and Rob jumped into the ring to hug her, and Rob picked her up from her waist to celebrate her first victory. The win was the best moment of her life. She had been waiting to get the chance to prove to herself that she could win since she became a professional boxer. She had photographers taking pictures of her with Simon and Rob on either side and singles for the promoters.

After leaving the arena, the three of them went out for dinner and celebrated her first victory. They spent the night in Vegas and returned to Los Angeles the next day at 1:30 p.m., still feeling a victorious ending and only the start of her career.

CHAPTER SIX

Rose was happy to get back home in LA, especially with a big victory. She didn't have to go back to work or train until Wednesday because Simon had told her to take Monday and Tuesday off. Rob took advantage of their evening by taking Rose to a very nice restaurant and had dinner. Rose had a small bruise on her right cheek from one of the punches that Keyanna had thrown that got through and made contact on her cheek. All Rose did was cover it up with makeup to blend it with her skin, so it was no big deal to her. After having dinner, Rob took Rose to a movie. Right after watching the film, they went home to enjoy the rest of the night, doing nothing but celebrating her victory with a bottle of wine and enjoying the moments together. Rose had a lovely evening out with Rob, and she had planned a surprise for him when they went to bed. And it was a surprise for him as she told him she would.

On Wednesday, she was back to her training routine, starting with jogging before going to the gym. She was still full of energy and glory when she arrived at the gym. Simon was in his office already, working on a new training schedule for Rose's next event and his fighters. He had made some phone calls and got hold of a boxing event in Arlington, Texas, that would be held within the next three months, so he made arrangements for Rose to be added to the event. The second one Simon scheduled was in California within three months following the one in Texas. He was trying to get at least four bouts scheduled for the next twelve months. Rob couldn't make it for her training on Wednesday because of his work being extremely busy, but for the rest of the week, he would be able to spar with Rose and show her some of the moves she did wrong in her last fight so she could refine the movements. Other than that, she did what it took to win the fight.

During the next few weeks before her next fight, Rob had shown her several new moves. Her condition escalated above her expectations because Rob made her go six three-minute rounds every session that she sparred with him until she could go the distance without any fatigue. She was in the best condition ever, thanks to Rob.

The month passed quickly and now it was the last week before leaving for Texas. The plans were to leave on Tuesday, which would give them four days prior to the event. That was enough time for Rose to get ready for the event and relax and workout the last two days before the fight. The night before leaving LA, Rob and Rose did the last-minute packing of their clothes and items needed for the trip to make sure they didn't forget anything. Rob tells Rose that she needs to relax and get some sound sleep so she would be ready to travel tomorrow because it was going to be a hectic day for her.

The girl that Rose was fighting was from Alabama. She was a southpaw fighter with a record of 6 wins and 2 losses, but she was known to have the reputation of pushing her opponents, trying to get them off balance and then hitting them as they lost their balance. Her name was Liz Palmer, but they called her "The Rock" because she was solid as a rock, buffed and had tattoos all over her body.

The next day, they were off to Arlington and arriving around 1:45 p.m. at Fort Worth International Airport. From there, they would have a taxi take them to the hotel. After arriving and checking in at the hotel, they all settled into their rooms and relaxed for the rest of the day.

Rose was up by 5:00 o'clock in the morning, taking a jog wherever she could run. When she returned to the hotel, Rob was just getting up. Rob was heading toward the coffee maker to make some coffee as Rose was walking in.

"Good morning, my dear love. How are you this morning?" asked Rose.

"The mattress was too soft for me, and my neck hurts a little because of the soft pillow," Rob answered.

"Poor baby! Come and put your head on my shoulder so I can rub it," Rose made fun of him.

"It's not funny," Rob sobbed. "I still think that you should rub my neck. It really hurts."

"Ok, come here, then." Rob scooted closer to Rose as she rubbed his neck for about ten minutes. Rob sighed with pleasure, making him feel relaxed.

"That feels so good," commented Rob. "Thank you so much my love."

"You're very welcome my dear. Now go take a shower so you can feel even better afterwards."

"Okay, I will. Thank you."

Simon's room was six doors down the hall. Rob called his room to see if he was awake after taking a shower.

"Hello, Simon," said Rob.

"Good morning, Rob," responded Simon.

"Just calling to see if you were up and ready to start the morning."

"Yes, I am, Rob. Thank you for asking. I've been up for an hour already and drank all the coffee in the room, so I'm wide awake now. How about you guys?" asked Simon.

"Rose has already returned from her morning jog and is now taking a shower. I guess she'll be ready when she does her girly things if you know what I mean." Rob chuckled.

"We should have a light breakfast this morning. Rose must get weighed today for her fight. Today is the weigh-in at two o'clock, so she can't overeat to ensure she's at her weight. I don't think she'll have any problem making weight. She's cautious when it comes to her weight."

"That's Rose for you. Always cautious," said Rob.

"Yup!" Simon laughed.

After the weigh-ins, Rob had a surprise for Rose waiting for her at the hotel. He snuck the gift into the room without Rose knowing what he had done. He hid it in the closet and covered it with a towel just in case Rose happened to look inside the closet and see the gift on the shelf. When Rob and Rose went back to the hotel room, they talked for a few minutes before Rob decided to give Rose her surprise. So, after having a conversation with each other, Rob walked to the closet to get Roses' gift. He returned to where Rose was sitting on the couch. "This is for you, my Love." He surprises Rose unexpectedly. Rose looked at Rob as he gave her the surprise and her eyes opened widely with an exciting expression. "I thought you might want to use this tomorrow night. Go ahead and open it!" Rob tells her. Rose rose from the couch and held on to her surprise.

Rose didn't know what to say. It was totally a surprise for her. Her eyes sparkled, still wide open with a cheerful smile. The present had a fresh pink rose attached to the top of the box. She didn't have the slightest clue when he had done that. She picked up the pink rose and smelled the aroma of the flower as she put it closer to her nose. Then she started unwrapping the present. As she removed the wrapping from the gift, she saw a beautiful pink robe and picked it up. But it wasn't just a robe. Her name was written on the back like a rainbow over an embossed pink rose as large as a basketball. It looked beautiful, and Rose loved it when she first saw it. She then slipped it on with the help of Rob, and it fit perfectly. "Rob, this is so beautiful, and I love it. That is so thoughtful of you to get this for me. How in the world did you manage to get this without me knowing about it?" asked Rose.

Rob commented, "It wasn't easy because we're always together, but I figured out how to do it with the help of Simon. I think you deserve it, and I wanted the crowd to see and remember the name of the next world champion." He chuckled. "What I had them do though, I shortened your name to "The Rose." I thought if your fans would see your name on the back of your robe, it would remind all the people and fans watching you tomorrow night, who you are and how beautifully the rose reflects you and your name." Rob, with a broad smile, looked at Rose and saw the happiest smile that he had ever seen of her.

Rose cuddled her arms around Rob and gave him a massive kiss on his lips. "Now I have to win this fight for you, my love. I guarantee it. I dedicate this fight to you—or, should I say, I'll win this for you," said Rose.

"Remember, Rose, from now on, you will be called 'The Rose' because this is how the crowds will remember you, okay?" answered Rob.

"I will, my Love, and thank you so much. I love you, my Love." Rose embraced Rob snugly against her body with her warm hug, lasting for a few minutes longer.

"I love you, Rob. I'm glad I met you." Rose whispers in his ear passionately and kisses his ear with her warm lips.

CHAPTER SEVEN

The day and time had arrived. The event will take place soon with the preliminaries fighting first, and then the night's main event will start right after. Rose will be the third fight in the preliminaries. So, this gives her more time to warm up and get her adrenaline worked up and ready for her battle.

The waiting time was hard for Rose because she was anxious and the adrenaline was flowing one hundred miles an hour through her body, eager to get started and confront her opponent in the ring. She was serious about her fight and wanted to prove to her fans that she was here to fight and entertain them. She had about an hour before her scheduled bout. Simon wrapped the tape around her hands and an official scribbled his initials across the tape as a mandatory ruling before Rose could put on her gloves. Then Simon had her shadowboxing and hitting the warm-up mitts with Rob to help her loosen up her muscles and continue the flow of her adrenaline.

Rob was getting his things together for the corner of the ring with water, tape, scissors, and a small jar of Vaseline needed for cuts or unexpected bruises occurring at her corner after warming Rose up with the mitts. He also had her new robe ready for Rose to put it on as soon as Simon finished with her. Rob was happy that he got the robe for Rose. He was very proud of her and loved her like no other man could love a woman.

The time was now for Rose to step into the ring. As Rose walked down the aisle wearing her new robe and carrying a single pink rose in her glove, the crowd noticed her name on the back of her robe and started yelling, "R-o-s-e! R-o-s-e! R-o-s-e!" until she climbed into the ring and walked around, carrying the flower. Liz was in the ring already and waiting for the bout to start, as anxious as Rose.

When the ring announcer finished with their introductions, the referee went over the rules and then had them go to their corners until the bell rang and then shouted out the command to "Box!" the second he heard the bell ring. Liz didn't waste any time, charging Rose with a right swing and then a left, but Rose reacted as quickly as a cobra, striking back with jabs, and targeting her midsection. Soon, it became like a street fight, punch after punch after punch, like two rams clashing their horns at each other, but instead, it was gloves with power thrusting to the faces. Liz kept holding on to Rose's arms to slow her down because many of Roses' punches were connecting on her face. The round ended, and they both went to their corners. The four rounds scheduled for this bout were just two minutes long with a minute in between for a break.

Rose will most likely win this round by making more contact with the punching and controlling the round, which the judges look for, and the aggressiveness of the fighter by their actions.
Rob advised Rose, "Keep jabbing and step back then let her come toward you. That's when you give her a combination. Wait for her to come back with her swing, and when she does, set her up with a couple of left jabs and come up with your uppercut on her jaw. You got that?" yelled Rob.
"Yes!" said Rose.
"And put some power behind it," Rob yelled once more. Then Rose rose from her stool and waited for the bell to ring to start

round two and listened for the command to box from the referee.

They both met at the center of the ring and started where they left off. Liz was a little more aggressive this time and surprised Rose with a punch that got through to Roses' jaw. Rose expressed the pain by the look on her face. Rose held on to Liz's arms this time to give her some time to recover from the hard blow. As the referee broke them up, Liz shoved Rose back and tried to hit her as she got off balance. The referee noticed that, so he gave Liz the first warning about the illegal push. They returned to throwing jabs and combinations, but Rose was getting the best of them. Liz started to push Rose away from her, trying to hide it from the referee so he couldn't see anything from where he was standing. She was trying to get Rose off balance and hit her at that moment of the shove again. This time, Rose was ready for her. Rose kept jabbing and throwing straight hard punches at Liz' s face. Liz tried to protect herself from the punches coming at her, but she was unsuccessful. Rose was landing and scoring with every punch that she was throwing. When Liz tried to shove Rose again, the referee looked closely at Liz when she was thinking of doing it again. That's when the bell rang to end the round.

Both fighters went to their corners to recoup from the round and listen to their coaches for any advice they could give them and watch out for, besides wiping the sweat off their faces and rinsing and drinking some water.

Then the bell rang for the third round and the referee yelled out, "Box!" The third round started, and Liz looked like she didn't have the energy she had initially from the start. Rose still looked like this was her first round. She was glad Rob had pushed her to her limit, making her go the six rounds every time he sparred with her. Now she was in top condition, physically and mentally alert, because of what he made her do.Rose's adrenaline burst with energy that made her aggressive. She charged Liz with punches, landing combinations with lefts and rights to the face and at her liver. Liz tried to hold on to her, but Rose was too quick with her jabs. Rose found an opening between her gloves when she pounded her stomach and then went straight to the eye, making Liz raise her arms to guard her face. That's when Rose went for the uppercut and got through to her jaw and knocked her on the mat. Liz went down hard, and it looked like she wouldn't be getting back up. By the time the referee was at the count of eight, Liz was still struggling to get up from the canvas. She never made it up before the count of ten, so the referee waved his arms crisscross, stopping the bout, and indicating that it was a knockout. The bout was over, and Rose had just won her second fight as a pro with a knockout. Her record was now 2–0 with two knockouts as a professional. She was thrilled to death and was already thinking about her next fight in Sacramento within nine weeks.

Nine weeks passed, and Rose won another fight in Sacramento by a TKO in the fourth round. Rose was well-conditioned during that fight, and her adrenaline was still flowing from her last bout. In the next three fights that followed, she won, two by way of knockouts and one by a decision. Her record was now at 6–0 with five knockouts. She was becoming an attraction to many boxing fans, and her true fans followed her wherever she was fighting.

CHAPTER EIGHT

One evening, after Rose got home from her training, Rob walked up to her as she walked in the door, grabbed her hand, and then said to her, "How would you like to go for a walk around the neighborhood, close to where we live, and enjoy the evening together in a nice quiet place to have dinner?"

"I would love that, Rob," answered Rose with a kiss on the lips. "Let me get ready and shower so I can change into my comfortable clothes, and then we can go, okay?" said Rose as she stripped off her top, covered with sweat from her workout. She continued toward the bathroom, dragging her body slowly to the shower.

"Don't take too long," said Rob as he walked to the kitchen. "Would you like something to drink?" asked Rob, his voice raised a little louder because she was in the bathroom.

"Yes, I would. Thank you, Babe," answered Rose. "But wait until I'm finished taking a shower."

"What would you like: water, Coke, or a beer?" yelled Rob.

"Water is fine," she said loud enough for Rob to hear.

Rob waited until he didn't hear the shower running. Then he walked around the corner from the kitchen toward the bedroom door, carrying a glass of cold water in his hand when Rose came out flying through the bathroom door and almost collided with him.

"Holy shit! I almost spilled the glass of water on you. Are you okay?" asked Rob.

"Yes. I'm okay. And you're lucky you weren't walking any faster. I would've been pissed-off at you if you would've spilled a cold glass of water all over me," remarked Rose.

"And what would you have done to me, my dear?" asked Rob.

"Punched you in your stomach then I would've given you a great big kiss on your lips. How's that for punishment?" said Rose.

"Sounds like maybe I should've done that." Rob laughed. "Are you ready to go?"

"Give me another five minutes and I will be," responded Rose.

Rob waited patiently.

"Okay, I'm ready. Let's go," answered Rose as she picked up her purse sitting on a chair by the door.

So off they go, strolling down the sidewalks of the town, looking at things displayed in store windows, and occasionally, Rose would stop and admire some of the clothes displayed on the mannequins. She would stare at Rob with a sad and begging look, hoping it would make him feel bad for not buying it for her, just like a little kid begging her mommy, asking her if she could have it. But Rob didn't give in so easily. He always gave her a hard time before he was conned into getting it for her; Rose always ended up getting it.

After walking several blocks, enjoying every minute as they held hands, they decided to return to the apartment. Just as they were three blocks away, Rose thought she heard some mariachi music coming from a nearby place but wasn't quite sure. Then she asked Rob, "Do you hear what I think I'm hearing?"

Rob listens and hears what Rose was saying to him. "It sounds like it's coming from that direction."

As they got closer, the music became louder. Rose could hear a strong Mexican voice and trumpet playing. It was a mariachi band playing at this little restaurant. Rose became anxious and curious to see who these musicians were. It reminded her of home. She never told Rob that she was from Mexico. All she told Rob when they first met was, she lived in Texas with her mom and wanted to be on her own, so she decided to travel to LA and start a new life without the help of her parents. She also told him about her endeavors to LA and how she met and made friends with Amber when the bus stopped in Arizona to pick up the people traveling to other places besides LA, which ended as good friends until she disappeared with her boyfriend.

Rose was absorbed with the music as they sat down to listen to the mariachi band. Rob looked at Rose as she enjoyed the music. It was like something had captured her mind and taken her to another world. They listened for an hour when Rob had an idea and wanted to share it with Rose.

"Rose!" Rob said it loud enough so she could hear him because of the loudness of the music. "I think I have a great idea about this band. What if I could get this band to play one of your favorite Mexican songs in front of you as you walk up toward the ring? And you know the rose you usually carry into the ring?" Rob stopped to get Rose's attention, looked her in the eyes, and continued to get her full attention. "Well, what if you stopped at a random side of the ring with your back against the fans and threw the rose out to the fans? Just like throwing a bouquet at a wedding, as a symbol of your name, the Rose. What do you think?" As Rose stared back, Rob kept looking into Rose's eyes with an exciting and enthusiastic expression on his face, waiting to hear a response from Rose.

Still staring into Rob's eyes, Rose let out a big smile and said, "You are brilliant. You know that. I love the idea, and I can see myself walking down the aisle in my robe and hearing a piece of Mexican music and the people shouting out my name, 'The Rose.' Do you think it would be possible? And can we afford it yet?" asked Rose, intrigued by Rob's idea.

"I can surely try, but I think you should go with me so they can see who this beautiful lady they'll be playing for. How can they resist you? Besides, what if they only speak Spanish?" Rob smiled at Rose, telling her what his chances were by having her next to his side. "What do you think?" asked Rob.

"I can handle that," replied Rose.

"Let's go talk to them," said Rob.

The idea worked, and they both agreed to do it in her next fight. Rob, especially Rose, got excited about the idea and could hardly wait for it to happen at the events.

"So, my dear Rose, are you ready to go home now?"

"Yes, I am, my dear handsome man. Let's go, and I'm ready. And thank you for this lovely evening. I love you, Rob," Rose whispered in his ear as it was emotionally and affectionately coming from her heart. The night turned out to be a wonderful and enjoyable evening for them. They had successfully made a deal with the mariachi band to play for Rose at her fights. Rose was thrilled to death, excited about the brilliant idea, and loved Rob even more than ever for doing what he did.

As they walked home, holding hands, the glowing moon brightened the sky, creating a warm evening. After they went inside and did their things before getting into bed, Rob started kissing Rose on her cheeks and ended on her lips. Rob had drunk a little too much but was feeling good, and so was Rose. The next thing, they were in bed, cuddling, kissing passionately and ending the night with a romantic and loving end.

Rose had another vigorous workout at the gym the next day with Simon and Rob. She learned a few different moves that Rob had up his sleeve. Her next fight was going to be in Las Vegas again with a fighter from Hawaii. Rose was confident with herself, knowing and feeling ready with her physical condition and stamina, no matter who they put in the ring with her, she felt ready.

Simon met with Rob in his office in the morning to tell him that he had one of his fighters scheduled to fight in Los Angeles the same day, so he wanted Rob to manage Roses' fight in Vegas.

"I got Jerry, a cutman, to help you at Roses' corner, and I know he's experienced because I've used him before you started helping me. Are you okay with that, Rob?" asked Simon.

"Sure. I don't have a problem with it," answered Rob. "Does Rose know? You know how she is with surprises," said Rob with a worried look.

"I don't think she'll have a problem either. As a matter of fact, I had mentioned it to her about a month ago that I was setting up a fight with one of my other male fighters around the same time, but it wasn't a set deal at that time. That was the only date they had available. Now here I am, with two fights scheduled at the same time, and the only way I can work this out is by having you take care of Rose for me. I have a lot of confidence in you, Rob, and I know you can do it." Simon stared at Rob when he finished explaining the situation to him.

"Do you want me to tell Rose what's going on or shall I have you mention it to her first?" asked Rob.

"Go ahead, Rob. She'll be okay with you telling her. She'll probably be happier about it when you tell her yourself," Simon tried to convince Rob that he could handle it and not to worry.

Later that evening, as Rob and Rose were just about to finish eating their dinner, and Rose was sitting across from him, Rob laid his silverware on his plate after taking his last bite. Then he looked at Rose straight into her sparkling eyes and paused, wondering how he would open the conversation about him being her manager for her next fight. He looked at her, cleared his throat, and then took a deep breath.

"Rose." He said her name with a soft-spoken tone of voice. "On your next fight, Simon asked me last night to be at your corner to take care of you because he has to manage his other fighter in Los Angeles the same day as your fight. It just worked out that way. He didn't have a choice because that was the only time to schedule his fighter. He didn't want to wait any longer for another chance to open and lose the opportunity for his fighter to fight for the number one ranking contender." He paused. "Oh! I almost forgot to tell you that Simon made arrangements with Jerry to help me."

Rose took a deep breath and said, "I already had a feeling about this because Simon had mentioned it to me, but at that time, he wasn't sure, and I hadn't forgotten what he told me, although I was wondering what he was going to do, and he hadn't said anything about it. But now I know for sure. Thanks."

Rob was relieved and then asked her, "Are you okay with that?"

"I couldn't be happier or luckier to have you at my corner." She rose from the table, walked around Rob's side and wrapped her arms around his shoulders. She leaned over to the right side of his cheek and gave him not one, two, or three, but four warm kisses. Then he turned his head around and went straight for her lips and plunged his lips right smack into hers. "Let's clean up the kitchen and what do you say we go to bed and call it a night?" said Rob.

"Why do we need to clean up? We should call it a night and worry about cleaning tomorrow." Rose silenced his conversation with another kiss, not letting Rob say another word and leading him to the bedroom. From there on, the night ultimately became a night neither one will forget, ending with a romantic and passionate love that each other had for one another.

There were five more days before the forthcoming event in Las Vegas. This time, Rob, Jerry, and Rose were the only ones going. Rob felt confident that he could handle Rose's corner with the help of Jerry, the cutman, so he wasn't worried. The only fear he had at first was telling Rose about being at her corner without Simon. It turned out to be easier than Rob expected. She was completely confident in Rob. That was a significant relief for him.

The night before leaving for Vegas, Rose had a hard time sleeping. She kept thinking about the girl she was fighting and how she would counterattack her style. Rose gave Rob a nudge to wake him up, telling him that she couldn't go to sleep. Rob opened his eyes and felt Rose's hand touching him. He rolled over to face her, asking her, "What's wrong?"

"I can't sleep. I keep thinking about the fight," responded Rose.

Rob got closer to Rose's body from behind, holding on to her and cuddling for a while. After 30 minutes, Rob's warm body next to hers made her forget the fight and finally managed to fall asleep.

The following day, she woke up with a bit of a headache, just trying to rationalize the strategy of her fight. Rob, lying behind her in bed, opened his eyes facing Roses' back and had his arm across her stomach and whispered in her ear, asking her to turn around so she could look at him, and then noticed something was wrong by her confused look on her face. Rose never wakes up this late and is usually consistently energetic in the mornings, but not this time. Her facial expression showed that she wasn't the same Rose as before. Rob asked her if she was all right.

"Of course," she said, "Yeah!"

"Well, you sure don't look like it," remarked Rob.

"You're right. I don't feel that great, but I'll be all right," said Rose. "I just had a long night thinking about the fight. I'm getting up." She rolled over toward Rob and kissed him on his lips, and then moved back to her side of the bed and practically jumped out, trying to arouse herself from her moody behavior.

She went straight to the kitchen and started heating the water in Keurig and added the gourmet pod. She was still half asleep and dragging her body around the kitchen, waiting for the coffee to finish dripping into her cup, and then she went to the bathroom to do her girly things. Meanwhile, Rob was slowly crawling out of bed, concerned about Rose's feelings. He wasn't prepared for the day to begin like this. He got out of bed and dragged his body to the kitchen, smelling the aroma of the gourmet coffee pod Rose had made for herself. He got himself an empty cup from the cupboard and replaced the pod with a full one in the Keurig, and then added the cream and sugar. Rose managed to get into the shower by the sound of the water trickling and splashing the side walls of the shower. Rob sat on a stool at the kitchen table, waiting for Rose to finish taking a shower and meanwhile, he had some toast ready for her. It was just a few minutes later when she stepped out of the bathroom with a towel wrapped around her body and her hair partially damped, carrying her cup of coffee, and said to Rob that she was freezing. "I just want to say good morning my Love."

"I smelled the aroma of the coffee, and I just had to rush to the kitchen to get a cup," said Rob. "I made you some toast."

"Thank you so much, Rob. You're an angel in disguise." She wrapped her arms around Rob, gave him a big smack on his cheek, and went right back to the bathroom to finish drying her hair and dressing into something comfortable.

It took her another fifteen minutes to finish doing what she had to do, and then she came walking out of the bathroom with a smile and a change of attitude from the time she had gotten up. Rose walked to the table where Rob was waiting for her and sat across from him.

"Do you feel a lot better now?" asked Rob.

"Yeah," replied Rose. "While taking a shower, I thought about you and how confident and comfortable you will make me feel having you at my corner. I thought about how you have changed and motivated me to be who I am now. You put me at a higher level of life and opened my eyes to the dream I have longed for since I got here. I'm so happy to be with you. I love you for what you have done for me."

Rob sat quietly and listened to Rose saying words he wasn't expecting at this moment, but she made him feel like a proud and lucky man as she finished saying what was on her mind. Rob stood up, walked behind Rose's chair, and wrapped his arms around Rose.

As Rose tilted her head far enough to get a better look at Rob, Rob kissed her on her forehead. Then he leaned over a little more to reach her lips. There was a little silence between them, and not long after that, Rob wanted her to go back to bed with him, but she knew there were things to do this morning, and she couldn't afford to take this time to do what sounded so comforting and plea-surable. She had to talk her way out of it without hurting Rob and making him understand that it wasn't him.

"Rob, I would love to take you into the bedroom right now and make love to you for a very long time, but as you know, I have a hectic day ahead of me, and right now, it isn't a good time. Do you understand?"

Rob kept kissing her lips and cheeks, yearning to make love to Rose.

"Okay! Okay! I understand," answered Rob with a disappointed tone of voice. "I apologize for being so selfish. I got lost after listening to you say those loving words to me. I'm sorry, Rose."

"You're right, but I won't forget what you just told me." Rob gave Rose a flirtatious smile as Rose knew what he was referring to.

"Maybe, just maybe, after we arrive in Vegas and settle in for the night, I'll show you and treat you to a wonderful night you won't ever forget. How's that sound to you?" Rose said in a sexy and loving tone.

"I can hardly wait," answered Rob, his eyes sparkling. "Okay! I can live with that!"

"I want to do the same thing, but I think we should take care of business first to make sure we are ready for the trip. We can finish what we both want once we get to Vegas. Is that okay my Love?"

"Yes, I'm okay with that."

Before leaving for Las Vegas, she wanted to take care of some of her things that she didn't have for the trip. The flight leaves LAX at 5:00 p.m. and arrives in Vegas around 6:35 p.m. That would give them enough time to settle in and relax before the fight. Then he asked her if she was ready to start getting her things together. She replied, "As soon as I finish drinking my coffee, I'll start doing my things."

"Okay, I'll go ahead and start with mine, and then I'll help you with yours," said Rob.

It was almost time for them to take off to the airport to catch their flight. It took the cab twenty minutes to get there. Check-in time was two hours before taking off. Now they had to wait another hour and a half before taking off. Jerry was going to meet them tomorrow in Las Vegas. When they got to Vegas and checked into their room, it was about 8:00 p.m. Both were exhausted, but they remained in a good mood because they had finally reached their destination.

The following morning, Rob discovered that he was alone in bed, and Rose was not at his side. He knew that she was probably out doing her routine jogging. He then smiled and whispered aloud to himself, 'That's my Rose,' and then jumped out of bed, went straight to the kitchen, and started making some coffee. It wasn't long before the door opened, and Rose walked in. She was taking her shirt off, sweaty from the jog. Rob was sitting at the table, waiting for her while drinking his coffee. As she passed by him, she kissed him on his head and continued to the refrigerator to get a water bottle. Rob got a whiff of her sweaty odor as she got close to him, but it didn't matter to him. He knew she was constantly pushing herself to exceed her conditioning limit and maintain her endurance.

Her opponent was a girl from Hawaii with a record of 8–1. She went by the name of Monique Stafford, a blond-haired fighter with eyes like the color of the sky on a clear day. Besides being very aggressive, she had a powerful left-hand punch that stopped most of her opponents in the ring. She had moved to the USA from Germany six months ago and settled in Hawaii to get her training. She was determined to bring her ranking high enough to become a contender, making her eligible to fight for the world championship in her division, but Rose intended to get there first. She had a different style than most other fighters because she was a southpaw and had a reputation for pushing the fighters with both hands to get them off balance after holding on to the fighter's arms and stepping on their feet. Her move was to hide and position herself with the referee behind her to create a blind spot for him, making him unable to see the illegal movement and letting her get away with it. Rose was prepared for her, knowing the type of fighter she was after watching some of her previous fights on video. Rob had prepared her for that move with a technique to counteract her style. They figured out a way to overpower her action so it would backfire on her when she attempted to use it on Rose.

The fight was to take place at 6:00 p.m. as a non-title fight. The one to follow their bout was going to be for the featherweight division, which was the main attraction for the night, meaning that

Echo was fighting to defend her championship title. Echo was why Rose wanted to become the best she could to become and earn her way to be the top contender so it would allow her to challenge the champion, Echo. Rose has worked hard and is determined to reach that goal of being in the ring with Echo. Rose was not too far from reaching her goal of accomplishing her dream. Winning her next fight tonight would put her in a position to move her up to that level status.

Meanwhile, back in the dressing room, Rose was preparing for her bout. After wrapping her hands with tape and the official putting his signatures on the tape, Rob had her warm-up after putting on her gloves and doing some shadowboxing. He then had her striking the sparring mitts until she started to sweat a little to get her adrenaline going. Rose was eager to begin her bout, ready to release her energy in the ring and win her fight. Rob held the robe he had gotten her, waiting for her to finish warming up. As soon as she was ready, he helped Rose put on her robe and then put the hood over her head. The large pink rose embroidered on the back of the robe with her name is as visible as the sun on a sunny day. Rose was ready to walk out to the ring to face her opponent with all the confidence in the world. She also carried a fresh red rose in her glove to throw out to the fans as a trademark for her name.

As she walked down the aisle, the mariachi band sounded off their music in front of her, loud enough for everyone to hear. The fans knew she was on her way to the ring as soon as they heard the Mexican music coming down the aisle. When they saw the entrance of Rose coming down the aisle, most of the crowd stood up, yelling, cheering, and whistling out her name as she passed them. Some waved mini-Mexican flags as a sign of their country. Her fans loved her for who she was and were hoping she would become a world champion one day.

Rose was a beautiful girl with long brown hair. She always braided her hair before her fights, so it wouldn't interfere with her vision and block the way of a coming punch. When Rose made her way through the ropes as Rob was holding them apart into the ring, she walked around the ring, waving at all her fans with her arms high and holding the rose that she was throwing at her fans. The next thing she did was stop at a random place in the ring. Then she stood holding on to the rose as the fans waited for her to throw it. With her back against the crowd, she threw her rose over her shoulder toward the fans as the fans reached out to catch it. That was her trademark, and the people loved it.

A lot of the people in the crowd were already half-drunk and were usually the ones that were boxing fanatics. They attended most of the scheduled fights, especially tonight, with Rose being in one of the fights. They knew it would be a challenging fight for her but entertaining for the fans, and the other was the main attraction. The featherweight championship title was at stake. Now Rose would have a chance to see the champion, Echo, fight for the first time in person. Everyone hoped and wished her opponent would knock the crap out of Echo. Most fans wanted to see the champ get her butt beaten to the ground once and for all. Rose was facing a fighter more of her caliber, so this wouldn't be an easy night for her.

As the ring announcer finished stating the introductions for both fighters, the referee had both fighters go to the center of the ring to explain the rules for the fight tonight, and then told them to return to their corners and wait for the bell to ring. The bell sounded and the referee shouted out the commanding word, "Box!" That's when both fighters rushed to the center of the ring where they made contact. Monique threw the first hard punch to Rose's face and followed with some combination punches that Rose wasn't expecting. It caught Rose off guard. The crowd came to a sudden silence when they saw it happen. For a minute, they were shocked to see this happened to Rose. But it didn't take long before Rose returned with a solid jab to the right side of Monique's head that made her sway back and took her a few seconds to regain her stance. Rose didn't waste time and followed with a punch to her gut which took the wind out of her. Rose quickly took advantage of the situation of not letting Monique get her wind back and immediately came up with an uppercut that sent Monique to the mat.

The referee jumped in front of Rose to back her away to start the count on Monique. She was on one knee, trying to regain her wind back. At the count of eight, Monique rose quickly to avoid a knockout. The referee checked her to confirm that she was all right to continue fighting. Monique was okay and ready to defend herself from Rose. She was still trying to recuperate from the punch that Rose shot to her stomach. Now all she was doing was protecting herself from Rose's punches. There were thirty seconds left in the two-minute round and Monique was trying to survive through this round. The bell sounded and saved Monique from a knockout.

As both fighters sat in their corner stools for the one minute break that was allowed after every round, Rob told Rose, "Back away from her and let her come towards you with a few steps then charge at her with a jab to set her up for a left hook, and when you do, I want you to put all your power behind it and connect it to her jaw. It must be fast and quick but keep your arm and elbow protecting yourself from her right swing."

After the minute was up, the referee had them wait at their corners until the sound of the bell. Then shortly after, the bell rang for the second round. Again, both fighters rushed toward each other in the middle of the ring, like they were ready to knock each other's brains out with their first punch. Rose was able to get the first solid punch to her body again, and then she followed with some combinations to her face. Monique's legs buckled a little, but she kept clinching on to Rose. The referee broke them up, and Rose went right back to jabbing Monique's face. The referee was keeping a close eye on Monique because she was only protecting herself from the punches and not fighting back and was getting a beating from Rose with power punches and combination shots to her face. The referee was concerned about her ability to fight back or not. He was giving Monique another minute to see if she was going to counter. Monique was still a little confused and didn't entirely recuperate from Rose's punches. She kept holding on to Rose's arms, trying to keep Rose from throwing punches at her. The referee again broke them up and commented to Monique that she had to box and not dance with her opponent then let her return to the fight. The round was almost over, and Rose couldn't knock her out. The round finally ended, and the bell again saved Monique.

Both fighters were tired, but Rose seemed to have much more energy than Monique. When the bell rang for the third round, even though you could hardly hear it because of the crowd being so loud and yelling and screaming their lungs out, both fighters went straight back to the center of the ring and continued fighting with what they had left. Rose was more aggressive this time because Rob had told her to finish her off so they could go home. He knew Rose was a better fighter and had more scoring points than Monique up to this round. Rose attacked Monique with everything she had. She landed some hard hits to her side, then her body, and ended with combinations to her face. Rose kept jabbing left and right as Monique tried to protect herself the best she could. Although Monique had a difficult time keeping away from Rose as Rose continued hitting her hard with flurry shots from every angle and connecting and scoring with every punch Rose was throwing. Rose just wanted to knock her out that minute. Surprisingly, Monique came up with a hard blow to Rose's face and stunned her a little, but not enough to damage Rose. She went back and gave Monique an uppercut, just like Rob told her, but this time, it was effective.

Monique's body fell straight to the canvas, landing next to the ropes. She struggled to get back up as she grabbed and pulled herself up with the ropes. The referee was on the eighth count by the time she completely stood up, trying to regain her focus. The referee looked at her and decided to check to see if she was capable and strong enough to continue the fight. He decided to stop the fight because he felt she wasn't going to make it another round and considered it a knockout for Rose.

As soon as the referee crossed his arms to let the officials know that the fight was over. Immediately, the crowd stood up and let out their joy for Rose by yelling out her name as they clapped and whistled as loud as they could. Rob jumped into the ring, rushed toward Rose, and embraced her. He couldn't be a happier guy than he was tonight to see Rose continue to win her fights. Rose was even more pleased when she saw Rob's expression on his face with a huge smile. Then she whispered into his ear and said, "I told you, this win was for you," and smiled then kissed him on his lips. The crowd was glad to see Rose win tonight and build their hopes for her to become the next champion contender against Echo. The fans wanted Rose to dethrone Echo from her title and knock the crap out of her. They knew that Rose would be the one to do it.

When Rose was officially announced the winner by the ring announcer, she walked around the ring a few times, thanking the crowd, then stepped out of the ring to walk back to her dressing room. Her mariachi band started playing her favorite song and led her path to her dressing room. She raised her arms high in the air, waving at the crowd and paced down the aisle until she disappeared into her changing room.

As Rose passed the champion's dressing room, the door swung open. Out came the champion in her robe, looking for one of her trainers. Rose stopped and turned around to see her. The champion closed the door behind her and noticed that Rose was staring at her. They immediately made eye contact. Echo wasn't quite sure who she was because she had never seen Rose since the incident at the restaurant, but she heard a lot about Rose through the news media. Echo continued eyeing Rose and had a feeling about who she was, thinking that she had seen Rose somewhere, but couldn't remember where.

Rose hated Echo more than anything in the world, and now she is another step closer to getting a match with her. The retribution with Echo will be the most satisfying moment for Rose when she strips Echo of her title in front of all the crowds, which many boxing fans were looking forward to seeing because of her reputation. She didn't deserve to be called a world champion. Rose kept her cool as she continued to her room. The champion turned around after Rose continued walking toward her room. Echo kept wondering where she had seen Rose.

Twenty minutes later, and just by coincidence, the champ, Echo, walked out of her room to head toward the ring for her fight as Rose also stepped out of her room. Echo started walking down the aisle to the ring entrance as Rose walked a short distance behind her to go back to her hotel room. Echo wasn't aware Rose was walking behind her because she had her robe with a hood over her head, blocking the view. Her robe had a bright red lightning bolt running at an angle across the back with her name written inside the lightning bolt. Rose was planning to go back to her room right after her fight, but after seeing Echo walking in front of her, she changed her mind and decided to stay and watch the title fight. Rose thought watching her fight tonight would give her a better idea of how she fought her opponents. It would allow Rose to study her style for when the time comes to face her in the ring.

The other reason she wanted to stay and watch the fight was because she was hoping and wanted to see her opponent knock her butt to the canvas, but she was too optimistic to think that way. It made her think about when she first met Echo at the restaurant, but at that time, she didn't know who she was. All those memories that Echo painted on her mind were a nightmare for Rose. She was hoping that one day she would meet her again, but in the ring, to erase those horrible memories embedded in her mind.

The first fighter to enter the ring was Christi Keener from Chicago. She had a record of fourteen wins and two losses, six being knockouts. A few minutes later, Echo started her entrance to the ring. That's when the noise, booing, and yelling started getting louder. Echo walked down the aisle toward the ring, ignoring the crowds as they yelled profanity words at her. The arena got so loud that it felt as though it was ready to tumble. The crowd had not stopped yelling rude names at Echo when she entered the ring. After a few minutes, the ring announcer had to ask the audience to stop yelling and screaming too loud so he could introduce the fighters. It took another few minutes to manage and control the crowd. They finally calmed down to hear the announcer with the event introductions.

The main attraction for the night finally started, and the champ allowed her opponent to hit her with a few punches before Echo belted Christi on her side and a power punch to her body, which caused Christi to gasp for air. Then the champ gave her an uppercut that sent her to the floor. The referee stepped in front of Echo before starting the count and told Echo to return to her corner. Then he began the mandatory count on her opponent while she struggled to stand up. Christi was trying to get her breath back and regain her composure. She slowly made her way up, and the referee grabbed her hands to see if she was able to continue. He felt that her strength was enough to continue and brought both fighters to the center of the ring to continue the fight.

As Rose and Rob watched the fight, her anger escalated as the champ punished her opponent. Christi clinched Echo's arms to keep her from hitting her body and face. But Echo was too sharp and fast. Her punches were filtering through her opponent's blocks and scoring. The first round finally ended, and Christi was lucky that it did because she was on the verge of collapsing. Christi, still confused after a beating from Echo, managed to walk back to the wrong corner when her manager yelled at her to come this way to her corner. The minute flew by too fast for Christi; it didn't seem to be long enough for her to recuperate all the way. The bell rang, and Christi charged Echo with what she had left, showing more confidence and being more aggressive. She started throwing more punches at the champ's face, scoring points. The champ wasn't too happy about that. You could see on the champ's face that she was ready to murder her. Echo started to punch her opponent with some illegal too-low blows. The referee didn't see it because she hid the punches from his sight by blocking his vision. Christi stooped over a little, and the champ took advantage of her position, clobbering her on the face. She followed with combinations and punches to her stomach, and then on her face again. Christi's legs started to buckle as the champ kept throwing a flurry of punches, making contact, and scoring. With one minute left in the round, all she could do was clinch on to Echo's arms to slow her down.

When the bell rang, the champ couldn't help but give her another low blow after the bell sounded. The referee saw it this time, so he went up and warned her. He decided to take a point off her score for misconduct. The crowd loved it when the referee deducted the point from Echo. They kept yelling at her with boos and calling her profane names.

It didn't take long before the bell sounded off for the third round. The crowd finally mellowed down and waited for Christi to give her a hard punch, enough to knock the champ out for good. But it didn't look like it was going to happen. The champ still had too much energy left and kept on punishing Christi. This time, she gave Christi a hard punch on her left eye, making a small cut above her eye that started bleeding. The blood quickly ran down her eye, interfering with her vision. The referee reacted as the blood ran down her eye and stopped the fight to check on her. He had her go to her corner so the doctor and her trainer could have a look at her eye. After the doctor wiped some of the blood from the eye, he evaluated the cut over the eye. She was okay to continue fighting.

The champ waited impatiently for Christi to continue because she wanted to get this fight over with. As soon as Christi was face-to-face with the champ again, Echo went straight for her eye again and succeeded, hitting Christi on the same eye with the cut and making it bleed again. Echo intended to do that. Christi tried to protect it but couldn't do it because the champ was too fast with her hands. Suddenly, Echo managed to throw a hard punch that connected to Christi's jaw. Christi's body dropped like a falling stone, hitting the canvas hard, bouncing a couple of times when she landed. The referee quickly stepped in front of the champ and pushed her back to her corner. It took a few seconds before he returned to Christi to start the mandatory count. Christi was still struggling to get up, but she wasn't going to make it this time. With her eye bleeding and after the hard punch, there was no way that she would get up. The referee was on the eighth count, and Christi couldn't even sit or attempt to get up. She was too hurt to continue. The bell rang, and the crowd started to boo again, showing anger toward the champ. They hated her and were hoping to see her get knocked out for once. Although like before, this didn't happen. She still retained the title of world champion.

Rose sat and watched the fight come to an end. She was furious, wanting to go up to Echo and ram her fist in her face. Rose had to control herself. When the time came to be face-to-face, she wanted to put her ass on the canvas, after punishing her. The champ walked around the ring with her arms in the air and a smirk on her face, being sarcastic about her win. She was letting the crowd know that she was still the champion, knowing how the crowd would react to her victory and showing her glory. She didn't give a damn about what they thought about her. She just wanted to torment the crowd by displaying her ego as always. Rose's anger increased every minute she watched Echo walk around the ring with her arms raised in the air. She despised her for how she was trying to represent herself to the people.

As soon as the ring announcer mentioned Echos' name and declared her the winner, the referee raised her arm in the air. That's when the crowd booed and screamed profane names at her again, even louder than when she entered the ring. Echo finally decided to step out of the ring as her staff put her robe around her. Then she climbed between the ropes and strolled down the walkway to the lockers. As she took a few steps down the aisle, she passed right by where Rose was sitting and caught her staring at her. Rose stood up and looked straight into her eyes without fear, not saying a word. Rose was trying to control herself from doing anything foolish at that time.

Echo knew who she was now. She remembered the day when she knocked her ass on the floor at Maria's Café where Rose used to work as a waitress. She also knew that Rose would become the first contender to challenge her for her title by the way Rose was winning all her fights. Echo finally opened her mouth and commented to Rose, "You're no different than any other fighter. I'll be waiting for your time to come if you make it. And if you do, I'm going to knock the crap out of you to the ground until you can't get up anymore. You'll be lucky if the doctors will be able to do anything for you at the hospital." Rose, still trying to control herself, couldn't let her walk away without saying anything to her and remarked, "I can hardly wait to see your ugly face in the ring, and if you think that you're a badass, wait till that ugly, badass becomes your face. I'll be waiting for that time to come, and you're damn right that I'll be there to do it."

Echo's manager had his hand on Echo, holding her by the shoulder, ensuring that nothing would get out of control. The staredown lasted for a few minutes, then Echo turned around and continued walking down the aisle toward her dressing room.

The crowd continued to yell and scream profane names at her; others tried to reach out to hit her. Luckily, she had her managers and guards around her to protect her from harm. Rose never sat back down on her chair. She stared at Echo as she made her way back to her room. Rose's thoughts swept her away; she was thinking about the day of confrontation with Echo in the ring. She couldn't forget what Echo told her before being escorted out of the restaurant: "I'm not finished with you yet."

Now she was a couple of fights away, and Rose was determined not to let anything get in her way of winning the next two fights, no matter what. Rose can't wait for this face-to-face confrontation with Echo to happen, so she could knock the brains out of her. Then she stepped onto the aisle and left the arena to go to her hotel room with Rob.

CHAPTER NINE

Rosalinda became to be known as "The Rose" throughout Los Angeles and Las Vegas. Her name was very popular with many Latinos who were the majority of the crowd attending the event. She was a threat to many boxers because of her skills and her 14–0 record with eight knockouts. Many managers wanted to put their fighters in the ring with her to see if they could beat Rose. But there was nobody yet that could stand up to her.

The champ, Echo, was hearing a lot of talk about the Rose. Echo wasn't worried, but she became jealous because Rose was getting most of the publicity. Echo was getting fed up and tired of listening to the people talking about Rose or how great she was and hoping that someday, Rose would be the next champion of the world.

Before fighting the champ, the next two fighters scheduled to fight Rose would be the worst and dirtiest recognized fighters to fight in the ring. One was from Texas and the other from England. The one from England, Rose thought, is the toughest and strongest of the two. The fighter from England used tactics that were as illegal as they could get if she could get away with it. She had two losses on her record. She was disqualified for using illegal punches several times on her opponents, and the other was the loss to the champion, Echo. In either case, Rose felt confident and ready for either one. She continued working vigorously every day with the training of Simon and Rob. Her endurance was building more and more every day, and she was learning the techniques Rob and Simon trained her to do, over and over until she got it almost perfect. Her body conditioning developed into a strong cardio to go the distance of twelve rounds if it were the case. Simon and Rob always tried to give Rose what they felt would be the best way to counter-attack her next opponent by reviewing the video. That helped prepare Rose for any unexpected punches or moves the opponent would use against her.

A few months passed, meaning that Rose's next fight was close for the event to happen. She felt ready for the next fight because she couldn't afford to lose either fight because a loss would set her back, destroying her chances of fighting Echo for the title. Rob pushed Rose beyond her limitations when Simon wasn't around to train her.

The next fight, which will be the co-main event, was going to be in Houston, Texas, on a Saturday night. The promotion of the fight was a success for the event. It attracted thousands of fans attending and thousands of viewers, making this event a mega fight. When the day came for Rose to fly to Texas, she felt well prepared and was calm and confident against her opponent. She just wanted to get this next fight over with a win and eager to face her next opponent from England. Her adrenaline kept flowing in her body, rushing to her heart, creating activity in her brain, and sending all the power of energy throughout her muscles. She was saving all this built-up energy for that day to be in the ring, face-to-face with the champ, Echo.

The best thing about this fight for Rose would be a fight closer to face Echo for the retribution and satisfaction of stripping the title from Echo and feel the joy of humiliating the champ in front of her fans. Rob and Simon were excited and optimistic about

Rose winning her fights, but first, she must win this fight in Texas and then defeat the fighter from England, which would be the most important fight in her life because it would make her the next contender to fight for the featherweight world title, against Echo, the champ.

CHAPTER TEN

It was Wednesday in the afternoon when they arrived in Houston, Texas. This gave her enough time to chill and settle in the hotel before her fight on Saturday. She had been here a couple of other times before because of two other fights in the past. She liked coming to Texas because it reminded her of her hometown in Mexico. The last two times that she fought here made her feel closer to her home after seeing most of the fans were of her nationality, Mexicans. They seem to be very proud of her for being who she represented and showed their support with cheers and standing ovations both times she fought here. This weekend was not any different than the other times she fought here. She still felt the support of her Mexican fans who attended.

On Friday, she had her weigh-in day and was on target and so was her opponent, Kelsey. This was the first time they had seen each other face-to-face. Rose's confidence was at her utmost readiness for her opponent. She had viewed her opponents' techniques and knew what to expect. Kelsey Fernandez is also a Mexican fighter and a native of Texas. She was well-known by her nickname "The Cobra."

Before every fight, providing that she had the time, Rose would make a point of going out to the fans and signing autographs for the people. Meeting fans was one of the good things she liked doing for the people; they loved her for taking the time to do that.

After the weigh-ins, Simon and Rob took Rose out for dinner and had a great time wandering the city for the rest of the evening.

"I'm so happy that I have both of you guys with me and at the corner of the ring. You guys mean a lot to me. After tomorrow's win, we can begin focusing on my next fight, and I promise you, I will win that too." Rose was being optimistic because she believed in herself. "Then, the most important fight of my career will come when I have the chance to face Echo. That's my goal, and I'm making sure that I will be in the ring with her. That's another promise I will keep."

Simon and Rob were astounded just listening to Rose about how determined she was to make it happen by beating Echo for her world title. She was not letting anything get in her way to meet face-to-face with Echo. Simon and Rob believed that she could do it and will do it when the day comes to be in the ring with Echo.

CHAPTER ELEVEN

The time had come for Rose to eliminate one more fighter with a win and then face the biggest challenge of her dream. This was a must-win fight for Rose; defeating this opponent would mean having one more fight to win and being the next in line to fight the champ for the title.

Rose had to focus on this fight first. It had to be a win. Both fighters were in their rooms getting ready. As Kelsey walked out to the ring, down the aisle, she was welcomed by many of her fans. There were a few who booed her, but she ignored them. The crowd then heard Rose's mariachi band playing. That's when they knew Rose was coming down the aisle at any moment. As she approached the aisle to the ring, the crowd cheered with excitement and yelled "Rose!" as loud as they could. Rose felt appreciative to be around a crowd that made her proud to represent her country. She was proud to be who she was. She entered the ring and the audience continued cheering for Rose. As always, before the start of every one of her fights, she stopped at a random side of the ring, turned around with her back toward the crowd, and threw her rose out to the crowd of her fans, a symbol of her name.

The ring announcer started his introductions for both fighters. During the announcement, you could hear a lot of hurrahs and very few boos from the crowds because they were both liked. Plus, this was Kelsey's hometown, and although Kelsey wasn't the favorite, they wanted Rose to win because they knew she had a better chance than Kelsey of fighting against the champ, Echo. After the introductions, the referee sent the fighters to their corners after he finished going over the rules and told them to always protect yourself at all times. And then he had them wait for the bell to ring.

The bell sounded and both fighters went to the center of the ring after the referee shouted, "Box!" Both fighters attacked each other like wild roosters. The fighters went out swinging with all their power and were already trying to knock each other out. Since they were both experienced fighters, it was difficult for either one of them to find an opening for a solid hit and throw that knockout punch. Rose backed away to see how Kelsey was going to bring her counterattack to her. Rose let Kelsey come close to her with her punches, then Rose responded with some of her hard shots to her side, then countered with some jabs to her face. The Cobra backed away and eased up on her throws. Rose didn't stop jabbing and continued with some flurry of punches pushing Cobra against the ropes, hitting her face and scoring points with every punch Rose threw. The Cobra tried to protect herself by clinching Rose's arms. It was only the first round, but the Cobra looked like she was already running out of energy. Rose wasn't as tired, but she was starting to breathe faster than normal because the Cobra gave her a fight for the money. The bell rang to end the first two-minute round.

Rob and Simon talked to Rose as she sat resting on her stool and wiped the sweat off her face, waiting for the next round to start after the one-minute break.

"Don't forget that she can hurt you if you let her find an opening, so keep giving her combinations to the face and lower body to keep her from using her left hook. If she starts to use it more frequently, back off and let her come to you, then try to get her against the ropes to slow her down. You got that?" Rob trying to get

Rose to listen and does what he tells her to do.

The bell sounded and the referee yelled out to box. Both fighters returned to the center of the ring to continue where they left off. The Cobra started jabbing Rose with two combination shots with her right arm. And then she started using her left arm, trying to set up Rose for her kill. She scored with a couple of good hard punches against Rose, catching her off guard. Kelsey surprisingly snuck a left to Rose's jaw and stunned her. As the Cobra got aggressive with her punches after she gave Rose that left hook, she kept on punching Rose's face with combinations, punch after punch. Rose was trying to protect herself from the Cobra's blows. This time, Rose clinched Kelsey's arms around the Cobra to avoid getting hit by the flurry of punches thrown at her. This slowed her down enough to let her catch her breath, but the referee broke them up.

It was only halfway into the second round when Rose finally managed to find an opening to hit the Cobra on her face, which sent her back against the ropes. Rose followed through with a few more punches, but the Cobra wasn't giving up. She kept fighting Rose, landing solid punches on her face, but Rose was doing the same thing, scoring points. As they were beating each other with hard blows, one after another, the time ran out to end the round. Both fighters were exhausted again. Neither one had the strength to knock each other out. The first round had to go to Rose. She was the most aggressive and scored the most points with her punches. The second round would turn out to be even if it was scored accurately by the judges.

Simon was a little frustrated with Rose because she left herself open for that left hook that got through after telling her to watch out for that move.

"You must focus on her style. She will knock your ass on the canvas if you ignore her left hook." Simon tells her. "Don't blow your chance with your ignorance because it only takes one time and a few seconds to destroy your opportunity for your next fight. If you want to win this fight, listen to me and do exactly what I tell you. Focus! Damn it. Focus! Look at me, Rose! Are you listening to me?" Simon looked straight into her eyes.

"Yes! Yes! I'm listening. Focus! Focus! I got it." Rose got up from her stool and jumped around to keep her adrenaline going after Simon tried to encourage her and make her understand how important this fight was to her.

The bell rang for the third round and Rose was ready this time. Her adrenaline had kicked in. She was ready to knock her opponent's ass to the canvas. The Cobra wasn't a piece of cake when she returned to the ring to face Rose. She must've had a good talk before returning for the third round, like Rose in her corner. The Cobra was firing back at Rose with all she had and was doing a good job at it. This time, Rose focused on Cobras' move, watching out for her left hook. She was trying to set up her uppercut to knock the Cobra out as soon as she could find an opening. Cobra was doing a good job of defending herself defensively against Rose's punches. Rose kept throwing combinations shots at Cobra, targeting her face and delivering some hard blows to her side and stomach, but the Cobra clinched Rose's arms to slow her down. Rose kept pushing the Cobra away from her to set up her uppercut. The referee saw what was going on, so he broke them up, which gave Rose the advantage of setting herself up for the kill. The Cobra was hurting and seemed like she was out of energy. Rose took advantage of her weakness and found an opening at the face when the Cobra lowered her arms to protect her body. Rose instantly reacted with her right arm and threw an uppercut to the jaw that sent the Cobra to the canvas. The Cobra landed on her back and bounced a couple of times. The way her body hit the canvas, she wasn't likely to get up anymore. With Rose's power punch that made contact, the Cobra was out and wasn't going to stand up for another round. The crowds were on their feet, knowing that Cobra wouldn't get up in time at the count of ten like the way she went down. The whole stadium was roaring with excitement because they knew Rose had won this fight. They were just waiting for the referee to reach the count of ten for the official knockout. Rose knew from this moment on, she needed one more fight to win to become the next contender for the title.

All she heard was the crowd yelling her name. Her mariachi band started playing as soon as the referee reached the count of ten. Simon and Rob jumped into the ring as Rob grabbed Rose and raised her up on his shoulders to celebrate her victory again. Rose waved to all her fans as she sat on Rob's shoulders. The Mexican fans yelled with pride and waved the mini-Mexican flags with joy. Rob walked around the ring with Rose on his shoulders. Rose was emotionally moved by her fans, seeing how they believed in her and supported her every time she fought. The Cobra had to be helped up by her managers and taken back to her corner. She was still trying to recuperate from Rose's hard punch on her jaw.

As soon as the crowd settled down, the announcer went to the center of the ring, where Rose was standing, to announce the official winner of the bout. The crowds were still celebrating Rose's victory. The ring announcer finally started his announcement and declared Rose the winner by way of knockout, and then the referee raised her arm high in the air. The crowd got louder. Winning the fight tonight was another giant step forward for Rose and one more fight closer to the title shot. As Rose walked down the aisle to the changing room, the mariachi band led the way, and the crowds kept yelling her name as loud as they could, "Rosa! Rosa! Rosa!"

When they returned to their hotel, Rose was still excited about her win, even though she had a swollen eye, and her side was hurting from all the punches the Cobra had given her. She was so exhausted from the fight that she asked Rob, "Can you hold me in your arms for a moment? And kiss me gently on my lips? I love you, Rob! And thank you for being there for me. You mean so much to me. I wouldn't have been here if it weren't for you. I love you, Rob," she whispered into his ear.

Rose embraced Rob tightly, and Rob held her for a minute and then told her, "I love you too, Rose. You mean so much to me too. All my life, I have always wanted to find someone like you. I wouldn't have given you up for anything in the world, not now, not ever. We've been through a lot, and right now, I think that we have something special between us that changed our lives. Something we love doing. I love you, Rose." Rob held Rose gently and then kissed her on the lips as Rose asked him to do. Shortly afterward, Rose showered and got ready for bed. Rob did the same, as Rose waited in bed for him.

They lay in each other's arms and made love the rest of the night until they fell asleep, listening to romantic music.

CHAPTER TWELVE

Rose gained recognition as a great fighter all over the States. She was known for her undefeated record in the ring since she started fighting. She now has an unblemished mark of 15 wins, 8 of which were knockouts and no losses. Many fighters wanted to get in the ring with her to see if they could beat her, but everyone who tried failed.

There was a rumor surfacing, meanwhile, about Rose's background, especially from the place where she was born. They were talking about her expired visa and the probability of her chances of not being able to fight in the United States. She was considered an illegal immigrant. Rose did not have a clue; she hadn't heard anything about the rumors surfacing about her.

Two days after Rose had won her last fight in Texas, Rob was walking to the gym with his friend when he asked Rob if he'd heard any rumors about Rose's background. Rob was shocked to hear him say that to him. "What do you mean rumors about Rose?" Rob responded. "What are you talking about?" He wasn't too happy when his friend asked him. He couldn't believe what his friend had just said. It got Rob worried. That was not a laughing matter but something serious that could hurt Roses' status or her career. Rob sped toward the gym to find out if there was any truth to this rumor. His mind was still in shock, but he was furious at the same time and was hoping it was just a misunderstanding. When he arrived at the gym, he looked for Rose. She was nowhere in sight. Then he went to Simon's office to find out if he knew anything about the rumor. Simon was sitting behind his desk working on Rose's schedule for the coming fights when Rob walked into his office. Rob had a worried look on his face, and Simon noticed how serious and worried he looked as he entered his office. Simon was baffled and confused and had never seen Rob look so bewildered. Simon then asked him, "Is there something wrong that's bothering you, Rob?"

"Yes, there is. My friend just told me something that I hope is not true."

"Well, what is it, Rob?" asked Simon.

Rob didn't know how or where to begin to tell Simon. "Simon..." Then he paused for a second. "Have you heard any rumors or conversations about Rose's background?" asked Rob.

"No, not a word. Why?" asked Simon.

"Well, as I was saying, my friend just told me there were rumors about Rose not being a US citizen. Either her visa is expired, or she is an illegal immigrant. I hope this is not true because you know what this will do to Rose's career. Not at this time of the game. For God's sake, I hope not," Rob finished talking.

Simon didn't know what to say. He was trying to understand what Rob had just told him and hoping that it was just a rumor.

"Where's Rose?" asked Rob.

"She went out for her routine jog. She should be back any time now," answered Simon.

They both didn't know whether to be frustrated or angry with Rose. They just had to wait until she got back and hear the truth from her.

Ten minutes later, Rose stepped into the gym, sweating, and carrying her top jersey over her shoulder. As she walked toward Rob and Simon, who were standing in front of the office, she noticed they had different and awkward expressions on their faces. They did not say the usual comment, "How was your run this morning?" As soon as she was close enough to Simon, he told Rose that he needed to talk to her in his office as soon as she refreshes herself a little. Rose didn't know what was going on. She walked to the restroom with a puzzled look on her face. She knew that it must be a serious matter that made Simon concerned. 'They didn't look so happy about something. It was probably something that happened here at the gym.' This was a thought that crossed her mind.

Rose walked to Simon's office after doing what she needed to do to get refreshed from her jog. When she stepped inside the office, Simon was behind his desk and Rob was sitting on a chair facing Simon and an empty chair next to him for Rose to sit. Simon remained quiet and calm, but Rob was anxious to ask Rose for the truth about the rumor. Rose walked up to Simon's desk as they both stared at her as she took her steps towards them until she stood in front of them and without any hesitation, she asked Simon, "Did I do something wrong? Why are you both looking at me that way?"

The first thing Simon asked Rose to do was to have a seat. The room suddenly was in silence, and they were all feeling a little tension among them. Rob and Simon were hoping the rumors that were spreading in the city and no telling who would know how far the news had already traveled, was just a joke. Rose, sitting quietly now, didn't know why they wanted to talk to her. Simon was dreading asking Rose about the rumor, but he had to find out if it was the truth or just a joking rumor that was going around the city. "Listen, Rose," Simon pauses and stares at Rose into her eyes and begins his conversation. "We have been fair to you and given you all our time to make you who you are today. You have proven to us that you have this passionate gift of fighting, and now we're just around the corner to make you the next contender to fight for the title. Then you will have your dream come true and make your people proud of who you are, and what you're fighting for. There is something that has surfaced about your background. I want you to be honest with us, and I want you to tell us the truth when I ask you a question about a rumor going around town about you in the streets and among other cities. Rob heard a disturbing rumor about you from his friend this morning on his way to the gym. He wasn't too happy when his friend told him. But he said that you are not a legal US citizen, which means you can't fight here in the US without legal papers or a legitimate visa. I want you to be honest with us and would like to hear the truth from you. Do you understand how important this is to us? This could change the whole situation about your next fight or any other fight, especially for the title bout. Do you know what I mean?" Simon finished explaining the circumstances to Rose.

Rose remained silent for a few seconds, thinking, feeling nervous and scared, then turned toward Rob and looked at him like she wanted to burst out crying at that very moment. "Rob, I didn't realize it would ever get to this point. I'm so sorry that you had to hear it from someone from the streets. I didn't mean for it to get this far. Everything was starting to come together for me, so I lost track of time. I wanted to tell you Rob, but I couldn't at that time. I needed someone in my life to be with, and when I first saw you and spoke to you, I got this feeling about you right away. After talking to you, I knew you were a good person that I could trust. I felt safe being around you. Since then, I have loved you." Rose tried to apologize to Rob for not telling him everything about her.

"The rumor that you heard is true about me. I'm so sorry, Rob." Rose burst out crying and leaned on Robs' shoulder. After Rose calmed down, she added, "I did have a visa card, but it had expired two weeks after I got to Los Angeles, and I didn't want to go back to Mexico, so I had to find a way to stay low and keep myself away from trouble so they wouldn't find me. I found a Social Security number in the streets, so I used it to apply for jobs. Since then, I have been using it. I don't even know who this person is that had this Social Security number. I just used it," answered Rose.

Confused about the situation, Rob turned toward Simon and asked him, "What do we do now, Simon?"

"Well..." answered Simon as he paused for a second and thinking about how to handle this. "I think we need to continue what we have been doing with the preparation for the next fight and start looking into some legal advice from an attorney to help us figure a way to get Rose some legal papers as soon as possible. Maybe if things don't get out of hand too quickly, we can keep her scheduled bout with the fighter from England without any interference from managers and coaches who will try to push this situation further. We have come a long way with Rose, and I don't want anything to prevent her from fighting for the title. She deserves a chance to fight for the title, and if she does get that opportunity, I know she'll beat the champ and establish a name for herself. That's why we must keep going as far as we can." Simon sounding worried but hoping that all this won't affect Roses' chances of fighting for the title soon.

Rob followed with a comment. "I think you're right," and turned around to look at Rose. Rob was upset with Rose because she didn't tell him the truth about her real background. But now it was too late. He had to think about what to do next. He wasn't going to give up on Rose just like that. He loved her too much for him not to try and help her out in any way he could, especially at this point. He found it in his heart to forgive her for not telling him everything about this matter. He looked at Rose and embraced her for a while as tears ran down her eyes and waited until she could talk about the whole situation.

The conversation continued with Simon agreeing to continue to keep doing what his plans were with the training until he figured something out to resolve the situation with the visa. So, the plan was to keep training Rose as they were and prepare her for her next fight.

CHAPTER THIRTEEN

They continued their regular training routine for the following weeks and tried not to let the shocking and disturbing situation interfere with the preparation workouts for the next fight. Simon did get calls from some coaches who told him that Rose should be disqualified from fighting in the United States. These threatening remarks made Simon furious and angry that he wanted to beat their brains out, but instead, he controlled himself from making the situation worse for Rose. She was still bothered by her feelings of not informing Rob about her background of living in the US with an expired visa and false social security from someone else. She felt bad that she had let Rob down by not telling him. She had to overcome that situation, or else it would cause her to lose everything that she had fought hard for up to this point of being so close to becoming the next contender fighting for a championship title.

Meanwhile, as time passed, rumors continued spreading throughout the city of LA and several other cities where Rose had fought. Simon and Rob were hearing more and more talk about Rose's citizenship, which made them seriously worried. Coaches and managers of several boxing gyms were questioning whether she even had a green card. Some were okay with that, but the fighters that lost to her in the past wanted to take the opportunity to do something about it. They wanted her disqualified and out of the picture because that would increase their chances of going higher up in their ranking. They were the ones taking actions against Rose by digging into her background and trying to find any information that would incriminate her with the findings and disqualify her from boxing in the United States.

The problem now with all the rumors going around the city of LA, the rumors had traveled and heard at other states. Somehow, it reached the office of the Federal Boxing Association. This triggered an investigation on Rose. They searched on her background but couldn't find any paperwork proving that she was a legal US citizen. They also discovered that the Social Security number she used belonged to a deceased man in Texas. Because of this uncovered discrepancy, they set up one of their associates from the Immigration Department to continue the investigation. So, the associate went searching for Rose to pay her a visit and get some more information from Rose and answer questions the associate will have Rose verify and confirm her stay in the United States legally. They wanted an explanation from Rose to prove that the Social Security number that she was using was hers. If she couldn't provide enough evidence that it was hers, then the next step they would take is the deportation back to Mexico.

Meanwhile, Simon and Rob started searching for an attorney to help them with the legal aspect of the situation. Rob remembered an attorney that helped his friend get his green card in a hurry after being caught without having legal papers on him, so he told Simon about him.

"I think I can get a hold of him and talk to him about Rose's situation tomorrow," said Rob.

Simon remarked, "If you get hold of him, let me know as soon as possible so we can get this mess sorted. We can't waste any time."

Another month had passed, but Rose kept training as much as she could to stay in good physical condition for her coming fight, and training with Rob every minute they had for Rose to know her opponents' style inside out. The fight was going to be in Los Angeles this time.

During this time, the Immigration Department had planned for an Immigration officer to drive to LA where Rose was doing her training after they gathered some of Roses' information from the Boxing Organization. When the Immigration officer arrived at the gym, Rose had already gone with Simon and Rob to the arena for her scheduled bout with the fighter from England on Saturday.

The boxers who were training at the gym didn't say much to the officer as soon as he told them who he was. They all clammed. The officer was trying to find out where he might be able to locate Rose and then asked to see the owner of the gym. The boxers didn't volunteer any information that would jeopardize Rose. They just played dumb and pretended they didn't know anything about where she was other than she just trained here at the gym. One of the boxer's trainings across the boxing ring where the officer was standing commented, "She's a damn good boxer too! She's one of the best fighters around here." He quickly clammed up just like the other fighters after saying that. The officer heard some laughter and giggles after they heard this comment. The officer looked around to see who had said it and stared at the boxer, who he thought might be responsible, but he didn't say anything and walked away.

The officer was frustrated because he wasn't getting anywhere with any of the boxers, and the type of responses they gave him had no respect or cooperation with him. He finally gave up and rushed out of the gym, thinking they were disrespectful to someone of his stature. He planned to go to a nearby restaurant or any obvious location where he thought he might be able to get better information about where Rose might be or if they've seen her around lately. He walked the sidewalk for about an hour, asking people that passed him randomly for any information that might lead to the location of Rose. Most responded, "Yes, I know her, but I don't know where she is," or "I haven't seen her in a while, but I know that she is a great fighter."

This wasn't helping with what he wanted to know. He finally gave up and went to a nearby restaurant to have dinner. As he waited for his dinner, he just happened to look at a poster pinned to the wall near his table. He noticed the girl in the poster resembled Rose, the one he had been looking for. The poster had her name written across the top of the poster, Rosalinda "The Rose" Escobar. He immediately walked toward the poster to get a better look. This was the girl that he had been looking for. He was pleased that he finally got a lead. The only bad thing, after reading the information on the poster, Rose was scheduled to fight that night at the arena, and her bout was starting at 8:00 p.m. He looked at his watch and discovered that it was 7:00 p.m., meaning the fight would begin within the next hour. He decided to cancel his dinner and drive to the arena to find her.

By the time he arrived at the arena, the fight was about to begin. All he could hear from the lobby as he was buying his ticket to go inside, was from the fans yelling out Rose's name repeatedly. The fans were whistling and waving their mini-Mexican flags with pride. The mariachi band had just finished playing a Spanish tune for Rose as she entered the ring.

Rose was at her corner hearing her fans still yelling out her name when the officer finally entered the arena. Roses' adrenaline was flowing throughout her body, just waiting for the fight to start. Nothing was going to stop her at this critical time of her career. She was determined to win tonight after hearing her name yelled out loud a hundred times from her fans, but the most important reason Rose wanted to win was because of Echo, which would make her the top contender and next in line to fight the champion, which would be Echo. She must also win this fight for her people and the fans that have been following her throughout all her fights.

Meanwhile, the officer worked his way close to the ring to get a better view of Rose to confirm that she was the one who he was looking for since he hadn't seen her before in person. He approached the ring and walked around to see what corner Roses' corner was. As soon as he saw Rose standing next to the referee, he was pretty sure that she was the one. The only thing he could do now was wait for the fight to end.

The officer looked for a place to sit after recognizing Rose, close to the corner where she was going to be sitting in her corner, but he was having a hard time because so many people were walking around, looking for their assigned seats. The only seat he could buy at the entry office was a seat on the very top of the balcony, so he bought it, just to go inside the arena and find Rose. He wasn't planning to sit there, but only to walk around the arena and get as close to Rose as possible.

The Immigration Officer looked around for a vacant seat near Rose's corner so he could keep an eye on Rose when the fight ended. It took him a little while to look around the ring to see if he would see an empty seat that wasn't taken by someone. After waiting patiently for another few minutes, but anxiously hoping to find a seat before Rose started fighting, he noticed an empty seat near Rose's corner. He rushed over to get it and waited for a few minutes to make sure that there wasn't anybody coming to claim it. He waited for a few more minutes and decided to grab the seat and sit on it, hoping that nobody with a ticket would come and say that it was his or her seat. He sat nervously, still hoping that no one would come and claim it; but no one came, so he continued to sit there throughout the fight.

CHAPTER FOURTEEN

Simon and Rob had already contacted an attorney two weeks ago to start processing the paperwork for Rose before this fight. It wasn't going to be an easy task for the attorney because of the legality of the process, finding information about Rose and tracing her background to Mexico. It would take some time to put all her paperwork together, maybe even a month. No telling where Rose might be by this time, most likely back in her hometown of Mexico, if she couldn't prove her citizenship.

The crowd of fans slowly began to fill the arena. There was cheering, yelling, and whistling as loud as they could let out while waiting for the fight to begin. Some were already half-drunk, but others were there mostly because Rose was fighting. The fans were anxious to see her win this fight because they knew if she won this bout, her next fight would be the biggest fight that Rose will be facing; the chance to become a world champion, but for Rose, Echo was the one she wanted to settle a retribution that has been haunting her for a long time and now she has the chance. Both fighters had entered the ring with the thoughts of winning the fight, but at the end, the skills and determination of the fight will seize the victory.

Rose was ready and eager for the fight to begin. The England fighter was in her corner, waiting for the fight to start. The crowd booed the England fighter when she had entered the ring, yelling at her to go back to her country where she belongs, among other rude names.

When the ring announcer finally came to the center of the ring, it took him a few minutes before he could calm the crowd enough to make his announcements and began with the tale of the tape; a brief background of the fighter; weight, reach and height, and stats of their number of wins, loses, and knockouts or draws if they had any, and where they are from.

The name of the fighter from England was Meagan Dawson, but she was best known as the Vipress. She appeared like a man because of her short blond hair streaked with black, like a zebra. Her face was like a stone, unfriendly and evil in appearance, with tattoos covering her right arm and down to her ankle. She liked staring at her opponents to intimidate them by looking straight into their eyes. Her body was as solid as a rock, with hardly any body fat. Her muscles formed around her bone structure like an outline of a bronze statue. Her record status was 19–1, with 12 knockouts, and the only loss she had was to the champ, Echo, a year ago.

Megan was determined to win tonight because if she did, her chances of winning would make her the next fighter to fight for the title, just like Rose. She knew it wasn't going to be a nice and pleasant welcoming because of her reputation with the crowd tonight. The Vipress was used to a crowd treating her that way, and she didn't give a damn what the crowd thought about her. All she cared about was to punish her opponents, hoping to hurt them bad enough so they wouldn't be able to climb back into the ring to fight again. That was her mentality of thinking, and she was doing a good job. That's how she intimidated most of her opponents in the ring with her. She had a worse reputation than Echo, the champ.

The bout, which had ten two-minute rounds with a one-minute break between each round was about to begin with both boxers standing at the center of the ring and staring at each other as the referee explained the rules for the bout. Rose kept her control as her adrenaline flowed through her body while the Vipress stared into her eyes, trying to intimidate her. When the referee finished explaining the rules, he told them to protect yourself at all times. Then the referee asked them to go back to their corners and wait for the bell to ring, but first, he asked the fighters to touch their gloves as a respectful good luck to their opponents. All they did was look at each other, knowing there was no way in hell it would happen. It wasn't in the Vipress's nature to do that, and Rose knew it, so she just ignored her and went to her corner.

The bell rang and both fighters returned to the center of the ring, looking at each other, waiting for the other to throw the first punch. Soon they started throwing jabs at each other; it progressed to harder hits and more aggressive punches. The Vipress started punching and landing hard hits on Rose's face, scoring points. Rose protected herself from some punches, but the Vipress found some openings and landed the shots for points. Rose came up with a strong left hook and caused the Vipress to stagger backward. Rose followed through with more jabs to her face. Rose had the Vipress against the ropes, pounding with left and right punches as the Vipress protected her face from Rose's flurry of punches. The Vipress interlocked Rose's right arm and held it tight against her, trying to keep Rose from landing any more punches to her face and body, but continue throwing with her right arm at Roses' face. Rose pushes the Vipress away to cut loose from the interlock position and gets aggressive and continues delivering hard shots and combinations for the rest of the round. It ended up with Rose having more points on the scorecard for the first round.

Rose knew that the Vipress didn't like the way she got punished on the first round, so Rose was mentally prepared for the Vipress to start fighting dirty anytime now. After their one-minute break, the referee had them wait at their corners and wait for the bell to ring

The bell rang for the second round, and the referee yelled, "Box!" The Vipress walked straight toward Rose, ready to slice her in half. When she reached Rose and faced her straight on, she came up with a right punch that connected to Rose's chin and stunned her, causing Rose to go backwards and lose her balance. Her reflexes grabbed the ropes since she was close enough, but her right knee went down to the canvas and was considered a knockdown. The referee rushed toward Rose because he knew the Vipress was attempting to do something else to Rose. The referee quickly jumped in front of Rose facing the Vipress and told her to go back to her corner to start the mandatory ten count. When he had reached the eighth count, Rose stood up on her feet. This was the first time that Rose had been dropped to the canvas. She wasn't completely focused but was trying to protect herself as much as possible and make it to the end of the round. Now she was the one that was holding on to the Vipress's arms, trying to keep herself from getting hit on the face and body.

The Vipress kept hitting Rose with low blows and was trying to give Rose headbutts by leaning forward with her head and make it look like it was unintentionally. As the Vipress made her dirty moves, she hid them from the referee's view. She had Rose against the ropes while pounding her with hard punches and jabs, scoring points, and weakening Rose. As soon as the referee separated them from the clinching, the Vipress went back and continued hitting Rose in her face with a flurry of jabs and shots to the body. All Rose could do was protect herself from the hits and hold on until the round was over. With only ten seconds left in the round, the Vipress snuck an upper punch into Rose's jaw that stunned her badly and sent Rose to the floor again. This time, Roses' body was completely on the mat. Since Rose hit the mat before the bell rang, the ruling of the mandatory count of ten must continue. Rose got up after a few seconds, but the referee still had to check Rose to ensure she could continue for the next round. This was considered another knockdown, and an extra point was taken away from whenever there's a knockdown; meaning each round is on a 10-point scoring system, and since Rose was knocked down, the score would be a 10-7 scoring round in favor of the Vipress. Rose managed to drag herself to her corner.

The crowds were shocked and quiet, looking at Rose as she got up from the mat. Simon and Rob were inside the ring, waiting for Rose to return to her corner. When Rose made it to her corner, still feeling a little confused, Simon and Rob worked on her, doing what she needed to regain and revive Rose back to her focus on the fight. It took a little time to bring her back to herself again. When the bell rang for the third round, Simon and Rob talked to Rose about what had just happened and how to prevent it. They managed to revive her enough to go back and try to finish the fight before the Vipress did something worse to her. Rose was focused, alert, and ready to finish the Vipress this coming round. She realized that she couldn't afford to lose this fight. That's when her adrenaline kicked in. Her body was aching with determination, energized, and ready to put the Vipress's ass to the canvas.

The bell rang for the third round. The Vipress charged Rose with all she had and attacking Rose with a flurry of punches. The Vipress was trying to give Rose a low blow; she was known for executing it and hiding it from the referee at a certain angle. She hadn't used it on Rose yet, but it looked like she was trying hard to use it this time.

As the fight continued, the Vipress was still given Rose a hard time. By this time, the Vipress was ahead of Rose on the scorecard. Rose knew she was behind and needed to start doing something to catch up to her by being more active with her shots or knock her ass to the canvas as soon as possible, but that wasn't going to be easy. Rose kept hitting the Vipress with jabs, some were getting through to the Vipress, but some of the shots were blocked and were ineffective; they were not connecting to give her points.

Things started crossing her mind about why she had to win this fight tonight. Her focus was now on winning and not protection. She started to move around the Vipress, being more aggressive with her punches. The crowd started to notice how Rose had regained her strength and responded by moving around the ring vigorously and countering most of the punches the Vipress was throwing. The crowd began to get louder and louder, yelling Roses' name to give her motivation and let her know that they were supporting her. Rose kept hearing her name coming from all around the arena, making her adrenaline flow through her body again, making her realize why she was there and what she had to do. She took the pain, the adrenaline, and the stamina within her and then started to show some strength, fighting back like a furious bull. She started hitting the Vipress with combinations, giving her a hard left uppercut to send her straight to the floor. The referee jumped in front of Rose to keep her away from the Vipress, telling Rose to return to her corner, and started his mandatory count. The Vipress struggled to get up and was using the ropes to lift herself from the floor as the referee kept counting to ten. When he reached the count of nine, she had gotten up completely, so the referee reached for her hands to check the strength of her grip and decided that she was okay to continue fighting. Then he took both fighters to the center of the ring and had them continue fighting. This time, Rose was in control of the fight. The Vipress tried hard to fight back, but Rose kept attacking her with a flurry of punches and hitting her face with left and rights. Somehow, the Vipress snuck a low blow to Rose's lower body that knocked the wind out of Rose and made her stoop over for a few seconds, but Rose recovered quickly. They both started to swing at each other, connecting with every punch they were throwing. Rose got the best of it. She finally was able to find an opening in Vipresss' jaw, and as soon as she saw this opportunity, she swung with all her power and connected perfectly on the jaw, which sent the Vipress flat on her ass to the canvas. The crowd jumped up, yelling as loud as they could and screaming out Rose's name triumphantly.

All the fans had on their minds was, "I hope she doesn't get up." The crowd wished for a victory for Rose. The crowd started to count with the referee as he was at the count of five, and the Vipress struggled to get up from the mat. The count continued, "Six, seven, eight, nine, and ten!" The referee then crossed his arms to end the fight. The bell sounded, and the crowd got louder than before, celebrating her victory. They were so proud of Rose!

The mariachi band started playing her music. Simon and Rob jumped into the ring to embrace Rose for her victory. She was still exhausted from the fight but knew what she had accomplished. Rob rushed toward Rose at a fast pace that he stumbled and almost fell but managed to balance himself before reaching Rose where she was standing and then picked her up and sat her around his shoulders. Simon was right behind Rob, carrying a rose for Rose. She grabbed the rose from Simon as Rob walked around the ring with Rose on his shoulders. Then Rose asked Rob to stop at a random spot so she could throw the rose to the crowd.

It didn't take long before the media and photographers swarmed around Rose in the ring, snapping shots of her and asking questions about her next fight, which was now the biggest, most important fight—a shot for the world title. This was her dream. "I still can't believe that it finally happened," she said as her thoughts exploded in her mind. She had been waiting for this moment to happen for a very long time, and now, she realized this was a dream come true.

After a while, her thoughts faded. Rob still carried Rose on his shoulder. Shortly afterwards when Rob let Rose down off his shoulders, they announced the official winner of the fight, with the referee raising Roses' hand high as the winner. The ring announcer asked Rose questions about the fight tonight and if she was ready for the bigger fight of her life; at shot at the world title championship.

When all this was done, Rose, Simon and Rob got ready to return to her dressing room. When she climbed through the ropes to get out of the ring, she noticed a man dressed in a suit standing close to where she was going to walk down the aisle to her room. As she started walking toward the aisle, the man approached her and asked if he could speak to her as soon as she changed back to her regular clothes. That's when Simon stepped in front of her and demanded the man to identify himself and explain why he was bothering Rose. The man took his ID from his wallet and presented it to Simon.

"My name is Joe Salazar, and I'm from the Department of Immigration." Simon looked at him and asked him if there was a problem, even though he knew what it was, asking him for his reason for being here and his ID.

The man responded, "I'll explain the situation to both of you, if you can just meet me at the front of the arena as soon as Rose gets ready."

Simon stared at the man and didn't say anything to him and then he turned around and walked with Rose to her dressing room. The man stood there for a few minutes, and then decided to walk outside to the front of the arena and hoped that Simon, Rob, and Rose would meet him there.

Rose got dressed and went to the lobby to join Simon and Rob so they could talk to Joe, the man from the Department of Immigration waiting for them outside in the front of the arena. The man was standing in front of the arena when all three walked outside. "There he is," Rose said, as she recognized and acknowledged Joe.

They walked toward him as Joe saw them approaching him. When they met, Simon, Rob, and Rose were a little tense and nervous because they didn't know what to expect from Joe. After greeting each other, Joe opened a folder with him and pulled out some information about Rose's background. It had a picture of her and some other information that would probably get her in trouble because it showed that her visa card had expired. The Social Security number she used belonged to a man who lived in Texas, but the bad thing was that this man was already dead.

Joe wanted to ask her about the Social Security card she was using and how she got hold of it. After they heard what Joe had to say, Simon told Joe that he had an attorney to take care of this situation as soon as possible. Joe understood what Simon was saying, but he had to indicate where she could be found in his report because she didn't have legal status or any evidence to verify that she was legally in the US. He also told them that she would be deported back to Mexico as soon as the report was processed.

"I don't have any control of this situation because I'm just doing my job," Joe explained. "They'll be sending some staff members to escort her back to Mexico once they get my report, and then as soon as they finish processing the paperwork, they'll come looking for her," Joe explained his responsibilities and circumstances of the situation.

Before Joe left, he complimented Rose's fight. He told them that he hadn't seen any other fighter fight with so much determination to win for the people. He told her that she was the best female boxer he had ever seen in the ring. Rose didn't know what to say to his compliment other than to tell him thank you.

Joe was a boxing fan of male fighters and never had the opportunity to see many female boxers in the ring, especially someone like Rose who fought like she just did. The other thing about Joe was, he was of Mexican descent, and it bothered him to do that to one of his countrymen, especially now that he had met Rose. He didn't have a choice in this situation. He was just doing his job. Something had crossed his mind; he was thinking that maybe he could pretend that he hadn't seen her or still couldn't find her anywhere in the city or didn't know where she could be hiding. After a while, he realized that it was wrong even to think that way, so he walked away to a nearby taxi, which took him back to his hotel, and returned to the Department of Immigration office in Sacramento.

Simon looked at Rob and Rose as they held on to each other as though they saw a car crashing into a building, not knowing what to do. Simon told Rob that they should get together tomorrow and make a plan to figure out what their next step would be. This had become an urgent situation and there wasn't much time to waste. They needed to get things rolling with her paperwork. Rose looked at Simon and Rob, knowing and feeling that she wasn't safe anymore. She was worried about the agent coming back to get her and sending her back home.

Rose was saddened because she knew the consequences and how hard she had trained to get where she was. That was a painful thought that crossed her mind for it to happen now and it would keep her from fulfilling her dream and chances to win a world championship title; losing everything she had dreamed of. Getting the bad news after a great outcome was not how Rose expected the night to end. But the good part of the night, Rose had won.

They got into the cars, Simon had driven his and Rob drove his with Rose and left the arena and went home.

CHAPTER FIFTEEN

It had been three weeks since the official from the Department of Immigration, Joe Salazar, had talked to Simon and Rose. Simon hadn't forgotten about Joe saying they were supposed to contact him or Rose within a few weeks, but he still hasn't heard a word from them. They seem to think that maybe Joe had a good heart and decided to delay the information he had about Rose and immediately changed his mind about reporting her to the Department of Immigration. They were trying to think positive, hoping this would be the case, allowing them the time for the title fight. Simon knew she deserved the chance to fight for the title more than any other fighter in her division.

During the waiting period of getting a response from the official, Rose continued to train hard and stay conditioned to withstand all the punches that Echo would throw at her. She couldn't think of losing to Echo, the fighter she despised the most. Losing to Echo would destroy the dreams Rose has been following and would shatter a lot of people's wishes if Echo remained the champ. Rose felt obligated to do it, and there wasn't any other alternative but to win. Besides fulfilling her dream of beating Echo, it would be the biggest dollar amount she would ever make in her career when the event takes place. That meant a lot to her because her mom and family back home in Mexico barely had enough money to live on, so winning the fight would help take care of them financially.

The negotiation with the world championship event was set to happen within six months from now. The fight will become the biggest fighting event that the public had read in the sports section of a newspaper in a long time. Most boxing fans had been waiting for an event like this to happen because of it being a female fight and because it was a world title at stake. But the best thing they wanted to see was someone like Rose take on the champ. As the fans were predicting, Rose was the only one capable of defeating Echo and stomping her butt on the canvas. Tickets were selling faster than almost any other fighting event that had ever happen in Las Vegas.

Most of the news in the sports section of the newspapers and television coverage was about Rose. The champ was upset and jealous about all these articles and TV shows that only talked about Rose doing this and doing that, nothing good about her. Echo was tired of hearing Rose's name everywhere she went. The only thing now for her to do, she thought to herself, was to break the bad news to the people in the ring and prove to them that she would be the one who steps out of the ring after punishing Rose and retaining her title belt and be considered as the world champion.

CHAPTER SIXTEEN

The title fight was just a month away, and they hadn't heard a word from the Department of Immigration. Simon and Rob couldn't figure out why they weren't getting any phone calls like Joe had explained. Simon and Rob didn't care, though. Whatever their reason for not calling, they only hoped they didn't hear from them at all.

After Rose finished training at the gym, Rob asked her if she would like to go for a fun walk downtown after she showered and changed into her regular clothes. Rose got excited and answered Rob. "I'd love to have some fun with you, just the two of us and doing nothing but being together, enjoying each other. It's been a while since we went out and enjoyed our evening together."

Of course, she didn't decline Robs' request. Rob responded and said, "You're on, baby. Hurry and get dressed so we can get started with our romance walk," and then he chuckled and gave her a gentle and sweet, but sweaty kiss on her lips.

That evening, Rose and Rob were walking in their neighborhood, enjoying the nice cool breeze as the stars shone brightly in the sky. They walked hand and hand, like a newlywed couple on their first honeymoon. They weren't too far away from where they lived when they noticed a dark old Cadillac with tinted windows cruising very slowly alongside the street and staying with the pace of Rob and Rose. Rob and Rose continued their conversation and held hands as they started walking at a faster pace down the sidewalk. Suddenly, they both got this strange feeling that this wasn't a good thing—something wasn't right. Rob looked at Rose and told her to keep walking straight as if they didn't notice them driving alongside them.

After walking another short distance, the mysterious car had stopped a few yards by the curb in the direction of their walk. When Rob and Rose reached the point where the car had stopped, Rob noticed the rear window of the car was being rolled down and saw a rifle barrel coming out of the window, pointing straight at them. Rob reached out to Rose to grab her by her shoulders and pull her toward him to cover her body, but it was too late. The sound of the rifle made a blast, sending a bullet toward Rose, hitting her shoulder. And then a second shot followed, but this time, it hit her side as she was falling from the first shot. The impact of the shots sent Rose backward away from Rob, who was trying to protect Rose before anything else happened. The blasts of the wounds caused blood to gush out from her shoulder and smeared Rob's clothing and spotted the sidewalk with blood when she fell. Rob fell on top of Rose to protect her from any other shots. A third shot fired was attempted to hit Rob. But he was lucky that it missed him. Then the car took off, tires spinning and squealing, leaving smoke and odor of burnt rubber as the car raced down the street.

Rose laid on her back with bullet wounds on her shoulder and her side by her hip, bleeding profusely while Rob was trying to find something to apply pressure on her wound. A bystander just happened to be nearby. Rob saw her and told her, "Call 911. Quick!" He was doing everything that he could to stop the bleeding. He noticed a little market just a few feet away, so when the lady finished calling 911, he told her to go into that market and get any gauze, cloth, or whatever she could find so he could use it to apply pressure on Rose's wounds. She quickly reacted to Rob's request and rushed to the market. When she returned from the market, the ambulance had arrived and started the emergency protocol for a shot victim. The EMT told Rob to step aside so they could take over the situation. Rob stepped back as the medics told him, but still worried about Rose. He kept asking them if she was all right and they told him they were doing everything they could for her. After they got her situated with the oxygen mask and all that applied to the bleeding, the police arrived.

The incident just turned her life around within a few seconds. She was in a critical and life-threatening situation because she lost a lot of blood as she laid there. Rob was praying as he watched the paramedics executing their protocol, getting her ready to take her to the hospital.

The police started asking and looking for anybody who saw or knew anything about what happened. Rob, of course, stepped forward and told them that she was his girlfriend. So, they started asking him questions. As they questioned Rob, the EMTs were putting Rose on the gurney as he was listening and answering the questions for the police report. He was watching Rose as the medics put her inside the ambulance, wanting to be by her side. Rob kept asking the police if they were finished asking questions because he wanted to be with Rose. They told him to answer a couple more, and then he could leave. The police asked him if there were other witnesses to the shooting. Rob told them about the bystander he had called 911 for him, and maybe she might have a better description of the car or the shooters. The bystander who Rob mentioned as a possible witness was standing close by. As soon as the police questioned Rob, they thanked him and talked to the witness.

By the time they finished, the medics had put Rose into the ambulance and started taking off to the nearest hospital that was six blocks away. Rob ran to the ambulance as they were leaving and tried to get the EMT's attention by knocking on the window. The ambulance driver rolled down his window and Rob asked him which hospital they were taking Rose to be admitted.

"She'll be at the Joseph Memorial Hospital, about six blocks away from here," the EMT told Rob.

"Sure, I know where it's at," said Rob.

Then the ambulance took off, and Rob immediately ran back to his apartment, four blocks away, and got his car. Rob was still in shock about what had happened to Rose and couldn't figure out why they shot Rose and tried to shoot him too. He didn't have the slightest clue who would do this or why.

Rob raced down the street in his car, trying to get to the hospital as soon as possible. All he had on his mind was Rose, not paying attention to the traffic flow or stop signs. He sped through the streets, hoping a cop wouldn't stop him from going too fast. He just wanted to get there. When he was one block away from the hospital, he came to an intersection street where he was supposed to make a right turn toward the hospital; the stoplights were red. His mind was so focused on Rose's incident that he didn't even think to stop and run the red light. There was an oncoming car crossing simultaneously, and by the time he realized what he had done, it was too late for him to avoid the accident. He was hit from behind, causing him to oversteer the car, which sent him straight toward the car coming in the opposite direction and crashing head-on.

Rob wasn't moving and immediately went unconscious. He remained trapped in the drivers' seat, not moving a muscle, while the other persons in the other cars managed to get out of his car, struggling until the pulled themselves out of the car and slowly staggered to the sidewalk nearby. By then, someone had already called 911 to the scene. Rob remained in his car trapped while a bystander checked on him, trying to open the car door, but he couldn't because the door was severely damaged and pushed inward, trapping Rob on his seat. So, he had to wait until the fire department got there. The fire department personnel arrived within a few minutes later, and then the ambulance. The police got there shortly after. They had to pry the door open using a hydraulic jaw to get Rob out of his car. He seemed unconscious; he was unresponsive to any of the questions they were asking him. So as soon as they were able to get him out of the car, they rushed him to the same hospital where they had taken Rose.

By the time the ambulance arrived at the hospital with Rob, Rose was already in the surgery room being prepared by the nurses for the surgery as the surgeons stood by to begin the operation on her wounds. Rob showed bodily injuries and bleeding profusely from different parts of his body. He was immediately sent directly to the surgery room. The EMT medics had already started IVs on both arms and administered medications through the injection ports on the way to the hospital. He remained unconscious, and the doctors feared that he might be paralyzed from the neck down because of the hard whiplash he suffered from the impact of the car that hit him from behind, injuring his spinal cord from the accident. Due to the impact from behind was the first indication for the whiplash as the doctors assumed that was the case. There were other injuries the doctor discovered after the evaluation of his body before the surgery was performed.

The surgery for Rose was ready to begin. She had been losing a lot of blood, and they had several pints of blood on standby, plus they had already given her two pints of blood. Simon wasn't even aware of the incident because it all happened so fast. Rose and Rob were at the same hospital at the same time, both in critical condition. Rose was having surgery, and Rob was prepped to have surgery as soon as possible. By that time, word was already out in the streets that Rose was shot and taken to a nearby hospital and Rob was involved in an accident. It didn't take long before the media got hold of the news and had it shown on TV.

Meanwhile, as one of Simon's boxers was working out with the weight equipment and watching the news at the gym, he thought he heard Rose's name mentioned. He focused on the TV to ensure he heard it right the first time. It was true, so he yelled out loud to Simon, who was still in his office, and had him watch the news. They were both shocked and couldn't believe this had happened to her.

Simon ran into his office and tried to get hold of Rob on the phone to tell him about Rose, but he wasn't answering. He wasn't aware that Rob was also involved in an accident. He gave up trying to get hold of Rob. So, he got his car keys and ran out the door to the hospital to see Rose.

When he got there, the lobby was surrounded by several reporters just waiting to get a story of Rose's condition, and they also knew that Rob was involved in a car accident. Simon wasn't aware that Rob was involved in an accident until he heard someone mention his name. That's when he started asking around to confirm Rob's story about his accident. It was true, and he couldn't believe the night had turned into a disaster and a trauma case; he was traumatized and sad to hear the worse news anyone could get. It was like a nightmare for Simon to hear all this simultaneously. He was devastated and had to sit down to get hold of himself before trying to get information at the registration desk. They didn't have any information yet. But the nurse told him that he could go up to the third floor and wait in the patient waiting area, where the surgeon would come out when he's finished with the operation to let him know how she was doing. Then he asked about Rob. She told him the same thing, but it would be a little later after Rose's surgery.

Simon went up to the third floor and waited. He sat in the waiting room, exhausted within those few hours, worried about them. Three hours had passed since they'd been operating on Rose, yet no one had come out of the surgery door to say a word to Simon about her condition. He thought about leaving for a few minutes to get a cup of coffee, but he was afraid that as soon as he stepped out of the waiting room, he might miss the doctor coming out to the waiting room to tell him the condition about Rose. So, he decided he would rather not leave; even though he was mentally exhausted, worried, and hungry, he waited patiently.

A nurse came passing through the waiting room to the surgery corridor. She noticed Simon slouched on the couch with his eyes closed. Instead of just passing through, she stopped to ask Simon if he was all right and if she could get him anything. Simon opened his eyes immediately because he was wondering who was talking to him. When he looked up, he straightened up on the couch and apologized to her for sitting like he was. He explained to the nurse how long he's been waiting and asked her if she knew anything or had any information about Rose or Rob.

At first, when Simon saw the nurse standing in front of him, looking right into his eyes, he thought he was dreaming. He was attracted to her. He wanted to know her name that second, although he knew this was a serious medical conversation, and he was supposed to be asking her about Rose's surgery and Rob's condition.

When he mentioned Rose's name, she knew exactly whom he was talking about. "It just happens that I'm one of the nurses in Rose's surgical room," she told Simon. "They're just about finished with the procedure, and it will probably be another half an hour before they'll send her to the intensive care unit for recovery. The only thing, she will not be allowed any visitors while she is in the intensive care unit for at least eight hours or depending on her condition if it's stable or not," the nurse explained to Simon.

She advised Simon, "Continue waiting for the doctor who performed the surgery and as soon as he's finished, he'll come out to the waiting room and explain how Rose's operation went and in what condition Rose will be."

Simon didn't have a choice but wait for the doctor. At least now, he knew how much longer he had to wait for an answer. Then the nurse told Simon that she had to go into the surgery corridor and maybe she'll talk to him about the surgery. Simon was still in a dream world about the nurse that talked to him and didn't even get her name.

The door coming from the surgical side finally opened and a doctor stepped out. The doctor wasn't sure who was waiting to hear about Rose's surgery, but he asked if anyone in the waiting room was waiting to hear about Rosalinda Escabar.

"I am, Doctor!" Simon said.

Then the doctor walked straight to Simon and asked if he was a family member. Of course, he said no, but told him that she was his fighter.

"How is she, Doc?" Simon asked worriedly, wishing that he had good news to tell him.

"She's going to be just fine. She did lose a lot of blood, but we replenished what she had lost, which was six pints of blood. She'll be taken to the critical care unit (CCU) area so that we can monitor her for the next twenty-four hours or longer if we need to. She is very lucky that the bullets missed any vital internal organs on her side, but the bullet that hit her on the shoulder tore a lot of her muscle tissue. Simons' mind didn't want to believe what the doctor just told him.

"With a lot of therapy on her shoulder, it might be at least six months to a year before she would have the full strength of her arm," explained the doctor to Simon. "Then she might be ready to go back to boxing."

Simon's thoughts of her becoming a champion diminished instantly after the doctor told him how long the recovery was going to take. This wasn't the best news Simon wanted to hear, although he was thankful that Rose was all right and not in a life-threatening situation.

When the doctor explained Rose's condition, he asked if he knew anything about Rob Anderson.

"I heard one of the other surgeons mentioning his name and said that he was in a critical status if it's the same Rob we are talking about. His condition wasn't too promising because of the hard whiplash he got in the accident. He had a bad head injury as well, and they believed that he is paralyzed from the neck down," the doctor finished telling Simon the rest of the bad news. Simon was devastated once he was told the bad news about Rob.

This had been a long day for Simon. He was exhausted because it was late and he had been at the gym all day with his boxers, training for their upcoming events. Simon was mentally exhausted and overwhelmed with all this bad news tonight. He didn't know

what to think anymore. As soon as the doctor told Simon the circumstances about Rose and Rob, he left the room. Simon stayed sitting
on the couch for a few minutes before he got up and walked out of
the waiting room slowly, thinking about how all this happened so
fast.

As Simon stepped out into the elevator lobby from the third
floor, he saw the nurse who talked to him in the surgical waiting
room. She was having a conversation with another nurse carrying a
clipboard, who was getting ready to hand it to the nurse that talked
to him. Simon couldn't let this opportunity pass without knowing
her name before he left the hospital, so he waited until she finished
talking with the other nurse to talk to her. As soon as she finished the
conversation with the other nurse, he approached her with a smile
and walked gracefully toward her, wondering if this was a good idea
or not. She was still standing behind the counter when he got there
as she was focused on her clipboard. Then she raised her head to see
who was standing before her.

"Oh…hi!" she greeted Simon, surprised to see him so soon
after they had a brief conversation in the surgical waiting room.
"Did you get good news about Rose? And if I recall, your first name
is Simon, right?"

"Yes, it is! You have a good memory." He gives her a smile
and thought about what else he could say to her. "I was on my way
out of the hospital because there's nothing else, I could do for Rose
or Rob. I'll check tomorrow first thing in the morning to see if there's
any progress on either one of them."

The nurse noticed a worried expression on Simon's face. "Is
there anything that I can help you with, Simon? Maybe I'll check in
the ICU first thing in the morning before I start my routine checklist
and check the progress report for an update on both, and then I'll
have them give you a call. Or if you want, I'll call you myself and let
you know the status on both. If you like," she spoke to Simon with
a soft and caring voice.

"That would be nice if you wouldn't mind," answered Simon. "There's one more thing I would like to know before I take

off. May I ask you what your name is? That was the main reason I walked over here," asked Simon. Then he smiled at her.

"My name is Amy. Amy Whitson. And I work here." She smiled at him and laughed because she had told him where she was working. He was aware of that. And then she laughed.

"Oh, by the way, you'll need my phone number to call me," said Simon.

"That would be a good idea, wouldn't it?" She smiled at Simon. "Do you have a piece of paper so I can write my phone number for you?" Simon asked.

"Yes, I do. And here's a pen." Simon writes down his number and adds a little note saying that it was nice to meet you. Then he gave her his phone number, still admiring her beautiful looks.

They talked for a short while because she had to continue working. After that brief conversation, they both agreed to get together on Friday at a nearby restaurant when she got off work and have a nice dinner while getting acquainted. Simon walked out of the hospital after talking to Amy. He was thrilled that he had enough courage to ask Amy for her name. She made him feel a lot better after all that was going on that night. Then he went home.

The next day, Simon called the hospital to check on Rose and Rob because he hadn't heard from Amy. After waiting for a few minutes because they had put him on hold, a nurse answered the phone and told him the status of Rose and Rob. He got some good news and some bad news. First, the good news: Rose was progressing very well but still a little groggy from the medication they had given her, but it put her in a stable condition. The bad news: Rob was still in critical condition. His head injury was way worse than they thought at first. He was still in the ICU area and monitored twenty-four hours a day. They had to keep him alive by using a respirator. Simon had a hard time accepting his status after they told him that all he could do now was wait. He couldn't see Rose because she was too drugged to talk to, so he thought he would wait until tomorrow and check again to see how they were doing.

Simon started thinking about Amy and why she hadn't called him this morning as she said. An hour later, he finally got a call from Amy.

"Hello!" said Simon. He sounded a little disappointed to get her call just now, after waiting all this time.

"Hi!" answered Amy. "I'm sorry to call you this late, but we had a fatal car accident emergency brought into the hospital, so they asked me to help them with the traumas. That was why I didn't get a chance to call you as soon as I walked into the hospital. It took us a while before we had all the people involved in the accident stabilized and taken care of, except one person. We did all we could to save his life, and he was too traumatized with injuries."

Then there was silence on both ends. Simon felt bad because of what happened, but it also explained why she hadn't called. He was relieved because he thought something had changed her mind about getting together soon.

"I haven't had a chance to check on Rose or Rob. That's why you never received my call," explained Amy.

"I'm sorry to hear you've had a tough morning already. I called the hospital this morning to check on Rose and Rob. Rose is doing fine, but Rob is still in critical condition. They told me Rob has a slim chance of surviving due to his head injury. I'll have to keep checking on his progress every day."

Amy interrupted and told Simon that she'd keep him informed of Rob's daily status.

"Thank you, Amy. I appreciate your caring for my friends. They both mean a lot to me. Rose is like a little sister to me. We've gotten so close ever since I met her. And Rob has been a lifesaver, being around Rose and helping me with her training. I just hope he'll fight to survive. I don't even think Rose knows anything about Rob's condition. I know as soon as she is stable enough to think straight, the first question she'll ask is, 'Where's Rob? And why isn't he here with me?' She's going to be devastated once she finds out what happened to him." Simon let his feelings out to Amy.

Amy listened to every word Simon told her on the phone. It made her feel like she wanted to be in his arms to comfort and keep him from feeling so helpless.

Amy answered him with a soft-spoken and gentle voice, telling him, "Whatever I can help you with, let me know, and I'll be there for you. Call me tomorrow to let me know how you're doing, Simon, or I'll call you if you like."

"Thank you again, Amy. Go ahead and call me if you hear of any other information about either one of them. I'll probably call the hospital first thing in the morning anyway to see how they are coming along."

"I sure will, Simon," answered Amy.

"I guess I'll talk to you tomorrow morning, one way or another. Okay?"

Simon agreed and said goodbye to Amy and hung up the phone.

After talking to Amy, Simon sat for a while before getting dressed to go to the gym. He had to ensure that his boxers kept up with the conditioning for their coming fights. He was trying not to overthink Rose and Rob, even though it was hard for him not to. When he got to the gym, Simon continued training his boxers the best he could, but his boxers noticed that Simon wasn't the same person he was yesterday before he got the bad news. They knew what was going on and were very understanding. They were all saddened by the incidents with Rose and Rob. But they had to continue, without any distraction because of their coming events. The whole gym was in a quieter mode. All you could hear was the sound of the leather punching bags and the barbell clinking as they were lifted and set back on the rack. Simon was in his office, sitting on his chair thinking about Rose and Rob, hoping that tomorrow when he called the hospital, they would have some good news to tell him.

Simon suddenly heard a knock on his door that made him snap out of his thoughts about Rob and Rose and saw three of his fighters walking into his office and asked about Rose and Rob. Simon looked up at them as they walked toward him. He then explained what had happened and what their conditions were up to this point. He told them that he would keep them informed on their progress. The fighters also asked Simon if they were able to see them at the hospital. But Simon told them that nobody was allowed in their rooms until they were stable enough to talk.

CHAPTER SEVENTEEN

The next morning, around eight o'clock, Simon was on the phone calling the hospital after he had his two cups of coffee, which is his normal routine when he gets up every morning at six. He was a little hesitant at first because he was afraid that they would give him some bad news about Rob and not Rose, and that's not what he wanted to hear first thing in the morning. When he called, he waited patiently for the nurse to get the information about Rose and Rob. It seemed like forever. Then he heard the nurse pick up the phone.

"Hello! Are you still there, Simon?" as the nurse remembered his name.

"Yes, I am," answered Simon.

"Well, there's good news, and then there's bad news. As for Rose, she is recuperating very well from her shot wounds and is alert and talking. As for Rob, he's still in critical condition, in a coma, but we must keep monitoring for at least another day or so, depending on how he does with some medications that we have given him. He's still in a coma, though."

After Simon listened, he knew there wasn't anything else that he could do for him. He was saddened with the bad news and all he could do was wait, but for how long was his question on his mind. Simon went to the gym right after he talked to the nurse.

When he got there, he gathered all his fighters and told them the situation about Rose and Rob. There was silence for a few minutes once Simon explained Rob's condition. Simon tried to convince them that there was still hope for Rob and Rose, so pray for their recovery. The room got quiet as the fighters listened to Simon telling them the condition of Rose and Rob. Then the boxers walked out of his office with their heads down, showing sadness and concern. Simon remained seated on his office chair as the fighters left his office as he sat worried and concerned, thinking about what he would do next without Rose or Rob being around the gym. Then he started thinking about the Department of Immigration, wondering why they hadn't called him.

He finally snapped his thoughts about Rose and Rob and talked himself into returning to the ring and continued training his fighters, especially those scheduled to fight within a few weeks. One was in the main event held in Las Vegas, fighting for a world middleweight title. He was the one who Simon trained most of his time in the ring because he knew he had a very good chance of becoming the champ in his weight division. Simon put a lot of time and effort into his fighter while Rob helped with Rose and kept her conditioned for her next fight, which was for the title.

There were just two of his fighters still training with the punching bags and the other two were sparring in the ring. Simon observed their techniques throughout for the rest of the day, and it was getting late. Simon decided to call it a night because it was going on eight o'clock and he wanted to call the hospital before it got too late. It was hard for him to finish his day because, occasionally, his thoughts would take him back to Rose and Rob, wondering how they were doing. He had to overcome his thoughts to stay focused on his fighters.

Everyone finally left the gym except for Simon. Then he went into his office to call the hospital.
Just by coincidence, as he reached for the phone, it started ringing. So, he picked it up and answered, "Hello, this is Simon."

"Hi! Simon. How are you? It's Amy."

"I was just getting ready to call the hospital to check on Rose and Rob. Your ring startled me as I was reaching for the phone," said Simon, smiling because he was glad to hear Amy's voice on the phone.

"I'm sorry! I was going to call you sooner, but I have been busy. It's been a nightmare all day. I've been here since eight this morning and it's now going on eight this evening. That's how busy it's been. How about you, Simon? How are you doing?" asked Amy.

"I'm okay. I made it through the day, but all I had on my mind was Rob and Rose. I was hoping for better news this morning from the hospital when I called to check on them. I just wanted to know how Rose and Rob are doing. You probably haven't had a chance to check on them, as you mentioned how busy your day has been. I understand if you haven't," answered Simon.
"I thought I was going to get a chance to look at their status, but that's when an emergency arrived, and a stat was announced on our pagers, asking for anyone available to help out with the situation," explained Amy.

Simon waited for Amy to finish talking. Then he answered with a gentle voice, telling her that it was all right and for her not to worry.

"Give me about fifteen minutes so I can check in the ICU report for any information about them, and I'll call you right back as soon as I find out anything about their condition," said Amy.

"You've had a very long and exhausting day and I want to thank you for doing that for me, so why don't you just finish your day with what you have to do because I know you're probably tired by now. Why don't you transfer me to Rose's room in the ICU if you can? Then I'll have them tell me the status of her condition, and then I'll ask about Rob's. I'll be fine with that. Is that okay with you, Amy?" asked Simon. "I just want you to slow down and relax."

Amy agreed with Simon and thought it was a good idea to do that.

"I still would like to get together this coming Friday and keep our dinner date at the restaurant you mentioned. Do you still want to do that, Amy?"

"Yes, I do. I think it'll be fun to get to know each other. I think about you more than I thought," Amy said.

"That was nice of you thinking like that," responded Simon. Amy then told Simon to hold on so she could transfer him to the ICU. When Simon made connections with the ICU, he asked about Rose. She put Simon on hold to get Rose's chart. When she returned the phone, there was good news about her condition. The nurse told Simon that Rose was progressing very well, and she was able to see visitors anytime now. The nurse told him that Rose was transferred from the ICU ward to a regular room. That was a big relief for Simon. He was dreading the next question he had to ask the nurse. He knew that it wasn't going to be good news. Then he asked her if she knew anything about Rob Lee Anderson. She heard of his name, but he was in a different unit and being monitored 24/7 because of his condition. All she knew was that he was still in critical status.

"Would you like me to forward your call to the main desk for any other information they might be able to help you with?" asked the nurse.

"No, that's okay. Thank you for your help. I'll keep checking back later to see if there's any progress about him. I know I can't be of any help to him right now, so thank you again."

Simon calmly said goodbye to the nurse and hung up the phone. Simon remained seated quietly in his chair after he had talked to the nurse. He felt overwhelmed, thinking about everything that was going on. He felt alone as if he had just lost all his best friends and had nobody to help him. But then he started thinking about Amy. That helped him feel better. He knew that he had to overcome that feeling of devastation, fighting his feelings to accept of what has happen to Rose and Rob.

The one good news in his favor was Rose was going to be all right. Whatever it would take to get her back on her feet and the time to recover from her wounds, he was going to be there for her. Whether it took six months or a year, it didn't matter to Simon. He had decided the day would come when she would walk back to the gym and step into the ring once again and continue where she left off training to become the next world champ.

He got up and started moving around his apartment, trying to keep his mind occupied with something else, other than all that's been happening, lately. He decided to visit Rose tomorrow morning at the hospital now that they allowed visitors in her room. He was hoping to see Amy while he was there, before or after visiting Rose, depending on how busy she'll be, just to say hello to her. She was the best thing that has ever happened to him, besides training Rose. Simon jumped into the shower and got ready for bed. It was after 9:00 p.m., and he felt mentally exhausted. He finished taking a shower, turned off the lights, and then dragged his body to bed. It didn't take him very long before he was sound asleep.

CHAPTER EIGHTEEN

The following day, Simon was up by six o'clock, as usual. He planned to visit Rose at ten this morning, but before that, he went to the gym and gave his fighters the plan for the day. When he arrived at the gym, his fighters were waiting at the front door, ready to start their day of training. One of them, Tony Brown, was the one who would be in the main event for the title shot. Boxing was Tony's passion, so he always pushed himself to become better and better with every day that passed. That's why he is so successful now. Rose was just like him, constantly giving herself all she had to become better than the other fighters.

After giving his fighters their training schedules for the day, Simon left for the hospital. Along the way, he stopped at a flower shop close to the hospital to get Rose some flowers. As soon as he entered the hospital doors, he saw Amy passing by the front desk with a clipboard in her hand, getting ready to see one of her patients on the second floor. She noticed Simon entering through the front doors, so she stopped and waited to say hello to him.

"Hi, Simon," Amy greeted him with a happy smile.

"Hi, Amy," responded Simon. "I was hoping to see you while I was here visiting Rose. How are you?"

"Fine. Thank you. Those are pretty flowers. I know Rose will be happy to see you and enjoy the flowers you got her. I overheard a nurse talking about Rose this morning and said that Rose was recovering from her trauma very well. I was glad to hear that, too. I know how concerned you are about her condition. I'm just glad she's going to be all right," said Amy.

"I am too! And you're right about how I'm concerned with her condition. Now I only want to hear some good news about Rob. Have you heard anything yet?" Simon asked.

"The last thing I heard from a nurse in the ICU about Rob was he's still in critical condition and connected to the ventilator because he was having some complications breathing on his own. So, they won't have any good news to tell you. I'm terribly sorry, Simon," said Amy.

"There isn't much I can do but wait and hope for a miracle. Now the problem is, what should I tell Rose about Rob? Where do I start? She's going to have a nervous breakdown when I tell her that Rob might not live, or she'll never get another chance to speak to him anymore. I think it's going to be the hardest thing that I'll ever have to do, ever," Simon sadly tells Amy.

"I know it's going to be a heartbreaking moment for you, Simon, to tell Rose this devastating news. Would you like me to be there when you tell her? I don't mind. I know she doesn't know me, but I would love to meet her with you being there, so you can introduce her to me. What do you think, Simon?" asked Amy.

Simon wasn't sure if this was a good idea at a time like this. He wasn't sure how Rose would react to the bad news about Rob. He thought for a minute and then agreed with Amy.

"Okay. I guess it's not going to hurt anything. I'll introduce you to Rose before I give her the bad news. Then maybe that'll help her ease her emotions, seeing you by my side and knowing who you are."

"Okay," answered Amy. "It sounds like that would be a nice way of meeting her and getting to know her. Let me finish checking some of my reports, which will take about fifteen or twenty minutes, and then I'll be able to go with you to see Rose in her room. Okay?"

"Okay. I'll wait for you in the lobby. Let me know when you're finished," answered Simon.

The minutes went by fast and Amy was in the lobby within twelve minutes. She had rushed to get her reports done so she didn't have to keep Simon waiting for a long time. She knew how important it was for him to see Rose after not being able to see her for the last three days. Amy was excited to meet Rose. She felt like she had known Rose for a long time, even though they hadn't met yet. Simon always talked about Rose's past and how passionate she was about boxing when they were together or on the phone.

When Amy finished her reports, she walked to the lobby to meet Simon. Simon was sitting in a chair, reading a magazine, and waiting patiently for Amy when Amy walked behind him and whispered in his ear, "Are you ready?"

As Simon heard her soft voice in his ear, he turned around to acknowledge her with a big smile. He was thrilled that she could go with him to see Rose. They went up to the second floor to Rose's assigned room.

When they entered the room, Rose was lying on her bed with her arm in a shoulder harness and eyes wide open, as if she was expecting Simon to walk into her room anytime. They both walked toward Rose carrying the vase with a beautiful bouquet as she smiled. She was thrilled and so happy to see Simon walk into her room. Simon walked up to her, leaned over her bedside enough to embrace her and kissed her on her cheek. Rose held on to Simon, not wanting to let go of him. Simon just held on to her, waiting for her to let go and knowing what she had gone through. After a few minutes, tears started running down her cheeks and sniffing to keep her nose from running. Rose finally let loose of Simon and then lay back. Then she noticed Amy standing by Simon's side.

"Hi, Rose," said Amy.

"Oh! I'm sorry, Rose," Simon intervened. "This is Amy. She's one of the nurses that was in the surgery room when you were having surgery. I met her the day you were having surgery and she happened to be passing by after she came out of the surgery room into the waiting room when she stopped to see if I was all right or needed anything. I couldn't take my eyes off her, and I knew I had to find out who she was from that moment. Since she informed me of your condition, we've been in touch since we met. She wanted to meet you as soon as you were able and strong enough to talk."

"Hi, Amy," said Rose. "It's very nice of you to come by and say hello. I'm glad that you and Simon got together. Simon is a very good man, and handsome too."

Simon blushed when Rose said that, and then looked and smiled at Amy.

"He also has a good heart when it comes to helping people," Rose finished, embarrassing Simon in front of Amy.

"It's a pleasure to meet you. I hope to see more of you and get to know you even more when you get out of the hospital. And by the way, your progress is coming along very well, so I think you'll be able to leave the hospital soon."

When Rose heard Amy, her thoughts immediately zoomed into the boxing ring. It gave her hope of returning to the ring soon. When she thought of getting better, Rob suddenly crossed her mind.

"Where's Rob?" asked Rose as she looked at Simon, realizing that he wasn't here with Simon.

That was the moment Simon was dreading the most. The time had come to tell Rose the bad news about Rob. Simon turned around and looked at Amy then turned back to face Rose as she lay in her bed. Simon paused for a few seconds, wondering how to begin telling her about Rob.

"Rose," said Simon in a very soft-spoken voice, "Do you still remember the night you and Rob were walking together downtown, close to where you live, and someone in a black car came by and shot you but missed Rob?"

"Barely," replied Rose. "Why?" asked Rose curiously.

"There's a witness the police talked to at the site of the incident. She saw what happened," Simon said.

"Anyway," said Simon, "Rob was okay until he was driving to the hospital to be with you, but the only thing is that he was in such a hurry to get here and driving so fast that he didn't stop in time to avoid an accident at an intersection. He was just a block away from here when he was involved in an accident. He's here in the hospital but in critical condition. They say he has a bad head injury and thinks he might be paralyzed from the head down. But it's not positive yet if that will be the case."

Rose looked confused and worried. She didn't want to accept what Simon had just told her. Tears ran down her face as she reached for the box of Kleenex next to the bed. She was shaking her head from left to right, telling herself that this was not true. Then she stared at Simon, asking him, "This isn't true, is it?"

Simon went speechless, not knowing what else to tell Rose. She burst out crying after Simon failed to answer her, not denying her question. At that point, she knew that something terrible had happened to Rob. She still didn't know whether he was alive or not. Simon reached out to hold her when she started crying and held on to her for a few minutes until she calmed down. Amy got closer to Rose and then put her hands on her head, whispering to Rose that he'll be fine, although Amy had a bad feeling that Rob had a slim chance of surviving. They were trying to comfort Rose the best they could. Simon knew she would react as soon as he told her about Rob's accident. There was nothing else he could do for him. Rose was devastated and shocked, not knowing what to think.

Rose gradually calmed down and fell asleep. Simon and Amy stayed in her room until they knew she was okay and waited until she had fallen asleep. There was nothing else they could do for her tonight.

It was about 10:00 p.m. by the time they left Rose's room. Simon walked Amy to her car, spent a few minutes talking about how to approach this situation tomorrow, and then said they good night to one another.

CHAPTER NINETEEN

Simon went to his gym the next day to see how his guys were doing. He had given a gym key to Tony, one of his fighters, so he could open the gym for the other fighters who were training that day. He wanted to ensure that Tony was ready for the fight of his life because it was for the top contendership.

Some of his boxers asked Simon if they could see Rose and Rob at the hospital. He commented, "You can visit Rose, but not Rob because he's still in a critical condition status and is not allowed to see anyone just yet."

The boxers in the gym were attached to Rob and especially Rose. They missed them being around the ring and were worried about them.

As the day went by, Amy gave Simon a call at the gym to update him on Rose and Rob's condition. She didn't have any different news other than Rose was doing just fine, but Rob was still in a critical stage of his life. Things were not looking good for him. There were no indications of him getting better, only getting worse. They talked for just a little while because Amy had to go back to her work.

Later that evening, Simon went to visit Rose at the hospital. On his way to see her, he picked up another bouquet. He always thought that it would make her feel better and create an easier way to start a conversation, plus it would also keep her from thinking about Rob while he was visiting her.

When he got there, she seemed to have calmed down from the night before after he had told her the news about Rob. She had been devastated afterward, crying her heart out. Simon was glad to see her wide-open eyes as he walked in with the bouquet of roses. She gave him a little smile as he approached her and remained quiet until he was next to her.

"These are for you since you're as pretty as a rose. I thought they would be appropriate for you." It put a bigger smile on her face when he told her that.

"They're beautiful, Simon. Thank you so much. I love them," responded Rose. "Will you put them in that vase over there? Someone left it without any flowers, so now I think it belongs to me. What do you think?"

"I think that's a good idea," said Simon. "I'll put them next to the other flowers I got you." Rose watched Simon arranging the flowers and chuckled as Simons' face looked confused trying to figure out how he was going to do it.

"I'm glad that you came by Simon. Where's Amy?" she asked, noticing she wasn't with him.

"She's still working and should be getting off soon. She said she'll try to come by as soon as she got off work. That's the only thing with her schedule, she never knows when she has to stay later because of an emergency at the last minute, which will delay her hours before she could be off," explained Simon.

"I like Amy," Rose tells Simon. "She seems to be a very nice and polite person. I'm glad that you met her. I think you guys make a perfect couple."

"I think she is too. I have never been with a girl that I cared for as much as I do with Amy, even if it hasn't been that long since I met her. I think she's the one." Simon ended with a huge smile.

They continued their conversation for about twenty minutes before Rob's name was mentioned. She quietly asked Simon how he was doing. Simon hesitated for a few seconds, dreading telling her the bad news again.

"There's no sign of him getting better. His condition is still being monitored and remains in critical status. Amy keeps me informed of any changes that occur or if they need to get hold of me immediately in case of an emergency."

Rose turned her head to face the wall, lying quietly, not saying a word to Simon. It was devastating and painful for her. She was heartbroken to hear bad news about her loved one. Simon could see through her. She was silent for a few minutes while Simon held on to her hands, knowing she was hurting.

Simon knew Rose was a strong and determined girl. He knew that she would overcome this tragedy once she got well. But now, she had a hard time dealing with Rob's condition.

Simon tried to deter her from thinking about Rob by changing the subject. He told her about his fighter that will be fighting in two weeks for the top contendership and how his other fighters are getting better by the day.

Rose remained in silence, listening to Simon talk. Shortly, she turned around, looked at Simon, and said, "I have to get better, Simon. Whatever it takes, I will get better. I still think about my dream, the dream that will become my reality, something that will make me proud to be me. I will get better."

Simon was right. She was determined to make her dream come true. She was a fighter who would never give up.

CHAPTER TWENTY

The next day, Simon got a call from Joe Salazar, the official he talked to in Los Angeles from the Department of Immigration. Simon explained the situation to Joe. Then Joe told Simon that he had finished the report and was ready to pursue her deportation. But he told Simon that he had delayed his report for a couple of weeks, trying to give her time to continue her boxing events. That's when they will start the process of picking her up and deporting her back to Mexico.

After the conversation, Joe called the hospital where she was admitted, and they confirmed the information that Simon had told him. Then he made arrangements with the hospital to let him know when she'd be strong enough to be deported to Mexico. He contacted Simon later to let him know what his next step was going to be with Rose. They figured it would be another week before they'd be ready for deportation. Now Simon had to tell Rose about what was happening with her immigration status. Once again, he had to tell Rose the bad news about the immigration. She was already dealing with a life-threatening situation with Rob. But it had to be done, as much as he hated to tell Rose.

The following day, Simon had made special plans to visit Rose at the hospital. He worked around his schedule from the gym just to take care of something he dreaded doing was telling Rose about another bad situation with her deportation status.

When Simon arrived at the hospital, he came across Amy as she was going to check on a patient at the same level where Rose was recovering. Amy joined Simon since she had to go up to the same floor and had a chance to talk for a few minutes on the way up. Amy wanted to go with Simon to see Rose, but she had already planned to check on a patient on the same floor. It couldn't wait because of the patient's condition. Simon continued walking to Rose's room after talking to Amy. When he walked into the room, Rose was asleep. Simon found a chair to sit on and waited for her to wake up. He didn't want to disturb her as she slept, so he kept himself busy by reading magazines around her room, trying not to make any noise. He noticed that she began to move around a little. Then she opened her eyes.

"Good morning, beautiful," Simon whispered to her. "You look like you were enjoying your sleep this morning."

"Yes, I was," answered Rose. "How long have you been here?"

"Around thirty minutes or so. I'm glad that you got some rest."

Rose yawned and stretched with her good arm; the other arm was in a sling. "Why are you here so early this morning?" asked Rose.

"Well, do you remember the guy Joe Salazar from the Immigration Department?"

"I think so. It seems like a long time ago, though."

"Well, they're going to deport you because of your expired visa. They will start the process as soon as you can move around and are strong enough to travel. My Attorney and I have begun the visa application for you so we can bring you back to the United States as soon as possible. The only thing is that you might have to reapply for your visa card in Mexico, and hopefully, they'll give you at least a year or more with your approved application. It will take another few months before you can come back and depending how well you do with your therapy. Meanwhile, I plan to communicate with you a lot, and fly to Mexico for a few days to be with you to ensure your recovery is progressing with the right equipment and therapy. I'm not giving up on you, Rose. I guarantee you that!" Simon's sensitivity showed toward Rose, assuring her that he's doing everything he can to help her come back and let him know that he would always be there for her.

"Thank you, Simon, for being my friend."

"We'll get through this. It'll take a little time and patience to deal with the paperwork. For now, you need to get better and get that arm moving again. Take good care of it. Call it your dream arm. Without it, your dream won't come true. You know what I'm saying?"

Rose looked at Simon and felt like she was the luckiest girl to have someone like Simon next to her.

He stayed there another thirty minutes talking to Rose before telling her he had to leave and take care of business at the gym. Rose was exhausted with all her bad news happening all at once.

On his way out of the hospital, Simon saw Amy again, but this time, she was sitting behind the counter, writing her report. Simon walked toward her to tell her that Rose was fine after spending some time with her and talking about the other bad news: her deportation. "I think she's going to be okay for now. She understands the reality of it all and seems to accept the circumstances about Rob and the deportation."

"I'm glad to hear that. I'll try to visit her before I leave the hospital. Will you call me tonight, Simon?" asked Amy. "

"I sure will. Say about eight o'clock!"

"Okay then. I'll talk to you later." Amy said goodbye to Simon.

For the rest of the day, Simon thought about how long Rose would take to get better. He didn't want to see her leave. Rob's condition was not getting better. He was a little worried about him too. His problem was going to be with Rose. He questioned his mind about whether she would be able to continue her career as a boxer.

One thing that crossed his mind that bothered him as he thought
deeply into her boxing career: 'Will she be focused and think straight
during her training without Rob by her side in the ring anymore if he
doesn't live?'

CHAPTER TWENTY-ONE

After three days lying in the hospital bed, Rose felt stable enough to get out of bed and move around the room. As she walked freely and very slowly in the room, taking short steps at a time, she felt a little pain in her left side of her hip every time she took a step, but it wasn't painful enough to keep her from walking. Even though she felt like she was fully recovered from her gunshot wounds, she wasn't, and she knew the scars still needed time to heal.

The hospital had not called the Department of Immigration yet because they wanted to give her a few more days to recover enough to make sure the stitches were healed enough before putting any pressure that might open the incision if she walks on it too much. Rob's condition had worsened within those few days. Rose had tried to see him, but she was denied her visit because of his critical condition. She was a little upset, but that's the way it was. The protocol had to be followed by the hospital rules on patient care.

It was Friday when Simon and Amy went to see Rose. Amy was off that day and wanted to go with Simon to visit her. When they arrived at the hospital and walked into her room, Rose was sitting on a chair, reading a magazine. She was in her hospital gown with the sling holding her arm to immobilize her shoulder from moving. She was ready and anxious to leave the hospital because she was tired of lingering around her room, waiting to get better. She was not the type of person to be idle for a long time, but to keep active most of the time.

"Good morning, Rose. How are you doing this morning?" Simon asked.

"I don't feel too bad. I'm ready to get out of here," said Rose.

Rose stood up as soon as she saw Simon and Amy walk inside her room. She was thrilled to see them again. She walked up to Simon with a little limp and hugged him with her good arm because her other arm was still in a sling and hip was still healing. Then she turned around and hugged Amy too.

"I'm glad to see you, Amy. Thank you for coming and to see you with Simon." Then they all chuckled.

They exchanged conversations about what would happen as soon as they released her from the hospital. After they enjoyed talking for thirty minutes, Simon and Amy said their goodbyes and left.

Rose wouldn't be released until the doctor signed a form stating that she was strong enough to be moved. So, that Friday afternoon, the doctor checked on Rose to see how she was doing. Then he told Rose depending on how she is on Monday after he examines her again, he'll sign a form stating her release if he determines that she's okay and her stitches are healed enough to be mobilized when she needs to move around.

On Monday, Rose's doctor checked her condition around noon. After he had examined her, he couldn't find anything that would do any physical harm to her body if she had to travel to Mexico, so he was going to released tomorrow. Then he told Rose, "I have to notify the Department of Immigration to let them know of your release," he explained to Rose. "I think you're well enough to be moving around, but you still must be cautious of what you're doing to make sure you don't agitate the incisions. You got that, Rose?" The doctor specifically wanted Rose to do as he says.

"Alright. I'll do it," said Rose.

After the doctor left her room, it left her thinking about what's next in her life after she has gotten this far in her career. She was already aware of circumstances and prepared for this situation that was coming about being deported back to Mexico, although Rose knew it was her fault for not taking care of this matter before all this happened. Now she was paying the price.

The doctor told Rose that the hospital would let her know when the Department of Immigration would arrive to transport her back home after they would contact the Immigration office.

"So meanwhile, Rose, you know that you can't go out of town or anywhere besides your apartment," said the doctor. "I'm supposed to let them know where you'll be staying. Tomorrow, when you get ready to leave, can you have Simon come and pick you up?" asked the doctor.

"It shouldn't be a problem," answered Rose.

Knowing that Rose was a boxer and Simon was her trainer, the doctor told her that there wasn't much he could do to help her escape this predicament. He was doing what he had to do.

"I wish I could tell you something different," said the doctor. "But I have to do what I have to do. All I can tell you is that I hope you have the best of luck, and I think your day will come when you'll be back in the ring and fulfill your dream."

"Thank you, Doc," responded Rose.

"I have to go now, and if you need anything, please let one of the nurses checking on you know what you need. Okay?" The doctor waved at Rose as he stepped out into the hall and closed the door.

Rose laid in bed, wondering about what the doctor told her and what she would do next. Then she began to think about Rob and asked herself: 'Is he going to be all right when I leave for Mexico? Who's going to take care of him?' She was concerned about Rob. Rob meant the whole world to her, and he was the closest friend and lover that she had ever had in her life. This even made it harder for her to not be with him.

Rose was going to ask Simon to watch over him while she was gone. She knew that he would take good care of him. Rose had a phone in her room, so she went ahead and called Simon to let him know what the doctor had just told her. She called Simon, not knowing whether he would be too busy to talk because of his time with his fighters. She was lucky that he was in his office at that time when Rose called him.

"Hello, Simon!" said Rose. "I wanted to call you and let you know that the doctor gave me the okay to leave the hospital tomorrow. I was wondering if you could pick me up around nine o'clock tomorrow morning. That's when he's going to release me. Will that be okay with you?"

"You bet, Rose. I'll be there to pick you up at 9:00 a.m. Do you need me to bring anything?" asked Simon.

"Not really. I just want to go home." Her voice sounded weary and anxious.

"Okay, Rose. I'll be there."

"Simon!" said Rose. "There are a few other things I need to talk to you about tomorrow when I get home. Okay?"

"That'll be fine, Rose. Get some rest, and sleep well. I'll see you tomorrow. By the way, If you think of anything else, call me, okay?" Simon finished the conversation with Rose and said goodbye to her and then he hung up. Rose left him wondering what she was talking about when she told him she still had things on her mind, as he walked to get a glass of water.

The following morning at 8:30 a.m., Simon drove to the hospital to pick up Rose and take her home. Rose had gotten up early and had everything that belonged to her ready and waited for Simon to get there. Simon knocked on her door with a soft tap to let her know that he was there. When he opened the door to her room, Simon walked in and went straight to Rose to give her a hug, as Rose told him how happy she was to see him and was ready to go. Rose couldn't believe she was going home. Simon noticed that her eyes were a little red and teary. Simon asked her if she was all right. And then she told him that she was thinking of Rob before he arrived and asked him if there was a chance, she could see Rob before she leaves the hospital.

Simon looked at her, feeling compassionate and bad about the situation. "They're still not letting anyone see him because he's still in a critical status and a coma." Her head fell on Simon's shoulder to let her emotions out. Then Simon told Rose they should go while she had her head on his shoulder and sniffled. Simon could almost feel her pain and heartbreak that was going through her body as he held on to her.

A nurse arrived with a wheelchair to transport Rose to the car parked in front of the hospital. This was a hospital policy after being discharged. Rose wiggled her body onto the wheelchair and waited for the nurse to start moving. "Is this all you have, Rose?" asked Simon, referring to her belongings. "Is there anything else in the closet?" he asked.

"No, that's all. I already checked," replied Rose.

"Okay! Let's go," said Simon.

Off they went to the elevator, down to the first floor, and then out the front door where Simon's car was parked alongside the curb by the entrance door. Simon opened the car door as the nurse helped Rose step off the wheelchair. Then Simon turned around and held on to her by her good arm, ensuring she didn't bump her injured shoulder in the sling. When Simon knew she was completely inside, he closed the car door, thanked the nurse for all her help, and then left the hospital.

Rose had called her mom from the hospital a few days ago and talked to her brother, telling him that she'd be going home soon but didn't know when. She was close to her brother; they did many things together when they were growing up and helped each other if they needed help with anything. Sometimes she would go with him and watch him spar with the other fighters at the gym. He was well known for his fights in Mexico, and he had a scheduled fight to happen soon. The times Rose went with him to the gym, he had her jump into the ring to show her some protection moves, so she knew how to defend herself in case she would come across someone that might put her in harm's way.

Rose had already told her mom about what happened to her and Rob that night of the incident, and she was being deported back home soon. Now that she is okay to travel, she told her mom that she will be staying with her for a while because of the injuries. On the way home, Simon and Rose talked about the things she had to take care of before going back to Mexico. She had already told Simon about her brother being a boxer, which made Simon feel good, knowing that she would be around her environment. That was one of the things that made her feel comfortable being close to a gym.

They finally arrived at her apartment and Simon got everything that belonged to her out of his car, which wasn't much. They talked for a little while longer once they were inside the apartment and made a list of the things Rose needed for the trip.

"Rose! Is there anything else that I could do for you before I leave," asked Simon.

"Not that I can think of. You have already done more than enough and appreciated you for being here for me and taking good care me like you have." It made Simon feel wonderful and happy when she told him that.

"In that case, I will go now, and if you need anything, just give me a call without hesitation, okay?" Then they said their goodnights and he left.

He was going to ask Amy if she wouldn't mind helping him get all the things that Rose needed and wanted Amy to go with him shopping for Rose. He wasn't used to doing this type of errands for anybody, especially for getting things for a female since he lived alone and wasn't much of a shopper. He just did whatever he wanted and got whatever he needed.

That evening, he called Amy and asked if she wouldn't mind going with him shopping for Rose. Simon lucked out because she didn't have to work the next day. So, she said yes, just like Simon was hoping. The following day, Amy went to Simon's apartment to start their fun shopping day. First, they were going to stop at Rose's apartment to see how she was doing and if there was anything else on the list she forgot to add.

When they arrived at Rose's apartment, Rose opened the door, and all you could smell was the breakfast she was cooking; scrambled cheese egg omelet with pieces of ham, bacon, and toast, and alongside the plate was the aroma of a hazelnut cup of coffee. She had been up since six and still in her pajamas, making breakfast for herself. The pain in her hip didn't seem to bother her that much, but she still had to wear the shoulder sling to keep her arm as immobile as she could because she knew that if it wasn't on a sling, she would use it and make it worse or prolong the healing.

"Come on in, you guys. Have a seat. It's sure nice to see both of you this morning."

"Would you guys like for me to make you some breakfast?"

"We're good, but thank you for asking, Rose. Although, it does smell delicious," commented Simon. "We stopped by to see if you needed anything else that you might have forgotten to add to your list," Simon asked. "You know what, Rose? I changed my mind. Maybe I will have a cup of your Hazelnut coffee since it smells so good. How about you, Amy? You want a cup too?"

"Sure. Why not," Amy responses.

"Great!" says Rose. "I'll get them for you."

"To answer your question, Simon. No…I can't think of anything else right off my head that I need at this moment," said Rose. "But thank you for asking."

Shortly afterward, Amy and Simon were off running errands for Rose. That took most of the morning to get everything she needed at home. When they returned to Rose's apartment, they helped her put everything away and talked about her transition back to Mexico.

Simon mentioned to Rose that the only thing he could do now was wait for the phone call from the Department of Immigration. The hospital was supposed to call the Department of Immigration and let them know about Rose's release. Then they would tell Simon when they planned to pick up Rose at her apartment and transport her back to Mexico. Rose knew the circumstances and she was coping with them reasonably well. She knew it was her fault, and now the reality was happening.

After Amy and Simon spent time with her, Simon had to tell Rose that he had to go back to the gym to work with his fighters. He had to take care of some important things with one of his boxers. Amy also had to go because she had some of her things to take care of when she had her days off. So, they hugged Rose and said goodbye to her, knowing she was doing fine and had all the things she needed for the moment.

The next day, Simon received a call from the hospital to inform him that the Department of Immigration had arranged to pick up Rose at her apartment four days from now at 10 o'clock in the morning.

Later that evening, Simon was dreading calling Rose to tell her the bad news, called Rose to tell her that he was going to her apartment to talk about the phone call he got from the hospital. It was about 8:00 p.m. when Simon arrived at Rose's apartment. She was expecting him but wasn't sure when because of his schedule at the gym. She knew what it was like with his fighters; she could relate to his plans.

"Hi, Simon," said Rose as he walked in. "How are you?"

"I'm all right, I guess. It's not the best reason for coming over with the news, but here I am," Simon spoke with a soft tone, not wanting to tell her about what she didn't want to hear from him.

"I guess you heard from the Department of Immigration, didn't you?" asked Rose.

"Yes, I did," said Simon.

"Well?" asked Rose.

"Well..." Simon paused. "They're supposed to arrive at 10 o'clock in the morning within four days. They made special arrangements for you since they're aware of who you are and take the extra precaution of getting you home safe. Are you going to be able to get hold of your mom and let her know that you'll be arriving in Mexico within the next four days? You'll also need to arrange for someone to pick you up at the Immigration office."

"I was waiting to find out exactly when they would do that. Now I know," said Rose. Then there was a little silence between them. Rose was getting a little nervous, but she was trying to be strong and not show how she was feeling at that moment.

"Okay." Rose paused. "I'll get hold of my mom today and let her know. She'll tell my brother to pick me up at the Immigration office. I don't think there'll be any problem picking me up when I get there," said Rose, trying to assure Simon.

Rose had accepted the consequences of her transition within the next four days. She wasn't thrilled about all the traveling, but she didn't have a choice. Now it was time and patience. She had to look at the bright side of things and go forward.

"I'll start getting most of the things together that I'll need to take back with me. I don't even know how many things they'll permit me to take back with me on this transport. Depending on what I'm allowed to take back with me now, maybe you can take the rest when you visit me. I'll call my mom later," said Rose. "There's one more thing, Simon. I haven't forgotten about Rob. Have you heard anything else about his condition?"

"As far as I know, he's not getting better. I checked yesterday, and he still hasn't shown any progress. He's gotten a little worse, though, to be honest with you. He hasn't been breathing independently, so they've had him on a ventilator. That's not a good thing." Simon hated to tell her that, but she had to know the truth, so it wouldn't be a shock to her if he didn't make it. At least, if she knew this, she would be aware of the worst scenario that could happen to Rob.

Rose was drawn back to Rob's condition, when she started thinking about him. It was an emotionally hard feeling for her to accept this devastating and heartbreaking moment. It was a good thing that Simon was there to help Rose overcome the sadness and heartbreak that she was going through. With Simon's support, he encouraged her to be strong and needed to look at the bright side of this because Rob wanted her to become the greatest female fighter in the world of all times. He's words meant a lot to her and had a meaningful inspirational feeling, and she took it well, understanding what Simon was saying to her.

Simon got ready to leave after he saw Rose feeling better, and asked Rose if she wanted or needed anything done before he left.

"Not at this moment. I don't have much to take with me but my clothes, and I know which ones I'm taking. I might need a small cosmetic case to carry with me, though. Maybe some type of handbag big enough for the things I need to use immediately. Those types of things," Rose said.

"Anything else?" asked Simon.

"Nope," answered Rose, "I think that's it."

"Okay. I'll see you tomorrow morning. Meanwhile, if you think of anything else, call me. You have my number."

"Simon…I'm truly sorry for what I did. Telling you and Rob the truth from the beginning would've prevented all this from happening." Rose took a big swallow as she paused for a few seconds.

"I will make it up to you by getting myself back to where I used to be and prove to you and will get you the championship title when I return. I promise you, and Rob deserves this." Rose was emotionally taken from thinking about Rob.

"I believe you will, Rose. I know Rob would be proud to see you win the title if he's with you. Now, get some rest and sleep well for tomorrows another day to live for."

And then Simon said goodnight to her, hugged her, and left.

CHAPTER TWENTY-TWO

Today was the fourth day when a special transport vehicle was arriving at 10 o'clock in the morning to deport Rose back to Mexico. It was 9 o'clock when Simon and Amy arrived at Rose's front door. Amy didn't have to start working until noon, so she had some time to see and talk to Rose before the Immigration transport arrived.

Rose opened the door as soon as she heard them knocking. Amy was holding on to a handbag to give to Rose, and Simon had a single rose to give Rose for her trip. "Come on in you guys," said Rose. "I'm glad to see."

"Here, Rose. Simon said you needed a handbag to carry your cosmetics and things you needed right away, and I thought this will serve its purpose. It's one of my extra cosmetic handbags, large enough for your makeup. I hope it works for you," Amy tells her.

"I hope it wasn't too much trouble. But I really appreciated you for bringing the bag. I think it's just right." Simon looked on, holding a bright red rose to give to Rose for her trip.

"Okay, Rose, what do you still need to do before the trip?" asked Simon.

"I got most of the things together. I was just hoping you didn't forget this bag, which you didn't, and I really appreciate you getting this for me, Simon. Well, maybe for telling Amy about what I needed. Thanks to her." Rose laughed.

"I really didn't have much time yesterday to look for a bag for you when I left your house. So, I called Amy when I got home and explained to her about what you wanted. I just lucked out. She had this extra bag in her closet that she wasn't using so it looks like it's going to work out for you just fine," said Simon.

It was almost ten in the morning as they waited for the Department of Immigration to arrive. Meanwhile, Simon got the address to her mom's house in Mexico so he could visit her as soon as possible. He wanted to be certain that Rose was all right and had the proper therapy and exercising equipment for her shoulder and hip in Mexico to help her recovery the best way possible and as soon as possible. Knowing that her brother was a boxer with a great trainer, Jimmy, because Rose had mentioned him before, made Simon feel at ease. He wasn't going to give up on her that easily, and Rose knew it. Simon told Rose that he'd try to visit her the first chance he got, hopefully within two weeks, when he could get away from his gym and things calmed down for his fighters. Rose got excited when Simon told her his plan.

By the time they were finished talking, they heard a van drive up to the apartment. Two staff members from the Immigration got out of the van and walked toward Rose's door. Rose stood up and began to get a little nervous. Simon and Amy stood up right after Rose. Rose walked to the door to let them in. As soon as she opened the door, there stood two officials looking at her, displaying their badges on the shirts. One of the officials was holding a letter of deportation on a clipboard.

They both acknowledged themselves with their credentials and asked her if she was ready. Rose nodded her head up and down slowly, not wanting to say that she was ready. She was having a hard time saying yes, but with a soft tone of voice, she answered, and said yes.

Now the time had come for Rose to start her journey back home: Mexico. Simon got both bags that Rose had packed and the ones she'll be using mostly, and leaving the rest of the things she wouldn't be needing or using right away. She had asked Simon if he could place the rest of her things in a storage facility until she got back. Rose was determined to return to the US to fight again, no matter what.

Amy walked out with Rose to the van as Simon followed, carrying her bags. Rose hugged Amy and then turned to Simon to give him a hug before she stepped into the van. She had tears running down her face. Simon told her that everything was going to be all right and to stay strong, and he'll be here for her if she ever needs anything.

The officials were already in the van, ready to take off. As the door closed, Simon and Amy stood beside each other, wondering if Rose could see them because the van had tinted windows. Simon and Amy waved anyway as they heard the van's engine start. Then the van started moving at a slow pace down the road. Amy and Simon remained standing side by side each other, watching as the van went farther and farther until it made a turn and then vanished. Simon and Amy were terribly sad to see her go, and it was hard for them to accept her departure. Amy had some tears running down her face. She was trying not to show her feelings, but she couldn't help it. She had gotten so attached to Rose that it felt like she had known Rose for a long time instead of a few months.

They both stood there for a while, looking down the road where the van had disappeared, embracing each other, and thinking about Rose, trying to look at the positive side; the day she would return. Then they went to Simon's apartment where they talked for a little while before Amy had to go to work.

CHAPTER TWENTY-THREE

Rose called Simon as soon as she arrived at her mom's house, just to let Simon know that she got there okay and that her shoulder and hip were a lot better. After a brief conversation between them, Rose thanked Simon for all the help he had given her and asked him if he could come to Mexico within the next two weeks. Of course, Simon didn't hesitate to say yes, but he needed to assure that the gym and fighters were set up with their training and gym would function smoothly while he would be gone.

Simon started making his plans to travel to Mexico and making arrangements for his fighters to keep them busy while he was gone, which was for five days, starting on Monday and returning on Friday.

Two days later, Simon received a call from the hospital updating him with Rob's condition. It was not good news. They told him that Rob might not make it for another week. After getting the information from the hospital, he decided to wait awhile before telling Rose. Simon knew that if he told Rose right now, she would be devastated once again, but in a worse way because all Rose knew was that Rob was in a critical status but not on his dying days.

Simon waited another two days before telling Rose the bad news, just in case Rob's condition got better. He was trying to look at the brighter side of things but had a bad feeling that it wasn't going to happen. Simon then called Amy at work to confirm the information the hospital just told him. When he called, Amy was in a room taking care of a patient, adjusting the medications per doctor's orders. She answered her cell phone and was glad to hear Simon's voice. The only thing, she asked him if she could call him back in a few minutes because she was right in the middle of a patient care. Simon felt bad for calling her at the wrong time and apologized for his interruption with her patient.

"Don't worry Simon. That's okay. I don't want you to feel bad about it. I'm glad that you called, but it's a little hectic right now. So, if you can give me a few more minutes, then I'll be able to talk to you, okay?" said Amy.

"Okay. But will you call me back instead, so I won't interrupt you again if you're busy? Finish what you need to do first, then call me," said Simon.

"I will," answered Amy.

Ten minutes later, Simon received a return call from Amy. "Hi, Simon. I'm sorry I couldn't talk to you when you called me a little while ago. You said you wanted to ask me something about Rob. Is he okay?" asked Amy.

"Well... I had just finished talking to one of the nurses from the ICU right before I called you, and she told me that Rob might not make it the rest of the week. I was going to see if you can verify this information for me, instead of me waiting and wondering if this is true or not." Then Simon paused for a few seconds. "Can you call me back after you confirm this with the nurse in the intensive care unit? It will assure me if you check yourself. I trust you."

"As soon as I have the chance, I will. I'll give you a call right after I find out what's going on. Okay?"

"Thank you, Amy. You're the best. I'll be waiting for your call." Then Simon said goodbye to Amy.

Later that afternoon, Simon was at the gym, training his boxers when Amy called.

"Hello, Simon. I just finished talking with the nurse in the ICU, and she did give you the right information. He might not live the rest of this week. They were looking for the next of kin but couldn't find any information listed or didn't have a clue. They did find you in the emergency list to call, if they needed someone urgently," Amy finished telling Simon the bad news. "They'll probably be calling you soon to let you know the status of Rob and give you the actual information about him."

Simon kept quiet for a few seconds, thinking about what to do next. "How am I going to tell Rose about this?" said Simon. "Now there's this dilemma I have to deal with, something that I dread doing again. But I think this time it's going to break her heart."

"Simon, maybe you shouldn't say anything to her just yet. Give her some time to settle down this week, and by the end of the week, things might change, but for the time being, Rob has a very slim chance of living to the end of the week."

"I think so too," responded Simon.

"I have to go back to work, Simon. Maybe we can connect later this evening."

"Okay. I'll talk to you later." Then he said bye to Amy, feeling a little distraught about all that's been happening lately.

Three days passed before Simon decided to call Rose to let her know that Rob didn't have that much time to live. After Simon compassionately told Rose the sad news, Rose broke down in tears, wanting not to believe it, even though, she knew that she might not see him again. She was emotionally hurt and had a hard time with the bad news when Simon told her, but after Simon talked to her for half an hour, he finally convinced Rose that she had to remain strong and continue with her life, and he'd always be there for her whenever she needed him. There wasn't any other way that he could've told her. There was nothing else he could do. He felt bad for her and tried to say it the best way he could, but it's all bad news, no matter how you say it.

Rose trusted him and believed in whatever he said to her. By the end of their conversation, she had calmed down, realizing and understanding what Simon was saying.

Another three days went by after Simon talked to Rose about Rob. Simon was walking into his apartment, after training his fighters all day long at his gym, when he heard his phone ringing. He rushed to answer it.

"Hello! May I speak with Simon please," were the first words that were said when he put the phone to his ear.

"Yes! This is he. Can I help you?" asked Simon.

"I have bad news about Rob Lee Anderson. Your name was written on his report as the only reference contact number in case of an emergency," said the nurse. "I just wanted to inform you that Rob died an hour ago of complications. We couldn't do anything else for him to keep him alive. We did everything we could, but he was not responding."

Simon remained in silence and devastated for a few seconds before he responded. "I understand, and I was already informed that he might not make it for the rest of this week, so I was aware of this situation happening at any time. Thank you for calling. I'll get in touch with you soon to figure out where to send his body."

Simon hung up the phone without saying goodbye to the nurse and sat in his chair quietly, feeling sadness for his lost friend. Rob was his right-hand man. He took good care of Rose while he trained his other fighters for him. But now he had to tell Rose the bad news once again. This time, it was going to be the worst news anybody can receive when it comes to losing someone special in their lives and Rose was the one this time.

He called Amy after sitting on the chair for ten minutes, thinking about how Rose was going to cope with this devastating news. When Amy answered the phone, she had just gotten out of the shower.

"Hello, Amy. This is Simon. Were you busy?"

"I just got out of the shower. Anything wrong?" asked Amy.

"Well, the hospital just called me to tell me that Rob died about an hour ago."

"I'm so sorry to hear that, Simon. Are you okay?"

"Yes, I'm fine, but devastated when I got the bad news. I'm worried about Rose, though. Just thinking of telling her is breaking my heart, and I can imagine how it's going to affect her emotionally when I tell her."

"Have you decided when you're going to tell Rose?" asked Amy.

"Sort of," responded Simon.

"I was thinking of asking you what your thoughts were about this. I was going to wait a little longer, but then she has to know sooner or later. What do you think?" asked Simon.

"I think it's a good idea if she knows now, instead of waiting, so we don't keep contemplating on when we should tell her. That would be my thought," said Amy.

"I think you're right, Amy. I'll tell her tomorrow night after I finish at the gym. Today has been a long day, and I feel exhausted. After I got this news from the hospital, it drained the rest of my energy from my body," said Simon.

"I can understand why. I think you should take a shower and get some good sleep tonight and start fresh tomorrow morning. You're going to have another long day tomorrow, and right now, you need all the sleep and rest you can get. Oh, one more thing, Simon, are you going to be the one who will take care of his funeral services?" asked Amy.

"I think so because they didn't have anyone else to call. They tried locating some of his relatives but couldn't find any information of anyone living close to him. So, I told them that I'll be taking care of it."

"That's good of you to do that. You're a good man, Simon."

"Thank you, Amy. I'll talk to you tomorrow. Thank you for understanding."

"You're welcome. I'll talk to you tomorrow then. Good night and sweet dreams." Then they hung up and went to bed.

The next day, Simon told Amy that he was going to wait a few days before he would tell Rose about Rob's passing.

CHAPTER TWENTY-FOUR

After a couple of days had gone by, Rose had settled down in her mom's house and moved around without any problems, even though she felt a little soreness on her hip where she was hit. Her recovery was coming along very well, and she was already thinking about her workouts.

Rose started getting anxious being around the house and thinking about her training and how she needed to stay in good condition and not let her body whither down slowly causing her to lose her strength. So she decided to go visit her brother, Rudy, at the gym and watch him train and work out. When she got there, Rudy was sparring with another one of his partners. As soon as the boxers training at the gym saw Rose walk in, they froze for a few seconds. They couldn't believe how beautiful Rose turned out to be since the last time they had seen her here at the gym. They stared at her until she reached the ring and waited for Rudy to stop sparring so she could talk to him. Rudy stopped as soon as he saw her and made his way out of the ring to talk to her.

"Hello Sis! Did you have a hard time finding the gym?" asked Rudy. "Ok you guys! You can continue training." Rudy yells out to the fighters training. "I think you know who this is."

"Not really," Rose responded. "I hadn't forgotten the location of the gym. It was pretty much a straight shot from the house, and mom kind of told me where it was, thinking that I might've forgotten."

"I'd like you to meet Jimmy. He's in the office right over there," as he pointed in the direction of his office. "Let's go meet him." Rudy made his way toward Jimmy's office as Rose followed right behind.

"Hey, Jimmy, I want you to meet my sister, Rose, the one I told you is a boxer."

"It's a pleasure to finally get the chance to meet you. I've heard so much about you, and I watched all the fights you've had and of course, all the great things Rudy told me about you. I hope you'll make yourself at home. *Mi casa es su casa*, as they say in Spanish; My house is your house."

"Thank you so much, Jimmy," answered Rose. "I can hardly wait until I get started again so I can get back into my rhythm. Thank you for inviting me and letting me use your gym." Rose looked around the gym while talking to Jimmy.

"Rudy! Why don't you show Rose where everything is located so she can get an idea where to go and get the equipment that she needs to work out when she's ready to start her training."

"Okay, Jimmy. I will," said Rudy.

"This isn't quite what you expected to see, right Rose?"

"Not really, but it will serve its purpose for now," responded Rose.

"But it's kept me in shape, and the equipment is good enough to train and workout," said Rudy.

She wasn't really impressed with the equipment in the gym, but she saw the trainees working out without any problem. It didn't matter to Rose at this time of her healing process because her shoulder was still in the healing phase and still couldn't work out if she really wanted to. She looked around to see what else they had in the gym and figured that it was going to be good enough for her to train for the time being. This wasn't anything like Simon's gym, but she knew this was Mexico, and to be able to find a gym around here was like heaven to Rose. Most of the equipment Jimmy had been worn out, but it was better than nothing. It was equipped with old weights and a bench press with worn-out leather and partially coming un-threaded around the edges. The ring was okay, just a little worn out, and she noticed a small tear on the canvas at one of the corners. The ropes around the ring were a little loose but tight enough to be safe when you would lean against them. What mattered to her was it was a gym with some exercise equipment to help her condition and strengthen the muscles in her shoulder and side.

Rose was anxious and ready to start training again. Rose was comfortable with Jimmy's personality. She was grateful that he was letting her use his gym and equipment. The healing process was the only factor that was stopping Rose from starting her workouts right away, even though she felt fine and thought she could start anytime today.

Meanwhile, back in the States, Simon kept hesitating to call Rose because he wasn't sure how Rose was going to react this time. He was dreading giving her the bad news about Rob. He really didn't have a choice but to tell her. There were no ifs or buts about it. This was the day he dreaded the most.

When he got off work, the first thing he did was call Rose at her mom's house. After two rings, Rose was the one who picked up the phone.

"Hi! Is this Rose?" asked Simon.

"Yes, it is," answered Rose.

"This is Simon. How are you?"

"Oh! Hello Simon! I don't feel too bad, a little anxious about not being able to train, but I'm getting a lot better. How are you? I'm so glad that you called. I was just thinking about you and wondering why you haven't called."

"I'm fine, thank you. Is everything going all right for you so far?"

"Yes. So far, so good. Thank you for asking."

"Rose…" Then he paused. "I need to tell you that Rob passed away three days ago. I was going to wait another day until you had settled down at your mom's, but I thought it's best for you to know this now than later. They tried to do everything they could to keep him alive, but he was having too many complications with his head trauma." Simon waited for a few seconds and couldn't hear anything from Rose. Then he heard Rose burst out crying, which was expected of her. He waited for a few seconds more before he continued talking.

"I'm so sorry, Rose. He meant a lot to me too. I was devastated myself when they told me." Simon could relate to her feelings.

"You know what, Rose? I made plans to travel to Mexico to see you in a couple of weeks." Simon tried to distract her from thinking about Rob. He still couldn't get her to say anything, so he waited for a few more seconds. He could still hear her crying, but not as loud.

Rose immediately felt a pain like someone had just penetrated a knife into her heart. It was worse than Simon thought it was going to be. She had laid the phone down on the table, trying to grasp her feelings and stay strong. Simon was not aware that Rose had done this and just kept talking to her, but Rose didn't hear a word that he had said to her. She was not able to keep her emotions from her thoughts of losing Rob and not accepting that he was gone forever.

"Are you okay, Rose? I need you to talk to me. I wish I was there to help you share the tears and sorrow, but I need you to be strong right now and think about what I just told you about my trip to see you soon." Rose still wasn't responding. "Talk to me, Rose!" Simon raised his voice with concern and getting worried, waiting for a response from Rose. He finally heard her voice responding with sniffling and sobbing as Rose wiped her running nose and teary eyes.

"I'm sorry, Simon. I can't believe he's gone. He just meant the whole world to me. I feel so alone now, like part of me just vanished and took my heart and soul. I will miss him, Simon." Rose's tears ran down her cheeks. She kept sniffing, trying to hold her feelings back so she could talk to Simon.

"I don't know if you heard what I said about going to Mexico to see you in a couple of weeks or not. But I already decided to go to Mexico."

Rose listened and responded this time. "It would be nice of you to come see me soon. I would really like that." Rose was still sniffling, and her eyes had turned a little red because of the crying.

"Just let me know when, so I can plan for the day you'll be coming. Okay?"

"I will," answered Simon. "I'm planning to take the trip within two weeks from now, and I'll let you know for sure within the next two days to confirm the time and day."

"I can hardly wait to see you," said Rose.

"One more thing, Rose. You mentioned that you went to the gym where your brother is working out and training. Is there any exercising equipment that you would need to help you with your therapy? Look around the gym and let me know so I can send them to you, or you can wait until I get there, then we can decide what equipment would be best for you to work out with. Okay?"

"Okay. I will. Maybe I'll just wait until you get here. I think you would be better of evaluating the equipment that I should need because you would know more about what exercise equipment I really need for my therapy."

"Okay. I'll call you again in a couple of days, or if you think of something that you need sooner than two weeks, give me a call. You take good care of yourself. Talk to you soon."

"Bye, Simon," and she hung up, sniffling and wiping her running nose and teary eyes redden from her thoughts of Rob.

Rose was eager to start training before Simon had told her about Rob. Now her mind was all about Rob. But she also knew that she had to continue training and not let her emotions jump to conclusion and make her overwhelmed with her feelings. After she had talked to Simon last night, she stayed awake for a long time, thinking about what they had talked about before she fell asleep. It took a while before she calmed down and realized that Simon had made a lot of sense about what he said to her.

Simon, on the other hand, felt what Rose was going through last night and was hoping that she would think strongly about what they had talked about and not let her feelings affect her mind with depression or have trouble controlling her emotions, like Rose's thoughts.

Rose had trouble sleeping for the next two nights thinking about Rob and knowing that she would never see him again or have him next to her every day or night. Simon waited to talk to Rose because he got so busy with his fighters and had to plan for an event that he had scheduled the week after visiting Rose in Mexico. Simon finally had the chance to call Rose. When he did, Rose was glad and got excited after he told Rose that he was coming to see her in another week and was looking forward for that day. Rose told her mom all about Simon, which made her mom as excited as Rose. She asked her mom, Francis, to help her move things around the house because she wanted to make Simon feel comfortable. Since they didn't have a lot of furniture to move around, other than a few knickknacks, it didn't take them very long to rearrange the furniture in the house. Roses' family didn't have a lot of money either, but they had a good heart and cherished what they did have at home.

Meanwhile, Simon was planning to leave the following Tuesday and return on Friday. He thought it would give him enough time to see how Rose was doing and what training equipment she needed at the gym and at home to help her strengthen her shoulder and hip. He wanted Rose in a workout routine as soon as her wounds healed enough to start her body conditioning and do her moves without disturbing the hip wounds.

The first thing Simon had to take care of was Rob's funeral. Since they couldn't find any information about his relatives anywhere, he thought the best and easiest thing that he could do for Rob was to have him cremated. Simon had called Rose to tell her what he was going to do. He explained the situation to her, and she seemed to be okay with it since she couldn't go see him. It was heartbreaking for her, but she had no choice but to accept the reality of the situation. She had already gone through a lot from the first time when she got the news about Rob being in a car accident. It was now a reality that had broken her heart emotionally, but she grasped her feelings and continued to move forward; painful to think about it, but she knew that Rob wanted her to become the best female boxer that ever fought in the ring.

For the next few days, Simon had made all his arrangements for his boxers, their schedules, and training routines. He gave the gym key to one of the longtime boxers, Tony, whom he trusted. Simon had asked Amy if she would like to go with him to visit Rose, but unfortunately, because of her schedule, she wasn't able to go with him this time. Although, she was going to make arrangements for the next time Simon decides to go back, possibly within the following month.

CHAPTER TWENTY-FIVE

Before leaving the United States to visit Rose in Mexico, Simon had talked to the attorney about Rose's visa. His Attorney told Simon that he was still working with the Immigration Department, trying to get Rose's visa forms completed, and hoping to process her visa card as soon as possible. They were treating it with a little more priority and it seemed that it wasn't going to be any problem, except for the waiting period, which would take another month or so, since she'd had a visa before and had become a celebrity, per se. The attorney knew about the P-1 visa, which was made for special athletes to compete in sports in the United States. Simon was elated and excited when the Attorney told him about the visa. Rose still needed a little more time to heal her wounds anyway, so a month wasn't an issue, although her healing process was going to take a lot longer.

When Rose told her mom, Francis, that she will be staying for around a month, she got all excited and thrilled to have Rose stay with her during her recovery. She wanted to help Rose get better as soon as possible by taking good care of her or whatever it takes to get her back into the ring. She was proud of Rose for being who she was and prayed for that one day when she could fulfill her dream like she talked about. Francis wanted Rose to continue boxing as a career because she had already established herself as an inspirational icon to all the city locals. The residences around the area near her and Mexico City are very proud of her. Her fans and followers knew that someday she would become a champion of the world in her weight class.

Finally, Simon was on his way to see Rose in Mexico. When he arrived at the Acapulco Airport at 6:00 p.m., which was the closes airport to get to Chilpancingo, the airport was crowded with people going out and people coming off a flight, rushing to get out of the airport, just like he was, and the outside weather was still blazing hot. He looked for a taxi as soon as he walked out the front door of the airport lobby to take him to Rose's mom's house. He was a little tired from the flight, which took about four hours. Now Simon had to travel at least 45 minutes to get to the city of Chilpancingo, a population of 166,795, on a Mexican Federal Highway 95, and then it will turn into a bumpy and dusty road in a taxi for another 15-minutes or more to get to the house. Simon wasn't aware of how bad the road was going to be until the taxi got closer to Roses' moms' house.

The sun was blazing hot, and Simon could feel the penetration of the heat through the windows, even with the air turned on high. The cab driver had to drive another two miles off road in the outskirts once he was in Chilpancingo on a paved two-lane road. The closer the taxi got to Roses' mom's house, the more the road had areas with potholes, which made it a little rough and bumpy. There were a lot of cactuses alongside the road that were of different sizes, and some even looked like little trees. The house was a few yards off-set on a dirt road, which was even bumpier and dusty.

When the taxi arrived at her mom's house, the first thing Simon saw were kids playing outside the yard, running, and chasing each other and enjoying their youth activities. They were dressed in raggedy clothes, as if they had found them in a trash can that someone had thrown away, and some had rips on their clothes while others were wearing clothes that didn't match, although that didn't seem to bother them. They were just having a lot of fun. When the taxi came to a complete halt, Simon stepped out of the car. The kids playing and running around the yard stopped and ran toward the taxi to see who was going to get out of the car. They gathered by the door of the cab and saw Simon making his way out of the car and stared at him. The kids got curious right away about who this stranger was and what he wanted. There weren't too many new faces that came to this part of the land, so the kids were waiting and staring at Simon as he made his way out of the car.

When Simon was completely out of the cab, he noticed a little girl standing in front of him, asking him questions in English, but with a strong Mexican accent, about what he wanted and who he was looking for. She wasn't shy but curious. Then Simon asked her if this is where Rose lived. The little girl just looked at him like she didn't know the person he was looking for.

Then she shouted out with her strong Mexican accent. "Oh! You mean Rosalinda?" Simon could barely understand her, but clear enough to communicate with the little girl.

"Yes," responded Simon. It dawned on him that he and the others back home called her Rose, but in her hometown of Mexico, they only knew Rose by her real name, Rosalinda.

Simon talked to the little girl and answered some of the questions that she was asking him, feeling like he was being interviewed by a reporter with all the questions the little girl was asking him. Although, he was enjoying listening to her asking all these questions like a grown-up with a serious expression on her face, making him chuckle as he answered her questions. Simon had to stop the little girl from asking too many questions so he could find out what house Rose was living in because there were two other houses next to each other. She finally pointed to the one where Rose was staying. Simon walked up to the house and knocked on the door. Rose's mom opened the door, not knowing who it was.

"Hi! My name is Simon, and I was looking for Rose. Is this where she lives?"

Rose's mom knew a few words in English, so she understood Simon and told him, "You mean Rosalinda?" saying it with a Mexican accent and with the tongue roll when she pronounced Rosalinda's name.

"Yes," her mom answered Simon. "Enter," she tells Simon with a real soft-spoken voice. "Me not know too much English. Please come in. She is in back room reading. I go get her," She tried to communicate with Simon the best she could. He understood her enough to know that she was going to tell Rose that he was here. It took about a minute before Rose appeared in front of Simon.

"Hi! Simon. So glad that you made it okay. I was expecting you a little later because of the drive from the airport. But you're here, and that's a good thing."

"It was a little bumpy and hot getting here, though," said Simon.

"I guess you already met my mom, Francis?" said Rose.

"I assume that she was your mom, and I think we understood each other with some words, here and there. She did understand me when I was asking for you. So, now she knows who I am." Simon smiled at Rose and walked up to her to give her a hug.

After Rose officially introduced Simon to her mom, they went to the kitchen and sat down to have a drink of water and talked for about an hour. Simon tells Rose, "There was this little girl who kept talking and talking, asking all these questions about who I was, what I was doing here, and who I was looking for." Rose laughed and got a kick out of it as Simon described the little girl. "I had to stop her or else, no telling how long she would've kept asking me more questions." They both chuckled for a minute.

"I think I know who you're talking about," said Rose. "She's my sister's friend's little sister that lives next door. She's a wonderful little girl. And yes, she's curious about a lot of things and is not shy and real talkative." Rose chuckles again.

Francis, sort of knew Simon by the way Rose described him before he arrived. While Rose and Simon were catching up on Rose's condition, her mom had excused herself from the conversation so she could start making dinner. Rose had Simon go with her to the living room so her mom could have the kitchen and make something to eat. She knew Simon was probably starving after traveling for several hours and she was also a little hungry herself.

Francis was an excellent cook and loved cooking. Rose's brother, Rudy, who is twenty-four years old was at the gym, training and working out as he usually does. He usually gets home around this time of day. Rose also had a younger sister, Anna, who was twenty-one years old. She adored having her around to do things together, but Anna was more of an outgoing type of person who liked boys and flirted with them quite often. Rose wasn't as outgoing as Anna, but more of a home body that helped her mom take care of things around the house.

Later, that evening, Simon met Rudy and her sister, Anna, when they got home. Simon enjoyed meeting them, and they all had a very pleasant conversation that evening, getting to know each other. Simon had planned on staying with them the duration of his visit, and Rose made arrangement for him to sleep in her sister's bedroom room. Anna was staying at her friend's house to spend the nights during Simons' visit, which was next door.

The next day, Rudy, Rose, and Simon all went to the gym together. Rudy had an old 2011 F150 pickup truck that got him around wherever he wanted to go. His longest drive was going to the gym. The drive took them thirty-five minutes and during that time on their way to the gym, Rudy briefly talked about his events coming up soon and what his plans were with his boxing career.

When they arrived at the gym, the first thing Simon saw was an old building that used to be a storage building. Rudy had told Simon before arriving that it needed some TLC, and that was Simons' first impression of the gym when he saw it. But, when Simon walked inside the gym with Rudy and Rose, his eyes widened as soon as he got a glimpse of the workout equipment and the two boxing rings. Rose noticed Simon's facial expression and whispered to him, telling him not to say anything. Rudy took Simon and Rose around the gym, showing him the equipment available that they had for training and the boxing rings. Then they saw Jimmy coming out of his office, so Rudy hollered softly to get his attention.

"Hey, Jimmy! I want you to meet Simon, Rose's trainer, from the US." That got Jimmys' attention, so he walked towards them.

"Hi! Nice to meet you," said Jimmy. "Rose told me a little about you and said that she's never met another man as kind and caring as you have been to her. She also told me how great of a trainer you are, and she owes her career to you for all the hard work you've put into her training and conditioned her into a top contender." Jimmy paused. "For now, I'm so glad that you could come and visit her. She must be a very special person to you."

"She sure is! She's one of the best female boxers that I have ever come across, and I consider myself very lucky that I met her first before anyone else discovered her. She's a very determined and strong-willed person who is always willing to learn and does not give up easily. That's what I like about her," responded Simon.

"What do think of the gym, Simon?"

"So far so good," said Simon, trying not to really say anything that would make Jimmy feel embarrassed. He had to think about where he was and what the people had to do to earn a living. He noticed the equipment that needed replacing and add some additional equipment he thought Rose might need to help her train and work out to strengthen her shoulder muscles.

Inside the gym was very warm and all they had were three free-standing fans on pedestals: two facing the ring and the other toward the direction of the boxers' training equipment. Simon then knew that this was another problem with the gym, so he kept that in mind to add to his list of things the gym was lacking. He looked at Rose and saw sweat running down her face. Simon then asked Rose if she wanted to drink some water. He pulled out a handkerchief that he carries in his back pocket because back home, he sometimes sweats and likes to wipe the sweat off his face, and then gives it to Rose.

"Jimmy! Do you have any cold bottled water anywhere near?" asked Simon.

"Yes, I do. It's in my office in the small compact refrigerator.

I'll take you there," said Jimmy.

"Perfect! I'm glad you do, Jimmy," Rose tells him. "I drink a lot of water during my training."

Meanwhile, Rudy got into his workout clothes and started training on the weights. Simon and Rose went and sat down on some old chairs that were located near the ring and watched two fighters spar with each other. Simon was impressed with their boxing techniques, and it seemed to him like they had been boxing for a while because of the way they were jabbing and punching each other, blocking each other's punches.

Simon and Rose sat for about half an hour and then decided to let Rudy know they were getting ready to leave. Rose wanted to show Simon around town, which wasn't much other than a gas station and a small grocery store, among other small retail markets. Rudy let Rose use his truck to get around while he worked out at the gym.

Later that afternoon, around four o'clock, Simon and Rose returned to the gym to pick up Rudy. Rudy was in the ring sparring when they arrived. He was pushing himself like Rose does, to better himself and be prepared for his coming fight in a month. After Rose and Simon had their discussion about Rose's therapy and plans about how Jimmy was scheduling her training to get her back to her boxing condition, they went home. Rose knew that Francis was making another good meal for all of them when they returned. By the time they got home, her mom had started making dinner.

Simon was excited to get a homemade Mexican meal because Mexican food was one of his favorite foods, especially when it was homemade and spicy. She had made brown rice, spicy frijoles, and her homemade tortillas, the best tortillas Rose has ever tasted, and had some leftover tamales that she had made the day before, but they tasted like she had just made them. Simon was in heaven as he ate every bit of his food on his plate. After having a wonderful home-cooked meal, Rose helped her mom with the dishes while Simon and Rudy discussed some of the ways that he could help Rose get better.

As soon as Rose finished helping her mom in the kitchen, she went to the living room where Simon and Rudy were talking about her workouts. Simon had made a list of the equipment that he thought might help Rose regain and strengthen her muscles, and he planned to send them to her as soon as he went back to the States. Rose got there at the end of the conversation and wanted to find out what Simon and Rudy had talked about. Rudy had told Simon a little about Jimmy and where he came from. He told Simon that Jimmy used to be a boxer himself who fought for four years before he got injured when he was fighting to be the top contender. But because of an awkward punch that landed on his side of his face, lost his balance, and fell with his knee buckling underneath him, creating an injury to his knee. From there on, he couldn't fight for a long time, so instead he set his mind on becoming a trainer, just to be around the boxing ring and train fighters to become champions, which he had done twice since becoming a trainer.

After hearing this from Rudy, it made him feel better about having him around Rose as a trainer. Simon went over the rest of plans with Rose. She was excited to get started, but first, she had to strengthen her muscles on her shoulder and hip injuries before she could even start working out. That was killing her to even think that she had to wait until then.

Another day passed, and Simon had finished listing the type of equipment Rose needed for the gym to help her with her exercises and therapy. Simon had a scheduled flight to return to the States early Friday morning, at 6:00 o'clock, so he wanted to get all his things packed and ready to leave in the morning. He asked Rudy if he could drive him back to the airport in the morning. Rudy didn't mind at all. They got along very well with each other, and Rudy appreciated Simon for taking good care of his sister. It meant a lot to him since Rose and him had a very close relationship as brother and sister. Simon had to get up by 4:00 a.m., because it took 45 minutes to get to the airport, and then he had to check in.

CHAPTER TWENTY-SIX

Simon got home safe and was not as tired as he was going to Mexico. After he rested and unpacked, the first thing he wanted to do was browse through his list of equipment Rose needed at the gym and home. But before that, he had promised Amy that he would call her as soon as he returned from Mexico, so he got his phone and called her. There was no answer when he called, so he just left a message for her saying that he was home and would try again later. Then he planned of going to the gym to see how his fighters were doing since he had been gone for four days.

When he arrived at the gym, all his fighters were busy training like he was hoping to see them actively working out. He felt good about it, knowing it all went well while he was gone. He had left Tony, the fighter he left in charge, and did an excellent job for him. Now he can trust him with confidence and not worry for the next time he goes back to Mexico.

While he was walking around the gym, Tony, his best fighter with the most boxing experience, was sparring in the ring with another one of his better fighters to give Tony a good workout. Tony had been training for the last four years with Simon. His coming fight, if he wins, would make him the next contender for the title shot in the lightweight division. Simon had been waiting for this moment for a long time. The first time Tony had a shot for the title was last year, but he was outscored in the fourth round because one judge gave him fewer points that could've made the difference if Tony would've won that round. That's how close the fight was, and the people felt that Tony should've won that fight. Three Judges who are approved by the boxing commission and sit along the ringside to score the bout, but are spaced apart a little, sometimes view the rounds differently than the other judges. One judge could favor one of the fighters that would give the fighter the edge of winning the round.

Simon stopped and talked to Tony for a few minutes to see if he was still on the training schedule that he had made for his coming up event.

The next thing Simon wanted to do was call Amy again. He hadn't talked with her since going to Mexico because he had been so busy with Rose and Rudy. He felt bad about not calling her, but he did tell her before leaving that depending on how it went in Mexico, he might not be able to call her, but Simon promised her that it would be the first thing he would do when he returned to the States and touch base with her. Amy understood and was okay with it. When he attempted to get hold of Amy again, she still didn't answer her phone.

By four o'clock in the afternoon, Simon had gotten everything on his list to send to Rose. He also arranged for the equipment he bought to be shipped to Mexico as soon as possible. It was going to take three days to get there. Simon called Amy again at about 5:30 p.m., but she still didn't answer her phone after he let it ring about five times before hanging up the phone. He assumed she was probably very busy with patients and decided to wait another hour before calling her back. Simon left another message for her to call him back when she was free to talk for a few minutes and let her know that he was back from Mexico. It wasn't until an hour later when she returned Simons' calls as soon as she was free. Simon answered.

"Hello Simon! It's Amy. I'm so sorry I couldn't answer the phone the first time you called me. We had an emergency just a few minutes before you called. You know how my schedule changes unexpectedly from one minute to another, and it gets hectic at times. I never know when something like this will happen," said Amy.

"Yes, I understand, and I know what you must do. I just wanted to let you know that I had arrived safely. I promised to call you as soon as I got back."

"Thank you, Simon," said Amy. "I'm glad that you're back. I missed you. How was your trip, and how's Rose doing?" asked Amy.

"She's doing great but anxious to start training. You know how she is; she never wants to stop training. Always on the go."

"I know," said Amy.

"It's pretty late now, so what if we get together tomorrow night and have dinner? Then we can talk more about this," said Simon.

"I think it's a great idea. What time is a good time for you, Simon?"

"What about seven?"

"Sounds good to me," replied Amy.

"Great! Then seven it is."

The next day, Simon picked up Amy at her apartment around 6:45 p.m. He was planning on taking Amy to dinner at a nice, cozy Italian restaurant near her apartment. Amy loved Italian food, especially pasta salads. It wasn't Simon's first choice of food, but because he knew it was Amy's favorite dish, he decided it was best to go there. His favorite dish was Mexican food because he liked the spicy taste the most. He usually drank a cold beer to soothe the afterburn of the hot and spicy flavor.

They had a lovely evening dinner and talked about his plans with Rose. Simon had asked Amy if she wanted to return to Mexico when he decided on the date, which he plans to return within three weeks. She was ready to go as soon as Simon confirmed the date for the trip. All he had to do was tell her what days he was planning on going so she could request those days off.

Amy spent the night with Simon since she didn't have to work the next day. Simon did have to work tomorrow but that didn't stop him from staying out late and enjoying the night with Amy. He was in love with Amy and would try to be with her any time he had the chance to be at her side.

A few days later, Rose called Simon to thank him for the equipment he had sent to her mom's house and some to J'S Gym, the name of Jimmy's gym. Rose was surprised when Jimmy called her to tell her that the equipment Simon had ordered had arrived at the gym. Now she would have some new and updated training equipment to help her get started as soon as possible. It was the only gym around that was close to the city. That's why Jimmy was doing so well, besides being an extraordinarily good trainer with his skills from the past as a fighter. He was another example of how Simon trained his fighters. Jimmy had some outstanding fighters besides Tony. Rudy, Rose's brother, was one of the other better fighters that Jimmy trained. Rudy had been boxing since he was ten and loved what he did. That's why Rose had the same love for boxing. It ran in the family.

When the equipment arrived, Simon had sent Rose a letter to tell her what equipment to use for her shoulder and side. He wanted Jimmy to help her with her routine and stay on schedule. If she had any questions, Simon wanted her to give him a call no matter what day or time it was. He just wanted her to get well, back to her normal condition, and training routine as soon as possible. Simon wanted Jimmy to start Rose at a slow pace and keep an eye on her progress with her training.

It was another two days before Jimmy decided to let her start exercising and working out in the gym. Rose was finally happy to get her hands on the exercise equipment, but the first thing she wanted to do was lift the weights. Jimmy told her no, as Simon requested. Rose was disappointed, but then she realized he was right to deny her request. Jimmy started Rose at a slow pace, doing stretches and sit-ups, and had her run slowly around the gym to build her cardiovascular strength back to where it used to be. From that point on,

Rose didn't hesitate to do whatever Jimmy wanted her to do. She put all the energy into her training to get her body conditioned as much as she could to get to where she was satisfied.

Rose had her mind set to go beyond her limit to exceed everyone's expectations of just being a female boxer. She wanted to become the world's best fighter in her weight class. Rose wanted to excel her skills beyond what she used to be, so when it would be time to face Echo for the world championship, she would be ready for anything Echo would bring to the ring. Rose hadn't forgotten her past with Echo; a retribution was all Rose could think of to settle what Echo did to her in the restaurant. The more Rose thought about her, the more it pushed her beyond her limit. She continued with her exercise as planned and finished her first day of body conditioning, making her feel lively again, full of energy, and ready to take on another day tomorrow.

CHAPTER TWENTY-SEVEN

Simon had scheduled to visit Rose in Mexico three weeks ago, but this time, Amy was going with him. She had made the arrangements at the hospital to be off for five days; three for a visit and two for traveling and recuperating when she returned from the trip, to relax and enjoy a cozy night with Simon. Simon already knew what to expect on the trip, except for Amy. The trip to Mexico was her first trip out of the country, and it made her excited to do so, especially having Simon by her side.

Time flew by fast that it was time for Simon and Amy to go visit Rose in Mexico. When they arrived in Acapulco airport later that afternoon, Amy was a little tense and a little jet lagged from the flight. It was an experience and a very different type of environment to be in. It wasn't as she expected, but she was glad that Simon was at her side and felt safe having him next to her. The populated site of the people who were walking around the airport were a mixture of different cultures, and when they walked outside the airport to catch a taxi, she saw people selling anywhere from fruit to hand carved furniture.

Simon had a taxi drive them from the airport to Rose's mom's house. He knew this would be an experience for Amy because she had always been a city girl and had never been on a rough dirt road like the one that will take them to Rose's mom's house. He thought this would be a different experience for her. Although now she will see how some of the Mexicans and other cultures live and survive with what they had to do to keep their families from starving.

It took them another forty-five minutes to get to her mom's house. Simon felt a little bad for Amy because it was a rough road, dirty and dusty, besides being bumpy.

When they finally reached Rose's mom's house, the same kids who'd been playing around the front yard the first time Simon visited Rose saw the taxi approaching, they recognized Simon in the cab, so they ran toward the taxi and waited for Simon to get out. Amy was with him this time, so she was a new stranger to the kids. They surrounded the cab and greeted Simon as he got out of the car and looked at Amy, wondering who she was. The kids quickly noticed that Simon had his hand around Amy's waist and figured it was Simon's girlfriend, so they said hello to her and accepted her as a friend.

Rose heard the kids from inside the house talking loudly outside, so she peeked out the kitchen window and saw Simon and Amy walking toward the front door as they pulled their luggage and a carry-all bag strapped on Simons' shoulder. She immediately rushed to the door to open it before Simon and Amy even got halfway to the entrance and stepped outside to greet them. Rose approached them, hugged Simon, and then smiled and hugged Amy. She was thrilled to see Amy visit her with Simon.

"I'm so glad to see both of you. You made my day. Let's go inside so you can relax and tell me how the trip was for you. Okay?" said Rose.

"Hey, you seem to be moving your arm and walking a little faster." Simon commented on Rose's condition. This was a good sign for Simon to see her energetic and seemed to be happy.

"I feel a lot better since the last time I saw you. I'm ready to get into the ring." Rose chuckled as Simon copied.

During the next few hours, Amy met Rose's mom, Francis, her brother, Rudy, and sister, Anna. She enjoyed talking to them every minute of their conversation, even though Rose had to interpret a few words for her mom. During their conversation, Francis excused herself from the room and went to the kitchen to start dinner.

At about 7:00 p.m., Francis finished making dinner for all of them. She loved cooking, whether it was breakfast, lunch, or dinner. They all had a wonderful homemade dinner, and now they could hardly stand up because of all the food they had eaten. All the food Francis had made was so delicious that they couldn't resist having seconds.

The following day, Simon was up early as usual, but he needed his cup of coffee to get him started, so he went to the kitchen, and when he got there, Rose had already started brewing the coffee.

"Good morning, Simon," said Rose.

"Good morning, Rose." He scratched his head. "Boy! I think I ate too much last night. I still feel full." He rubbed his stomach.

Rose laughed and told him, "I told you not to get carried away because I know how you like Mexican food and if you're hungry, you'll end up overeating, just like you did last night." Rose jokingly put a big smile on her face.

"Okay. You're right. I ate way too much, but I enjoyed it." Simon laughed. "The first thing I want to do today is go to the gym and see how the equipment I sent to the gym is arranged and talk with Jimmy. I'm sure he has the equipment set up in the best way possible that will benefit you the most. I just want to talk to him about some other things I have in mind and ask him how long he thinks it'll take to get you back into the ring," said Simon.

"We'll have a fun day today after we take care of business with Jimmy at the gym, and then I would like to show Amy around, with your help, of course, and take her around town and let her see what Chilpancingo city is like," said Simon.

"There's not much here to show her, but I think she'll get the feel of what the people have to do to survive and what they're doing for a living to buy food for their families," commented Rose.

Rudy had a newer car, a 2010 Toyota Corolla that he drove downtown, instead of his old truck when he wanted to have fun with his friends. He had let Rose borrow this car frequently before she went to the United States. After they had coffee and some Mexican pastry, they hopped into the car and drove to the gym.

When Simon, Amy, and Rose arrived at the gym, Simon had a look at the new training equipment that he bought Rose. Jimmy had already set up the equipment in a designated area for the trainees and Rose, knowing where he was going to start Rose exercising. Right after looking around, Simon walked into Jimmy's office to talk to him, which lasted for about an hour. They both agreed on her routine; saying that it would take another month or two before she could start sparring in the ring, depending on her progress. Jimmy agreed with Simon to stay in touch with him and inform him of her progress, and then they would decide whether she was ready to begin sparring.

Amy sat alongside the ring while waiting for Simon to finish talking to Jimmy and Rose in his office. She was amazed how the fighters hit each other hard and did not feel the pain they were getting from one another. She had never been this close to boxers fighting in the ring, but she was impressed with the fighters' abilities to move all around the ring and throwing punches at each other. It was a little entertaining for her, but she also thought how brutal the sport can be for a fighter to absorb all the punches they get from their opponents.

Amy saw Rose walking out of the office as Simon followed. She assumed they had finished talking, so she stood up from the chair and walked toward them.

"What do you think of the boxers?" asked Simon.

Amy replied, "I just don't know how they can stand being hit like that. It looks like it's too much pain for me when you get punched." Amy chuckled and squinched her nose.

"They get used to it. I'm pretty sure the fighters feel the power of the hard punches they're getting," answered Simon.

"Are you ready to see the town, Amy?" asked Simon.

"Yes, I am," replied Amy.

"Okay. Hey, Rose! How about you? Are you ready to go?"

"I'm ready," said Rose.

"Well, let's go!" said Simon.

Then they all got in the car and drove off to town. Amy wore a pair of old jeans and a light blouse with short sleeves because it was too hot to wear anything too heavy.

After walking around town for an hour, the sun became intolerable. Amy's arms were getting sunburnt, and her face was getting a little red around her sunglasses, leaving the outline of the glasses. She hadn't prepared to get a sunburn so fast; she hadn't even thought of bringing any sunblock to protect her from the sun. When Simon looked at her and noticed that she was getting a sunburn, he asked her if she wanted to get some sunscreen at the store just a short distance from where they were.

"That will be great, Simon. Thank you." Amy appreciated Simon for thinking and doing that for her.

At the end of the day, after walking around two hours, looking at the shops and eating, all three had enough of the town. Amy was ready to go back to the house, so they called it a day and went back home to Rose's mom's house. They had a long and well-spent day doing what Simon wanted. They were exhausted and Amy's arm got sunburned a little too much, but she survived the day.

The next day, they spent the day at her mom's house, wandering around the property, talking, and meeting her neighbors. Rose and Amy watched the kids outside enjoying their time with each other, playing, and running about the property. After watching the kids, Rose and Amy went inside to help her mom, Francis, cook some meals for lunch. They also prepared the food they would have for dinner later that evening.

The following day, Simon helped Rose set up the exercising equipment he had bought for her to use at home. No big equipment because of the size of the house they lived in, but a jump rope, a set of dumbbells and a punching bag he attached at the back of the house under a canopy to keep the sun from radiating Rose when she works out and a small mat for the sit-up bench.

After the third day, Rudy and Rose drove Simon and Amy to the airport in time to check in their luggage. They got there early and had some time to talk. They mostly talked about their next visit. Within thirty minutes of their conversation, they announced the boarding flight overhead, so Rudy and Rose said their goodbyes as they boarded the plane and watched as it took off and disappeared in the sky.

CHAPTER TWENTY-EIGHT

The trip for Amy will be one of the most memorable and great experiences that she's had in a long time. One that she will cherish forever especially having Simon by her side throughout the trip and Rose as the best friend that she has ever had.

When they arrived at Los Angeles Airport, they were dreading looking for their luggage because they knew it would take them another hour before they would be able to find them on the unloading conveyor belt. Once they found them, Simon had Amy wait for him to get the car and pick her up. Simon then drove Amy home and unloaded her luggage and all her items and took them inside the apartment. They had a brief conversation before Simon said goodbye to her. They were both tired and Simon had a long day the next day at the gym. Amy had another day off, so she could rest and catch up on her sleep if she needed to.

When Simon went to the gym the next day, a note from Rose's attorney was sitting on his desk. He read the note, saying that he wanted Simon to call him as soon as he returned from the trip. A lot of thoughts went through Simon's mind before reading the note. It made him think of the worst scenario that could happen to Rose's visa; it might not be approved. But that was only a thought, a fearful one.

Simon got his phone immediately and called the attorney.

"Law office of John and Associates, this is John. May I help you?"

"Hello! John, this is Simon. I got your note saying that you wanted to talk to me about Rose's visa. I hope you have good news to tell me?" Simon asked.

"Oh! Hi, Simon. I do! I was going to tell you earlier, but I heard you were gone on a trip to Mexico to see Rose. How did that go?" asked John.

"It was an excellent trip, and I took my friend Amy with me. We had a wonderful time together and did things with Rose. She's doing great and is getting better by the day. She already wants to get back into the ring and start sparring. But I had to tell her that it's not going to happen until she takes care of her injuries completely," said Simon. "Anyway, what did you find out about her visa?"

"They approved her visa and she'll be able to return to the United States sooner than I expected. It won't be until another month by the time they get the paperwork ready. But it's been approved, and that's all that matters," said John.

"That is good news! I'll call Rose as soon as we hang up. She asked me when I was in Mexico if I'd heard anything about her visa, but I didn't have an answer for her. Now I do," said Simon.

"I'll inform you if they need anything else to finish getting the visa completed."

"That would be great, John. Thanks for taking care of that for me. I appreciate you following through with it. I owe you." Simon finished the conversation. After Simon hung up, he called Rose to tell her the good news.

"Hello, Rose! It's Simon. We made it back okay. I just finished talking to the attorney. He had good news for you. I couldn't wait to tell you so that's why I'm calling you now. They approved your visa. How wonderful is that!" Simon was so excited to tell her the good news. Simon heard Rose scream with excitement.

"That is so wonderful, Simon. Thank you! Thank you! Thank you!" Rose couldn't believe the good news. It made her day.

"Now you have to get better and take care of yourself as we discussed. Stick with our plan, okay?" said Simon.

"I will, Simon. I promise you," replied Rose, still excited with the good news.

"I'll call you as soon as I can to let you know when my next visit to Mexico will be. Probably within the next three weeks would be my guess. For the time being, I want you to take care of yourself and not reinjure your shoulder or hip, okay? And stick to your plans."
"Okay. Thank you again for the good news, Simon. You're the best. Bye!" Rose hung up the phone.

Two weeks had passed, and Rose never stopped exercising because she was determined to get back in shape mentally and physically. Her condition was getting better with every day she trained. Her shoulder improved with the light exercises Simon had her do, as the repetition increased slowly, which improved her arm strength and became easier for her. Jimmy had her training on a light set of bench weights among other exercising equipment Simon had gotten for her, strictly for the arm strengthening. Her hip movements were showing progress of moving around from side to side and foot work without any sign of pain, and it seemed to be getting better at a faster rate than her shoulder. The equipment Simon bought helped her a lot. With the assistance of Jimmy, he told Rose what and how to do it right. She started jogging two miles a day but at a slow pace because of her hip injury and preventing any further damage, and to help her get used to the heat outside and elevation. Then return to the gym to and continue her workouts.

The town discovered Rose was training at J's Gym and word started to get around other small towns nearby. Many Mexican natives knew who she was since she was born in Mexico and heard of her through the media as one of the best female fighters in the world. It made Mexico proud to have a female fighter to represent their country. Within another week, some fans who used to watch her fights had the chance to see her workout at J's Gym in person. She wasn't sparring yet, but she was getting close to that phase where she was anxious about starting. She felt that she was almost to the point of getting in the ring.

Simon had called her two weeks later to let her know he was planning on going to Mexico next Friday to see how she was doing. She was excited and wanted to make him proud of her progress. What she had in mind was to convince him to let her start sparring. For the rest of the week, Rose pushed herself, preventing injuries to her shoulder. She knew Simon would never forgive her if she were to do something to reinjure the shoulder by not following the exercises he told her to do. Jimmy was keeping an eye on her just to make sure.

Simon had asked Rose to see if Rudy or Jimmy could pick him up at the airport this time instead of having a taxi take him when he arrived next Friday at ten in the morning. She told him that Rudy would probably be the one who would pick him up, but they'll be someone there, even if she had to do it herself. Amy couldn't take some time off to go with Simon on this trip but said that she went ahead and requested some time off for the following trip within the next three weeks from this coming Friday, when Simon was planning to go back to Mexico again.

Rose was trying to convince Jimmy that she could increase her weight by another ten pounds from the current lifting she had been working with and run for an additional mile or two, farther than the two miles she had already been running. Jimmy gave Rose a chance to prove to him that she was ready to move forward with her workouts and training. He had her do some repetitions in the gym to evaluate and prove her endurance and strength. After two days of observing Rose, she showed Jimmy that she was ready to move forward with her exercise. So, he let her advance a step forward but cautioned her about how important it was to follow his routine. He would only let her advance with her exercise by agreeing to his terms, which was no problem.

Rose made a habit of getting up at five in the morning and running for 45 minutes before driving to the gym and then running again in the evening. She wanted to be ready to show Simon by next Friday how well she had strengthened the muscles in her shoulder and conditioned her body. She kept pushing herself to the edge and wanted to go beyond her limit, but at the same time, she feared re-injuring her shoulder if she pushed herself too hard. So, she had to discipline herself, when trying to surpass her limitations.

By Thursday evening that week, after Rose had finished working out before going home, she walked to Jimmy's office to talk to him. Rose knocked on the side of the door since it was already open. When Jimmy looked up from reading some paperwork on his desk, Rose was standing in front of the door.

"Oh! Hi, Rose. Come on in," Jimmy acknowledged her and told her to have a seat. "How's your shoulder feeling?"

"That's why I'm here. It feels good and I was just wondering what your thoughts would be of me?" Rose paused for a short moment because she was a little nervous to ask this question. Then she continued, "Would it be possible if I could start sparring at a slow pace sometime next week with one of your fighters, so I can get myself back into a boxing mode?" She hesitated to ask Jimmy his opinion since she knew he was busy with an upcoming match.

"I'm sorry, Rose. My mind was still on my fighter's next event. I heard some of it, but I thought you said you wanted to get back into the ring next week?"

"Yes. I want to return to the real world of boxing, and I think I'm ready. Don't you think so?" asked Rose. Jimmy was silent for a few seconds, thinking about what she was asking him. He wanted to be sure and had to think about what Simon would say.

"I think you're ready, Rose. The only thing now, I have to let Simon have the last say when he gets here next Friday. If it's okay with him, it's okay with me. You'll have to prove to him and demonstrate the abilities of your progress. I don't think you'll have any problem with how you have been working out and lifting weights. I think you're ready, but I have to wait until Simon gets here so he can agree with me." Jimmy voiced his opinion.

"I have all this energy inside me waiting to exert from my body, and the only place I could think of is in the ring." Rose was a little disappointed with his answer.

"You understand, Rose. It's not that I don't think that you're ready, it's Simon who wouldn't forgive me if something happens to you because I allowed it to happen." said Jimmy.

"Okay. I understand. I don't blame you for refusing. That's okay then." Rose was silent with discouragement. "Oh! Jimmy, Simon called me the other day with some good news. He told me that my visa was approved, and they should finish all the paperwork soon. That has given me a reason to focus and train harder to go forward another giant step."

"That is good news, Rose. I'm glad that it happened for you," said Jimmy.

Throughout the following week, Rose worked hard to make herself physically conditioned and trained her butt off to get back in shape and get her endurance and mobility like she was before, but better.

It was Friday, 9:30 a.m. at the airport as Rudy and Rose waited for Simon to arrive from his flight at ten. They didn't have to wait long but wanted to ensure they were there when he came. They saw his plane landing, and Rose started to get excited, making her happy to see Simon again as they waited for him to pass through the arrival gate. Rose saw Simon and waved at him to get his attention, which Simon did acknowledge her.

"Hi, Simon. So glad to see you. I'm so happy that you're here. I've been waiting to see you." Then she hugged him.

"It's so nice to be here by my champion." He smiled at Rose.

"You look great, Rose! How are you, Rudy?" said Simon, shaking hands with him.

"Great!" answered Rudy. "Are we ready to go?" Simon traveled light with just a carry-on bag, so he didn't have to drag any luggage around with him. It didn't take long before they were on their way back home and having a short conversation about her training before they got home.

When they arrived at her moms' house, Francis had made a

quick breakfast to satisfy their hunger until it was time for dinner.

For the rest of the day, Simon and Rose spent the day talking about all the good news about her visa and when she might be able to go back to the United States. In between the conversations, Rose exercised for an hour with the training equipment Simon had sent to her moms' house, and Simon observed Rose while he evaluated her strength. Then Rose went on her routine jog for half an hour. By that time, it was almost dinner time. Since it was sweltering outside, Simon felt sweaty and wanted to shower before dinner. He didn't want to smell like sweat while sitting at the table with everyone.

Her mom, Francis, had made Simon a delicious Mexican dinner, one of Simons' favorite dishes - spicy sauce, enchiladas with rice and beans with salsa on the side dish. And what Francis added to the dinner this time was a couple of beef tacos on the side, which made Simon feel even better because he was starving.

After dinner, they talked a little more about what they would be doing the next day. The first thing Rose wanted to do was show Simon how well she had progressed with her body conditioning. She was excited because getting started sparring in the ring meant a lot. She hadn't told Simon about her wanting to spar in the ring, but it was in her mind to tell him when they go to the gym tomorrow.

Before going to bed, she exercised with a few weights and did sit-ups to keep up with her conditioning. She had been doing this for the last three weeks. It was part of her routine. She had a room in the back with the new equipment that Simon had bought and sent her just for this purpose. They were up early and ready to start the day the next day. Rose had gone for her regular jog, which she started at six in the morning, followed by her everyday exercises before going to the gym. Simon got up at six, just as Rose was going out for her run.

Around eight in the morning, Rudy, Rose, and Simon got into the car and drove to the gym. When they got there, Jimmy was in his office doing some paperwork and a couple of fighters were just getting ready to start their workouts. Rose greeted Jimmy in his office and then excused herself from the conversation to get her workout clothes from her locker. Rudy had put on his workout clothes before going to the gym, so he was ready to start his training when he got there. Simon stayed talking to Jimmy in his office and spoke about how Rose was coming along.

Simon began asking questions about Rose's shoulder. Jimmy's comment was convincing enough for Simon to see Rose work out with the weights and her body conditioning. The conversation lasted for about fifteen minutes and then they walked to the training area to see Rose working out. Simon was impressed with the way Rose was lifting the weights as he watched her lift without any struggle. He had already seen Rose lift a light number of weights at her mom's house, but he still wanted to see her workout with the weights at the gym in front of Jimmy. She confirmed Jimmy's comments about how well her progress was coming along.

"There's one thing I want to ask you, Simon," said Jimmy. "Rose and I had a discussion yesterday about her sparring starting next week. I told her how I viewed her performance and said she was ready, but we wanted you to see for yourself and decide if you agreed with me. I think you should consider letting her start next week."

"Well, she executed the weights and showed no problem with her body conditioning. I'm convinced she's ready too." Simon smiled at Jimmy and then turned to look at Rose. Simon watched Rose doing her workouts and stood by her side as he evaluated her shoulder and then her side. He saw no problem with her moves.

After thirty minutes, Simon approached Rose and asked her to go into Jimmy's office with him. Jimmy was already there.

"Have a seat, Rose," Jimmy said.

"Rose, after watching you in the training area doing your workouts, Jimmy tells me you want to start sparring next week. Is that right?"

"Yes!" answered Rose.

"Do you think in your mind that you're ready for this? Because once you start and it doesn't work out for you, and then you tell me that you can't do it, you will not get another chance to train with Jimmy or myself again. So, if you think you can, let me know now, or if you want more time, I can live with that, but don't tell me yes unless you think you can. Do you understand what I'm saying?" said Simon.

There was a little silence for a few minutes. Rose looked at Simon in his eyes and began saying how she believed in herself.

"I know I'm ready, and that's what I want to do. That's all I think about doing, and as for my condition, I would say that I'm at 99 percent ready, leaving the one percent in the ring for sparring because I haven't had the chance to start where I left off. Then I'll be able to say that I'm 101 percent ready. That's what I think of myself when you ask me if I'm ready," answered Rose.

Simon and Jimmy stared at Rose, thinking the same thing. Rose had convinced them that she was serious about what she just told them. It made sense to Simon and Jimmy, and now it was all in the Rose's training that would make the difference to get her to the top level of a champion. Simon and Jimmy agreed to do whatever it will take and train her to succeed.

The rest of the day, Simon and Jimmy stayed in the office planning Rose's monthly schedule. Meanwhile, Rose continued her regular workout routine while Simon and Jimmy finished working on her schedule. By that time, the day was almost over. They decided to celebrate a new beginning for her future boxing career. Simon wanted to treat Jimmy, Rudy, and Rose at a nearby restaurant that Jimmy told him about because it had great Mexican food, Simon's favorite. It was also Jimmy's favorite restaurant. He takes his wife out to dinner there and knows the owners.

The first thing Rose heard was a four-piece mariachi band, Rose's favorite type of music, and Simon always enjoyed listening to that type of music. They sat and listened to the music as they waited for the food they had ordered. Simon ate his favorite Mexican food and drank a beer to rinse the hot and spicy hot chili sauce. While they were eating, a girl selling roses came by their table, so Simon whispered to her, asking her to give Rose the giant rose she was carrying in her arms. It surprised Rose and made her a little embarrassed when the girl gave her the rose, but she appreciated Simon doing that for her. She stood up from her chair, went over to Simon and hugged him, thanking him for making her evening so wonderful.

"I'll have to come back to this restaurant the next time I come back and bring Amy. I think she would love this place like I do," said Simon.

"I hope you invite me too," Rose made a remark.

"You know I will, Rose." They all chuckled.

Thirty minutes later, they finished eating their meal and were ready to go back home. They all went home feeling stuffed with the food they ate.

CHAPTER TWENTY-NINE

The first thing Rose did when she got up at five in the morning was put on her jogging clothes and go for her three-mile run. Simon and the rest of the family were still asleep, so she walked around the house as quietly as possible so she wouldn't wake anybody up. Before taking off, she made a pot of coffee for Simon so it would be ready by the time he woke up. When Rose returned from her jog, Simon and Rudy were up and drinking the coffee Rose had made. She walked in with sweat running down her face and her top was drenched with body sweat because it was already hot outside. "Good morning, Simon!" She shouts out to him breathing mildly but with deep breaths from the heat exhaustion. "You too, Rudy. Is Mom still asleep?" Rose took her shoes off inside the front door, and then took her sweaty top off, leaving the tank top she was wearing underneath.

"Good morning, Rose!" Both Simon and Rudy responded simultaneously.

"And yes!" Rudy answered Rose's question if Mom was still asleep.

"How's the coffee? Not too strong, is it?" asked Rose as she passed by them going to the bathroom to take a shower.

"Very good! Thank you for making it this morning. That

was thoughtful of you," Simon said as he watched her pass by him and then disappear as she went into the bathroom, not saying another word but breathing a little heavy. Meanwhile, Simon got all his things together and got ready to go back home.

By the time Rose got herself ready, Simon was ready. Francis walked into the kitchen, scratching her head and said good morning to everyone. She noticed Simon had his luggage by the front door and ready to go back home. "Did you sleep well last night, Francis?" Simon asked her.

"Si," she told him in Spanish. "Do you want me to make you a good breakfast this morning?" she asked in Spanish. Simon understood what she was asking.

"Thank you, Francis. But I'm okay," Simon told her in Spanish.

He walked up to her, hugged her, kissed her cheek, and told her that he would be back soon.

Rudy and Rose walked with Simon outside to get in the car. Rudy was going to drop Rose off at the gym and then take Simon to the airport instead of taking a taxi.

On the way to the gym, Simon told Rose that he'd be returning within the next three weeks to see how she's doing with her training. "Don't forget Rose, if you feel any type of discomfort throwing punches when you start sparring, I want you to stop immediately and back off from sparring. All it will do is prolong your healing and I don't want that to happen. I have plans for you soon and I want you to be ready, you understand?"

"I understand Simon."

"Good." Simon continued his advice and told her, "If you need anything, please call me, okay, Rose?" said Simon. "Don't forget what we talked about your training. Keep that in mind, and the best thing to do is not to do anything beyond what you think you can do that would cause injury to your shoulder. Be careful. I also want you to pace yourself at a slow and with moderate punching. Don't overdo it, even if you think you're able to. I know you."

Rose responded, "I won't let you down, Simon. I promise. "

Rudy dropped Rose at the gym to start her training with Jimmy to stick to the scheduled training plan and Simon said good-bye to Rose and gave her a hug. Then Rudy continued taking Simon to the airport for his return flight to Los Angeles. Rudy stayed with Simon and talked until it was time for Simon to board the airline and then went back to the gym.

When Rudy first dropped Rose at the gym, Rose had gone straight to Jimmy's office to find out if he had someone in mind, he thought would be the first fighter to spar with her. When she walked in, Jimmy already knew what her question was going to be, and he was right. He had already decided on the fighter who would be the best match against her sparring abilities and who would give her a good workout and challenge that would help her get back on track with her moves and build her endurance of what she had been.

Not knowing who Jimmy had in mind, Rose would be surprised when he told her who the fighter would be.

"Hi, Jimmy," said Rose.

"Hi, Rose! How's everything going today?" replied Jimmy. "I think I know what you're going to ask me, Rose."

"What?" responded Rose.

"Sit down, Rose," said Jimmy. "Correct me if I'm wrong. You want me to tell you who your sparring partner will be, right?"

"Yes. That's right." She was surprised that Jimmy beat her to the punch. But she was glad that he had already made plans this fast to find the one he thought was comparable to her.

"Well, I'm not sure what your response will be when I tell you who I think you should begin sparring. I initially thought of Eddie, but the more I thought about the idea, I think it would be better if you started with Sara for this week. Out of all the female boxers, she's the best female fighter that will give you a challenge. She's been here the longest and has more experience in the ring than the other fighters. I want to see if you still have your moves and how well you protect yourself against her, for starters. I don't want you to think that I don't respect you as a great boxer, but I want to see you spar in the ring and see how your shoulder will withstand the punches, movements, and rotations of your arm. I plan to keep you sparring with her for this week, as I mentioned, and then I'll see how everything goes," Jimmy explained his plans to Rose as she listened to him, wanting to say something halfway into the conversation. Rose was a little disappointed, but she understood Jimmys' concern for starters. She accepted his terms and went right along with his plans.

"Well, I wasn't expecting to spar with a female fighter at first, but if you think that's where I should start, then I think that's where I'll start. I'm okay with that."

"Then, starting tomorrow, you'll be in the ring with Sara, but for now, just work on your routine workouts and be ready for tomorrow," Jimmy finished explaining the plans for Rose and had Rose start her workouts as planned.

The following day, Rose and Rudy arrived at the gym by eight o'clock in the morning after Rose had run for three miles at her mom's house. Jimmy was already getting everything ready for his fighters and posting their training schedules. Rose walked into the gym, full of energy and eager to start as Rudy followed. Jimmy heard the door slam as it closed behind them, which got Jimmy's attention to see who was entering the gym. He noticed it was Rose and Rudy.

"Good morning, Rose!" he greeted her as she walked toward him. Jimmy noticed sweat running down her forehead as she got closer to him. "How are you doing, Rose?" he asked her.

"I don't feel too bad. A little thirsty, though," Rose responded.

"And good morning to you too. How are you, Jimmy?" asked Rose as she walked by him, going to her locker, showing how energetic she was by her body movements and the adrenaline generating throughout her body. She was ready for the day to begin, especially knowing that she would be in the ring from here on.

"I feel great, as a matter of fact," answered Jimmy. Then Rose stopped to listen to Jimmy.

"Sara should be here anytime, so go ahead and get dressed for your workouts. For the meanwhile, warm-up, and workout with the punching bag. She should be here by the time you finish."

"Okay!" answered Rose and continued walking toward her locker to put on her workout clothes.

Rose finished warming up after ten minutes of her workout to keep her adrenaline going and then had Jimmy help her put on her sparring gloves and headgear before jumping into the ring. She had started moving around, shadowboxing, and getting used to the ring as Sara entered the gym, carrying her bag to one side. She looked at Rose as she got closer to her and said good morning to her, and then turned around to say the same to Jimmy but in a louder tone of voice because he was just to the other side of the ring picking up some towels left on the floor by some of the boxers that stayed late.

It took Sara about ten minutes to get into her workout clothes, and then she had Eddie help her put on the gloves and headgear. Sara felt Rose wasn't going to be an easy sparring partner. She knew a little about Rose and knew how good she was in the ring. Sara had only seen her working out a few times at the gym and saying hello to her, but never officially met her.

Sara was glad that Jimmy chose her to spar with Rose. She felt honored to be able to spar with Rose. It would be an experience and challenge for her to see how she would stand against an almost world champion, she thought to herself.

Sara climbed into the ring as Rose watched her enter. Rose had been waiting for this moment to come. It had been almost six long and stressful months for her to deal with her wounds, but it wasn't as hard as losing Rob because he was her best and closest friend that she had ever met, and he meant the whole world to her. She was thankful that Simon and Jimmy helped her deal with her loss and wounds. With Simon's support, she managed to deal with it, even with the situation and circumstances with the Department of Immigration. As for Sara, she was happy to get the chance to be in the ring with one of the best female boxers in the United States, including Mexico. So, it was a big moment for her to be able to spar with Rose.

"Good morning, Rose." Sara approached Rose to shake her hand and meet her since they hadn't officially met.

"Good morning, Sara," said Rose. "Jimmy told me your name, and he said many good things about you. It's a pleasure to meet you, and I'm glad that you were the one he picked to start my day. Shall we get started?"

Jimmy was standing right below the ring, waiting for them to begin.

"Okay, girls! Let's get it going and save your talk for after the workout, okay!" Jimmy's tone got a little loud, making the other boxers turn around to see what was going on.

That was one of Jimmy's habits when it came to boxing; he was always serious about his boxing life. He always focused on the boxer's talent. Either he had it, or he didn't. If they did, he would do the utmost to help them get as far as they could with their talent, just like Simon did with his boxers.

The girls began their sparring. At first, they started jabbing lightly and slowly got into a more aggressive challenge. They started punching each other with more power behind their punches as they defended themselves. Jimmy watched as they battered each other. He focused on Rose and wanted to see how her arm delivered her punches or if she was having any problem moving from one side to the other because of her injured hip. As she displayed her moves, Jimmy couldn't see anything wrong that would keep her from continuing to spar the rest of the week.

Jimmy saw enough to be convinced that she was ready to start working out harder each day of the week. He planned to keep Rose sparring with Sara for the rest of the week. Then his next plan for the following week was to have Rose spar with one of his better male boxers to give her the feel of harder punches and extend the rounds from three to five. If she continued like she is doing now, not having complications with her shoulder, Jimmy would follow his plans of letting Rose spar with one of his male fighters next week.

Every day that passed, Rose was improving her speed and showing great power behind her punches. It didn't take her long to get used to gracefully moving around the boxing ring without any problems. Sara was the right choice of a boxer to get Rose started in the ring.

By the end of the first week of sparring with Sara and evaluating Rose's moves, Jimmy was convinced that Rose was ready for his male fighter, so he scheduled his male boxer to step into the ring with Rose next week. He wanted to see how she would respond to a different type of hard punching power.

"Well Rose…I think you convinced me with the past few days that you are ready for feel some power punches from my male fighter, so starting next week, you'll be in the ring with him and take it further with your endurance. So, in the meanwhile, finish up today and I'll see you on Monday to start the week like you wanted. Get some rest this weekend, but you still need to take care of yourself and not do anything to your shoulder…okay?" said Jimmy.

"I will…believe me, I will!" Rose remarked.

On Monday morning, Rose was ready to take on the male fighter that Jimmy had scheduled to spar with. Rose did her usual warmup exercises before entering the ring for her first sparring session. Eddie was the fighter who would enter the ring with her, who Rose hadn't officially met, but had seen him working out in the gym before. Fifteen minutes later, Eddie walked into the gym with an enthusiastic mood, his everyday mood, saying good morning to everyone that was in the gym. He saw Rose in the ring shadowboxing, so he walked up to the ring to say hello to Rose.

"Good morning, Rose." he called out. "How are you this morning? You seem to be ready for me. Jimmy told me about you, so let me change and warm up, and I'll see you in the ring as soon as I'm done and ready for you."

Rose stopped shadowboxing to greet Eddie and responded with an okay and continued her shadowboxing. Jimmy was at the ringside helping Eddie put on his gloves and head gear, while Rose waited anxiously to get started.

"I'll be right there Rose. Just give me a minute," Eddie yelled out.

Eddie jumped into the ring and tapped gloves before starting the sparring session. It started at a slow pace with punches being thrown lightly for the first three minutes, and it continued for the next two three-minute rounds. The power punches were starting to progressively increase in the fourth round. Halfway into the fourth round, Rose comes up with a powerful uppercut and knocks down Eddie flat on the mat. Eddie never saw it coming and then he got up slowly. That's when Jimmy yelled, "That's enough for now. Take a short break." Jimmy couldn't believe what had just happened. He was impressed. "Are you okay, Eddie?" asked Jimmy.

"Yes. I'm all right. Man! Does she have a mean uppercut," said Eddie as he climbed out of the ring to get some water.

"Listen, Rose. I want you to fight another one of my male boxers in an hour. Do you think you can do that again?" asked Jimmy.

"Maybe I was just lucky. And yes, I'll be ready within an hour," said Rose.

One hour went by fast for Rose, but she was ready for the next boxer. Jimmy introduced David to Rose. David had a little more experience than Eddie, so it was going to be a tougher challenge for Rose to see how she would defend herself. Jimmy had a feeling about Rose, and he thought that by putting David in the ring with her, it would bring out her past experiences and force her to use the skills like she had before against David. David climbs into the ring and faces Rose for the first time.

"Okay! Let's go, you guys!" yelled Jimmy. "Are you guys ready." Both responded with a "Yes, I am!"

"Okay. Let's get started then," said Jimmy.

They began jabbing at each other and David threw the first hard punch at Rose and forced her to step back from the power punch, which hit her on the right side of her face. She bounced right back, protected her face this time and started throwing some of her hard punches to his body, and then focused on his face, throwing straight shots, and connecting. David didn't hesitate to respond with his hard punches, but Rose protected herself very well.

After four three minute rounds of sparring, Jimmy stopped them so they could take a breather. Then he told them to continue after a few minutes. About two and a half minutes into the fifth round, Rose snuck an powerful hook to David's jaw and sent him to the floor, just like she did to Eddie. Jimmy couldn't believe that she had done it again. He immediately yelled, "Stop the fight!" He was convinced that she wasn't just lucky the first time. He jumped into the ring again, hugged Rose, and said to her, "You just made me a believer in what you can do in the ring. I'm so proud of you."

CHAPTER THIRTY

By the end of the week, Rose had a rigorous workout and footwork improvement as she was determined to make herself go the distance with every three-minute round for eight rounds and refresh her skills. Jimmy was impressed with her performance. He was convinced that he had made the right choice of selecting Sara for her first challenge and was glad that he did. Then by giving her the chance to fight a couple of his male boxers, he justified his decision to have her fight two of his male fighters. It had paid off.

Jimmy planned to have Rick step into the ring the following week with Rose. He was his best fighter in the ring and thought he would help Rose improve her skills. He just wanted to see if she could take a little more punishment with harder punches and how she would protect herself against him. Jimmy had talked to Rick about Rose and what he expected him to do in the ring against Rose and how hard to use his punching power. Jimmy wanted to see how Rose would react with her skills and if she could take it. This would continue for a week, and then he was putting Rose back in the ring with Sara the following week.

Rose didn't know with whom she was going to spar on Monday. All she knew was that it would be one of his better male boxers and she didn't care who the boxer would be. All she wanted to do was get back into the body condition, endurance and cardio, like she used to be before everything that changed her life within minutes.

Jimmy was waiting for her in his office when she walked into the gym the following Monday. When Jimmy heard the door slam after she walked in, he stepped out from his office to meet her.

"Good morning, Rose!" said Jimmy. "I'll introduce you officially to Rick in a little while. He went for a short jog until you arrived. He should be here any time now. I know you've seen him in the ring, sparring with one of the other boxers, but you haven't had a chance to meet him one-on-one, so when he comes back, I'll introduce you to him, okay?" said Jimmy. "Go ahead, get ready and warm-up. By the time you finish, he should be back."

"Okay," said Rose.

Ten minutes later, Rick walked into the gym, sweating from his thirty-minute jog because it was already hot outside, as always. Rose had just finished warming up by stretching. She was walking toward the speed bag when she heard Jimmy calling her. "Rose! Can you come over here, please?" Rose was walking toward the punching bag across the gym, so he yelled a little loud so she would hear him.

Rose heard Jimmy, and then she walked toward him and noticed Rick standing next to him, waiting for her. Rose looked at Rick as he stood next to Jimmy, and for some reason, Rose thought he wasn't bad looking. Rick was thinking the same thing about Rose.

"Rose, I want you to meet Rick, your new sparring partner for this week."

She smiled and greeted Rick, "It's a pleasure to meet you. Now it's official." Rose chuckled and kept starring at Rick as she greeted him. Rick returned a smiled as he shook hands with Rose, making him think what a beautiful boxer she is. Rose felt something different too as she shook his hand, something special about him that she hadn't felt in a while.

Jimmy helped Rose and Rick put on their headgear and gloves and told them to get into the ring and get started. As Rose was getting ready to climb into the ring, Rick held the ropes apart for Rose to enter the ring. Then Rick climbed into the ring.

Jimmy wanted Rick to let Rose warm up first with the mitts before they start sparring, which they did for ten minutes, and then Rick switched to his regular gloves for sparring. Jimmy had a discussion with Rose before her sparring with Rick, so she knew what she had to do and what was expected of her.

They were now ready to start punching each other after warming up with the mitts. It started at a slow pace, jabbing, and throwing punches with some power behind it, but not with all they had. After a few minutes, the punches became more powerful and aggressive, connecting at the body as Rose focused on her moves.

Rick was throwing his punches and testing her responses to see how she would react to the hard blows. Although Rick weighed a few more pounds than Rose, Rose returned some of her hard punches, and Rick felt them. Rick began to tell Rose, "Let me see what kind of punching power you have, Rose. Show me what you got and give it to me." Rick talked to her while he jabbed at her face and occasionally hit her on her shoulder. He was just trying to intimidate her into seeing how she would react and if she would control her actions with her punches. Rick wanted to see how much power she had behind her punches and how she would move to avoid being hit. Whatever Rick was doing to her was working. Rose was returning her punches with all her power, and Rick was beginning to feel the power behind her punches when she connected. The impact of the punches caused Rick to step back as he protected himself from the punches Rose was delivering. Rick was impressed from that moment on; it made him believe in Rose's ability to become a great boxer.

Jimmy watched how she handled herself, moving around the ring and protecting herself against one of his best boxers. That was an impressive sight that he had just witnessed. Jimmy was blown away because he has never seen a female boxer deliver punches like Rose. He knew now that she would be ready to go against any female boxer within a few weeks. He could hardly wait to see Simon's face, when he arrives within two weeks from now and see how she has been doing.

Simon had been communicating with Jimmy for the past two weeks, ensuring Rose was on the right track of conditioning her shoulder and hip. What Simon was hearing from Jimmy was that she was doing great, gaining her strength back and moving around the ring without complications. Those compliments made Simon feel satisfied and anxious to see her. He was content with the progress and was fortunate to have Jimmy as her trainer.

Simon wasn't aware of Rose being in the ring with a male boxer this week. It was Jimmy's last decision when he decided to do that. He was going to tell Simon about his plans, but after watching Rose spar with his two other male fighters and now Rick, Rose wasn't having any problem changing her style to counteract Rick.

By the third day, Rose was getting used to being around Rick. She was improving and learning new moves she didn't know she had. Her punches became twice as powerful and accurate than before the more she sparred with Rick. She thought he was a great mentor to be in the ring with her and was glad that Jimmy had chose him as her sparring partner.

That same day, Simon called Jimmy to see how she was doing. Jimmy was pleased with Roses' progress and eager to tell Simon that she was doing an outstanding performance in the ring without any difficulties. Jimmy felt confident telling Simon that he had made a last-minute change in her schedule when he started talking to Simon and the reason for doing it.

Simon listened to Jimmy with his changes. "Simon. I have a confession to tell you." It got Simon's attention quickly and was curious as soon as Jimmy said that, but he remained quiet and told Jimmy "I'm listening." Simon responded.

Jimmy continued. "I started Rose sparring with my more experienced female fighter, Sara, but then I decided after watching Rose sparring with her, I liked her progress, so I had two of my male fighters, face Rose in the ring afterwards last week, and she knocked them flat on the mat. It proved to me that she was ready for someone else with more experience and skills. On Monday I had my best fighter, Rick step inside the ring with her. I thought he might give her a better challenge and apply more pressure to see how much she could take. Before Rick jumped into the ring with Rose, I explained to Rick what I wanted him to do and how much to push her. So far, it's been a learning experience for Rose, and I'm glad I did it. I think it's paying off because she seems to respond quicker, and she learned to deliver her punches with more accuracy and connect to the body with power punches."

Simon listened to Jimmy's reasoning and justified his change of the scheduled plan. The more Simon thought about it, the more it made sense to him, and he was glad that Jimmy did what he did with the change of plans.

"I think it was a great idea, Jimmy. Good job." Simon replied.

"I guess I'll see you and Rose real soon. Amy will be with me this time. She can hardly wait to see Rose too."

"That will be great. So, I'll see you next week." Jimmy hung up the phone after saying goodbye to Simon.

Simon kept himself busy with his fighters in LA, but he always thought about Rose, wondering how she was doing. He was anxious about leaving soon and couldn't wait to visit her in Mexico again. Amy had requested those days off and got it. She was pleased they approved her request because she wanted to see Rose.

For the remainder of the week, Jimmy had Rose fight extra rounds to take her to another level of endurance. He wanted to build her body conditioning to withstand her opponent's pressure and not show any fatigue if she had to go all rounds of the fight, which could be eight or ten rounds, depending on what the promoters recommended.

CHAPTER THIRTY-ONE

The following week, Simon and Amy got their belongings ready to visit Rose in Mexico for a six-day trip. They planned on returning on Sunday, giving them the weekend to enjoy some fun time with Rose to do and see more things around Mexico especially for Amy. Amy was looking forward to this trip this time. She knew what to expect and how the traveling was going to be like.

Meanwhile, at the gym, Jimmy was planning to have Sara get back in the ring on Monday to spar with Rose, but instead, he decided against it since Rose was doing so well this past week, sparring with Rick. He felt that Rose was ready, well prepared, and it's time for her to return to the dream of her life where she left off and be that fighter to represent her country as a champion. Jimmy knew she was ready to take on anyone in her class, but he wasn't going to tell her that just yet. He wanted to ensure that she would be the best fighter she could be in her weight division.

It wasn't long before some of Rose's fans heard she was sparring at J's Gym. Some of them hung around outside the gym, by the front door, waiting for her to step outside so they could get an autograph. Word was spreading throughout Mexico that she was back in the ring. Many people knew who she was by watching her on TV and following her wherever she was fighting. Now that her fans heard where she was training and was back to being active in the ring, their hopes of having their hero become a champion was a big thing for Mexico. They were proud of Rose for representing Mexico. As soon as it reached the Mexico City, some reporters jumped at the chance of being the first reporter to get her story so they could have it printed in the newspaper's sports section. They knew who she was and how popular she was before her incident. It was like a race for the reporters.

Within a few days, reporters were swarming all over the front door of J's Gym, crowding her fans, hoping to ask Rose questions about her comeback. The reporters were trying in every way to get a piece of information from Rose for an exciting and great story for the newspaper; that was typical of a reporter, doing whatever it takes. Rose continued with her training at the gym not knowing the impact that she was creating on the outside of the gym. She was too focused and busting her butt to be the best. One of the trainees at the gym made his way inside, squeezing himself to get through the gym door because of all the fans and reporters outside. When he got inside the gym, he yelled at Rose to let her know that there was a swarm of fans and reporters outside the gym, wanting to get her autograph. The reporters hung around the front door with their cameras and writing pads, eagerly waiting to get her story about her come back.

By the end of the day, Rose picked up some good tips and had a very vigorous sparring with Rick. When she stepped outside the front door carrying a red nylon zipped-up bag with her training clothes, she acknowledged everyone in her path. She heard cameras clicking and voices coming from everywhere, asking questions about her training and when she would be ready to face her opponents. Rose suddenly stopped answering some of the reporters' questions and said to them, "I want to thank all of you for being here and making me welcome, and I feel very proud of my hometown. There's no better feeling than having all of you here to support and stand by me. I will make you proud when I get the world title. I feel good about myself, and I am confident that I will prevail in the title when facing the champion."

Then a reporter yelled out a question to Rose. "When are you going to fight your next opponent?" he asked.

Rose responded, "As soon as my trainer knows that I'm ready. I will be ready to face the best in the ring. I want to make my people proud of me and those who have followed and supported me throughout my past. There is something that I need to settle in the ring with someone when the time comes. I will be going now, so if you can excuse me for now, I'll be back tomorrow. Thank you all for being here."

Rose stopped talking and continued walking toward her car as she listened to her fans clapping and calling out her name as loud as they could. The reporters ran to their cars as fast as possible to take the story to the newspaper department to have it printed in the sports section as the main headline. Rose got into her car, waved at the fans, and took off to her mom's house.

Jimmy stood outside the gym's front door and watched Rose walking to her car with Rick to ensure that Rose would be all right. Some boxers peeked through the windows to view Rose talking to her fans and handling the reporters like a champ.

Jimmy and Rick stared at the road as Rose drove off until she vanished when she turned at an intersection. Then Jimmy looked at Rick and remarked, "This is only the beginning."

Rick responded, "I think you're right, Jimmy."

They both went back inside the gym and Jimmy went to his office as Rick got his things and went home. Jimmy waited for the rest of the boxers to complete their workouts so he could lock-up the gym and go home.

Rose was still thrilled about the crowd at the gym as she was driving home and couldn't believe how the crowd supported her. When she got home, she told her mom how the day had gone until the end, having her fans and reporters all around her, making her feel like a champion. It made Francis proud of her, knowing the day would become a reality of being a champion someday.

The next day, Rose was back at the gym before Rick arrived. She had already warmed up at home before she went to the gym. She had her routine every morning when she got out of bed by running three miles and working out for a few minutes with the exercise equipment that Simon had bought for her.

Jimmy was at the gym thirty minutes before Rose arrived. He was in his office when she walked in and as she passed by his office door, he called her to come inside his office.

"Good morning, Rose," said Jimmy.

"Good morning, Jimmy," replied Rose.

"Have a seat. I just wanted to ask you how everything is going for you. Over the past few weeks, you seem to be getting better and better with every day that passes. Your moves, punches, and focus on the fight are amazing. I'll talk to Simon when he comes and tell him that he should start thinking about scheduling you on a lineup with exhibitions in the United States. Of course, I need to convince Simon of my recommendation, but he must see how your progress is coming along and what you can do in the ring. You have to make him believe in your passion for boxing and how badly you want to be the world champ. Do you know what I mean?" asked Jimmy.

Rose responded quickly and then replied, "Simon knows me quite well and he knows what I can do in the ring. And yes, I do understand what you're saying. All the things that you have done for me, Jimmy, I couldn't have done it any other way. Your way of training reminds me of Simon. The patience, the demands, and training you gave me, have taught me a lot. And when you decided to put Rick in the ring with me, I learned even more about myself than in the past. Rick taught me to be a better fighter by building my endurance and fighting smarter in the ring. I thought I knew a lot, but now I feel so confident with myself that I have to agree with you about saying that I'm ready to go up another level. I do feel that way, Jimmy," said Rose.

Jimmy looked at her and remarked, "Thank you for saying that. But I'm also so proud of you, Rose. I know that Simon will also be proud of you when he sees you in the ring when he gets here. Continue what you have been doing, and don't ever stop doing what you love doing. You hear?"

"Yes, I do, Jimmy," answered Rose.

"Now go out there and do what you love doing."

After listening to Jimmy, she went to her locker and changed into her workout clothes, and it took her a few minutes to walk to the ring. Rick had just walked inside the gym as Rose was getting ready to jump into the ring filled with energy and motivation that Jimmy had just built her up to be. Then she starts warming up with some shadowboxing.

"Well, good morning, Rose," Rick yelled at Rose as he walked in. "You look like you're ready for me."

"Hello, Rick. I'm ready. Let's get it on!" responded Rose with determination in her voice.

"Slow down a bit, Rose. At least, let me get dressed and I'll be ready to take you on. Give me a minute and I'll be back, so be ready for me." Rose chuckled and Rick smiled at her.

A few minutes later, their sparring began as they started moving around the ring, looking at each other as they jabbed at one another with combinations.

By the end of the week, Rose had learned a few more tricks from Rick, but at the same time, she started to get a little attached to him. Rick had the same feeling for Rose. He seemed to be attracted to Rose by the end of the week.

On Friday, right after having the last session of sparring, Rick had asked Rose if she wanted to go out to a restaurant in Chilpancingo and have dinner tomorrow afternoon. It didn't take Rose very long to think about it before she found herself telling him, "That would be nice."

Then he responded, "I'll pick you up at six tomorrow evening, okay?"

"That would be great and thank you for inviting me. That's very thoughtful of you, Rick. So, I'll see you then."

Rose picked up her bag and left the gym while Rick had to go to his locker and get his things. Rose encountered a few fans waiting for her outside the gym and a couple of reporters wanting to find out if she knew when she would start facing her opponents. She told them that she still didn't know yet, but she was hoping it would be soon.

CHAPTER THIRTY-TWO

Rick was on the road to pick up Rose by 6 p.m., Saturday evening for his first dinner date with Rose. He had taken off early enough to make sure he was there in time because he's a person that doesn't like to be late anytime, he has a set time. The evening was a little warm, but it had a cool breeze of air blowing across the road path to Roses' moms' house as Rick made his way there When Rick arrived at Rose's house by 6 o'clock with a bouquet of flowers, Rose was still putting on her last-minute makeup on her face when she heard his car driving up the driveway. She asked her sister, Anna, if she could meet Rick at the door and ask him to come in. When Rick walked up to the front door, Anna opened the door for him when she heard him knocking on the door to let him in and told him to come in and have a seat until Rose finished getting ready. Her sister was well-mannered and talked and acted like a grown-up. Soon Rose stepped out of the bathroom into the living room where Rick was sitting.

"Hi, Rick," Rose politely said it in a soft tone of voice.

"Hi, Rose." Rick was a little nervous as he held on to the bouquet of flowers. "You look very nice. I am so used to seeing you in your workout clothes. Now I see who you are in your normal clothes. It's great. I mean, you look beautiful." He went speechless, only to say how beautiful she looked. "These flowers are for you, so I hope you like them." Rose was delighted and couldn't be any happier to see Rick stand in front of her.

"Thank you so much, Rick. You're making me blush. Would you like something to drink before we take off?" asked Rose.

"No, thank you. I'm fine. Thanks for asking, though."

"Are you ready to go?"

"Yes, I am," answered Rose.

It didn't take them very long before they were on the way to have a romantic evening together for the first time.

That night, they had a wonderful evening together. They got to know each other better and made another date to go out again, but they weren't sure where it would be. They haven't decided just yet but will talk about it at a different time. They had dinner at a Mexican restaurant called La Fiesta which had a cohesive look of a Mexico décor ambience atmosphere setting, with bold colors throughout the dining area, and lighting to enhance the concept of the restaurant. The last thing they added for enjoyment was a four-piece mariachi band that was going around playing for couples or whoever requested music to serenade them. Rose enjoyed listening to every song the group played as they ate their dinner. Rose was pleased and thankful that Rick had asked her to go with him, especially to a Mexican restaurant with a live mariachi band playing some of her favorite tunes.

There was a moment when the band started playing one of her favorite songs that reminded her when she was with Rob at a Mexican restaurant back in the US and enjoying the time they were together listening to a small group of a mariachi band and were as happy as can be. She withdrew from talking suddenly and couldn't prevent tears from trickling from her eyes. Rick looked at her and noticed the tears in her eyes but didn't know what to think. Rick was wondering why she had suddenly changed from her cheerful and laughing mode to a sad and tearful mood. Rose turned around to look at Rick and noticed that he was probably wondering why she was acting this way. Rose then explained to Rick the reason for the mood change, and he understood why, after the fact, and felt terrible. He reached across the table to hold her hands to help comfort her and understand her past. After a while, Rose realized that she had to overcome her memories of Rob, although Rose will never forget him in her heart. Rob was a very special person in her life when he was alive.

They sat holding hands, looking at each other, not saying a word for a minute until Rose realized she had to pay more attention to Rick and not let herself drift away with her emotions for Rob. Rick was attracted to Rose, particularly her personality. The chemistry with Rose worked itself into his heart. He had never felt this serious about another girl before meeting her. Rose was the one he wanted to be with, now and forever even though they had just met.

Rose was having a wonderful time with Rick and enjoying every minute. It finally dawned on her that she was getting the same chemistry as Rick, even though she didn't know how Rick felt toward her. Rick just watched her as she listened to the band. He considered himself lucky to be with this beautiful lady sitting across from him. Rick erased the person in the boxing ring and saw her as Rose, a lady who could be someone special in his life.

It was late, and the evening had to end, so Rick took Rose home. When they arrived at Rose's house, Rick walked her to her door. They embraced each other for a few minutes before she went inside. Rick whispered in her ear as he held her in his arms and said, "I should leave now. It's late, but I hope our next one will be as wonderful as we had tonight. We'll talk about it at another time to decide where we shall go. I will be looking forward to it coming soon. Thank you again for tonight and I really want to continue our friendship if it's alright with you."

"I'm looking forward to the next one too. And I really enjoyed your company, Rick. I think we should continue to see each other again. I feel comfortable with you, and it tells me something about who you are, so yes, I want to continue our friendship."

Rose got close to his ear and whispered in his ear and said, "I think I like you," and then kissed him on his lips and said good night to him, although, she had a hard time letting go of him, not wanting the night to end.

On Monday, Rose was at the gym on time, as usual. Jimmy had made a different type of schedule for Rose. Instead of being in the ring with Rick, he had her work out with weights and spent some time on the punching bag, plus other physical miscellaneous workouts. He knew Rose had to leave early to prepare the house for Simon and Amy because they were staying at her mom's house for the next six days. They were to arrive on Tuesday morning at the Mexicali Airport, and Rose was going to meet them when they arrived. She was as excited to see them again as Simon and Amy were to see her.

The first four days were going to be at the gym so Simon could observe Rose in the ring to see if she was ready to start fighting some opponents from around the nearby area. The last two days were going to be about having fun in Chilpancingo and eating out in restaurants, Simons favorite foods: hot, spicy, Mexican dinners.

CHAPTER THIRTY-THREE

The following day, Rose woke up with her eyes wide open before her alarm went off at five in the morning. The morning was cool outside, and it made the morning a perfect morning for Rose to do her routine run. By 6:30 a.m., she had returned from her jog, and it gave her enough time to think about Simon and Amy, which made her feel excited knowing that they will be visiting her soon. She was ready to pick up Simon and Amy at the airport. Rose had another hour and a half of waiting time before picking them up, but she had to allow fifteen minutes of driving through the rough, bumpy road to get to a smooth road before arriving in Acapulco. Meanwhile, Rose showered and had some coffee, a berry bagel, and a banana after drinking bottled water.

On her way to the airport, she thought about everything she was going to ask Simon. The most important thing she was hoping was that he would be pleased with her training and approved her to start fighting in some kind of exhibitions to show him that she was ready to face the top contenders to get back in track and climb to be the top contender again for the championship title.

She arrived at the airport a little before the plane landed after finding a place to park with so many people doing the same thing. Once she was inside the airport lobby, she waited for them in the area where Simon and Amy would be exiting the plane and into the lobby. The lobby was full and Rose was hoping they would be able to see her. She finally saw them walking down the plane exit aisle within a few minutes. She tried to get their attention by waving her arms over her head, kind of hidden with the mixed crowd doing the same thing. They both saw Rose waving at them to get their attention and acknowledged her by waving back with happy smiles on their faces.

"Welcome back, Simon. And it's so nice to see you again, Amy," Rose greeted them with a big hug and smile.

"It's so nice to see you again, too, Rose," replied Amy as she hugged Rose.

"I'll pick up the luggage so you two can jabber away, okay?" said Simon.

"We'll walk behind you, Simon, so you won't get lost," said Rose. She was teasing him and smiling as they walked behind Simon toward the baggage pickup area.

After getting their luggage and dragging them to Rose's car, they took off to her mom's house. Rose and Amy never stopped talking about everything they had done since the last time they saw each other. They were acting like they had known each other for years. Simon just listened.

When they got to the house, Rose's mom, Francis, had a big breakfast ready for them because it was only a little after 10:00 a.m., and her mom wanted to make them feel welcome at her home. She always loved cooking and enjoyed having Simon and Amy stay with them.

"Gracias," Simon tried to respond to her mom to make her feel good. He tried to be polite and respectful to her language, even though it sounded funny.

Francis did understand him and responded to him by saying, "De nada," (you're welcome), in Spanish. Simon had been trying to learn a bit of Spanish back in LA because he knew Rose's mom didn't speak or understand English very well. Rose wasn't aware that Simon was trying to learn some Spanish and was quite surprised and shocked when he responded to her mom in Spanish. She thought it was nice of him to try communicating with her.

After Simon and Amy settled down in their room and had a good breakfast, Simon asked Rose if she was ready to go to the gym to say hello to Jimmy. He wanted to talk to him about some important things, mostly about her scheduled training and possibly setting up some exhibition fights in the United States, depending on Rose, after observing how she did in the ring.

When they arrived at the gym, they saw Jimmy yelling at his fighter in the ring, but it was a good thing because he expected all his fighters to be and do the best they can in the ring to become just that, the best. Simon yelled out a big hello at Jimmy so he could hear him. Jimmy turned around and saw all three of them approaching him.

"Hi, Jimmy," said Simon. "You still remember Amy, my friend?"

"Yes, I do. How can anybody forget a face like that? So beautiful!" That made Amy blush.

"Thank you, Jimmy," replied Amy.

"Hi, Rose. You look nice too," commented Jimmy.

"That doesn't look like training clothes to me," Jimmy said jokingly because he knew what was happening.

"Thank you, Jimmy," answered Rose, smiling.

"Okay, girls, you can take off to the city while Jimmy and I talk about some business. It'll probably take about two hours or so. I'll see you girls later, okay?" said Simon.

"Be careful," said Jimmy. "Watch out where you're walking and keep your eyes opened around the surroundings wherever you're going."

"Okay, we will. Thank you Jimmy for your advice," Rose tells Jimmy.

Both girls took off while Simon and Jimmy stayed behind to discuss Rose's plans.

"Let's go to my office," said Jimmy. Simon followed Jimmy as his eyes wandered the gym before going into his office.

"Where do you think Rose would be at this point?" Simon asked Jimmy as he's sitting down on one of his chairs near his desk and starting the conversation.

"Well, for me, she has been progressing fast and seeing her in the ring with Rick this past week, I think she's ready. Her form, moves, stamina, and energy have been great. I don't think there's any problem in the ring. After watching her knock down some of my better male fighters, I think it's time for her to start moving to the real thing. We should start shouting out her name to fighters who are well-known in the ring. That would be my opinion," said Jimmy.

Simon listened to what Jimmy was saying, knowing that if anybody else knew Rose as he did, it would have to be Jimmy.

"You know what, Jimmy?" said Simon. "I believe you. I think she's grown on you as she did with me. Ever since I first had her go in the ring with one of my female fighters, I saw this female fighter for the first time in the ring, and the minute that she hit her opponent and knocked her down on the mat, I had a strong feeling about her that made me want to be her trainer. Although she hadn't had that much experience in the ring, it seemed natural how she was protecting herself against someone whose been in the ring for some time. It was like love at first sight. Of course, I'm referring to boxing."

Jimmy laughed and knew what he meant. Simon made that clear to Jimmy.

"Knowing Rose and what you just told me about her, I wouldn't even hesitate to say yes. Let's move forward with this, but I want you to see her spar a few rounds with Rick tomorrow. I think she would love to show off her progress in the ring to make her feel good and proud of her accomplishments and prove to you that she's ready for any challenge. Last, but not least, I think she would love to confirm your curiosity," said Jimmy.

"You're probably right, Jimmy," said Simon. "I started checking on some exhibition fights for Rose back in the States. The only thing is I was thinking more of three to four months from now, but after you tell me that she is ready to go forward, I might have to move them closer than four months. Two fights would be great for her to start, one within two months and the other, the following month. This would give her recovery some time. I'll check on them as soon as I return to the States. I'll try to start scheduling them a month from now. And don't say anything to Rose about the schedules because then she'll want to know all the details, and I'm not sure yet if I can get those fights changed to a month from now."

"That sounds like a good idea to me. I won't say a word to Rose. Just keep me informed about what is going on in the States so I can plan her training. I know she's going to be so excited when she finds out," said Jimmy.

Simon and Jimmy finished discussing Rose's future when Amy and Rose walked into the gym, hollering, "Hey, guys! Where are you?"

Jimmy jumped up from his chair in his office when he heard them, and Simon followed. They walked toward the open door of his office, and as they stepped out, they saw Rose holding a couple of bags filled to the top with stuff she had bought in the city. Amy had a giant sombrero on her head, smiling and giggling as she walked behind Rose.

"Hey, señoritas, I see you ladies made it back okay, and it seems you ladies had a good shopping spree!" said Simon. "But I'm glad you ladies made it back safely. It scares me to think you two are out there by yourselves, especially being so beautiful." Simon smiled when he said it.

"Simon!" Rose yelled out. "Don't forget what I can do," remarked Rose as she smiled with a big grin at Simon. "I was looking after Amy for you. I pretty much know this town of mine. As we walked into some stores, I had to stop and sign a few autographs for some of my fans. That was great, I thought."

"Okay, are you ladies ready to leave?" asked Simon.

"I think we are," said Rose.

"Well, let us finish our discussion in the office while you put those bags in the trunk of the car and give me about five minutes with Jimmy," said Simon.

"Okay. We'll be waiting for you in the car but try to hurry. It's pretty hot out there," said Rose.

"Will do," answered Simon.

It wasn't very long before Simon walked out of the gym, climbed into the car as the girls were starting to sweat, even with the air conditioning on and took off to Rose's house. Simon kept quiet about Rose's schedule and plans in the States. Rose tried to get information from Simon because she was curious about when they would let her box some real opponents in the ring. She didn't succeed with Simon because that was the plan and not let her know anything just yet until he was sure about her exhibitions in the States. He told her he wanted to see her fight in the ring tomorrow morning to see how her progress was coming along. That distracted her from asking too many questions about her plans to come. When they arrived at the house, it was a little late in the evening, and her mom had dinner ready for them. They had another delicious hot meal cooked for them; rice, beans, and enchiladas to go with some hot salsa set aside if they prefer to eat a little spicier food. After dinner, they talked for a while and then went to bed to get some rest for tomorrow morning because he knew it would be a long day, especially for Rose.

CHAPTER THIRTY-FOUR

By the end of the week, on Friday, Rose had displayed her abilities in the ring for Simon. She executed her moves and punches like a pro and never showed any weakness or fatigue. She proved that she was ready and anxious to go forward. To them, she was back to herself like she used to be, and ready to be a top contender. Jimmy was right about Rose. They both agreed that she was ready. Simon told Jimmy the first thing he would do when he returns to the States was considering of bringing her exhibition fights closer than two months. Jimmy agreed with what Simon said about allowing six weeks for the first fight and then another two months afterward for the second. This would allow enough time for her to return to being in the ring and boxing again in front of all her fans and viewers. The plan was to keep Rose from knowing what was going on. She's always curious about her schedules. Jimmy had to convince her that they were still working on plans and would soon have an answer for her.

The following day, Saturday morning, all three were going to enjoy the next two days as they planned: shopping, sightseeing, and just having a fun day being together. This time, Simon wanted to take Rose's mom with them in return for the hospitality she had given him and Amy, especially for all the great meals she cooked for them. Rose thought that it was a great idea.

"That is so thoughtful of you, Simon. My mom would love that," said Rose.

When Rose told her mom what their plans were, she got excited. She immediately went to her room and got herself dressed to go out with them. It only took her ten minutes to do so.

It took them about 45 minutes to get to Chilpancingo City. There were so many tourist people enjoying the city sightseeing museums, shopping centers, lots of authentic Mexican restaurants, Simons' favorites, among other historic buildings dating back to the 1800's. That day turned out to be an exciting day for Rose's mom. She has never been treated like Simon just did for her in her life. She thought it was the most exciting day ever. Rose went up to her and hugged her and Simon waited for Rose to finish so he could also give her a big hug too. Her mom had tears coming down her eyes, showing the affectionate and emotional type of person she was for everything they did for her today.

The next day, Simon and Amy were getting their things ready to return to the States. Rose had been up since 5:00 a.m. but had gone for her routine run. When she returned, Simon and Amy were having some coffee with her mom.

"Good morning, Rose," Simon greeted her when she walked inside and passed by them on her way to the bathroom to wash up.

"Good morning, everyone," answered Rose, drenched with sweat. After she came out of the bathroom, showered, and refreshed, and the first thing she did was go straight to the refrigerator to get a water bottle to quench her thirst. Then she went and sat next to an empty chair that was by Amy at the table.

"I see you guys got all your things ready for departure," Rose spoke. "I hate to see you guys go back so soon. It seemed like the time went by too fast. I really enjoyed having both of you come to visit me. I had a great time, and I hope I made Simon proud of my training."

"Indeed, you did, Rose. I was impressed overall. I think that you've made extraordinary progress with your therapy conditioning. I only wished I was with you more often than I've been here. I miss being around you and watching you train in the ring, thinking that one day, I'll be watching a world champion who worked hard and busted her butt to become a true champion," said Simon.

"Thank you, Simon." Rose was flattered and didn't know what else to say to him.

The time of their departure was 2:00 p.m. to LA. They had about two hours left to spend with each other, so they talked about when his next visit would be. Rose tried again to find out when they would let her go back to the States. Simon tried hard not to say anything about the exhibitions he was planning to schedule for Rose. All he told her was that he was working on some deals in the United States, but they weren't for sure. Simon didn't want her to give up her hopes of not being able to start her boxing dream again. He wanted her to continue focusing on her training until he found out when her first fight would be in the States. It was time for Rose to drive them to the airport. Her brother, Rudy, had asked if they wouldn't mind him going with them to the airport. Of course, they didn't mind at all.

When they arrived at the airport, there were so many cars coming and going every which way, and it made it worse to find a parking space so that took another 15 minutes before locating a spot to park the car. They all went inside so Simon and Amy could check in their luggage and wait for their flight, which was another hour of waiting time. Meanwhile, they talked more about what to do on their next visit. When they announced their flight, it was hard for Rose to see them leave. She hugged Amy, thanked her for coming again and hoping to see her soon. Then she hugged Simon, and he noticed tears running down her eyes.

"That's okay, Rose," Simon told her and then gave her his handkerchief. "Everything is going to be all right soon. Hopefully, I'll be back with some good news for you. I feel that you'll be going back with me on my next trip. So, be strong and focused, okay?" said Simon.

Once they boarded the plane, it took them about 15 minutes to take off down the runway and slowly lifted off the strip and into the air until they vanished in the sky. Rose and her brother, Rudy, watched them disappear, then they returned home.

CHAPTER THIRTY-FIVE

When Simon and Amy arrived in LA, around 7:00 p.m., they were a little exhausted. Simon was now dreading having to walk to the baggage conveyor belt to find their luggage and knowing that it was going to take him at least another 30 minutes, but they had no choice but to force themselves to get them. Simon found their luggage after 30 minutes and dealing with the other people crowding and reaching for their bags and listening to them grip about why they had to wait such a long time for the luggage to come down the belt.

Simon's car was parked near the exit airport doors when they came out of the lobby with their luggage. The traffic was terribly busy as the cars were coming and going every direction, making it harder for Simon to haul the luggage across the street, but they managed to make it to the car without anyone hitting them as they crossed the street to the parking lot. Thereafter, Simon took Amy home and helped her carry her luggage, among the other things she had brought back from Mexico, inside her house.

Simon went home after having a short conversation with Amy and telling her that he would call her later that night. Simon drove home tired, but he was still thinking about the trip and the enjoyable time he spent with Amy and Rose. He couldn't stop thinking about them, especially Rose. He thought about everything he wanted to do for Rose but the one thing he wanted to do was help her get back in the ring with someone challenging to see how she would handle the opponents.

When he got home, he forced himself to put everything away he had taken on the trip, knowing that it would be harder to do it later than now. Then he laid down on the couch for a few minutes to rest, feeling exhausted after all the traveling. Within 15 minutes, he dozed off for an hour when he suddenly snapped from a dream and jumped up from the couch, dazed for a few seconds, realizing that it was just a dream that he was having. He was glad that it was just a dream. This was because it was a dream about Rose entering the ring to fight Echo, her antagonist, her worse nightmare. Rose had been chasing Echo to settle a retribution from the start of her career and put an end to the chapter by defeating Echo in front of all the fans and show her who the real champion should be with the win.

"Man!" He shook his head from side to side. "Boy!" he spoke out loud to himself. He got up from the couch and went to the kitchen. He picked up a tall empty glass from his cabinet, walked straight to the refrigerator and got some chilled water from the water dispenser. It was 8:30 p.m. when he remembered telling Amy he would call her later.

After drinking the chilled water, he searched for his cell phone to call Amy before forgetting. And then he called. "Hello, Amy."

"Hi, Simon," replied Amy. "Anything wrong? You sound a bit shaken up. Are you okay?"

"Yes, I'm okay now. I just woke up from a weird dream thinking that I was in Las Vegas with Rose, and she was going to fight Echo for the title. It wasn't a bad dream, but when I woke up suddenly, I didn't know where I was or if it was the real thing or not. I'm okay now!" said Simon. "How about you? How are you doing?"

"I'm fine now. I laid down and rested on the bed after putting everything away. I didn't know I had that much stuff to unpack. It must have been all that shopping I did in Mexico." Amy laughed on the phone. "I was just waiting for your phone call."

"I was thinking that I should start working on Rose's plans and figure out how I'm going to schedule the dates when I want her to start fighting. I'm not sure of the day Rose will be able to come to the US. I have a pretty good idea of what I want to do, but whether they agree with the idea or not, I think I can still bring Rose to the US within the next two weeks and convince the trainers to agree with the dates that I want." Simon continued telling Amy about his ideas.

"Great! I think you should get started as soon as possible," Amy replied. She was very supportive of Simon since she was like a sister to her ever since she met Rose. If Rose needed anything to help her continue her boxing career, Amy would go that extra mile to help her in any way she could. She also kept in touch with Rose at least once a week to see if she was doing all right. Simon and Amy talked for another ten minutes and then they said their goodnights. Right after they finished their conversation, Simon got started on the plans for Rose and stayed up until 10:00 p.m. when he finished.

He was tired but glad that he had figured out how he was going to schedule her exhibition. With his plans, he was sure he would be able to bring Rose back to the US within the next two weeks. Rose had her papers for the visa, and nothing was going to stop her from coming here. The other thing he was happy about Rose was that she was ready to face any opponent that would step into the ring with her.

It didn't take Simon very long to fall asleep after he finished his plans. The first thing he did the following day was visit a trainer friend of his, Jeff Gentry, who he thought would look at his plans the way he did. They had been friends for a long time, and he figured it would be the best place to start. They communicated every so often and talked about the past and coming events. Simon even spoke to him about Rose and how her condition was progressing. Jeff knew

Rose because he would watch her spar when she was training at Simon's gym.

When Simon arrived at Jeff's gym the following morning, he walked straight to his office since he didn't see him around the ring. He was right. He was busy working on his schedules for his next event for one of his boxers.

"Hey, Simon! What a surprise!" said Jeff as Simon walked in. "It's great to see you again. How was your trip to Mexico?"

"Good!" answered Simon. "It was gratifying. Rose is doing great, and I think she's ready to start boxing in the ring with some challenging opponents. That's why I'm here. I want to bring her back to the States soon and I thought we could work something out with one of your best fighters to challenge Rose in an exhibition match."

"Don't you think it's too soon for her to start that quickly?" asked Jeff.

"Not really. If you could only see how Rose has improved from what she used to be. If you think she was good back then, you will not believe how she changed her style. If you put one of your better male boxers against her, she would give him a battle or knock him out. Trust me," said Simon. "She's ready."

Jeff looked at Simon and smiled at him, shaking his head. "I believe you," said Jeff. "I'll check the schedule of my best female fighters and try to arrange it. But it might be three weeks, so let me see what I can do. Okay?"

"Great! Perfect! I appreciate you doing this for me, Jeff. Rose will love you," said Simon. "Jeff, there's one more thing I would like to ask you. What do you think of getting her set up with one of Joe's girls?"

"Well, he does have a strong female fighter that would give Rose a challenge. I think it wouldn't be a bad idea if you inquire about her," answered Jeff.

"I just wanted to get your opinion. And I was right. We do think alike," said Simon and then smiled.

Simon took off to Joe's gym after talking with Jeff to see

if he would agree to have one of his girls get in the ring with Rose for an exhibition match. He was glad that Jeff okayed the match with Rose. Now he had to convince Joe to do the same. He wanted to confirm at least three matches for Rose before he told Rose his plans. On his way to Joe's gym, he was trying to think of another trainer that he could convince to let one of his fighters get in the ring with Rose for an exhibition fight.

When Simon arrived at Joes' gym, he walked inside the gym and saw Joe showing one of his girls in the ring on how to avoid being hit on the face by protecting herself with her hands and arms.

"Hey, Joe! It's me, Simon."

"Hey, buddy," Joe yelled back at Simon. "How are you? It's been a long time since I've seen you!"

"Yeah! It's been quite a while," answered Simon.

"What have you been up to, Simon?" asked Joe.

"I need to talk to you about Rose. Do you have a few minutes to talk?"

"Sure. Just give me a few more minutes and let me finish with my fighters."

"Okay, no problem."

"If you want to wait for me in my office, you can, or just hang around here until I finish," said Joe.

Simon decided to stay and watch how his fighters were sparring. It wasn't long before Joe showed his fighter some techniques in the ring and then climbed out of the ring to talk to Simon. Joe shook hands with Simon and led him to his office.

"Well, what's going on with you, Simon?" asked Joe.

"You still remember Rose when she used to box for me, right?" asked Simon.

"You bet! She was one hell of a fighter. Where is she now?" asked Joe.

"That's why I'm here. You know that she was involved in a shooting a while back. Then she was deported back to Mexico because her visa had expired. Now she has recuperated from her wounds, and her visa is being processed. Meanwhile, she's been training in Mexico with a boxing trainer that I've gotten to know very well, and I'm glad that I did because his techniques are similar to mine, and we can relate to each other. I'm trying to bring Rose back to the States and line her up with some exhibition fights so she can get back in the ring with some challenging opponents. That's when you come in. My question is, how do you feel about setting up one of your best girls with Rose? I'm looking at three months from now," said Simon. "It's because I already talked to Jeff about setting up an exhibition within six weeks, and then you would follow his schedule."

"Wow!" said Joe. "That is a surprise. But I think we can work something out. Three months will give me enough time to review my schedule, and then I'll call you to confirm it, okay?"

"Cool," said Simon. "I'll be looking forward to hearing from you soon. Thank you, Joe. I greatly appreciate it."

When Simon left Joe's gym, he felt better about the outcome. There was only one more exhibition to set up before calling Rose to tell her the good news. He wondered who might accept his idea as he drove home.

When he returned home, he went straight to his office and picked up some notes from Rose's past fights, searching for managers that might be interested in letting one of their boxers get in the ring with her. He sat on his chair behind his desk, searching through the notes in front of him. It was going on four o'clock when his phone rang.

"Hello!" said Simon.

"Hello! Is this Simon?" the person on the other end replied.

"Yes, it is."

"I don't know if you remember me, but my name is Ralph. I used to go to your gym occasionally to see how my competition was doing. I have a training gym for boxing, and I just finished talking to Joe. He informed me you were looking for someone to spar in an exhibition with Rose. I remember her and have always admired her for her boxing skills. She was an excellent boxer. Joe told me that she would be returning to the States soon and you wanted to get some exhibitions lined up for her. I want to see someone kick the shit out of the current champ, and most people feel the same way. I think if there's anybody that can do it, it would be Rose if she still fights as she used to before her incident."

Simon replied with confidence, "Thank you for your comment, and yes, I also think she's the one to do it." He paused.

"I have some good, experienced female boxers, but to be honest, not as good as Rose used to be. I'll let you know as soon as I talk to Joe and work with him on some dates with our schedules, and I think he said that you already talked to Jeff, so maybe we can get together soon and work something out, okay?"

Simon was very appreciative of Ralph. "You don't know how much that means to me. And of course, Rose will be the happiest female boxer on earth after I tell her the good news about how you guys reached out to give her a chance by helping her get back in the ring so quickly and by changing your schedules to accommodate hers. I want to thank you, Ralph, for stepping out of your way and helping Rose, and making this happen for her."

"I'm glad to help you, Simon. I think you're a great trainer and it shows by putting a lot of effort into your fighters and how much you care about your fighters to help them succeed. That's a very admirable way of thinking. Good luck Simon and we'll talk again soon."

CHAPTER THIRTY-SIX

Simon made arrangements for Rose to fly to Los Angeles within the next two weeks, right after he had talked to his attorney about the good news about the renewal of Rose's visa. It was approved for the next three years as a P-1 visa because of her status as a highly known athlete. When he called, it caught Rose by surprise as she was working out with the exercise equipment. Her first reaction she got after Simon told her was to let out a yell of excitement and feeling jubilant. Rose couldn't believe that she was going back to the States and continue where she left off. She felt like crying out loud but was holding back because some of the fighters near her were staring at her as she was yelling.

After Simon finished telling Rose the great news, she went into Jimmys' office and told him the good news. Jimmy was excited for Rose with the news, and he came close to telling her what Simon was doing in the States about lining up her exhibitions. But he also remembered that Simon told him not to mention anything to Rose about the exhibitions, so he didn't.

"Jimmy, I want to thank you and Rick for making me a better fighter than I used to be. I feel like I'm in better shape now and my endurance is extremely higher with my body conditioning as a fighter than I used to be. With all the training Rick pushed me to exceed limits every time we were in the ring, I feel like I'm a smarter and stronger fighter."

Rose would've jumped in the plane instantly if she would've had a chance to leave that minute. One good thing that crossed Roses' mind and made her excited was knowing that she would be fighting against some more experienced opponents, and she was looking forward to whoever entered the ring with her.

Meanwhile, Simon and Amy went apartment hunting the following day for Rose and to have it ready when Rose returns. They got lucky and found one that was not too far from his house and had it furnished within two days and ready for her to live in. This was another surprise that Simon had done for her, so Rose didn't have to waste any time getting settled when she arrives from Mexico.

The following two weeks, Rose had her visa in her hands to travel to Los Angeles and she didn't waste a second getting her things ready to travel and was at the airport in Acapulco after being in a cab for a little over an hour traveling from Chilpancingo. Simon had sent her the tickets for her flight a few days before leaving, so she didn't have to purchase them.

Rose arrived in Los Angeles on a Tuesday at 2 o'clock in the afternoon, and Simon was going to pick her up. Simon was as excited as Rose to return to the United States.
Rose looked through the side window of the airline as it got closer and closer to the landing strip of the runway. Her eyes opened wide as it got closer to the ground and finally heard the plane touch down, hearing the tires screeched on the runway and felt a little bounce. Then she heard the reverse engine thrust to help the plane slow down, making a loud noise from the deceleration. Rose still couldn't believe that she was arriving in Los Angeles after being gone for so long. She was eager to see Simon and Amy once again, but this time it will be in LA instead of Mexico. Rose was getting a little anxious just sitting in the plane and waiting for it to stop and thinking that it feels like it's taking forever to get there.

Simon and Amy waited for her at the gate where Rose would be walking down the arriving aisle. As soon as Simon spotted Rose coming down the aisle, he raised his arms to get her attention the second they made eye contact, and Rose weaved her way through the crowd toward Simon and Amy to greet them.

"You finally made it!" said Simon. "Did you have any trouble with the flight arrangements or visa?"

"No, I didn't. Everything went smoothly. I can't believe that I'm finally here," said Rose. "Thank you, Simon, for doing this. I'm so grateful for all that you have done for me. And, before I forget, my mom specifically told me to say hello to you. She really likes you and thinks highly of you."

"That was nice of her. The next time you talk to her, tell her I said hello," said Simon. "Let's get going. I bet you're tired, aren't you?"

"Just a little jet-lagged," answered Rose.

Then they took off from the airport. "By the way, Rose. I rented an apartment for you close to where I live, and Amy found it, thinking that you would like it. It's not huge, but it's in a nice neighborhood, quiet and peaceful." Rose was thrilled and surprised because Simon never mentioned anything to her about the apartment, so it was another big surprise that Rose wasn't expecting.

When they arrived, Simon helped Rose carry her luggage and garment bags into her apartment. He had already bought her a few pieces of furniture and some kitchen items, so she didn't have to take time looking for things to buy for the apartment. He wanted her to start going to the gym and working out with the exercise equipment as soon as possible to prepare her for the exhibitions. Simon had a brief talk about her exhibitions on the phone before she left Mexico. That made her even more excited about returning to the States.

Rose was aware that she would have her first exhibition in two weeks and wanted to start working out first thing tomorrow morning. She didn't want to wait any longer or waste any time than she needed to. She was ready to continue following her dream.

The following exhibitions were set to take place every six weeks for the next three months, or if anything changed from her fighting status, they would consider putting her on a main event card for that night.

The three weeks passed as if a gusty wind swept by and moved everything forward in a second. The media had already found out that Rose had her first exhibition at Jeff's Gym, where he often had other exhibition fights for fighters that wanted to become professionals. The gym was well known for these exhibition fights and people would show up to see them. Roses' exhibition caused a fan crowd around the ring to watch Roses' exhibition when she was scheduled to fight.

Reporters were swarming and crowding the fans among the crowd, trying to get as close to the ring as possible to take pictures of her and be the first to get the story on her return to boxing in the United States. They knew Rose when she was at her peak, on the brink of becoming a champion, until her incident occurred when she almost lost her life. But now, she was back, and the reporters wanted an exciting story to write about, so they followed her wherever she was scheduled to fight. They had lost track of her when they deported her back to Mexico and didn't know whether she had died or if she was ever coming back to fight in the United States.

Aside from the reporters lingering around the ring, waiting for Rose to step into the ring, there were other boxing managers who were interested in how she would do in the ring. She had become the talk of the city. One of the reporters who had a lead about her return to the States put a small article on the sports page, not knowing much about her condition, whether she was or was not capable of fighting like she used to.

All he wrote in the article was this:

"A girl named Rose from Mexico, who was a top contender, returns to the United States after being gone for almost a year to continue her battles in the ring. But my question is, "Is she still the same female boxer as she was back then? Will she begin where she left off or is she finished with what she used to love doing in the ring." We shall find out soon.

That's what attracted many sports writers and fans; they were the ones curious to find out if she was the same Rose as the reporter was talking about.

The reporters were swarming around the gym where she was going to have her first fighting exhibition with Sandi Carlson, one of Jeff's best female fighters. The reporters wanted to be the first to write an article about her return and how she takes on her first opponent in an exhibition after being gone for a year.

Her opponent, Sandi Carlson, had won six bouts and had one loss, but she is very aggressive and a hard puncher.

Flashing cameras were surrounding Rose as she stepped into the ring. This was an unofficial bout with six two-minute rounds. The reporters waited for the bout's outcome, not knowing if it would only be one round, two rounds, or all six rounds. The reporters wanted to ask her questions about her plans when the bout was over.

As the fight progressed into the second round, after the first round was more of a warmup round, Rose didn't seem to show any fatigue and was moving around the ring comfortably, but being aggressive at times to show some skills that she picked up from Rick. Some of her old fans watched as she fought, yelling their lungs out for her. They still hadn't forgotten about her. It felt like good old times for them.

Within a minute and a half into the second round, Rose kept looking for an opportunity to knock Sandi out, and after she saw Sandi throw a shot at her face and missed, Rose took all her power with her right hand and landed an uppercut to Sandis' left lower jaw and down went Sandi to the canvas. The referee quickly jumped in front of Rose and told her to go to her corner so he could start counting his mandatory ten count. Sandi never made it back up before the ten count and it was considered a knockout. She backed away from her opponent as the referee counted her out. Her fans got louder as her challenger went down to the mat and waited for the count. Then they all cheered for their hero once again.

Cameras flashed continuously at Rose as she walked around the ring after the fight. The reporters were impressed with the victory that Rose had given her fans to witness her first exhibition fight since she's been gone. The reporters scrambled through the crowd of fans and got enough photos and information about her next fight and were off to their offices, hoping to be the first to write the story. It would be a big thing for the reporter who could write about this huge story in the sports section and be the first one to do so.

After Rose finished talking with some of her fans and putting up with the reporters, Simon had her go to the dressing room to shower and change into her regular clothes. Then Simon wanted to take Rose to a restaurant with Amy to celebrate her comeback victory with honors. It was quite a night for Rose to be able to show the public and her fans that she was back like she was before and just proved to them that she is the same Rose and to answer the reporter who had questioned her in his newspaper article about whether Rose was the same top contender as she used to be.

Simon was so proud of Rose and how she handled herself in her first exhibition. She had listened and focused on the fight, just like they planned, and it worked. He was proud to scc Rose defeat her first opponent after being gone for a long time. She didn't show any sign of fatigue and moved around the ring gracefully, protecting herself defensively from the punches being thrown at her and making contact with most of her punches that she threw and scoring.

When Rose finished getting dressed, she met Simon and Amy outside the dressing room.

"Are you guys ready for me?" asked Rose.

"We've been waiting patiently for you. How are you feeling, Rose?" asked Simon.

"Not too bad. A little sore where the opponent hit me on my side, but other than that, I'm fine," answered Rose.

"Okay! Let's go then," said Simon.

Then they took off to the restaurant to have a nice dinner and talked for about an hour before going home.

The following Monday, they were back at the gym. Rose went straight to the weight machines to work out her soreness from the fight. Simon had one of his trainers stay at her side to help her with the weights. She had pain, but it wasn't stopping her from quitting. Rose wanted to keep her body conditioned, no matter what it would take; quitting was not in her vocabulary. That was part of Simon's plan for today; tomorrow, he was having her spar with some of his male fighters again. Simon liked what Jimmy had done to get her used to harder punches and different fighters. Then on Thursday and Friday, he made arrangements with some other trainers from nearby gyms to let Rose spar with some of their fighters to get her used to different fighting styles. Rose was excited to hear that Simon had done that. She was determined to get back in the ring with more experienced and aggressive fighters, whatever it takes to make her a better fighter. She was going to exceed her expectations.

Day after day, Rose continued to push herself to the next level that would make her unstoppable. She wanted to be ready for the next fight and knew losing was not an option.

Weeks passed, and she was ready for her next opponent, one of Joe's girls named Melissa Garza. This time, it would be at Ralph's gym since it was a little bigger and had a better fighting ring than Simon's.

Melissa had been fighting for a year, but she was one of the best fighters that Joe had. It didn't worry Rose about who she was or how good she fought. All she wanted was to fight whoever stepped in the ring with her. She felt ready and confident with herself. The media had found out about her second exhibition, and the sports writers were all around the ring, flashing their cameras and waiting for her to start and finish fighting so they could talk to her. Rose was used to it, and it didn't bother her having them around; plus, she also had some of her fans, mostly of Mexican descent, following her wherever she was fighting. That made her feel prouder about who she was which built her pride of being a native of Mexico.

As the fight was getting ready, Simon and his assistant, Alex, prepared Rose in her corner, anxious for the fight to start. Both fighters waited for the bell to ring at their corners. As Rose and Melissa heard the bell ring and the command from the referee, they rushed to the center of the ring and began throwing punches. Before the fighters would make their first contact, they usually butt gloves to respect each other, but in this case, Melissa, her opponent, charged at Rose instead with punches aiming at Rose's face followed by a blow at her side. Rose backed away from the punches that Melissa was throwing. As soon as she did, Rose stepped forward, attacking with short jabs that led to a solid hard punch to Melissa's midsection and then came up with a hard punch to her face. That sent Melissa to the ropes. Rose continued throwing a flurry of punches, landing most of them for points. Rose kept hitting her with left and right, as Melissa covered her face to block Rose's punches. Rose scored with every contact. The referee stepped between them to break them up because Melissa was not responding to Rose's punches. The referee had Rose go back to her corner so he could check on Melissa. She looked hurt and bruised, and blood ran down her face from a small cut above her left eye. The referee looked in her eye and then held her hands to see if she was still able to continue fighting. He determined that Melissa was okay and to continue the fight. The fight proceeded until the bell rang, ending the first round.

The first round was exhausting for Melissa. She rested and listened to her coach, as he advised her what to do next. In Melissa's corner, her cutman worked on her eye that was bleeding by applying Vaseline before it got worse, hoping that Rose wouldn't hit her there again, but it wasn't guaranteed if she would or not.

The bell rang for the second round, and they both returned to feeling each other, jabbing lightly, and looking for the right moment to land a hard knockout punch. Soon they started landing harder punches, but Rose delivered the hardest and most direct punches that were doing the most damage. Right before the two-minute round was over, and after Rose hit Melissa several times on her face, Rose catapulted her right fist with all her power and delivered a hard right punch to Melissa's left temple, sending her to the mat. Melissa never saw that coming. She laid on the mat, dazed and not moving as the referee jumped in front of Rose and stopped the fight. It was all over again. Rose raised her arms and walked around the ring as Simon climbed into the ring to hug her.

"You're awesome. You know that?" Simon shook his head from side to side, praising her for another victory and job well done.

CHAPTER THIRTY-SEVEN

The following day, the first thing Simon did was call Jimmy in Mexico. He was excited to tell him about Rose's second victory. Jimmy was in his office working on his paperwork when Simon called him at 9:00 o'clock in the morning.

"Jimmy! Good morning. It's Simon. How are you?"

"I'm fine. Thank you. What's going on?" replied Jimmy.

"I just wanted to tell you that Rose had another victory last night. She was outstanding and I'm very proud of her. I think she's on her way to becoming a champ the way she fought last night. You should have seen her!" Simon was still excited about Rose's victory with a victorious knockout and felt like he needed to let the world know.

"I know. I read it in the newspaper this morning. That goes to show you how fast news travels. Rose is the talk of the town. She's our hero," said Jimmy.

"Jimmy!" Simon intervened. "There's another thing I wanted to talk to you about. I was thinking about helping you and Rick get a working visa, so you guys could come to the United States and help me fulfill Rose's dream to ensure she reaches the top." That got Jimmy's attention immediately when Simon told him, then his eyes broadened, thinking that it was a great idea and hoping that it would happen. "If I can get you and Rick a working visa to come to the United States, will you come? I'm planning on going to the attorney tomorrow and talking to him about asking to see if he would help me get you guys a visa like Roses'."

"Yes, I would, instantly, and I'll work something out with Rick so he wouldn't lose out on his fights." Jimmy got excited, wanting to call Rick to let him know the news as soon as he hangs up.

"Rose doesn't know that I'm doing this, so please try not to say anything to Rose about what's going on if she calls you. I want this to be a surprise," said Simon. "And let Rick know not to say anything to Rose either, okay?"

"Don't worry, Simon. I'll keep this under my hat. Thanks for doing this. I really appreciate this a hundred times."

Meanwhile, Rose continued her training, lifting weights and jogging in the mornings. Simon started his plans to get the visas for Jimmy and Rick, hoping he wouldn't have any problems processing their paperwork. After talking with his attorney that evening, he mentioned that there might be a visa, EB-1, that will allow trainers or coaches to the United States without any trouble for a year. So, there might be a good chance of them coming to the United States and helping him with the training. That was good news for Simon. Rose had a vigorous workout as the day went by, even after her exhibition yesterday with Melissa. Winning every fight scheduled was on her mind. She wanted to be recognized as the undefeated female boxer in the area. After finishing all her fighting exhibitions, she wanted to become eligible to fight a high-ranking boxer.

Her next opponent was Rachael Martinez, one of Ralph's girls. She has more experience than Melissa because she has been boxing for the last two years. At one time, she had the chance to become the next contender to fight for a title bout, except she lost to a girl from Texas named Evett Perez, a top-five contender. She knocked out Rachael in the third round with a solid straight punch and never knew what hit her. Rachael is a southpaw fighter who throws hard and brutal punches that can do damage if she gets through to her opponents. Out of her last ten fights, she has had five knockouts by the third round, two being in the first. She was ready to take on Rose, knowing the type of fighter Rose has been with her known status.

Rose kept doing what Simon wanted her to do, and it worked. It kept her mind focused on her fighting. She was ready for Rachael, and her fighting record didn't bother Rose a bit. Once she got in the ring with her, winning was the only option in her mind.

The day had come for the two fighters to meet in the ring. Simon had been with Rose most of the time to ensure she was getting the proper training and ready for this fight. He had taken Rose further in her conditioning than he usually does, and she followed the training he expected out of her. That was one of Rose's most significant values. She would never complain and was always ready to do whatever it took to get there. She was fully confident in herself because of the training Simon had her follow, and she retained all the training Rick and Jimmy had given. He knew she was ready and wasn't worried about this fighting exhibition with Rachael.

On the day of the fight with Rachael, and before Rose entered the ring with Rachael, she was swarmed with sports writers and photographers again, trying to get another story from her for their sports section. Some reporters sent the information to Mexico with Rose's photos of her to keep them informed of their hero. Most of the crowd were her fans, besides the reporters. Simon and Ralph enjoyed seeing the crowd watching Rose fight in an exhibition. The fans would certainly go see her fight on her first return as soon as she is ready to go back in the ring and fight the higher rated opponents in her weight class.

The fight started with a flurry of punches between Rose and Rachael in the first round. The second and third rounds were similar with both fighters throwing about the same number of punches and scoring almost even. It was the last round that decided who the winner would be.

The fight with Rachael ended with a decision. Rose edged Rachael by two points, but a win is a win, and a loss is a loss. Rachael had given Rose the most challenging fight out of all the exhibitions that she fought. Rose ended up with a cut on her right eye that swelled severely. She didn't give in that easily and fought back like a champ. All her fans cheered like crazy, even though it was just an exhibition; they were happy and proud that she was back in the ring.

This was another victory for Rose, and she was already looking forward to her next exhibition fight within the next three weeks. She had to win the next two fights to prove that she was still the Rose from the past and that she was back to win the title.

Rose had no trouble winning the next two exhibition fights. She had earned her shot in the pro fights once again. She had proved she was a true fighter and challenger to any other female fighter who would step into the ring with her. Her name was being mentioned and heard throughout the streets and cities nearby. The sports headlines dubbed her the returning fighter who might be the next top contender in the super featherweight division. The promoters were already setting up an event for Rose to fight in her first big headliner. They were trying to set up a schedule to begin within the month. Prospects for Rose were being discussed to see who a good contender for Rose would draw a big crowd as a featured co-main event, besides having a title fight as the main headliner.

Rose was thrilled to learn what they were trying to do with her fights. She got excited and anxious to see when they would finalize the date and who her first opponent would be. Simon was busy negotiating the deal to ensure that Rose would remain the co-main event of the fight night and earn what she was entitled to from the attraction of the crowd that she would bring to the event.

CHAPTER THIRTY-EIGHT

It took a few days before the promoters and managers decided and finalized the event for Rose. Her first opponent was going to be a girl fighting out of New Mexico, with a record of eleven wins and one loss to a girl from Las Vegas that went by the name of the Blaze; a top ranking contender for a championship title fight. The girl's name was Victoria "the Red Slayer" Duran. She got her nickname because of her hard windmill swing punches, which she threw with all her might, like an axe slayer coming from nowhere, landing close to the temple and knocking out her opponents. Her hair was as red as a shiny apple. It was cut short around her ears, with a long blazing red ponytail that hung just below her neckline. Out of her eleven wins and one loss, she had five straight knockouts by the second round and the rest by unanimous decision. It didn't bother Rose when they told her about the Red Slayer's record. She was confident in herself and thought of the Red Slayer as just another fighter wanting to beat her opponents and hurt them as much as she could if she had the chance.

The fight was scheduled to take place in Los Angeles Sports Arena, starting with the preliminaries at 5:00 p.m. and ending with the main headliner event: a middleweight title fight in the men's division. Rose and the Red Slayer were the co-main event of the night. There were two more months before all this was going to happen. Rose continued training like always and focused on this coming fight event. Simon stayed on top of her scheduled training to keep her ready and conditioned, making sure that nothing was distracting her, especially if she thought about Rob.

The first six weeks went by fast, leaving two more weeks of training before the event. Simon and his team were ready and confident with the training they had given Rose. Rose was anxious and wanted to tell the world she was back in the ring and show them that she was better than before.

On Friday before the event, all the fighters had to be weighed to be officially eligible to fight in their weight category. During the weigh-ins, Rose had the chance to meet Victoria face-to-face as they both stared at each other, not budging apart from the closeness of their bodies as they stared at each with fearless expressions and readiness with thoughts in their minds that she's going to kick her ass in the ring tomorrow night and can't wait for it to happen.

Saturday, the final day was here for Rose. She was in her changing room getting ready for the fight as Simon and his assistant, Alex, prepared her for her battle. Alex used to help Simon when he needed help with his fighters a long time ago. And now that Rob is not here to help him, he called Alex to help him out.

As soon as the official put his initials on the tape wrapped around her hands, Simon had her hands slip into the gloves and tied them. Then he had her warm-up with Alex with the boxing mitts. Rose and the Red Slayer would fight in a 8-round two-minute bout before the main event, around 7:30 p.m. It was getting close to Rose's time to start walking to the ring. Simon was anxious to see Rose win, and Rose was ready to begin her return to the pro fights since she had returned from Mexico and finished all the exhibitions that Simon had arranged for her. Now was the time to show her fans that she was back.

When her time came to go out to the ring, you could hear the crowd roaring from every direction of the arena and her fans cheering for her as she walked down the aisle wearing the same robe Rob had given her. The Red Slayer was already waiting for Rose in the ring. Simon carried a red rose to give to Rose once she entered the ring so she could throw it to her fans, as she had been doing in the past. As Rose entered the ring, the crowd was still yelling and cheering for her. She turned around to find Simon to get the rose from him. Then she turned around with her back facing the fans and threw the rose over her shoulder to her fans. You could hear them yelling and screaming as they saw the rose heading towards their direction when Rose threw it as the fans reached out to grab it, trying to catch the rose when it was about to land in a fan's hand.

After the ring announcer stated the introductions of the two fighters, the fight was ready to begin. The referee had the fighters meet at the center of the ring to go over a brief ruling of the can and can't do during the fight with their punches and had them touch gloves as a respectful good luck greeting to one another. Then told them to wait at their corners for his command. He waited for the bell to ring and shouted the magic word, "Box!" in a loud tone of voice. Within seconds, immediately the fighters didn't waste any time and approached like wild bulldogs, throwing their best punches and jabs, landing and scoring points. Rose was finding openings and penetrating between the Red Slayer's gloves and making contact on the Slayers' face. Rose wasn't letting up, but the Red Slayer was fighting back, trying to send her windmill punches across Rose's head. Rose kept an eye for that punch because she knew how damaging it could be if the Slayer connected. Rose was moving around the ring, switching to the southpaw stance and then back to her orthodox stance. This was one of the new moves that Rose had picked up from Rick.

The Red Slayer was aggressive, yet she was cautious of Rose's hard punches because she knew Rose was known for those hard and direct power punches. The Red Slayer kept her distance as Rose followed her around the ring as she was moving from left to right and Rose would throw single jabs and throwing her combinations when she was close enough to stop the Slayer from moving around the ring. The two minutes went by fast, and the bell had rung in no time, ending the first round and it followed by a one-minute break.

Both fighters scored a few points by making contact in the upper and lower body, but it seemed that Rose outscored the Slayer by several points. Neither fighter looked to be tired as they sat in their corners, listening to their trainers.

The bell rang to start the second round after the referee yelled out, "Box!" Both fighters rushed to meet the other in the middle of the ring and went right back throwing hard punches, not wasting any time again. Rose took advantage of throwing a hard punch to the Red Slayers' lower body side to the liver, making Victoria stoop over a little as she tried to protect herself from the other punches Rose was throwing, trying to protect her side with her arm. It did a little damage to Victoria, but not enough to take her down as the Red Slayer clinched her arms around Rose's sides and held on tight to keep Rose from throwing more punches at her. The referee broke them up and had them go back to boxing again. Rose returned to what she was doing to the Red Slayer and continued throwing combinations this time. The Red Slayer responded with punches and jabs but weren't effective or hard. Rose was making contact with some of her hard flurry of punches that were weakening and wearing out the Red Slayer. She wanted to finish her off by the end of this round, but it seemed like it wasn't going to happen. With twenty seconds left, the Red Slayer was still fighting back, but she seemed to be exhausted and kept holding on to Rose. The bell rang and ended the second round, saving the Red Slayer from a possible knockout.

Simon had a brief but serious talk during the break with Rose about why she hadn't knocked her out yet.

"This time, go out there and finish her off. You can do this. She's not as good as you. When you switch to the southpaw, set her up with jabs and look for that opening. I noticed that every time you do that, she covers up and that's when I want you to use your power with your left punch and deliver it to her liver side and let her have it, okay, Rose?" Simon's voice rose high enough for Rose to hear every word he said.

"Okay! Okay!" said Rose.

The referee yelled out "Box!" as soon as the bell rang for the third round of the fight. Both fighters went to the middle of the ring and bumped gloves as a sign of respect for the fighter. Then they returned to where they left off, throwing everything they had. The Red Slayer tried throwing her windmill punches, hoping to land one on Rose's head and knock her out. Rose was still on the lookout for those punches and dodged a couple of them when the Red Slayer attempted to make contact. Rose started to move around and switched to the southpaw stance as Simon suggested. She noticed the Red Slayer was dropping her right arm when she switched and saw an opening, and shot a straight hard punch, landing hard right on the Red Slayer's cheekbone. The Red Slayer never saw it coming. She went straight down to the canvas, landing on her back and not moving a muscle. She was out. The referee jumped in front of Rose and had her go to her corner and wait. Then he started his mandatory counts on the Red Slayer. She didn't recover until a minute after the bell rang, as they doctored her to make sure she was all right. Her trainers helped her up from the mat and sat her on the stool. She was recovering slowly enough to be moved, but she was alright. Rose walked around the ring while they looked after the Red Slayer, ensuring she would be okay as Simon looked at Rose and feeling how proud he was of her.

The ring announcer got his microphone and stated his official outcome of the fight and announced the official winner of the fight, calling out Roses' name as the winner with a technical knockout with 90 seconds in the third round. Rose was the happiest fighter of the night, feeling an adrenaline rush throughout her body the more she thought of being closer to challenging the champion.

Simon wrapped his arms around Rose telling her, "I told you can do it if you listen to me." He continued hugging her to celebrate her first victory back from her long dreadful recovery. Rose was back and she let her fans know that she's moving forward from where she use to be, a top contender and a shot for the championship title.

"You're back, Rose. I think you still have it," said Simon. "Congratulations!"

Reporters flashed their cameras all around the ring and waited for Rose to step out of the ring and onto the aisle. They were yelling too many questions at once, wanting to find out when and who she wanted to fight next.

It was a madhouse with her fans cheering as loud as they could, shouting out Rose's name and celebrating her victory. This was a night to remember for Rose as she finished answering questions for the reporters and waving at her fans. Then she walked down the aisle to her dressing room to go home and enjoy her victory.

CHAPTER THIRTY-NINE

Another one of the toughest fighters that Rose was going to encounter in the ring was a girl named Vanessa "the Fearless Hurricane" Collins. She was originally from a small town in the Sun Valley in California, but spent most of her life in New Mexico, working as a bartender while training to become a full-time boxer. On her days off and before going to work, she spent most of her time in the gym, training every chance she could, and it paid off for her. She had validated her status as one of the best fighters around New Mexico and was well known throughout the states. She had a record of 10 wins and no losses and was determined to have an 11–0 record when she beats Rose.

Vanessa would be facing Rose in eight weeks in Las Vegas. She knew Rose was a tough fighter with hard and powerful punches and beating Rose would take a lot of her energy. On the other hand, Rose wasn't a bit nervous or worried, but confident enough with her experience for this fight because it wasn't going to be for a title fight, but she must still beat Vanessa to advance closer in the rankings to be a top contender.

Rose worked out as usual for the rest of the week to stay in good condition. One thing that kept her focus on her fights was calling Rick three times a week before her fights. She's been communicating with him for the past two months. He would always give her the support she needed, the motivation to continue fighting, and would give her advice on how to counteract the punches and moves by her opponents after she would tell him the type of fighter that she was going against. That helped her build her confidence before the fights.

The weigh-ins was almost the same as the last time when she faced Victoria with their expressions of wanting to beat the hell of one another.

The day finally came, the Saturday Rose has anxiously been waiting for after two months for the fight to happen between her and Vanessa. There were thousands of fanatic boxing fans, professional boxers, male and female, and celebrities who loved following the sport of boxing, especially well-known boxers. The arena was packed almost to capacity and a lot of the crowd had already drunk alcohol like water, anxiously waiting for the fight to begin. Not all fans watched the preliminary fights before the co-main event, but as soon as the main card event was starting, the rest of the crowd rushed to get their seats to watch the event, especially for the co-main event when Rose versus Vanessa and then the headlining main event that will follow.

Simon and Rose were talking as she had her hands wrapped by Simon to help prevent any injuries to the hand. A boxing official stood by them, waiting to apply the initials to the tape as a mandatory ruling in the boxing world. After Simon finished, the official legally signed off the wrapping with his initials and left the room. Simon had Rose throw warm-up punches on the mitts with his assistant trainer Alex to get her adrenaline flowing, loosening up and focused. Simon was confident with her abilities to beat Vanessa. He knew Rose could beat Vanessa if she stayed focused, fighting smart, and listened to him.

Vanessa was already in the ring, prancing back and forth at her corner, waiting for Rose to step into the ring. The crowd booed Vanessa as she paced the ring, but some of her fans cheered and proudly yelled her name. She wore red-hot boxing shorts, and her top matched her shorts. Her hair was a solid black color in a French-braid style, with the length of the hair extending below the back of her neck. And on her right leg on the calf, she had a tattoo of a colorful snake from her Achilles to right below the back of her knee.

It was time for Rose to walk toward the entry of the aisle that led to the ring as she shadowboxed in front of her, keeping herself stimulated to continue her adrenaline flowing. As soon as her mariachi band started playing, the music filled the arena to the liking of the Mexican people, as they yelled out Rose's name and waved their mini-Mexican flags to support their hero. The rumbling sound of her fans, yelling and whistling as loud as they could, knew she would be coming down the aisle. Once she reached the ring, she stepped into the ring as Simon held the ropes wide open for her to climb in. The crowd didn't let up on their yelling and whistling for Rose as she pranced around the ring, waving at her fans. Rose stopped at her corner to get a rose from Simon, and then walked to one side of the ring by the ropes, turned around with her back toward the crowd, and made her traditional throw of a rose to her fans.

After the ring announcer made the introductions for both fighters, the referee had them step to the middle of the ring to explain the brief rules of the fight and told them to always protect yourself at all times. Then he told them to touch gloves and go to their corners, wait for the bell, and wait for his command. The bout was for eight rounds, two minutes each with a minute break between the rounds.

The bell rang and both fighters approached each other, touched gloves, and then started with light jabs, trying to get an idea of how they would deliver the most critical punch of the fight—the knockout punch. Within the minutes into the first round, the light punches had progressed into power punches, making contact and scoring points as the round continued. Rose had landed a few more punches than Vanessa. Rose kept right on her face, not letting up and being the aggressor. Vanessa kept protecting her face as Rose delivered blows to her body and then some combinations, backing Vanessa against the ropes a few times. The referee had to separate them because Vanessa kept clinching her arms around Rose. The referee had them go to the middle of the ring and let them go back to fighting. With ten seconds left in the round, the bell rang right after, ending the first round just as the fight was beginning to get more aggressive. The referee jumped between them to stop the fight as soon as the bell sounded to make sure there would be no more punches thrown after the bell and make sure they went to their corners right after.

When Rose sat down on her corner stool, Simon began his advice to Rose. "Rose, you need to be focused more on her punches. She keeps herself open whenever she throws a combination, then drops her hands down for a few seconds. I want you to look for that chance to hit her with a hard straight punch, but make sure that it's going to connect. I think with your power and speed, you can knock her out. If you see that opening, take it! That's how fast you must do it," said Simon. "Do you understand?"

"Got it!" replied Rose.

The bell rang for the second round and both fighters waited for the referee to give them the sign to start fighting right after the referee said the command, "Box!"

Vanessa charged at Rose, not wasting any time and swinging at Rose with everything she had. She wanted to beat Rose so badly to earn the top contender's respect.

Rose was countering her punches as fast as Vanessa was throwing them. Rose was looking for that opening Simon had told her to watch out for and take that opportunity to knock Vanessa out. She threw some combinations at Vanessa, hoping to get her to do the same. Rose kept scoring with her punches and jabs, and Vanessa was also getting through and connecting for some points. One of Vanessa's punches managed to find an opening and forced Rose to back up a little, but she recovered after moving around from side to side until she got her posture back. Vanessa thought she had her now and continued forward with some combinations, confirming what Simon said. After throwing the combinations for a few seconds, Vanessa dropped her right hand. That's when Rose took Simon's advice and threw that hard straight punch that connected at her nose, sending Vanessa to the canvas. She laid there for a few seconds, looking unlikely to get back up. The referee quickly stepped in front of Rose and told her to go to her corner. Then he started his mandatory ten counts. By his ninth count, Vanessa was barely moving around the mat. She was trying to get up but didn't look like she would make it up by the count of ten. As soon as the referee shouted the tenth count, Rose raised her arms in the air and gave a big smile to her fans as they watched her win another victory and get closer to her championship fight. Simon crawled between the ropes into the ring and rushed toward Rose to hug her. Rose turned around to confront Simon and gave him a big hug.

"You're great! You know that! You did great, and I'm proud of you, Rose," said Simon as he hugged her. Rose held on to Simon for a minute because the announcer was ready to officially announce the winner.

"May I have your attention, please!" The announcer tried to soften the noise in the arena so they could hear him announce the official winner. Then he began, "Ladies and Gentlemen, the referee stopped this contest in one minute, thirty-five seconds in Round 2. Declaring the winner of this bout, Rosalinda 'The Rose' Escobar!" Then the crowd began to raise their voices as loud as they could, yelling out Rose's name repeatedly. She was swarmed with photographers from every corner.

The ring announcer walked up to Rose to get a brief interview with Rose. "Rose! Congratulations on your big win tonight. You have done what you wanted to do to get closer to fighting for a title. How do you feel now?" asked the announcer.

"I feel great!" said Rose. "Viva México!" Rose yells out to her fans and the fans respond with cheers. "Tonight happened like I wanted it to happen; with a win. I want to thank Simon and my team for letting this to happen like it did. Without them, I wouldn't be here tonight."

"When is your next fight and who is it going to be?" asked the MC.

"I have one more fight to win and I'm sure that I will win that one too. It will be my last fight before I will face the ex-champion, and nothing is going to get on my way to get there." These were the last words that Rose made before she exited the ring.

As she walked to her room with the mariachi band playing behind her, the crowd continued yelling out her name with pride and joy; that made Rose feel special, and she wanted to give them the fighter they had been waiting for to become the world champion. Simon wanted to let Rose have a good night's rest after all the activities that went on tonight because he planned to take her on a little tour around Las Vegas. He thought Rose would enjoy having some fun and enjoy the day doing whatever she wanted or enjoy watching some live entertainment.

CHAPTER FORTY

During Rose's fight in Las Vegas, Rose's victory drew the attention of a Las Vegas fighter, Maureen Miller, sitting, watching the fight. She's also a high-ranking fighter who has been waiting to earn her way to the top and become the number one contender to fight the champion. Maureen is one of the most formidable opponents for Rose if she has to face her in the ring. She is known to be a well-shaped and sexy fighter, more like a model, but is as tough as a bull. She goes by her nickname "The Blaze" because she has streaks of blond hair along each side of her temples that stand out like the stripes on the American flag. Her fighting record was fourteen wins and a loss to the ex-champ. She had been fighting since she was eighteen years old just to survive a bunch of wild and crazy girls who lived in her neighborhood.

The schedule of the event with the Blaze happened reasonably fast. There was no thinking about who Rose should fight next. Simon had already planned this event happening because this was the only fight left for Rose to win and winning this fight would make her the top contender to fight for the title against the Vipress, who is now the reigning champion after taking the title from Echo, who is now the ex-champion. The only thing that Rose wanted to do was fight Echo before fighting for the championship title against Vipress. Rose was in position now to fight Echo, even though it would not for the title, since Echo is not the champion, but for a revenge that Rose had been wanting and waiting a long time of facing Echo in the ring to settle a retribution from the past. Rose felt like she was in the best condition that she could be and confidently ready to take on any fighter in her weight class. She knew beating the Blaze would put her in a position to fight Echo. That's why losing wasn't an option for Rose.

The fight was scheduled in Las Vegas as a featured bout because of the popularity of the two fighters. It was a sold-out crowd because they wanted to find out who would be in the ring with the most hated and unlikable ex-champion, Echo, who was recently beaten by another unlikable fighter, now the new world champion, "The Vipress." The fans waited a long time to see someone stomp Echo's ass to the mat, and the Vipress had done it. And now the Vipress was the one to beat. Rose wanted to do the same to Echo; beat her ass to the canvas for the second time but with a little more punishment.

The two fighters were ready for each other, knowing it would not be an easy fight. There were no options but to fight with all they had to earn the respect of a top contender. Rose had to win this fight because it meant the whole world to her and have the chance to get even with Echo. If she loses, her chances of fighting for the title would be disheartening because she would have to start all over by fighting the fighters already rated at the top and waiting to take the place of the fighter who would lose. Rose didn't want this to happen to her. Rose had her mindset on winning because this was the only way she would be able to fight the ex-champ before fighting for the title. Now, the possibility of facing Echo was in place; Once and for all, she could diminish the nightmare that had been haunting her for a long time. But first, Rose had to beat the Blaze.

The months flew by fast, and now there were only three weeks before the event. Rose did not waste a minute of her time training, sweating, building her endurance with new techniques taught by Simon, and studying videos of Blaze's last fights. Rose was determined not to lose.

Rose's team traveled to Las Vegas once again. This time it was more important than the last fight she had with Vanessa. All the fighters for the event on Saturday had their weigh-ins on Friday. Rose and Simon were anxious to get this over. Simon put every minute he had with Rose to make sure that she stayed focused and talked to her about what she had to do to win.

Saturday's final day was here, and both fighters were in their rooms getting ready for the event. Rose stared at Simon as he wrapped her hands with the tape and the official waited to initial the tape. She was thinking about how Simon helped her through everything she had to deal with from the start of her boxing career. He'd been an angel to her, helping her with whatever she needed to succeed and keeping her focus on her passion for boxing. As Simon finished putting on her gloves, after the official put his signatures on the tape, he had her warm-up with his sparring assistant, Alex, and stretched for a few minutes to loosen her up to get her adrenaline flowing. The Blaze was doing the same thing as Rose, preparing herself for the fight because she also knew that this would be the fight of her life.

Shortly after the final preliminary fight had ended, the ring announcer made the next coming attraction, "Ladies and gentlemen, the next fight will be a fight that all of you have been waiting for!" The crowd yelled, whistled, and roared, ready to see an entertaining fight for the night. The fans have been hoping to see Rose step out of the ring with the win. Now, it was time to prepare for the next bout, which was Rose versus the Blaze. It was a non-championship battle, but the fight was expected to be just as good as a championship fight.

The ring announcer began his introductions for the fighters, Rose and Blaze to come to the ring. Shortly, the Blaze walked down the aisle. As soon as the crowd got a glimpse of her, most of them stood up, booed, and yelled names at her with every step she took toward the ring. With her streaked hair shining along each side of her head, the Blaze walked and looked straight ahead, trying to ignore the crowd's comments and screams. She knew she wasn't the favorite, but she was used to it and kept walking toward the ring. There were only a few steps left before reaching the ring when a man tried to grab her by the hand and hit her, but her guards reacted quickly, so he didn't get a chance to do anything to her. The guards slammed the guy to the floor, put the cuffs on him and took him to the security room for questioning. He was very intoxicated and probably didn't know what he was doing. The Blaze got a little shook up but she was surrounded by her staff, making sure that she was protected against any other attempts that might happen again. The Blaze looked around to see if everything was okay so she could proceed to the ring. Her manager checked with the security to clear her path for safety reasons and okayed her path to continue walking to the ring.

This was not a good start for the Blaze. It was the first time that this had happened to her. She settled down once she walked around the ring and the crowd's screaming put her back in focus on the fight.

After the ring announcer briefly stated a little information about the incident, the crowd heard the sound of Mexican music playing, and that's when the crowd burst and roared with cheers, hurrahs, and whistling, knowing that it was the Rose coming down the aisle. As she made her ring walk, Simon was at her side with Alex behind her. She had some security guards following her just in case there would be any trouble like Blaze had on her way to the ring. They were not taking any chances, especially when many of the crowd were a little drunk and could get out of control unexpectedly.

Most of the crowd were Mexicans, but they had followed Rose ever since she first started fighting as a professional in her boxing career. Rose was proud of who she was and fighting for her country of Mexico. That feeling made her adrenaline flow in her body like fast rapids flowing down a wild river, nothing blocking it from slowing down. She was ready for the fight.

The announcer continued with his introduction for the event with the tale of the tape; a brief background of each fighters' weight, height, age, arm reach, and statistics of their career fights they've had wins, loses or knockouts if they had any.

The time had come to find out who would be the last one standing. Now, Rose and Maureen stood face-to-face, staring at each other in the middle of the ring, trying to have the face of a fighter who thinks that losing is not an option, as Maureen tried to intimidate Rose with her smirky smile. They both knew they had to do whatever they had to do to be the winner in the end. The referee read rules about where punches were allowed during the bout and told them to protect themselves at all times. Then he had them step back to their corners until they heard the bell ring. Within a few seconds, the bell rang, and both headed to the middle of the ring.

Blaze charged with her hands protecting her face and ready to cock her glove to Rose's face and deliver her first blow of the night. Then Rose responded with her jabs, backing her up against the ropes. She was being aggressive and not giving Blaze time to think about her next shot. Rose kept jabbing her upper body and hitting her lower body with power punches. Blaze tried to block Rose's punches that kept coming at Rose as if she were hitting a punching bag. Blaze finally escaped by clinching on to Rose's arm to keep her from hitting her. The Blaze had enough strength in her to push Rose back and catch her breath. Rose charged at Blaze again, but this time, Blaze countered with her punches and started countering against Rose with jabs and combinations.

They both threw punches, left, and rights, trying to knock each other out. Rose was getting the best of it. Her punches were connecting more than Blaze. Blaze's left eye was starting to get swollen by all the punches that Rose was throwing and connecting, but Blaze didn't have any trouble seeing as she moved around the ring, trying to get away from Rose. Just as Rose was setting up for her knockout punch, the bell rang, and lucky for Blaze that it did because there was no telling what would've happened if Rose had connected.

They both went to their corners and had time to recover from the fight, especially Blaze, as her cutman worked on her swollen eye with an ice pack and Enswell, a flat cold metal tool applied to the swollen area of the eye and then rubbed Vaseline around her face to keep the glove from gripping her skin when she gets punched.

At Rose's corner, Simon told her to focus on Blaze's left arm. "Watch when she drops her left arm, and as soon as she does, I want you to take a quick and short step to your right and come over with a hard swing and aim for her jaw. She's been dropping her arm more frequently, giving you an open shot at her jaw. She should go down to the canvas with an accurate shot and not get up by the count of ten. You got that?" said Simon.

"Yes, I did," answered Rose.

"Then go out there and show me," said Simon.

The minute was up, and the bell sounded for the second round, and both fighters were back at the center of the ring staring at each other like they were ready for the kill. Rose was being more aggressive this time and started punching Blaze with short and effective jabs and followed with hard punches to her side. The Blaze felt every punch that was being thrown at her as Rose delivered to the upper and lower body. Blaze kept trying to protect herself, but Rose made it hard for her to stop some of the punches. Blaze, with a sudden spurt of energy, shoved Rose outward and leaped toward Rose. Then the Blaze connected with a straight shot on Roses' nose, causing Rose to step back a few steps against the ropes. That's when Blaze rushed toward Rose and tried to take advantage of her punches.

The crowd couldn't believe that Blaze got one of her straight punches to make contact and scoring. Rose protected herself from Blaze's flurry of punches thrown at her, still not believing that she let Blaze find an open shot and hit her smack on her nose. Rose wasn't giving in so easily and wasn't going to let Blaze take advantage of her punches. Rose clinched on to Blazes' arms to slow her down.

Then the referee broke them up. It gave Rose some time to breathe as she regained her composure and started to jab left and rights at Blaze, reversing the scenario. Her nose started bleeding more, and running down her mouth from the punch Blaze smacked her on her nose a few seconds ago, but all Rose could do was wipe it with her shoulder.

Rose was now the one throwing the hard punches and making Blaze back up against the ropes. Rose saw an opening when Blaze kept dropping her left arm and reacted quickly and came up with the short and powerful uppercut and landed on Blaze's jaw. Then with her left, she swung a wild punch to her temple on the other side of her face and sent Blaze to the canvas. The referee stepped in front of Rose and had her go to her corner before starting his mandatory counts. She waited to see if Blaze was going to get back up. Blaze was having a difficult time getting up, grabbing on to the ropes to pick herself up. The referee was at the count of eight as the Blaze tried pulling herself up, using all her energy, but it seemed like she was not going to be entirely up by the count of ten. Simon watched Blaze struggling to get back on her feet and hoping it didn't happen. It seemed unlikely that it would happen before the referee reached the count of ten. Simon was gripping the ropes as tightly as he could, not knowing that he was doing that because all he had on his mind was a significant victory for Rose.

When the referee reached the count of ten, it was too late for Blaze to continue. The fight was over. When Rose heard the referee say the last count, she jumped up and down, knowing that she had won. She raised her arms as high as she could in the air, and the crowd joined her by cheering her on, celebrating her victory with hurrahs and whistling.

At the sound of the bell, Simon jumped into the ring, walked as fast as he could toward Rose, grabbed her around her waist, and lifted her as high as he could. Rose waved to all her fans with pride and saw them honoring her as the winner. Reporters were all around the ring taking pictures and flashes coming from all directions. As soon as Simon put Rose back on the mat, she noticed the reporters waiting to ask her a ton of questions when she leaves the ring.

Her trainers, Simon, and the security guards kept the reporters away from Rose so she could breathe. A question from one of the reporters got her attention, asking about her next fight with the ex-champ and how she plans to beat her.

Rose thought for a few seconds, and then made a statement. "I have been waiting for this chance to settle something personal with Echo that has been with me since the day I started boxing. She is the fighter I will be facing in the ring next, and I can hardly wait for this to happen. If she's here now, I want to tell her this: "I'm going to do everything in my power not to let you forget who I am, and after I punish you, it will stay on your mind for the rest of your life, as it has been in mine.""

As soon as she finished making that statement, Simon took her hand and led her away from the ring. Her fans were still screaming out her name with excitement as she walked down the aisle to her locker and vanished from the crowd's sight.

Rose couldn't remember being as happy as she was tonight, other than the last time when she was with Rob. He will always be in her heart and will never forget him. If he were here, he would be very proud of her for her victory tonight. Winning tonight took her one step closer toward her dream.

It took a long time before the crowd dissipated. Simon and Amy took Rose back to her hotel. Before they left the arena, Simon had a long talk with Rose in the dressing room about her next fight with the ex-champ. As she listened to him, she felt proud to be with Simon and felt lucky that she had met him as her trainer.

The night came to an end when they got back to the hotel. When she walked into her room, she went straight to the shower, put on her nightgown, climbed into her bed, and fell asleep within a few minutes. She was exhausted from all the activities that went on tonight.

CHAPTER FORTY-ONE

The following morning at 8:00 a.m., Simon had room service sent to Rose's room with a special hot and fruity breakfast. Rose wasn't aware that Simon was going to do that for her this morning, so when she heard a knock on the door, it startled her. She was afraid to open the door or ask who it was. It wasn't until she heard the voice of a hotel staff member said loudly, "Room service!" That made Rose feel better. She then opened the door and let him in. The guy rolled in a cart with lids covering some sort of breakfast surprise and a pot of coffee next to it. She notices a note next to the covered dish and a red rose lying on top of the note. The guy was walking toward the door after he parked the food cart next to the TV when he heard Rose tell him to wait a minute. Then she went to her purse to get a tip for the guy and gave it to him. She quickly opened the note, anxious and curious to read it out loud:

Rose,

"Thank you for your hard work and for making me proud of you. You have been an inspiration to my boxing career, and I don't know of any female boxer who has as much dedication to boxing as you do. I do not doubt that you will be the next female world boxing champion. Keep up the excellent work."

Your one and only trainer,
Simon

When she finished reading the note, she had tears flowing from her eyes because it made her a little emotional. This meant a lot to her, giving her more incentive to continue what she loves doing. She had eaten most of her breakfast when she heard another knock on the door. It was Simon and Amy checking on her. The first thing Rose did when she opened the door and saw Simon and Amy, she reached out to Simon and hugged him and not saying a word. Then she hugged Amy. Rose got emotionally and teary eyes, a sign of a happy fighter. Then Amy reached out to Rose again and hugged her to congratulate her on her victory.

"Hey, Rose," said Simon. "Amy and I want to take you out to the strip and have some fun today and tomorrow and not think about boxing until we get back to LA. Is that okay with you?"

"Sure. That sounds like fun, and I think I need to do that. Let me put on some comfortable clothes. Just give me a few minutes, and then we can start our fun, okay?" said Rose.

"We'll be waiting for you at the lobby so you can get dressed and meet us there, okay? Take your time. We have all day." Simon smiled at Rose when he said it.

While Rose was changing clothes in her room, Simon got a call from Jimmy. Simon answers quietly, knowing what he was expecting Jimmy to say.

"Everything is good, and I'll see you when Rick and I get to LA. I can't wait," said Jimmy.

Simon replied, "Me too!" and hung up. Amy looked at Simon, wondering what was going on with the conversation that Jimmy had with Simon. He looked at Amy when he hung up the phone and told her, "I'll tell you later. It's a surprise that I have planned for Rose when we get back to Los Angeles."

"Okay," said Amy. "But don't forget to tell me."

The weekend they spent in Las Vegas was exciting and fun for all of them. Rose had a great time looking at various places, enjoying the entertainment, and gambling some of her money, which she liked doing, but she had to discipline herself not to get carried away with her money.

They had reservations to fly back to Los Angeles on Monday morning and arrive by 10:00 a.m. When they arrived in Los Angeles, they were tired, and all they wanted to do was relax and sleep for a little while before going out for dinner at the restaurant where Simon had made reservations. Rose didn't know that Simon had a surprise for her that evening. He had arranged for Jimmy and Rick to meet them at a restaurant near where they lived. He had been working on Jimmy and Rick's visa cards for the past two months and finally got both approved for a year with the help of his attorney. This was going to be a shocker for Rose. She would not know what to do when she first sees them at the restaurant. This would be one of the best surprises she would ever get and a memory in her life that she would probably never forget.

When Simon, Amy, and Rose arrived at the restaurant that evening, Rose was still excited about her victory. She talked about the fight during the drive from the apartment to the restaurant. Simon just let her talk his ears off because he liked seeing her happy. As soon as they walked into the restaurant, Simon inquired about the reservation that he had made.

"Oh yes!" said the hostess. "Please follow me to your table. I believe you already have some guests sitting at the table waiting for you."

It was good that Rose was busy talking to Amy, so she didn't hear what the hostess just said to Simon because she would have questioned it. When they got close to their table, Rose noticed two guys sitting there. Rose was a little confused when the hostess pointed to their table because it was already taken. But when she saw Jimmy and Rick look at her, she stopped and couldn't believe that it was them sitting there, here in the United States.

Jimmy and Rick stood up and looked at Rose with a big grin on their faces. Her hands immediately covered her mouth and shocked as she stood there while Jimmy and Rick walked toward her to embrace her. Rose was still in shock and couldn't believe that they were here as she saw them walking toward her. Jimmy was the first to hug Rose and kissed her on her cheek. Rick waited for Jimmy to finish hugging her so he could embrace her. Then it was his turn to hug her. Before he did, Rose looked at him straight in his eyes, gave him a big smile, reached out with her arms, wrapped them around his neck and kissed him on his lips. Rick anticipated her kisses, and they embraced each other for a few minutes as Simon and Jimmy watched.

Simon finally intervened and asked them to take a break. "So, now we can all sit down and talk for a while," he said it with a smile as he turned his head from side to side, knowing they were in love.

This night was a night she would never forget. As soon as they all finished talking and eating dinner, they stood up from their chairs, feeling stuffed from overeating food. They said a few more words before finally saying good night to each other as they walked to their cars and left the restaurant.

Jimmy and Rick had gotten a room in a nearby hotel, but Rick ended up going home with Rose to spend the night with her. Before going to sleep, Rick whispered in Rose's ear and spoke to her, "It's great to be back with you. I have thought about you back home, and I missed you so much."

"That's nice of you, Rick. And I missed you too. I'm glad you're here with me," responded Rose. And then Rose turned her back against Rick's body, closed her eyes, and fell asleep. Rick held his arm over her shoulder, holding her snugly to him, and fell asleep.

CHAPTER FORTY-TWO

The dream was becoming a reality for Rose. After training for four months, the event with Echo would happen within a few weeks. The thought of facing Echo in the ring one day had been the fight that was tattooed on her brain since day one of her fighting career. Her retribution would now be in the ring once she came face-to-face with Echo. Her name had been haunting Rose for a very long time. Rose is making sure she puts a closure on this chapter in her life after she punishes and beats Echo in front of all her fans, which wasn't many, and the audience that have been looking forward to Echo getting beaten again. There were now two weeks left before she was going to meet her nightmare. She trained rigorously harder than she had ever done before to make sure there was no way Rose was going to let Echo, walk away with her dream. Now she had Si-mon, Jimmy, and Rick by her side to make sure she was going to be in the utmost and best condition she had ever been.

For the rest of the week, Rose worked on her moves because Echo was a fighter who moved around the ring a lot and will try to sneak illegal blows by hiding them from the referee. She would try anything to win, whether it was legal or not, and try to get away with it, just like she did with her past opponents.

Jimmy and Simon worked together to make a strategic plan to counteract Echo's moves. Simon had gone to see the fight between the Vipress and Echo in the Las Vegas arena for the world title championship. That's when Echo got her first loss and lost her world title belt. The Vipress gave her a rough time for the first three rounds and punished her in the next two rounds. With only a minute left in the sixth and last round, the Vipress shot an unexpected punch on Echo's jaw, making contact and sending her butt to the canvas. She never recovered fast enough to continue the fight. She was dazed, and it took her a few more minutes before she recovered after the bell rang, but she was all right.

Simon had a better idea of Echo's techniques and moves after seeing her fight the Vipress. Observing the event helped him prepare Rose for the fight. He got Jimmy and Rick to help him with his new plans and execute the new moves to help Rose win the fight.

There was one more week left to work with Rose and prepare her for the fight. Rose was totally focused on the fight. She didn't do too much with Rick in her spare time that had to do with entertaining because she didn't want to be distracted or interfere with her training. Rick was understanding and knew what she had to do, and he admired her for doing it. He wanted her to win this battle to give her peace of mind and satisfaction, but mostly, revenge.

Jimmy and Rick worked hard to get Rose in the condition that Simon wanted her to be for this fight with all the training they put into Rose. Her condition was more incredible than ever before, and she moved around the ring like no other female boxer could do. Her power punches were more powerful than before, and her speed increased tremendously than ever. She was ready for Echo, and she felt very confident with herself.

The media surrounded the ring every time she was training and asking her questions about her coming fight with Echo if she was ready or feared losing to Echo. The reporters were impressed with her training, seeing no problem of beating Echo. The stories of Rose were mentioned right after the reporters got an interview with Rose in the sports page of newspapers. Her name was talked about and mentioned every other day in the headlines of the sports section. Echo, meanwhile, read the sports section every day to see if anything was said about her. All she read were articles about Rose, which infuriated Echo, and that's when she started to get angry with the media for not saying anything good about her. The only time she saw her name was when Rose commented that she had been looking forward to fighting Echo for a long time, and now she was going to settle and erase a bad memory that had been haunting her for a long time. It was more of a personal grudge with Echo.

The fight was just around the corner, and both fighters had done all they could to prepared for that night. Rose was going into the ring to settle a personal grudge, and Echo wanted to get back to being the top contender to have a rematch with the champion and try to get her title back.

CHAPTER FORTY-THREE

The T-Mobile Arena in Las Vegas was almost a complete sellout for the co-featured fight—Rose versus Echo. Even though they weren't the main attraction, they were the ones who brought most of the crowd to the arena. They had a men's middleweight title fight as the main attraction. Many people attending the fight were fans who knew and followed Rose from the start when she was well-known and up to the day when she was set to fight Echo for the world title. Rose never had the chance to face Echo in the ring because of the tragedy that happened to her and Rob. Rose was getting ready to face her most hated fighter in the world. Jimmy and Rick were at her side while Simon ensured everything was going as planned with the fight.

While Rick wrapped her tape around her hands, Rose looked at him like she used to look at Rob and reminded her of when Rob used to do that. The longer he did it, the more she thought of Rob. Rick spoke to her with a soft tone of voice, telling her not to worry and that she would be the one with the win. Rose listened to him and just stared at him as he talked to her, barely hearing what Rick was saying because her thoughts were with the memory of Rob for a few seconds. That's when Rick looked up at her and noticed something was wrong. He asked her if she was all right.

The minute he heard Rick ask her if she was all right, she snapped out of her trance and said, "Yes! I'm all right." She knew that she had to focus on the fight.

"What were you thinking?" asked Rick.

"I was…" Then she paused and didn't want to say anything to him about what she was really thinking about. "I was thinking about the fight. Today is the day for me." Then she looked at Rick and said, "Thank you, Rick, so much for being here with me. I love you. I'm glad you're here."

Rick replied, "I love you too, Rose."

She had not yet stopped thinking about Rob, but she knew inside her heart that she had to, or else she would be less likely to succeed. She scooted down a little toward the edge of the bed table, just inches from Rick and hugged him for a few seconds. Then she wiggled her butt slowly back where she was before. He wasn't sure why she had done this right now, but for now, he just wanted her to focus and win this fight because he knew it meant a lot to her. The official was there to mark the initials on the tape as soon as Rick was done wrapping her hands. Rick then put Roses' gloves on her as soon as the official initialed the tape and then put his practice punching mitts to have Rose get her adrenaline built up for the fight.

A few minutes after warming up, Simon walked into her room with a single fresh, long-stemmed red rose. He gave it to Rose and said, "Here, Rose, this is for you. I know you've been waiting for this moment, and it seemed like a long time for you, but this rose will remind you of your dream, why you're here today and deserve to be here. I know, and you know, that it's been a struggle for you to get to this point, but again, you never gave up your dream. I'm very proud of you." Simon gives her a hug and kiss on her cheek.

With that said, Rose got a little teary. "Thank you so much, Simon. This is my dream come true." She wiped away the tears from her eyes.

"Now I want you to go out there and kick her ass but think smart because she's going to try to do the same thing to you. Just beat her to the punch. Okay!" said Simon. "You have about ten minutes before you go out there." Simon made sure she was ready to step out to the aisle with a positive attitude and fearless walk to the ring to face her nightmare, a long and waiting retribution that had lingered in her mind for a long, long time. And today was that day.

Echo's real name was Jalali Quanzi. She came from Central America, a small Costa Rica country, and was known in the US as Echo. She'd been fighting for over four years and had the reputation of being the dirtiest fighter in several states. She had a 14–1 record, with eight straight knockouts, until she lost her title to the Vipress last year. She managed to use her headbutts to hurt her opponents when the referee couldn't see her execute them. Some of the fighters even refused to be in the same ring with her because they didn't want to risk getting injured and being unable to fight again. Other boxers hated her so much that they wanted to get into the ring with her just to beat the hell out of her and put her out of commission. But so far, only one fighter, the Vipress, has pounded her ass on the canvas and taken away her title. Today, she must beat Rose to earn the right to fight for the title as the top contender.

Simon had gotten the mariachi band ready to play her favorite tune as soon as she was prepared to start walking down the aisle right after they announced Echo to make her walk to the ring. Echo began her ring walk and as soon as the crowd got a glimpse of her, you could hear them booing loudly and yelling profane names at her. She walked down the aisle with a stoic look, showing no sign of fear because she saw herself as a fearless fighter, without any guilt for what she was planning to do to Rose. She wore a black robe and a hood that covered her head, displaying a red lightning bolt embroidered on an angle, symbolizing her strikes.

A few minutes later, after Echo had entered the ring, Simon had the mariachi band start playing Roses' favorite Mexican music theme. Rose got in front of the band and started walking to the ring. Rose felt like she was going to walk for a mile before getting there. The band continued playing as loud as they could and followed Rose down the aisle to the ring as she walked with her arms raised over her head, waving to the crowd and her fans, feeling proud and supported by her fans. Her music stimulated her adrenaline and made her feel at home.

Rick held the ropes spread apart to let Rose pass and enter the ring between the ropes. Simon was inside the ring already and waiting for Rose. She hugged Simon first and then turned to Rick and did the same. She carried a rose to throw to her fans as she walked to one side of the ring and threw the rose at a random spot as the fans reached out to catch it; A tradition the fans loved every time she did that and always waited for her to throw it.

The ring announcer started the introductions for both fighters. As usual, as soon as he mentioned Echo's name, the crowd booed loudly again to let her know she wasn't the favorite in this ring. Then he said Rose's name, and the crowd went wild, clapping, yelling her name, and whistling. After the introduction with the tale of the tape, the referee had the fighters meet at the center of the ring to go over the rules of the fight. When he finished, he told the fighters to always protect themselves at all times, and then told them to touch gloves as a respectful customary for fighters to do, but this wasn't going to happen between Rose and Echo. The referee then told them to go to their corners and wait for the bell to ring and his command to box. Within seconds, the bell sounded, and both fighters confronted each other with punches, and you could see the hatred in their eyes, wanting to tear each other apart.

Echo got in Rose's face and said something to her that caused Rose to push her back. The referee saw what Rose did, so he warned Rose not to do it again. They went back to punching each other and throwing everything they had, trying to knock out each other with a lucky punch. Rose backed away from Echo just to get a feel of what Echo was planning to do. Rose kept jabbing at Echo's upper body with combinations, trying to set up a hard straight punch, hoping to land one for a knockout. Echo countered when she was able because Rose was aggressive with her punches. This continued during the first round with Rose dominating the round.

Simon and Jimmy talked to Rose during the one-minute break about what she should do next since she did very well in the first round. Simon wanted her to set her up again, but this time in a southpaw position, then find an opening with a fake punch when she falls for it and swings, but make sure she misses you, and then throw your power punch when you see the opening with all you got and let her have it. If she's not falling for it, get close enough to come up with an uppercut and connect it to her jaw. "If that doesn't work, I want you to punch her in the gut with your left to get Echo to lower her arms, and when she does, come around with your right with all your power and connect her temple or behind her ear. Do you think you can do that? Because that's what I want you to do," said Simon. "Your timing is crucial for this punch. Just look for the right opening."

"Okay," said Rose.

Rose listened to Simon's plan but had already decided to do something else. She was going to do what Simon wanted her to do, but not immediately. She wanted to punish Echo as much as she could before ending the fight. She was going to make sure that Echo wouldn't forget her name and stay in her memory forever.

The bell rang for the second round and both fighters returned like they did the first round, throwing their punches with all they had. Echo looked more aggressive this time and Rose felt her power punches. Rose was the one protecting herself this time, covering up her face and backing away from Echo. That's when Echo tried to headbutt Rose. You could hear Simon, Jimmy, and Rick yelling at Rose to move around and look for a straight shot.

Rose finally broke away from Echo's punches and began throwing punches and jabs with some combinations. Rose connected a hard punch to her side, and then hit her with a hard right to her jaw. Echo felt that and quickly put her gloves in front of her face to protect herself. As Echo backed up against the ropes, Rose kept hitting her, pounding, and pounding as much as she could to punish her. Simon could see it in her eyes and knew what her intentions were, but he was afraid that she might get too careless and let Echo slip in a hard punch.

The referee got in between them because Echo clinched her arms around Rose to keep her from throwing more punches at her and slowing her down. The bell ended the second round, leaving Echo with a bloody nose and a small cut on her left eye from all the punches Rose had given her.

When Rose went to her corner, Simon looked at Rose and wanted to smile, but he knew what was going on in the ring, so he had to keep it serious.

"Rose, you're doing well out there. Keep up what you were doing. Just be cautious of her moves and stay alert. I don't want you to be surprised with an unexpected punch. Do you understand?" Simon said. "Don't forget what I asked you to do the last round."

"I know," said Rose. Rick looked at Rose and then at Simon as if they were up to something he didn't know.

"Here, Rose, take a little drink before you return," said Rick.

The bell rang to start the third round. Echo came out swinging at Rose, backing her against the ropes as Rose countered her punches, finding her way out. They both started throwing harder punches and getting closer to each other, trying to connect a good hard punch. Rose kept using her left and right jabs, following with combinations, and scoring points because they were landing hard on Echo's face. Rose was being more aggressive and stayed in front of Echo's face so she could see Rose punishing her. Rose kept pushing Echo against the ropes talking to her and telling her not to forget what I'm doing to you now, trying not to let her go so Rose could continue to punish her. Simon kept looking at Rose and knew what she was doing.

"Don't let her go!" yelled Simon.

Echo clinched her arms around Rose again, holding on to her so the referee would break them up, which he did. When they went back to fighting, Rose turned her head when she heard Simon say something to her. Echo took advantage of that split second, hit Rose as hard as possible, and sent her to the canvas.

The referee jumped in front of Echo and told her to go back to her corner. Rose was close enough to the ropes that she grabbed them and pulled herself up. The crowd was silent for a few seconds until they saw Rose getting up slowly. She waited for the eighth count to buy some time to catch her breath. The referee checked Rose to ensure she was all right to continue. He was convinced and let her continue fighting. That was the first time that Rose has been knocked down on the mat. She was aware of what she did wrong-always protect yourself at all times.

That irritated Rose. Her adrenaline kicked in and looked for an opportunity to throw a punch that will knock Echo out. She moved around the ring to give herself some time to catch her breath. She was ready to finish the fight, but she heard the bell as she was prepared to deliver her punch. The referee stopped the fight. Now she had to wait until the next round to finish Echo for good.

Rose didn't talk much in her corner because she knew what Simon was thinking.

"Listen, Rose!" said Simon. "That was just a lucky punch that she gave you, but you were strong enough to get right back in front of her face. If you had one extra minute in the round, I know you would have knocked her out. Now it's your time to finish her, got that?" said Simon. "Go kick her ass to the mat, and let's go home. Show her that you're not just an opponent but a true champion."

"You bet I will!" said Rose.

The bell rang for the fourth round and Rose had no other thoughts than putting Echo's ass to the mat. They didn't waste any time trying to kill each other as Echo went in swinging wildly and Rose fought back bravely. Echo was trying to headbutt Rose, but Rose was sharp and fast enough to see it coming and moved quickly to one side to dodge Echos' plan. When Echo tried to headbutt her again, Rose leaned to one side, tightened her right glove, and delivered it straight punch to Echo's nose, making a direct contact. The power behind the punch sent Echo to the mat, and you could see her eyes dazed from the shot as she went down and landed on her back, not moving a muscle.

The crowd rose from their seats, yelling and screaming, hoping that Echo would not get back up. The referee stepped in front of Rose and told her to go to her corner. As soon as she did, the referee started his mandatory count. Echo was struggling to get up as the referee continued his count. When he reached the sixth count, the crowd yelled out the counts with the referee, still hoping that Echo wouldn't get back up.

Rose looked on, wishing for the same. When the referee reached the count of nine and Echo still seemed dazed, Rose knew then that she wouldn't make it up in time. She heard the bell ring. It was all over. She had done what she wanted to do. She fell to her knees and put her gloves over her head, and tears started to flow down her cheeks as she sat squatted on the back of her legs, knees to the mat. This was the most glorious and victorious day of her life. Simon, Jimmy, and Rick made their way into the ring to embrace Rose for her victorious win. The crowd roared as loud as they could with cheers and hurrahs coming from all around the arena. Her Mexican music started playing full blast, making her fans proud as they waved their min-Mexican flags from side to side.

The announcer waited a few minutes for the crowd to settle down so he could make his official winner announcement. It took him about another five minutes before he could say what he needed to so the crowd could hear him announce the winner. As soon as he made the official announcement of the winner, the crowd continued celebrating Rose's victory with cheers, yelling out her name, "Rose! Rose! Rose!" repeatedly.

The MC had Rose go to the middle of the ring to talk to her.

"Congratulations Rose. Once again. You did what you wanted to do and came out with a win. How do you feel now?"

"I feel great and honestly, this is the best fight of my life. This is the one that I have been looking forward to fighting. And I am very satisfied with the result. I have never been so happy as I am tonight. I have accomplished half of my dream, and now I will face the champion when that day comes, and I will prevail to get the title for Simon, my team, and my country of Mexico."

"Well, good luck to you Rose, and the fans here and around the world, will be looking forward to that day when you'll be facing the champion for the title."

Echo remained in her corner with her manager and trainers because she was still recuperating from the hard blow that Rose gave her. Rose walked toward her and thanked her for the fight, even though they both knew it was just a customary and respectful thing to do for their opponents. Echo was still dazed and barely knew where she was, but she recognized Rose when she saw her standing in front of her. Rose looked at Echo as she thanked her for the fight, but Echo didn't respond to what Rose had just said to her. Echo ignored Rose by looking down on the mat. She was so upset that she had lost to Rose. This was a nightmare for Echo because now she had to live with it, which was a reality for her.

Rick stepped out of the ring to get something for Rose. When he jumped back into the ring, he brought Rose a large bouquet of roses and surprised her when he gave them to her. Rick handed the bouquet to Rose. She reached out to give Rick a big hug and a kiss. After all the hugging, Rose pulled out a single rose from her bouquet, turned her back to the crowd, and threw it to them, just like always, as her traditional thing with all her fights. Shortly after, they all got their things from their corner and walked back to her dressing room so she could change into her regular clothes.

The night ended, and half of her dream had been fulfilled by beating Echo. And now, being the top contender for the title, the only fight left will be against the world champion title holder, the Vipress. By winning this fight, she would finally fulfill her dream of becoming a world champion, but she knew it wasn't going to be an easy fight.

CHAPTER FORTY-FOUR

Three months had passed, and Rose never stopped training her heart out every day for at least three hours a day, except on Sunday. She felt confident with her physical conditioning and preparations for thc most rewarding fight of her life. She knew that beating Echo and putting closure to her nightmare had fulfilled only half of her dream. The final thing she wanted to do for her people in Mexico was to give them what they had been waiting for—someone they could be proud of and call their hero. Rose was going to fulfill their wish by wearing the world championship title belt around her waist.

The negotiations took place about a week after the fight with Echo. The promotors wanted this event to happen, knowing that it would be one of the best fights in history when they clash in front of thousands of people in the arena and thousands watching the fight on TV. They didn't want to waste any time letting the fans know that Rose versus the Vipress, the current champion, is going to happen soon. The promotions had started with a great headliner to feature one of the best and epic fights, Rose versus the Vipress, for a world championship battle. It was drawing the attention to all the boxing fans across the country and the world. The promoters are expecting a complete sellout at the MGM Arena in Las Vegas. Fans were already talking about the event and how it was going to be an epic fight of the year.

Another three months passed as Rose stayed on an intensity training regimen like Simon wanted, building her strength, speed, and endurance, besides the footwork. He built her defensive strategy and tactics to use against the Vipress.

There were conferences that were televised on the sports channels interviewing both fighters, listening to the bad mouth of the Vipress who was putting down Rose as just being an amateur compared to her. With all that being said, the interviews were the intention to promote the fight and build the hatred between them and excite the fans to see the war between Rose and the champion head-to-head in the ring. Simon had gone to see the Vipress fight Echo, but it was for Echo's moves, but at the same time, he remembered the skills that the Vipress had and figured out how Rose could outdo the Vipress and get the win. He had Rick train Rose for those moves over and over, plus found other ways to bring the Vipress down. The Vipress was the toughest fighter Rose had ever encountered before she would face Echo for the title. Echo was the champion during that time until Vipress beat her about ten months ago. All this happened during the time Rose had been in Mexico, recuperating and healing the wounds from the gunshot incident.

The Vipress had become a much better but dirtier fighter than she used to be. This was going to be a real challenge for Rose, and she knew it, but the longer she thought about it, the more confident she felt with the fight, making her feel stronger and fearless with the help of Rick and Jimmy.

Two weeks prior to the fight in Vegas, Rose, Simon, Amy, and Rick had planned on going to Vegas next Tuesday to get settled in their hotel room and prepare for the fight on Saturday. They arrived in Vegas on Tuesday as planned and got settled into their hotel rooms to relax and enjoy the day as a pleasurable day. The last two days, Rose worked out in the gym for an hour and ran for two miles each day. It kept her conditioned and her mind focused on her fight.

On Friday, Rose went to her weigh-in and was at her official weight class to fight. The Vipress was there too, and she was also at her weight, but weighed five ounces more than Rose. The stares they gave each other at the weigh-ins when they posed for the news media was like two bull dogs facing each with steam coming out of their ears, but the Vipress was the only one with a smirky facial expression, ready to tear Rose apart, but couldn't do anything until tomorrow. Saturday was the night when they would meet in the ring to release their adrenaline, and both were more than ready to kick some ass.

Later that day, when it was time to go to sleep, Rose was having a hard time falling asleep. Rick had fallen asleep, which didn't take him very long because he was so tired of walking all day, but Rose was tossing and turning, thinking of tomorrows' activities. Her mind was overwhelmed with her thoughts for tomorrow's fight. Rose decided to get out of bed and drink some water. *I beat her before and I can beat her again,* Rose whispered to herself and paced in the bedroom and into the kitchenette. She kept questioning herself about how the fight was going to end, if she would be the one with the championship belt strapped around the waist. This was not a good night for Rose to be thinking about the prediction of the results.

Rick suddenly opened his eyes and noticed how Rose was pacing the floor in the bedroom and back from the kitchenette. He finally had to intervene as she came back from the kitchenette looking as though something was bothering her and worried. Rick couldn't wait any longer to find out what was going through her mind. So, he jumped out of bed and stepped in front of her to find out what was going through her mind. When he stopped her, he put his hands on her shoulders, staring into her eyes, not saying anything to her. Then he asked her, "Rose, what's bothering you? I know there's something wrong," he paused and then waited for her to answer him.

Rose answered him. "I'm having a fear of losing, and I can't bear losing. What if this happens? Then what? I failed my fans, my country, you, and Simon. There's a lot of meaning in this fight. I can't lose." She leaned her head on Rick's chest with her arms around his neck. Rick comforted her and distracted her from thinking about what was bothering her. He then kissed her and told her how beautiful she looked. Rose held Rick snuggly, listening to him.

"You know what, Rose? I have a good feeling about tomorrow. I think you're going to have the best day of your life. I think you'll be stepping out of the ring as a world champion. A huge victorious night and fulfilling your dream. How's that for encouragement?"

"Thank you for thinking highly of me. That was very thoughtful of you," said Rose.

"I think you should lie down and get a good night's sleep. Tomorrow is going to be a hectic day for you. A lot of interaction is going to take place, and you need to be ready for it," said Rick. "You need to relax and get some rest. Everything is going to be all right. Believe me, it will. Simon has told me that you've fought the Vipress once before and beat her. That tells me that you can beat her again."

"I know I can," said Rose, assuring herself that she could.

Rose held on to Rick as he snuggled her in his arms, which made her feel comfortable and loved. It made her start feeling relaxed and sleepy.

"I think you're right, my love. Thank you for being here with me. I'm starting to feel sleepy. Can you keep holding on to me until I fall asleep?" as Rose held Rick tighter against her body.

"I sure will. Let's get back in bed."

Then they went to the bedroom and lay next to each other. The rest of the night, Rick held on to Rose as they both fell asleep snuggled next to each other.

The first thing in the morning, Rose woke up feeling great, thanks to Rick for making her feel ready for the day. Rose jumped out of bed as Rick lay asleep like a log and snoring a bit, and not moving a muscle when she got out of bed. Rose made some coffee for herself and read the morning paper, waiting for Rick to wake up to have a conversation about the day's activities. After having 30 minutes of quietness and tranquility, while reading the paper, Rose laid the paper down on the coffee table and saw Rick standing in front of the bed scratching his head with his hair sticking straight up like a porcupine.

"Good morning, my love," said Rose as she approached Rick in her pajamas to give him his cup of coffee and a lovely morning kiss and hug.

"Good morning, sweetie," answered Rick.

Rose felt less stressed, and Rick noticed how she moved gracefully around the room. "Why don't you put on some comfortable clothes, and let's go out and have a nice breakfast this morning!" said Rick. "I'll get dressed and we can go out."

"I need to go for a run and stretch this morning," answered Rose.

"That can wait. It won't hurt to skip just today for an hour or so. Then you can burn off what you eat." He smiled and laughed softly.

"Well, okay! I guess I could do that. Just this once. Just for you, okay?" And then she kissed him on his cheek and went to her bedroom to put on some comfortable clothes.

When she finished getting ready for breakfast, she asked Rick, "Hey, you know what? I forgot about Simon, Amy, and Jimmy. Aren't we going to ask them if they want to come with us?"

"I thought about that, but I think we should have some time for ourselves this morning, and then after the fight, we can all go out and celebrate your title and dream," said Rick. "I'll call Simon and let him know what we're going to do this morning, so they won't get worried. Okay?"

"Okay! I think that's a good idea, Rick. Thank you!"

After about an hour and a half and having a nice hot breakfast, although Rose didn't want to overeat because of her fight, they returned to the hotel. They talked for a while before Rose told Rick that she needed to start getting ready for her fight, even though it wasn't going to start for another six hours. She wanted to go out for a short run and do some stretching before going to the ring.

CHAPTER FORTY-FIVE

The big day and the time had come, the moment Rose had been waiting for the last few hours, but now it was just two hours away for a reality of a dream to happen to her. It had been one hell of a journey for Rose. With all the adversities that crossed her path, she never gave up or let any obstacles hold her back. Her determination, endurance, and all the support from her fans, who believed in Rose, made it all possible. But all the credit leaned toward Simon, who took her under his umbrella and trained her to be who she is now, and today, she must prove to the world, especially her country, that she deserves to be the world champion.

Jimmy and Rick were busy getting Rose ready for her fight. They were now just a little over an hour away from the main event of the night. Jimmy told her to start warming up and follow up with ten minutes of shadow boxing. Rick got all the things ready for Rose's ring corner with water, cold packs, towels, and other necessary items for cuts, bruises, or swollen eyes. Simon waited to talk to Rose after she warmed up so he could refresh Rose about some important details about the Vipress.

"Rose, I want you to be consciously aware of some of the things to keep in mind about what the Vipress will be trying to do to you. The Vipress is not going to be an easy fight," Simon tells her, and Rose knew it. "I've seen her fights the last couple of times. You must be smarter, and I know you're a better boxer than she is, so I want you to listen to me very carefully when I tell you to do something because I'm your eyes watching her moves. You got that Rose?"

Rose stared and listened closely to what he was saying. "Yes, I do," said Rose.

"The Vipress is not the same fighter who you fought the first time because she picked up some other illegal punches that she used to punish her opponents. In other words, she got worse than Echo. Watch out for her left hand because she tends to hold her opponents from behind the head on purpose, and punches the opponents' faces when she gets the chance, hiding it from the referee. She'll try to do this repeatedly if she can and as long as the referee doesn't catch her. Do you understand Rose? Just do what we trained you to do."

"Yes, I do," replied Rose.

"Just go out there and put her ass on the mat like you did Echo. I would love to see you do that again," then Simon and Rose chuckled for a minute. "Finish getting ready and show them, the crowd, who the real champion will be at the end."

The arena was a complete sellout and all you could hear was the crowd roaring and waiting for the fights to begin. This was going to be one of the most exciting, entertaining, and biggest fights they've had in a long time because it was a female title fight, and there weren't too many like these fights, headlining as the main event.

Winning this fight for Rose was going to complete her dream. She had worked rigorously with her training and gone through intensive workouts to get here with the help of Jimmy, Simon, and Rick. They made sure that she was physically conditioned to go the distance without having her run out of energy halfway through the bout. She had shown a slight weakness with her conditioning when she fought Echo. That's why they were concerned, so they focused on this matter.

The preliminary fights had ended, and the main card had begun. Meanwhile, Rose and the Vipress were getting ready and warming up with their trainers, waiting for their time to come. Rose would be the first one to enter the ring this time since she was the challenger. Then the champ, the Vipress, would make her entrance right after Rose stepped into the ring.

Three fights had already been fought in the main card, with two ending with a knockout and the other with a split decision. Now there was only the co-featured bout before the main event. Meanwhile, both fighters continued preparing for their fight. They were thinking that she was the one that would be stepping out of the ring with the championship belt, but the Vipress was the one that had the most pressure because she had to defend her title and didn't want to lose her world title championship belt, especially to Rose.

The crowd started roaring deafeningly, meaning the co-event was over. Then there was an announcement overheard stating the fight had ended with an unanimous decision. The fights were only scheduled for eight rounds. For the main event, it was scheduled for ten two-minute rounds with a minute break between each round.

Simon stepped out of the room to make sure that the mariachi band was there and ready for Rose the minute she stepped at the beginning of the aisle to do her ring walk. Simon had ordered some roses for Rose, and it just happened that the florist just got there in time to give Simon the bouquet of six roses. He took out one long-stemmed red rose from the bouquet because it was the one she would carry to the ring, so she could throw it out to her fans. This time, he changed the tradition. He got six red roses instead of just one. He wanted her to do something different.

Simon walked into the room with the six red roses and gave one to Rose. She was surprised because he normally brings just one red rose.

"This time, I ordered you six red roses since this will be the biggest fight in your life, not counting the fight with Echo. I thought you might want to throw more than one rose to your fans. It will give them something to remember you by and cheer about, so they will never forget this fight," said Simon.

"Great idea, Simon!" said Rose. "Thank you. These are so beautiful. And the fresh-cut roses having an aromatic fragrant scent smell, as always," said Rose. "You are too sweet, Simon," commented Rose. Then she gave Simon a thank you hug. "I'll make you proud and get you the title belt. I promise. Just for you, Simon."

Rose was in the best condition that she could ever be. With her training from Jimmy and Rick, she accelerated her speed, moved a lot faster, and delivered harder punches. In her mind, she was ready for the Vipress. Her fears from last night had disappeared after Rick helped her forget her worries about losing her fight today. She felt strong, confident, and optimistic about winning this fight. Her body was filled with an adrenaline rush, determination, and stamina, ready to kick the Vipress's ass.

It was time for Rose to enter the ring. Simon helped Rose put on her robe, which had an embossed red rose with her name written arched over the red rose. It was the one that Rob had given her. Simon had the mariachi band start playing her tune when they got in front of the band. As soon as the crowd heard the Mexican music, the crowd burst out cheering and yelling her name. Then she started the ring walk down the aisle, waving at her fans as she walked proud about who she was and represented Mexico. Almost everyone in the arena was standing up. Rick carried the flowers behind her until she got into the ring, then he gave them to her and snuck a kiss on her lips for good luck.

She walked around the ring and tossed the red roses, one by one, at each side of the ring. She kept one for Rick to hold on to until the end of the fight. As she walked around the ring, she noticed that Echo was sitting ringside, front row, opposite her corner. Echo stared at Rose like she was her worst enemy in the world, and it showed. Her thoughts of sitting and watching the fight, angered her mind, thinking that it should have been her instead of Rose fighting tonight for the title. Tonight, she was hoping that Rose would win. As much as she hated the thought, she was being optimistic about Rose winning because it was the only way she would get another opportunity to fight Rose again, but for the world championship title.

When the ring announcer mentioned Rose's name, the crowd rose from their seats and cheered as loud as they could and chanting out her name repeatedly. A few minutes later, the ring announcer introduced the Vipress as she made her entrance down the aisle. The angry crowd let out many boos as she got closer to the ring. The Vipress wasn't a very likable fighter, even though she was the defending champion. She wore a red cape with an embossed black viper snake, about two feet long, signifying who she was as she moved around the ring like a snake and then strikes fast with her punches. As the Vipress crawled into the ring like a snake, she glared at Rose, trying to intimidate her. Rose made eye contact with her and returned the same type of devilish stare.

When the time came for Rose to come face-to-face with the Vipress, she felt no fear. She was ready and nothing could keep her away from the title and wearing the championship belt around her waist. She was ready to make her country proud. Right after, the announcer read the tale of the tape introduction; a brief background about the fighters, indicating where they were from, city and state, the record of fights they had won and lost, plus the accomplishments from the past, were made for both fighters. Then after the introductions, the referee had them meet at the center of the ring to go over the rules of the fight and then told them to protect themselves at all times. After the referee finished going over some mandatory rules for the fight, he had them touch gloves as a respectful tradition for the sport, but in this case, neither fighter wanted to do that, so the referee had them go to their corners and wait for the bell to ring and wait for his command to begin the fight.

The bell rang, and the referee yelled out the command word, "Box!" Both fighters went straight with their punches, swinging as hard as they could and trying to knock out each other out and not wasting anytime to do so. Rose connected with more of her punches, scoring with hard jabs to the upper body, and then backed away from the Vipress. The Vipress stayed in Rose's face, trying to find a solid punch with a hook. Rose kept her distance far enough from the Vipress reach because she knew she would try to use her elbow and hold on to the back of her head, which was her strategy. She would hide it from the referee because it was an illegal hold. As Rose tried to punch her, she would move from one side to the other, avoiding Rose's punches. Rose jabbed with her left and came back with a hard right punch. Rose was trying to find a way to set up an uppercut, but the Vipress was moving too fast and staying away from Rose. Rose followed wherever she moved. Rose got her against the ropes, throwing shots to her side and uppercuts, making the Vipress protect herself. The Vipress covered her face and attempted to sneak some punches when she had the chance. The referee broke them up and had them move away from the ropes. They made their way to the center of the ring, but it didn't stop them from throwing a flurry of punches to the upper body and a couple to the lower body. Rose was getting the best of them. Rose continued throwing her jabs with some combinations to her face, but the Vipress responded with a hard punch to Rose's head and then followed by a power left punch. That caused Rose to lose balance for a few seconds, but she recovered instantly and went back swinging, landing her punches on the Vipress's face and side as the Vipress counteracted with her own jabs, blocking some of the punches.

Rose connected with her right swing to the head and then threw a couple of combinations that stunned Vipress. The Vipress tried to clinch her arms around Rose to keep her from sending punches to her head. That's when the referee intervened and broke them up again. Rose went back where she left off and continued to land more punches. The Vipress tried to get close to smothering Rose and keep her from throwing hard punches. Then the Vipress tried to hold on to Rose's head from the back and punched Rose in her lower body, and then her head. She was trying to hide it from the referee since it was an illegal punch and didn't want to get caught.

Rose pushed the Vipress away and followed with some combinations. The Vipress covered her face again with her gloves, attempting to block the punches flying toward her. Rose kept hitting her until the bell rang, ending the first round.

At the end of this round, Rose had a slight edge over the champ and dominated this round, except for a brief moment when the Vipress caught her with a hard straight punch. Their trainers took advantage of their one-minute break to cool them with ice packs and gave them water to rinse and drink a few swallows of water. They were also told what to do and what not to do against the opponent.

The bell rang for the second round as the referee shouted, "Box!" Both fighters started at a slower pace this time, jabbing lightly, single jabs and some double jabs, each feeling and waiting for the other to see what their opponent would do. Then Rose went in with a quick punch to the Vipress's side. The punch made the Vipress bend down a little because she felt the pain. Rose attacked the Vipress immediately, not allowing the time for the Vipress to breathe and continued throwing a flurry of punches to the upper body, not giving her time to recuperate. The Vipress managed to get away and move around the ring to give her some time to get her poise back.

Rose continued to put pressure by being more aggressive toward the Vipress. She wanted to put her ass on the canvas and finish her off. The Vipress got her energy back and responded with some jabs and didn't let up. Now they were both swinging at each other like two cats fighting in a locked cage, and there was no other way out except to finish with a knockout. The battle continued until the last second of the round. Then the bell rang, with both fighters using up most of their energy when trying to knock their opponent out. The referee had to jump in between them to stop the fight because if he hadn't, they would have continued fighting.

When both fighters went to their corners, Simon told Rose, "Throw a left punch at her lower right-side of the body on her liver to make her bend over a little to force her to drop her arms. Step back and swing with your right arm and as soon as she does that, punch her on the left-side temple of her head to knock her out. You've got to be quick and fast the minute she does that, okay?" said Simon. Rick was wiping the sweat off her forehead and giving her water to rinse and drink. "Use all the power behind that swing. Remember, be smart about it," Simon shouted at Rose, loud enough for her to hear him. Then the bell rang for the third round. The Vipress gave Rose a smirk as they confronted each other at the center of the ring. She was trying to intimidate Rose, but Rose wasn't feeding into it.

They both continued where they left off, being more aggressive and swinging their punches wildly. It didn't take long before the Vipress tried to hold on to Rose's head again when she got close enough to hide it from the referee. The referee couldn't see what the Vipress was doing, so she was getting away with it. Rose kept trying to push Vipress away from her to give her some room to punch. The Vipress pushed Rose against the ropes and pounded Rose with jabs, trying to hold her against the ropes to punish her. The referee finally broke them up and had them return to the center of the ring. The battle between the two warriors continued for the next minute until the bell rang again, ending the third and clashing round.

Both fighters seemed tired this time because they had used a lot of their energy throwing a flurry of punches and combination shots to keep from getting knocked out. This was a close round for them. Rose showed less fatigue than the Vipress, who was breathing heavily with her mouth slightly open. They both got freshened up with water and sweat wiped off their faces with Vaseline smeared lightly on the faces.

By the time the bell rang for the fourth round, both fighters had regained their focus and were ready to go back with everything they had, hoping to win this round with a knockout. They both started off slow, looking at each other, pacing in a circle, and throwing short and quick jabs. Rose began to throw some combinations. The Vipress reacted to her punches and started throwing some combinations of her own. The Vipress started getting close to Rose and looked to see where the referee was standing. As soon as she spotted him, she turned her back toward him and headbutted Rose, which made a small cut above her left eye. Rose backed away angrily because she knew that it wasn't an accident. The referee looked at Rose and noticed the cut on her head and stopped the fight to warn the Vipress to watch her head when making contact and looked at the cut on Rose.

The referee ruled it as an accidental headbutt and asked Rose if she's ok to continue fighting.

Of course, all she said was, "I'm Okay!" and continued fighting. Rose was furious, but she knew not to let it get to her because that would only mean trouble and cause her to throw a wild punch, making it easier for the Vipress to take control of the fight. The Vipress was a smart fighter and Rose was cautious of her.

Rose moved around the ring for a few seconds to see what the Vipress was going to do next, then she attacked her with some combinations, leading to some hard punches to the Vipress's side. Rose was trying to find an opening to hit Vipress with a killer punch and knock her out. But the Vipress kept fighting her back with hard jabs, protecting herself from Rose's shots. The round was almost over, and Rose could hear Jimmy and Rick yelling at her, saying, "Knock her ass down!" a few times.

Rose was trying, but the Vipress was not giving up. The Vipress was fighting back like a champ. The crowd was also yelling out Rose's name repeatedly, over, and over as loud as they could, "Rose! Rose! Rose! Knock her out! Knock her out! Rose! Rose! Rose! Knock her out! Knock her out!" The bell dinged, and the referee jumped in between them as soon as he heard the bell, broke them up, and told them to go to their corners.

The Vipress was tired and breathing fast and heavily through her mouth again. Rose started to breathe a little harder this time because she was using all her energy to knock the Vipress out. Simon talked to Rose as she sat on her stool, getting her eye worked on by Jimmy, trying to stop the bleeding from the cut she got when the Vipress gave her a headbutt.

"Rose, I want you to get close to her and throw a punch at her liver as hard as you can. Give her two, or maybe even three, if you get a chance, then step back away from her and come up with a hook to knock her out. Okay?"

"Got it!" said Rose as she was trying to get a drink of water.

Then the bell rang for the fifth round. The Vipress charged at Rose, wanting to finish her off as soon as the referee gave the sign to fight. She rushed toward Rose with all her power and energy behind her punch and went straight to Rose's nose, connecting and sending Rose to the ropes. Rose wasn't expecting this. The crowd responded with boos and started yelling Rose's name, hoping to get her going again. Rose held the Vipress's arms, trying to get her poise back as the Vipress tried to break away from Rose. The referee was getting ready to step between them and separate them when Rose pushed the Vipress away from her to let go and started jabbing once again. Both threw punches with combinations and jabs. Rose was trying to get close to the Vipress and punch her in the liver like Simon wanted her to do, but the Vipress kept moving around from side to side, avoiding some of Rose's punches.

Rose kept following her until she got her cornered against the ropes. Rose started pounding on her like a fighting machine, trying to punch her in the liver. She finally succeeded with a hard shot that got through and then came up with a hook. She made it happen. The hook punch got through to her jaw and made contact that sent her to the canvas. The referee jumped in front of Rose to keep her from throwing any more punches at the Vipress. He started his mandatory count as the Vipress struggled to get up. By the count of eight, she had pulled herself up by holding on to the ropes, and the referee checked to see if she was able to continue.

After the referee did a quick evaluation of her condition, he let her go back to fighting. Rose was waiting anxiously to finish her off. Rose rushed toward the Vipress and continued throwing as many hard punches as she could to knock her out. She knew that this was the time to knock her out. Rose executed her punches, one after another, with combinations and wasn't giving her any time to recover from the almost knockout punch that she gave her, even though she still got up. She was attempting to do it again, but this time, she wanted to make sure that she wasn't going to stand up anymore.

The Vipress tried to move around the ring as Rose stayed right in front of her, trying to set her up again. Rose continued to focus on her liver, looking for the chance to stab one hard punch to the spot again and succeeded. The Vipress felt it and backed away. Rose leaped toward her and threw a hard straight shot at her nose that connected and sent her flying to the mat. She landed hard and flat on her back. On the way down, her eyes had a strange look, as though she saw stars and was ready to take a nap. The Vipress lay on the canvas, not moving a muscle, as the referee started his mandatory count. When he reached the fifth count, the crowd joined him, counting, "Six! Seven! Eight! Nine! Ten!"

Then they heard the bell ring, ruling it an official knockout. The crowd went ballistic, wild, and cheering for Rose as the Mariachi band started playing loud. Rose was victorious once again. She felt like she was the happiest fighter in the world. She jumped up and down as Simon, Jimmy, and Rick made their way inside the ring to congratulate her. Rick picked her up on his shoulders and walked around to ring. The crowd kept screaming out her name, and some of the fans were waving a mini-Mexican flag in honor of her people. This day had made her proud of who she was, seeing that most of the fans were of her descent.

After walking around the ring, the announcer had to officially announce the winner of the fight, so he asked the crowd for their attention. It took him about five minutes to quiet the crowd enough to hear the announcement. After the official announcement was made, Rose asked Rick if he still had the rose that she had him hold for her before the fight began.

"Yes, I do," said Rick.

"Can I have it, please!" replied Rose.

"Let me get it for you. I left it on top of the corner stool where I was sitting. Hold on. I'll be right back," said Rick.

When Rick returned with the rose, he gave it to Rose. She took it gracefully from his hand and walked toward the corner where Echo was sitting. Then she looked at Echo and made sure she made eye contact with her, and then Rose swung her arm that was holding the red rose and threw it at Echo with a smile. It landed right in front of Echo's feet. Echo looked down at the red rose on the floor, then raised her head up to stare at Rose. Rose remained smiling at Echo because she knew that it was killing her to see what had just happened. And then Rose turned around and walked toward Rick, grabbed his hand, faced Simon and Jimmy, and told them, "My dream has become a reality. And I'm proud to be me. Thank you, guys." Rose couldn't be any happier to have all three of them by her side. "Let's go. I'm done here. Let's go celebrate," said Rose.

Echo stayed seated on her chair as she looked at the rose that Rose threw at her feet. She felt embarrassed to see Rose walk away with the world title and a championship belt. All that was going through her mind at that moment was a rematch. Now it was her turn for revenge.

They all walked out of the ring as Rose waved at all her fans and walked proudly down the aisle on her way to the dressing room, while the mariachi band followed right behind them, playing her music. The crowd stood up as she walked by, cheering for their hero, Rosalinda "The Rose" Escobar, who just made her fans proud and the pride of their Mexican heritage.

TO BE CONTINUED...

To the reader;

"I want you to follow my dreams. The passion and love that I have for the sport of boxing. I will take you with me through the adversities and struggles that I have encountered with my career. Let no one tell you that you can't do it because you can if you set your mind and heart to follow your dream. With the help of my Trainer, Simon, who believed in me and pushed me every day and every minute I had to give, he saw something in me that made me who I am now, a Champion. He put his belief and heart into me, knowing that I have what it takes to become a Champion. And I did, and so can you if you believe in yourself and follow your heart. Don't think you already know everything on how to become a champion because you don't. Without your trainer, the help of the assistant, and coaches, you can't do it alone. So, listen to them, and they will take you to the top with the training they believe is right when you face your next opponent. I have scarified my life, not because I had to, but because I wanted to. The pain, sweat, and blood I had to deal with, boxing is not an easy sport to make it a career. You will get beaten, punished, hurt, and feel the effects of it all, afterwards. Follow my journey, my dreams, because it's what I wanted, and I have accomplished my dream, but it doesn't stop here. I have challengers waiting to take my championship belt, so whoever steps into the ring with me, I will be waiting to prove to the world that I will not give up my title easily because I have trained too hard to get here, and I will do my utmost to defend it."

"If you want it, go get it."
"Always protect yourself at all times."

Rosalinda "The Rose" Escobar

About the Author: Jesse Moreno

I was born in Visalia, California, and now I live near the west coast of San Luis Obispo, California. I'm a veteran of four years in the Air Force and proud to have served in the era of Vietnam. I have been writing for the past 9 years and have been following the sport of boxing and MMA events for many years. This is the reason for writing a boxing story series that will help you understand the reality of a boxing sport. My inspiration comes from watching the award-winning movie "Million Dollar Baby," also a female boxer. Since then, I discovered that I wanted to become a writer and published author. Rosalinda The Pride of Mexico: Part One will be my first of the series with more to come. Follow Rosalinda's journey from being a waitress to becoming a champion boxer. I do encourage you to follow her dream and journey in the series to come.

www.ingramcontent.com/pod-product-compliance
Lightning Source LLC
Chambersburg PA
CBHW020742310726
48969CB00002B/371